DAUGHTER OF THE SWAN

Also by Joan Juliet Buck

THE ONLY PLACE TO BE

DAUGHTER
OF THE
SWAN

Joan Juliet Buck

WEIDENFELD & NICOLSON
New York

Copyright © 1987 by Joan Juliet Buck

All rights reserved. No reproduction of this book in whole or in part or in any form may be made without written authorization of the copyright owner.

Published by Weidenfeld & Nicolson, New York
A Division of Wheatland Corporation
10 East 53rd Street
New York, NY 10022

Published in Canada by General Publishing Company, Ltd.

Library of Congress Cataloging-in-Publication Data
Buck, Joan Juliet.
Daughter of the swan.

I. Title.
PS3552.U333D38   1987   813'.54   86-28302
ISBN 1-55584-118-X

Manufactured in the United States of America
Designed by Ronnie Ann Herman
First Edition
10 9 8 7 6 5 4 3 2 1

In memory of e.s.h.

PART ONE

1

WHEN I WAS SIXTEEN my father gave me a Roman ring. It was bronze, oval, heavy, and thick at each side. In the center was a broken seal; a blow had cracked away a third of the pale blue surface, and with it some of the design, but the image was still clear. A woman lying on a couch, with a swan beating its wings as its body rose from between her legs.

The brute conviction with which that scene had been cut into the sliver of stone some two thousand years before remained in the ring. It held my hand as its maker would have, his intentions clear. Its very shape, unwieldy, too heavy and too thick to sit well on my finger, distended the natural splay of my hand. The wide oval edges pushed my fingers out on either side, as a knee forces unwilling legs to open. It weighed me down with the promise of pleasures long banned from this world.

I wore it every day. Sometimes, forgetful for an instant, annoyed at some benign but graceless temporality, I would wave my arms and crash the heavy bronze against a rough wall, a hard glass door. And then I'd cover the ring with my hand, explore its surface to make sure it was intact, check the smooth tips, feel for the familiar scratches on the inset stone. I never dared look until I could see what I had with my touch. Nothing I did to it could ever hurt it.

On thick slow days at school, when the sky was gray and the air so full of matter that movements were tangled and slow, I would sit in class and cut away at the side of a nail until I had drawn blood. And then I'd spend the rest of the hour sucking the blood from my finger until I could taste in its thick salt the edge of another memory.

My friends in school wore gold chains, bright and new, pink lipstick, and brooches with hearts on them. They kissed boys and cursed runs in their stockings. They talked about staying out late in nightclubs. I longed for a superior man, and suspected that he might have to be a god in disguise.

I had a picture of Morpheus over my bed, the winged head of Morpheus. "At least it's not Jesus anymore," my father said. No one told me Morpheus was the god of sleep.

Through my childhood, I'd had a crush on Jesus, which I had caught from Bertha, who cleaned my father's house and took care of me. Bertha had a blue statue of the Virgin Mary that turned purple when the weather changed. Above her bed was a writhing Jesus on a white plastic cross. One Easter with my aunt in London, when I was eight, I spent a fervent day painting a picture of a smiling Palm Sunday Jesus. He was outlined in gold paint, his shadow was cobalt blue, and I attached him to the wall of my London bedroom with two straight pins. I knew the pins were delicate and the holes shallow in the wall; it was Divine Grace that would have to keep the picture there, not any skill of mine.

Even as a child I believed in giving providence every chance to show itself.

Once, waiting outside the headmaster's office, I became engrossed by the meaning of the black and white linoleum tiles on the floor. I stood on a black tile, and then moved both feet to a white one.

"You were meant to be on the white," I told myself.

Then I had a moment of doubt. I went back to the black.

That's what you were meant to do, a voice inside me said. It was no longer entirely mine.

I moved back to the white one, fast.

"There!" I thought. "Here?"

You were meant to do that too, said the voice.

I moved back and forth between the black and the white until the headmaster's secretary came out to find me in tears, rooted to a black tile, unable to move, whimpering: "I don't know what I should do."

My father dealt in antiquities. He kept an enormous file of statues from the ancient world, even the ones in museums. He took me to the shop that sold photographs of works of art. I went through the index cards under "Gods—Dieux Antiques"—and found Jupiter and Apollo and Mercury and Diana and Athena and the rest. I flipped through their names and then through the manila envelopes of shiny black and white photographs. Morpheus had a wing on his head. I thought he was the most beautiful man I'd ever seen.

He had a full lower lip, a straight nose, drooping eyelids over empty eyes, winding windblown hair. He had more dignity than the Kouros Dad kept in the front hall, who was too smooth and had a dumb plump smile, and eye makeup.

Morpheus was considered a step in the right direction. When I asked my father for a second picture to put over my bed at Julia's house in London, he gave it to me. I took Jesus off the wall and put him in the drawer of the bedside table. A few years later, on my birthday, I received the ring.

Not long after that I lost my virginity to the saddle of a horse. I came home from riding one afternoon and as I pulled down my underpants I saw a red stain. I thought it was my period, at last. At sixteen I was the only girl in my class who had not yet turned into a woman, and the wait was long and anxious. The spot of blood without pain disappointed me. I tried lying down with a hot water bottle on my stomach, but nothing more happened. I took a large pad of cotton wrapped in gauze, which had been in a box under the sink for three years, and attached it to the little elastic belt that came with the box; but although I looked wonderfully wounded and sacrificial in the bathroom mirror, puberty still eluded me.

I looked often at the ring and longed to be ravished by a swan.

When my Latin tutor led me to bed I wondered if it meant he loved me, while he did the things he wanted to do. Then, to my dismay, he put two fingers inside me and said, "You have no hymen."

The use of the antique word enchanted me, while the absence of the material membrane, newly revealed, brought back that peculiar afternoon.

"It must have been the horse," I said.

2

My MOTHER DIED WHEN I was born and then again when I was twenty. The second time she wasn't my mother, she was my aunt, my father's sister, Julia, who lived in London. My father didn't like or trust women, but his sister was as rare and strange as he was, and he loved her. In Paris there was Bertha to take care of me, but then she left and Dad hired a Vietnamese houseboy called Nguyen, and someone must have said that I needed a woman around me. So I started going to London.

The first time, Dad and Michel came with me. "You remember your aunt," said Michel. "She's very nice and she's very pretty." I wasn't sure. They took me to Julia's house and stayed for tea while I played with blunt wooden toys from Sweden that she had set out on her rug just for me. Then they went to the country, and I was left alone with Julia. "Come see your room," she said. I was five, maybe I was six. I wasn't interested in my room. "This is where you'll live when you're in London," she said. "Do I have to be in London?" I asked, and I cried and asked where my father was.

Julia was beautiful, like my father. They both had brown eyes, a perfect nose, dark red hair, like carnelian in the light. Julia's lids were arched, her hair was long and parted in the middle. Her hands were big and pale, her shoulders wide, her voice a little deeper than my father's. He was two years older than she was, but I think he was a little afraid of her. Each time he and Michel took me to the airport to go to London, I felt they were sending me into an exile that I had done nothing to deserve. "You'll have fun with Julia, you'll see," Dad would say. "You'll do things girls do." At home everything was dark and shining, there was talk about dowagers and houses and pieces from Tarquinia, Georgie and Alexis came to dinner, I ate olives from the bowl on the coffee table. "She'll give you chocolates, you'll wear dresses, you've got a pretty pink room," he reminded me each time he saw me off. I didn't want to be forced to eat sugar and wear pink frills.

When I came home, at the end of a weekend or the end of a week, I carried presents from Julia to my father, and things she'd torn out of the London *Times* for him. "Doesn't she know I get the *Times* here?" he'd say, but he looked at the torn newspaper anyway, and with a smile.

I didn't like London. I was never sure what people said because accents slid words into impenetrable sounds, and Julia's friends had children who were never there. In London you couldn't touch the buildings because most of them had iron railings and moats called areas, and the houses were ugly brick.

Julia was determined that I should love London. She took me to the zoo, to the theatre, to Kew Gardens to look at plants, and to the Chelsea Flower Show. From the time I started going to London to see my aunt I saw *Twelfth Night* nine times. She thought it was a suitable play for a child. I grew to detest Malvolio and dread his arrival in yellow cross garters, but I loved Viola, who had to dress as a boy to escape detection.

The first time I saw *Twelfth Night*, Viola had dark hair. The next time she was blonde. "That's because there are two different actresses," said Julia. "You mean different ladies can be the same person?" I asked. I didn't get taken to theatre in Paris. I didn't understand that different people could perform the same play. In terms of real life, that meant that I could wake up one day and find someone else being my father. I asked Julia about it. Finally, she said: "Look, it's like me and your mother. Your mother is . . ." and she couldn't say the word, but in Paris we weren't afraid of words like sick and dead, so that I said it, to help her—"dead"—and she gave a little start backwards and said, "That's it, and I'm not your mother, but I'm someone who is like your mother, even though I'm not her."

"So who was the first Viola, and how did she die?" I asked.

I knew, because my father had told me, and Michel had told me, that my mother was French and was called Elise and died while I was being born. There was a photograph of her on the dresser in Dad's room, a young French sort of face, thick eyebrows and thin lips and long black hair. She didn't come from Paris so we never saw her family. "Your mother is the only woman I ever loved," said my father. That was the truth. Before my mother, and after, my father had loved only men. He had lived with Michel ever since I could remember.

Julia was not married. "Your father's the married one," she used to say with a laugh, when I asked about marriage. She had almost married a lord, which was why she lived in London. The lord was called Leander Radford; because the English were so peculiar about the way names went I never was sure if he was Sir Leander or Lord Leander, and by the time I started going to London he had long ago retired to his estates in Scotland, with a Belgian woman whom he did marry.

When I was a child, Lord Leander Radford and my dead mother, Elise, were the two chances that Julia and Jacob had lost.

Their mother was called Olivia; she was very rich and very fat, and when the war was over she came to Europe with her children, and in one summer Julia and Jacob Ellis had become legends. "Everyone fell in love with them," Michel told me. Olivia went back to be rich in New York, and came to Paris every few years on her way to various spas, and brought me American dresses with detachable cuff links and washable collars. When she died my father and Julia divided up her things. Julia had the furniture that Dad called "good" and "serious," and Dad kept the fantasies, the bed with the ceiling on it, the chaise longue with an eagle's head and lion's feet. Julia's house was light and proper, while the apartment in Paris was full of surprises, mirrors, mother of pearl cabinets and screens, with the tall young Kouros guarding the front hall, living stone.

I couldn't ask Julia why she hadn't married the lord. There were pictures of her with him in silver frames on a long table in her bedroom; she wore sunglasses that looked somehow medicinal, he had a lock of pale hair across his forehead and big teeth. In one picture her hand was on her shoulder and you could see a ring shaped like a flower. "What happened to the ring?" was the most I dared to ask. "I gave it back," she said. "A lady doesn't keep things."

Julia worked. She designed printed fabric. There was a white room at the top of the house, with a long table under a skylight where she sat and painted flowers onto big sheets of paper. There were rolls of old designs on the shelves behind her, and swatches of the fabrics printed with her patterns. She used colored inks and the new felt-tip pens that had diagonal edges and little glass reservoirs that you could see if you peeled the plastic paint off the body of the pen. A white student lamp made a sharp angle over the table. Everything there was white: the plastic top on the table, the paper, the lamp and the light around her when she worked.

Sometimes she let me draw at her table, but I was better at putting makeup on my dolls with her felt-tip pens than at drawing things on paper. I was given a box of colored pencils and a pad of paper, and sometimes I copied what she did. She'd glance over at what I was doing and laugh—"No, no, do your own drawing." Which is probably why I drew Jesus.

"When you grow up you'll live with me," Julia said, the second or third time I went to London. It sounded solemn, a duty, a promise.

I was never sure if Julia loved me. The first hug that she gave me at the airport was always tight and strong, and her arms were comfortable and loving. But on the ride into London a distance took over between us, a nervous chill, so that by bedtime I didn't dare ask her to kiss me goodnight. When I was small she always held my hand while we crossed the street, and beneath the grip of her fingers I could feel her trembling.

The way Dad and Michel talked about her in Paris, Julia was the ordered, reasonable one, the one who had schedules and kept her accounts neat. They were happy to make her sound a little dull. I agreed with them at first, and then after more forced weekends and holidays I started missing her.

I became fascinated by Julia. A face just like my father's, but beautiful, strong where he was a little soft. I'd count the rings on her fingers and play with the chains around her neck, until she pushed me away with a distracted gesture, "No, Florence, come on." On Sunday mornings we'd have breakfast in her kitchen in the basement, with the English newspapers and their color magazines. Sometimes she invited people for lunch, and I helped her cook, chopping parsley very fine the way Dad did it, blushing when she told me I'd done a good job.

I wanted her to love me. I tried to sleep neatly so that my bed wouldn't be a nuisance for the charlady in the morning. I cleaned the bathtub after I'd used it, and rinsed the sink after I'd brushed my teeth. Most Saturday nights when I was with her she'd make two trays, and we'd have dinner on her bed, watching television until the priest came on to deliver a little sermon at closedown. I would pretend to be asleep on her quilt, and she would pull at my shoulder and say, "Florence, you have your own bed and your own room, go to bed now."

I wanted to sleep next to her, but she would scoop me off to bed and set me standing up, facing the door to the hallway and the bathroom.

"Go on," she'd say. "I'll see you at breakfast."

There were forced walks in the park, where Julia pointed out the trees by their names, and picked up leaves for their shape. We fed the ducks and swans in Kensington Gardens; I fed the ducks and Julia fed the swans. They came right up to her undefended bare hands and grabbed bread from her fingers. She wore an old leather jacket which made her look a little like a street cleaner on those walks. "Your aunt is an unusual woman," her friends said to me when I was older.

On spring evenings when the sky was light young men in sports cars sometimes came to take her out for drinks. Mrs. Smith, the charlady, would stay with me until Julia came home. I told Mrs. Smith about Paris. "Chinese gentleman to take care of you, well I never," said Mrs. Smith. "And I eat olives," I told her. "Don't like olives," said Mrs. Smith, who made treacle pudding.

The house was full of Julia: it wasn't just the little porcelain people from Dresden or the funny paintings she collected, of volcanoes and dark landscapes, it was that her things were everywhere. Capes and coats in the downstairs hall, white gloves and felt hats and evening bags hanging next to them, and shawls on tables, and lace pillows from her bed that found their way to the sofa. She kept crystal beads in a bowl on one of the small tables in the living room, and I loved to sit and fondle the cold transparent spheres. I knew I was not supposed to hang the beads around my neck, so I rolled them in my hand; the room was thin slices of gray and white in curves on their surface. I looked at her through the biggest, roundest bead. The fire was burning, she was reading in the chair next to me. "I want to always remember this," I said.

She looked up at me, and strangely. She was so still that I thought she was holding her breath, and her eyes looked absolutely flat.

"What's wrong?" I asked her. I was a little scared.

"Nothing," she said. The fire seemed hotter, and my heart began to thump in the center of my chest. I got up and went to get a cookie in the kitchen.

The only thing I didn't love about Julia was Trevor Blake. Trevor Blake was big and hearty. When he removed his coat, things fell off the hatstand. His gloves were enormous. His car was an antique. He wasn't as nice as the men who had come in little sports cars. He had a deep voice with various tones to it, and he'd stand at the bottom of the stairs and shout, "Julia!" and the air in the house would be a little damaged until the boom had died away.

Trevor Blake appeared when I was thirteen, but he must have been around before, too, because I thought I recognized him from pictures in Julia's frames. He had tightly curled hair that bunched behind his ears, and thick eyebrows, dirty grayish blond, and a round, red face. He had a stately home in the country and a good name, and he had been a hero in the war. He knew generals and field marshals, he voted Conservative and lunched with politicians at the House of Commons. And he had that voice: as a young man he had been an actor, before the war, and now he was something in advertising, and used his own voice to sell cat food, chocolate bars, and motor oil. He had dandruff on the velvet collar of his overcoat, he wore tweed jackets that smelled of dog, and he wouldn't leave Julia alone.

It never occurred to me that she liked him. After I'd met him a few times, we all went to his house in the country. The house had gateposts with eagles, a Palladian façade, not enough land, and death duties on it. He had two tall sons, who shot birds and drank whiskey: there was an ex-wife called Daisy, who'd bolted, one of the sons told me, years before. The house was freezing, there were hot-water bottles in our beds after dinner, and little tins of cookies by a thermos of water next to the beds.

They thought I didn't know she slept in his room. Her weekend bag was put in a room with roses on the wallpaper, and she'd call me in there to talk before dinner, to say, "Be nice to Trevor, don't sulk." But I saw her horsehair mitt in his bathroom when his sons took me up there to see the dirty engravings of people tickling each other in eighteenth century clothes. Her mitt, and her bottle of Mitsouko by the sink. Dad and Michel had told me all about sex so the engravings didn't shock me, but the mitt and the bottle did.

Trevor Blake called me "the little Frenchy."

"I'm not French, why does he say that?" I asked Julia.

"Because your mother was French," she said.

I told Dad and Michel how awful Trevor Blake was, as if they could save Julia from him. Dad must have said something, and done it wrong, because Julia called me from London. She was furious.

"If there's something you don't like about Trevor, tell me, don't tell your father. It's nothing to do with him."

I didn't think she would want me back in London after that. But a few weeks later, Dad gave me my ticket and took me to the airport again. And when I landed, Julia gave me one of her great warm hugs.

"You couldn't help it, you're just jealous," she said.

"Why should I be jealous?" I asked, trying to be light about it, to say it fast, the way Dad and Michel said things fast. But the words were difficult to say. I was jealous. Which meant I was in love with her, and that was sick.

When we got back to the house I waited for Trevor Blake to arrive and do his terrible shout up the stairs; I gave a start every time a car parked outside in the street, and Julia said, "He's not coming around this weekend, it would be too embarrassing for everyone."

"What are we doing tonight?" I asked. It was Saturday.

"We can have trays and watch television, the way we used to when you were a child," she said. I was fourteen by then.

I felt I'd ruined her weekend, and the next morning I didn't want to get out of bed. She came in to shake me at ten, at eleven. I didn't move. I was angry and embarrassed and wished I could be back in Paris without having to walk through her house. A little later Doctor Emery came, Doctor Emery who had seen me through chicken pox a few years before. He had a big schoolboy's briefcase and a reassuring way of sitting on the bed and just smiling at me before he took out his stethoscope. I saw Julia's shadow against the pink door-jamb, listening, just at the edge of the hall. Doctor Emery grabbed both my hands in his, read the title of the book on the table out loud, and said, so that she could hear him: "Julia, dear, there's nothing wrong with her. The girl is absolutely fine. She's been reading Colette, that's all."

When I was small she gave me organdie collars and little net bags, lace gloves and faded silk flowers that she said she had worn on her fur coat. As I grew taller and nearer her size, she gave me shoes, ghillies with intricate lacings, flat ballerina slippers, party shoes in dyed satin. Then belts, studded with silver nails or made of bright rope. And later dresses, skirts, blouses, things that had been hers. She had more bosom and more hips and less waist than I did. I didn't look like her unless I threw my head back and let the light draw cheekbones on my face.

I wore her clothes in Paris. One night, when Dad's Italian dealer, Erghi, came to dinner, I put on Julia's white silk blouse from the forties. I felt precious, young-lady, feminine. It was covered in frills. The frills from the cuff trailed in my soup, and Dad picked my elbow up and wiped the cuff with his napkin. "That's pretty, where did you get it? But you've got to learn to eat like a girl."

"It was Julia's," I said.

He held the napkin closed around my cuff. "Of course it was," he said. "I think I remember it."

"Ah, Julia!" said Erghi. "How is she?"

"She's wonderful," I said.

"She's wonderful, and she lives in London," said Dad.

"I'll never forget the way she looked in Rome," said Erghi, "with a cape. She had a cape and she sat on the Spanish steps."

The next time I was in London I sat on the steps of the house while I waited for Julia to come out. "Stand up," she said. "You make it look like a tenement, sitting there."

"You used to sit on the Spanish steps," I said.

"The Spanish steps are bigger," she said.

She had friends who went to monasteries in Greece, who walked across the Himalayas, who slept in the Sahara. They came to the Sunday lunches and over the roast lamb they talked about high places, adventure, lost treasures. When Trevor Blake was there he carved, and when he wasn't she did, but she also paid attention to what was being told, and would pause, knife in hand, to say—"Was it cold? What were the smells?" and also: "What did you eat? What do you eat in Ladakh?" Trevor Blake called the people who came to lunch wasters, bohemians. They came from good families, but they traveled and traded in rugs and miniatures. Julia went away to India several times with her partner Alistair; Alistair was the part of the business that printed her designs, and India was for cotton. And when she came back there were piles of bright necklaces and bands with little bells on them, for the forehead, strange pieces of old textiles, lengths of thin voile, all heaped in baskets in the living room. "Research," she'd say, "color."

She brought back kohl in little phials, and, from Morocco, once, uneven round clay discs, glassy brown inside; she showed me how to wet my finger and rub it on the shining surface, to turn the dry veneer to a wet red: "That's what Bedouin women use as lipstick," she said, and rubbed her finger on her mouth.

"It looks sort of cheap." I couldn't help it. The jam-red lips were horrible.

"How Victorian you are."

"It's just ugly," I said.

"We'll give it to Trevor, all right?" she said, and from then on things were better between us.

When I was fifteen London began to change. Julia took me to the King's Road, where we spent afternoons in the antique markets; everyone in the streets wore bright Indian shirts and there was long hair and incense and music all along the street. I made her buy me short skirts, and I did dance movements around the table at Sunday lunch, to catch the eye of the men who were there. "I suppose you don't meet anyone at home," Julia said, "not around Jacob and Michel."

"Lots of people!"

"You know what I mean," she said, as I helped her stack the dishes after lunch.

Trevor Blake was still a presence. I'd find new pictures of him with her, and sometimes his raincoat was in the hall even if he wasn't there. He'd leave bloodstock books lying around, or he'd call during one of my weekends, and if I answered he'd say, "Just tell your aunt I wanted to fix up Tuesday night," and hang up before I could say anything. One of his sons got married, the other was sent down from Oxford; he sold a Guardi from the house in the country and it was in the papers. Once we went out to dinner with him, but he said something about an actor who was "Queer as a coot," and because I knew what he meant I said:

"Some of my best friends are coots, and so's my father."

We finished the dinner in silence, and I didn't have to see him for another year.

Talk about love started with Geraldine, who was Julia's best friend. Geraldine was overweight and busy, with hair that was always a little dirty pinned up on top of her head. She had a husband who was a Labour MP, and five children. Sitting at the kitchen table with a glass of red wine in her hand, tucking a piece of hair back into place, she asked:

"Florence, are you going to be a career woman like your aunt, or do you want to get married and have children?"

"I'm sure she wants to get married," said Julia.

"Find the perfect man before you do it," said Geraldine. We were in the kitchen: it was Sunday afternoon. I was doing something with modeling clay, which I could never do in Paris because Nguyen didn't want the kitchen messed up and my room was too decorated to have wet clay on the desk.

I looked at Geraldine, subsided in the chair like a collection of pillows, her body all blown sideways and out by constant fullness and birth and breast feeding, Geraldine the real woman, with thick thighs and large low breasts, a body as radical as the Willendorf Venus. I didn't want to be shot full of babies and emptied every nine months, like a pond drained.

"Maybe I want to work," I said, "but I don't know what I'm good at."

"But if you meet the right man you'll want to get married," said Geraldine.

"I want to fall in love," I said.

"There's plenty of time for that," said Julia.

After my father gave me the ring I brought it to London, to show Julia. I held out my hand to her.

"What is that?" she asked.

"Leda and the swan," I said. "Roman." I was proud of its strangeness and hoped she would understand.

"Show me."

I slipped it off my finger and gave it to her. She closed her fingers around it and rocked it in her hand.

"It's good," she said. I told her to look at the intaglio, and looked over her shoulder as she stood by the window.

"Oh, yes," she said. "The transformation of Jupiter, up to his old tricks. Take good care of it. You'll have that forever."

I showed it to Geraldine.

"What is that duck doing to that girl?" she asked.

"It's a swan," I said patiently. "Jupiter made himself into a swan to visit Leda."

Geraldine put her glasses on to get a better look.

"My God, they're at it!" she said; and, to Julia, "I think your brother is putting ideas into her head."

"I don't know," said Julia, "I'd rather see her wearing the ring than a charm bracelet with Kiss Me Quick spelled out in rhinestone letters."

The first time Julia and I talked about love we stayed up all night. She was in bed with her lace pillows around her, and she gave me a bolster to lean on, and cashmere shawls to keep me warm. While we talked she buffed her nails with a little silver instrument that had chamois stretched across it. I wanted to see the dawn come up, I wanted to break through the night, and I kept asking questions to keep her awake.

"Have you known a lot of men?" I asked.

"Sometimes I think too many, and sometimes I think that I've never met anyone."

"Anyone?"

"The one I'll settle down with."

"The love of your life."

"No," she said, "the love of my life is something else. I mean someone I could bear to live with."

"So it's not Trevor," I said, reassured.

"Trevor's reliable, and he's good. That's important."

"So who was the love of your life?" I asked.

"Oh," she said, and took a white pencil from the silver tumbler on the bedside table, and ran it under her nails, looking down. "When I was twenty-two I was in love, and all my friends had been in love, at least once. And now that I'm forty, I've still only been in love once. I thought so much more was going to happen." I saw how thin the skin was beneath her eyes, how it crumpled when she leaned forward.

"But do you have to settle down?" I asked—"You've got your work, and the house, and your friends, and Daddy in Paris, and me, and your whole life."

"You mean I don't need anything else," she said.

"Well, you're perfect," I whispered.

"I wouldn't be too sure about that," she said. "Now go to bed."

"No, tell me more. Tell me about my mother."

"Your mother." She looked up at the ceiling as she spoke, fast: "Your mother was pretty, and French, and she died when you were born."

"Is that all?"

"Just about," she said.

"Why don't you live in Paris?"

"Paris," she said, "slows time while accelerating growth. Everything rots in Paris, especially Americans."

I found another position on the quilt, moved the bolster a little. "I want to know about love," I said.

"Later," she said, "when you're older. The sun's about to come up."

"I want to see that too," I said.

"You know"—her head was back on her pillows now, her eyes closed—"in India they say the sun only comes up because five million women beg it to rise every morning."

"But the sun rises anyway."

"So maybe they're just asking for what they know they'll get."

"How silly," I said.

"That's not silly. That's wisdom."

I wanted Julia to be loved. She was perfect in her solitude, but I hoped the best things would happen to her, so that I could be sure that there was some point to being brave and beautiful. I watched the eyes of her guests to see if they were in love with her. I read her mail when she was out to see if there were love letters, to read what a man wrote when he was in love. All I found were terse notes from Trevor, "Okay for Friday then? Sorry about last week," and a few pieces of paper with poetry on them, in a handwriting that was not hers.

She came to Paris several times a year, and we all went out, Dad and Michel and Julia and me. Dad and Julia would walk ahead of us, arms clasped around each other, like lovers, and I'd follow behind with Michel, feeling like an imitation, an afterthought. I would do my best to be seated next to her at dinner, to go through doors with her, to have her come to my room first when she came to see us at home. When I could I held her hand, to make sure she was more mine than Dad's.

"Look at them," Michel said, as they walked ahead of us. "You'd think they were twins. Heavenly twins."

I reminded him that Dad was two years older than Julia.

"Neither of them ever grew up," said Michel. He had a little more gray hair than Dad.

Julia's visits to Paris were occasions. We went to the best restaurants with great ceremony. Sometimes Georgie and Alexis came too. They both had a curious way of looking at Julia, as if they had to remember things about her.

I was seventeen and eighteen and I had boyfriends. Sometimes they came to dinner with Dad and Michel, if they spoke English and if they had what Michel called enough references to follow the conversation.

"Why don't you ask Philippe, or Jean, to come with us tonight, to meet Julia?" asked Dad.

I knew I didn't want her to see any of the boys I went out with. I couldn't explain it. I didn't want them to see her.

Girls my age in London had dances given for them; the invisible daughters of Julia's friends. "You're going to have a normal social life, I'm going to make sure of that," she said.

She showed me her evening gowns, crashing waves of tulle, liquid satin. I stroked the dresses and imagined a charming prince for every dance. It never quite happened. Julia said it wasn't seemly for someone who didn't live in London to have a dance.

When I told Dad, he said, "She's the rich one, she could do it."

I had more fun getting drunk with Philippe and sleeping with Jean than I imagined I would with the spotty awkward boys I sometimes saw in her friends' houses. But she promised, she kept promising something to me: that I would live with her when I had finished school, that I would have a regular life.

I stayed with her when I was eighteen; her chin had begun to sag and there were blue veins on her right leg, and still there was no one but Trevor Blake in her life. I remembered the way she had held the ring, kept it in her hand and known its weight. But time was short; her mouth was getting thin, her eyes looked fierce when she wasn't smiling. Her work was going well, and in those years she made a great deal of money. Dad kept talking about how rich Julia was. She bought jewelry for herself, and let me try it on. I looked at myself in her dressing table mirror, and crinkled up my eyes.

"What are you trying to see?" she asked.

"A tiara. If you'd married Lord Radford, you'd have a tiara. Wouldn't you?"

"I wouldn't necessarily be letting you try it on. What's wrong with the emeralds you've got on?"

"No one gave them to you. He was the love of your life, wasn't he?"

"Florence, what a way to think! He was not. He was glamour. He wasn't love."

I touched the emeralds. "So what's love?"

"Heat," she said, quietly, sitting on her bed.

"Heat?"

"Heat. Warmth. Light. I can't explain. You'll see."

"Heat," I said again. It sounded like cooking.

In Paris my school friends' lives were set: they would pass their *baccalauréats* and then go on a long holiday where they would forget their exams and acquire deep even tans. And when they returned to Paris in the fall they would go to the *faculté* or take courses to teach them how to cook, how to recognize good art, or how to become experts in public relations. I was going to go to London and live with Julia.

But instead of passing our exams that year, we rioted in the streets and some of us helped occupy a watch factory in the suburbs. We threw paving stones at policemen and screamed about freedom. It felt wonderful. I didn't come home for six days. "You'll have to take the whole year over again, that's all," said Dad, suddenly severe. His car had been set on fire in the Boulevard Saint Germain, and he was suing the government for restitution.

"Now if you hadn't made trouble, you could be with me," said Julia. "It's your own fault."

"But we all did it, it was everyone my age in France."

"There's no need to follow the crowd, particularly if it's busy looting and pillaging."

The paving stones were covered with tarmac and the old fan-shaped pattern was erased from the streets. The street corners were patrolled by CRS guards in tight uniforms. I went back to school. There were fewer weekends with Julia.

"My life's a little complicated right now," she said on the phone. "Come next month." And then the month after that. I saw her, briefly, at Christmas. The house looked different; there were new, oriental things in it.

"You have to spend New Year's Eve with your father and Michel," she said, as if that were important.

I went back to Paris a little bewildered. It had been as if she didn't want me with her.

She came to Paris in the spring. I was bored in school, but doing my duty. "I am coming to live with you next fall, aren't I?" I asked when we all went out to lunch and she and I were walking along the Rue Jacob, by Dad's shop.

"Of course," she said. She was wearing dark tights and flat suede shoes. I passed my exams and spent the summer in Provence, with Dad and Michel, as usual. When we got back to Paris in September she called and said, "Why don't you take a breather for a few months? Come in February. I'll give a party for you on Valentine's Day." I wondered if she was punishing me for the riots. They seemed a long time ago.

I worked in a boutique for three months, selling makeup. I didn't want to work with Dad. They teased me enough about London in the evenings, I didn't need to hear that during the day. Julia was lunching with all the right people so that I would be accepted at the Courtauld Institute to study history of art. "You could do that at the Louvre," said Dad, "or even in the shop." I was determined that I would live with Julia. I told my Paris friends that nothing I did counted, since I was about to move away. I broke up with Philippe, since I was leaving. Philippe was relieved, I think: he had just started a job, and had to work hard. I told Jean I'd see him whenever I came back.

A month before the move, in the beginning of January, I stayed a weekend with Julia. She'd put new curtains up in my room, and there was a new quilt on my bed. "Like mine, since you like it so much," she said. There were some books by a man called Gombrich on my desk, the name a solemn portent of hard work to come. I suggested I might work in a boutique instead. Julia was horrified. "You are not coming here to waste your life," she said. "Now when you come back, you're to bring the recipe for the soup that Nguyen makes. And write it down carefully."

I was happy. I felt I was almost home. From the new distance of almost being a Londoner, Dad and Michel seemed a little pathetic, a little too colorful. I was eager to give them up.

"You know," Julia said over dinner in her kitchen, "everything you want can come true."

"Really?"

Her smile was complete, her eyes a little dreamy. "Really," she said. "Really. Sometimes it takes a while, that's all."

She gave me a list of things she wanted from Paris: decanted perfume from Guerlain, some linen pillowslips from a shop on the Rue du Bac, and a necklace she had paid for but left to be repaired at a shop near Dad's, on the Rue Jacob. And some pale turquoise tights. "You can only get them in Paris," she said. "Send them to me."

The tights weren't easy to find. Once I bought them I left them lying in an envelope.

When I began to pack, my father took me into the living room and placed his hand on my shoulder as if he were knighting me. "You're going to be a very rich woman one day," he said.

His eyes looked beyond me to the torso on the console, the Buddha's head on the coffee table, the golden screen with storks on it. "It's true," he said.

I squirmed under his hands. The word rich always brought up my grandmother Olivia. I didn't want to weigh two hundred and fifty pounds, like she did. I shook my head and said, "Oh, no."

"I am just telling you this"—he was separating his syllables—"because you're going to be meeting all sorts of men, and I don't want you to fall for the first fortune hunter you run across."

"Julia's not going to let anything bad happen," I said. "She knows, she's got everything planned. And anyway, I'm not looking for a rich husband."

I wanted to call Julia to tell her what Dad had just said, and how weird it was. I didn't, because I hadn't sent the tights.

And then the next day, a week before I was supposed to arrive in London, Julia died in a car accident.

3

I was packing in my room, making little piles of what I would need and what could stay in Paris. I had felt a slight nausea since waking, and the cold claustrophobia of a hangover. My father had come in once during the afternoon, looked at my piles of clothes, and said, "You're going to have a very different life," and then stood there, a little liquid about the eyes, until neither of us could stand it any longer. Focused on sweaters, I was trying to decide how many to take, what I could borrow from Julia, and what she might buy me once I was there. I had the list she'd given me of things I had to bring over: the decanted perfume from Guerlain, the pillowslips from the Rue du Bac, and the set of trader beads. The list moved from my dresser to my table to my bedside table, like the turquoise tights, ever more important and undone as the days went by.

I heard the phone ring in the living room, just once, and someone picked it up, and I didn't hear my name called so I went back to the sweaters, but through my absorption in my clothes I heard steps running, a sort of cry. I thought maybe a statue had toppled, or something had broken, and Nguyen had been summoned with the mop. Such queens, I thought, with the vision of broken flowers and spilled water.

Then Michel was at the door of my room, and I looked up at him. His face was set, his features drawn back, as if a hand were gripping at his scalp. He said, "Julia's died. Julia's dead." I jumped up and hit him, because it was such a stupid, mean thing to say. I hit him on the shoulder and he caught me in his arms and said, "I'm sorry."

I pushed him out of the way and ran into the living room, where Dad was on the sofa, utterly still. His head was between his hands and his elbows on his knees. I sat next to him but couldn't touch him. There was a bronze wall around him. In front of us this gaping hole as if half the world had been cut off just beyond the sofa. The couch was the only safe place. Everything else in the room was suddenly evil.

"How," I whispered at last. Not even a question, just How.

"A car crash," he said from beneath his hands, and he put his arms around me. I put my head into his shoulder but it was a bad fit, he was hugging her and not me, I was hugging her and not him. When we cried our bodies went soft, and then his shoulder was familiar again.

The cologne, the linens, the beads came to me and I panicked. "I left them for the last day," I said.

"It's all right. Shhh," he went.

Michel came over with two glasses of brandy. On the window seat I looked out at the garden where dark magnolia trees marked the corners of the terrace. It was six at night, winter dark, and the light from the living room didn't reach to the hedge. There was just a black mass beyond the terrace. I felt the stuffing crumble in the yellow silk cushion under me.

I knew I had to go to her, but there was nowhere she was that I could go.

Michel was on the phone to British European Airways at the other end of the room, booking seats for tomorrow morning. That isn't fast enough, I thought. We'll miss her. And then: If we go tomorrow, I can bring the perfume and the beads. I can keep my word.

There was no time. It was an eight a.m. flight. Dad had been on the phone to Trevor Blake all evening: the crash had happened near his house. He was the one who'd called.

Dad did not want to stay at Julia's house and nor did Michel, and I could have stayed there alone but didn't want to. When the cab went past Hyde Park corner on the way to the hotel, I tensed for the turn to the right that didn't come. Dad squeezed my hand. I was already going down Grosvenor Place, the cab humming and choking past Halkin Street and Chapel Street, humming down past the brick houses with the white fronts and the bright doors, braking, twice, first a rubber bulb squeezed by a metal claw, then a squeakier contraction, followed by a lurch. I had my hands clenched around the five-pound note that got me to Julia's house, was sitting forward to pay, trying not to topple over, as I usually did, both knees on the grid of rubber ridges on the floor.

They were shaking me.

I should have gone to the house. I was twenty and did not believe in ghosts. I would have been near her that way. But I was scared.

I had never stayed at a hotel in London before, and the one we stayed at was bland and rounded, like a hospital. The hotel people were kind: the manager came up to Dad and said, "Mr. Ellis, I'm so sad to hear about your sister," and I remembered him from when Julia cashed checks there on the weekends.

A man from the police came to see us: the car was going at sixty-five miles an hour at five forty-five in the morning of January twenty-seventh, seventy-three miles from London, at the intersection of Tuddenham Road and the A12, and the right side of the car had been destroyed. "Very rare that, the driver's seat being the one to get it," he added. Dad went alone to see the body. He was the next of kin.

Trevor Blake and some of Julia's friends had decided on a Quaker ceremony. They must have asked Dad what he thought, but all he said to me was, "Her friends want it, and who am I to say anything?" As if he barely knew her. Maybe he didn't want to tell them to do it in a synagogue. She believed in justice, grace, and hope; how do you bury someone like that? A service was necessary, and the Quakers accepted all beliefs.

Michel and I ate lunch in the hotel dining room. He said he could think of more amusing places to go, and then, looking at me, he said, "It doesn't matter." I remember the Melba toast and the transparent smoked salmon. "You must eat," he said, sagely, French. There was a fog around me. Dad was with his sister, wherever they had put her. She was no longer my Julia.

Michel came back up to my room after lunch, and smoked cigarettes with me, and said he really had to stop smoking so much.

The winter light was a bright cloud at the window. Michel sat with his feet on the radiator, and he looked handsome, his face longer and paler than usual. He inhaled as if the cigarettes had an answer, and in the overheated room something settled between us that was warm and tense and strangely sexual. We filled the ashtrays. "Julia was a remarkable woman," he said from time to time.

I took a nap, rolled over on the couch that was my bed, and into a doze. I awoke when Dad knocked on the door. "Why are you in here, it looks like a gambling den," he said, coughing to make his point.

"How was it?" asked Michel, as if Dad had simply been to the dentist. Dad said nothing and sat next to me. He took off his shoes.

"I've got something under my sock, here it is . . ." He took a small ball of fuzz off the underside of his woolen toe. Tea was ordered. "Dark and hot," my father said into the phone.

"Make it light and cold," said Michel to make us laugh.

Tea came. "Trevor Blake was there," said Dad, testing the sand-wiches with his finger. He didn't take any of them.

"I hate him," I said.

"Du calme," said Michel.

"He's all right," said Dad. "He can't help it. He asked me round for a man-to-man talk."

"At Julia's?" I asked. "At Chester Street?"

"He's got a key, he was there yesterday."

I felt Julia being taken away from me, chipped away by the claims of others. "He's heartbroken," my father said.

Me too, I wanted to say. But that would be letting Dad know that I loved Julia more than I loved him.

I said nothing.

"Her partner, Alistair, is having her friends round for drinks," said Dad.

"Florence?" asked Michel.

"I'm staying with both of you," I said.

"But you know them all," said Dad.

"There's the lawyer," said Dad. "I'm seeing him tomorrow."

He made the words important.

"You know," he said, "you're going to be a rich woman."

I didn't want to hear that. Worse now than the week before, and worse because it had to do with Julia's death, and worse still because he looked proud. As if I had earned a prize. I got up and went to the bathroom, where I washed my face, and tried to hear what they were saying over the running water. When I came out Dad was talking about the house. "Apparently, by today's market value, it's worth seventy, eighty thousand pounds."

"We're keeping it," I said, "aren't we?"

"Why?" asked Dad.

"What if I go to the Courtauld?"

"Do you still want to?" asked Dad.

I didn't even know if I'd been accepted. "I don't know."

"You're not going to live alone in Julia's house in London just because you were going to stay with her for a year or so," said Dad.

A year or so. I had thought it was to be forever.

"It doesn't apply anymore," said Michel.

"You have to come over to the house with me to decide what you want to keep," said Dad.

"Aren't we keeping everything?" I asked.

"A lot of stuff will have to be sold," he said. "You don't want old saucepans and the maid's room bed. All that junk will go, and we'll bring the good stuff over to Paris."

"What if I want to live in London?" I tried one last time.

"You don't need a four-story house," said Dad, curtly.

"Whose is it?" I asked. I was furious. She didn't want him to have her things, I knew that, and the house was hers, not his. Maybe it was mine, but she had to give it to me. "There's got to be a will." I felt like a vandal asking for it. My father broke in.

"We have to sell the house, we don't need it. The money will be more useful. You're going to be . . ."

I put my hands over my ears not to hear that again. I could see his lips moving. Michel put his hands over mine and prised them off my ears. "People should be good to each other when someone has died," he said.

Doctor Emery came to the hotel, to hold our hands and give us a little bottle of liquid valium, which he said was better for the stomach. I had five drops in a glass of water, but I woke early, startled out of sleep by the alarming memory that Julia was dead. I stood by the radiator with the olive silk of the curtains bunched in my hands, watching the line of taxis waiting in the fog. I sat down at the table and tried to write something to say at the service, because Dad had said that the Quakers expected people to talk when the Spirit moved them. I didn't trust the Spirit to find me and move me in the right way. Nothing came.

I wrote Julia, Dear Julia, Julia I love you, Julia I miss you. The lamp made a flattened sphere of yellow light around me. The little room was hot, and the small words on the neat squares of hotel paper made no sense.

I put some clothes on over my nightgown and went down, through the lobby where a sleepy clerk was trying to look alert at the reception desk, and out into the cold where I got into the first cab in line. I had on my navy blue coat, the darkest thing I owned. I gave the driver the Chester Street address. The streetlights were orange, the sky impenetrable black. I was swept to the left as he turned into her street. I saw the house with my eyes closed, the lights on in the living room, and in the fan glass above the front door. I opened my eyes and it was as dark as every other house. "Aren't you getting out?" asked the driver. I told him to take me back to the Westbury.

At the revolving door of the hotel, I was suddenly conscious of the ruffled edge of my nightgown protruding below my coat, over my boots, and I ran through the lobby so as not to attract attention. We were meeting at eight for breakfast, a sporting idea of Michel's. I took a bath to pass the time, and tried again on the hotel paper, but still nothing came. I went to Dad's room. He was combing his hair; Michel was busy at the breakfast table. "Do you want to go over to Chester Street with me later, to choose?" asked Dad. I've just been, I thought. My little victory.

"No, I don't want to see it," I said. "You decide."

"You should go," said Michel. "There are bound to be things that aren't up to your father's high standards, but that you'll want to keep. You've got to stop him acting as if he's the main assessor for the Louvre."

"I don't want anything," I said, and sat down at the table.

"Trevor Blake probably wants a souvenir," said Michel.

"He's probably already taken several," I said.

"There you are," said Michel. "You don't want him stripping the house."

There was nothing left of Julia but the things in her house. I watched my father's agate hair, noticed how strangely rich brown gave way to black, how parts of it were almost blond. It made stiff little wings behind his ears. He caught me staring at his head: "I must have put too much junk on today," he said, with a helpless shrug. His face, still round and young then, was puckered around the mouth. His lips and chin were bloated, the skin too fine. He usually ate with coherent caution, was not above sniffing the meat or the fish, testing each piece of bread to find the freshest one, taking only the yellow leaves of salad out of the bowl. In his own kitchen he'd fillet a carcass and stuff a large fish with verve, while Nguyen made small precise piles around him, and Michel did herbal things to vegetables. But today he ate nothing, tried an edge of toast with one incisor, gave up. Watching him gave me something specific to do; eating was beyond me too. Michel ate scrambled eggs, and I despised him a little for his appetite.

Trevor Blake was at the door of the meeting house, accepting handshakes. Doctor Emery tried to pull him inside when he saw us arriving, but Trevor Blake held his ground, dignified, impeccable in a dark tweed coat, herringbones across his shoulders, a gray scarf tightly folded at his neck.

"Ah, Florence," he said. "My dear, how awful." It struck me as his cat food voice. He put his arms around me and tried to put his head on my shoulder. I stared into the hair of one sideburn and thought, You cannot have loved him.

Dad shook Trevor Blake's hand, Michel shook Trevor Blake's hand. I stood on the little step up near the door and looked for someone close to her, someone who really loved her. Doctor Emery stood next to me and patted my shoulder. "Geraldine," I whispered, "where is she?"

"I think she's just had another baby," said Doctor Emery. "She must still be in the hospital."

"Do you know where?" Perhaps I could see Geraldine later. I could sit on her hospital bed and it would stand in for Julia's. Then I could cry. "What hospital?"

"I'm afraid she's not a patient of mine," he said.

We went into a dark room where we had to wait for the Quakers. I remember it all as very brown, groups of people on benches. I stood and sat and stood. The arrivals were all hugging and kissing, and standing in an orange light, their shapes outlined in furry brown caterpillars. We filed into the chapel.

I wasn't sure which way the altar was, or even if there was an altar. There were no pictures, no stained glass, no decorations, not even a cross. The gloom in here was a little less brown, a little more green in the cool light from frosted windows. The Quaker ladies would know what to do, dumplings in dark coats with funny little hats and kind, deliberate expressions.

Julia was not in the room. I was in the front-row chair between my father and Michel. Trevor Blake had a perpendicular row all to himself, with his lawyer and his dentist and Julia's accountant, Mr. Leon, all wedged onto one end of it, as if they didn't want to be too close to him. They had introduced themselves to me, and Doctor Emery had explained who they were. Mrs. Smith, the charlady, sat behind Trevor Blake and smiled at me, holding a handkerchief to her cheek. This is absurd, I thought, and that was Julia's word. I had to breathe carefully. My hands came into focus at times, white things on my dark-blue lap. A man in a suit stood up and said we should speak when the Spirit moved us, and Michel leaned forward to look at me with an appreciative nod, pleased that the event matched its description. My father squeezed my hand. We waited. I heard my breathing, and my father's breathing, and then a foot shuffling and sometimes a cough. Mrs. Clarke, a Democrat Abroad, was sobbing uncontrollably.

I didn't cry. I wanted to know which of these people were Julia's real friends. I wanted to get rid of anyone there who had been less than loyal, less than good to her. The Spirit's refusal to move anyone to speech was due, I thought, to the amount of hypocrisy and social grace in the room. I wanted them out. I thought about the metal and the glass that had killed her. I said metal and I said glass. Behind the words, and in front, was the crushing empty space, a sky of boulders.

A silence spread through the room, hushing feet and sobs. I turned to Dad. He was impermeable, his head in his hands. Trevor Blake sat erect across the way, looking at his own feet. Somewhere in the room a throat was cleared. One of the Quaker ladies stood up. "I would like to say," she began, and there was a noise from all the coats sliding, turning in the chairs. The moment was saved. "I would like to say," the Quaker woman repeated, "that when I am sad, I always make a nice cup of tea and I find that cheers me up." She gave a kindly smile and sat down.

Mrs. Clarke began sobbing again, louder than before. Three weeks ago Julia had said, "Anything you want can come true."

"I want to see her before it's too late," I said in Dad's ear, and he quickly put his arm around me and held it there, warm on my shoulder. "Was she still beautiful yesterday, did she look beautiful?" I asked.

Trevor Blake stood up. He opened his mouth. Michel leaned forward, glaring. Get out, I thought. You weren't good enough for her. Trevor Blake opened his mouth, worked his jaw, and sat down again, wordless.

I thanked the Spirit for this show of solidarity. But I too was wordless. I felt the paper in my pocket. Not possible.

That was us and God.

God is the color of the sun.

After another long while, we stood up. There was a queue to get out. Trevor Blake had taken his dignity to the door and stood causing a bottleneck of murmurs and coats. Then we were out on the street and someone had thought of a car and we were in it and on the way to Golders Green, where a coffin slid along rails through a small square door into a furnace. It was only later that I learned that Jews are not supposed to be burned.

I went to the house, where Doctor Emery and Mr. Leon waited in the dining room on the ground floor while I went upstairs with a bunch of fluorescent green tags. The tags were for what I wanted stored. I was to put whatever small things I'd take back to Paris on the stairs, for Mr. Leon to have sent to the hotel. "Don't get your knickers in a twist," Doctor Emery shouted up the stairs after me. "Your father will evaluate everything later. Just take what you want."

I stood at the door of her bedroom, and registered the pictures of Mount Vesuvius, and the silver reliquary where she kept her jewelry. I put tags on them, and then I saw the bed, the bed where she slept, and I crawled into the hollow on her side and curled around the pillow and stayed there until I heard them shouting up the stairs, "Are you finished?"

So I shouted back, "Yes," and "Not yet," and put my feet on the floor and left the room without looking back.

I went into my room, and there were the pinholes from the picture of Jesus, and there were my London dolls and the puzzles that Trevor Blake bought me every Christmas. There were feather boas and the velvet hats that I wore only in London, and there was the copy of *Honey* that I had read in bed twenty days ago . . .

I climbed up to the top floor, to the white workroom. There were notes on the table, Xtra Prussian Blue, call Belinda Belville, 3 × 12 thread. I took the notes. Then I ran down the stairs and I threw the tags on the table.

"I can't do it," I said. "Dad will decide."

"But it's all yours," said Mr. Leon.

"Then I'll get it back in time. It will come back to me." I went past them, out the door, and turned right into Belgrave Square, no-man's land of creamy embassies.

On the plane Dad and Michel kept patting a package between them. "It's nothing," said Michel, when I looked at him, inquiring. Dad looked out the window.

"*Et ça?*" asked the customs officer, pointing to the package.

Dad looked at Michel, who looked at me. They asked if I could be let through. The customs officer said, "You're all together, you stay together. Open the package." Dad sighed. I think I already knew.

Michel began undoing the brown paper and the string. What came out was a small bronze urn, sealed tight. The customs officer tried to pry off the pointed lid.

"Don't," said my father. "It's ashes."

4

THE URN WAS PUT away, and we never discussed it. Sometimes I opened closet doors to look for it, rummaged behind old china. They had hidden it well. I didn't go back to London; the things, Julia's things, came to Paris. I wanted the paintings of Mount Vesuvius for my bedroom, but they were too big.

I was given papers to sign. "It's about the house," my father said. I asked who had bought it. "No one we know," he said.

"The jewels are in the bank," said Michel. I asked to see them, but he said, "Later." My father gave me a piece of paper to sign so that I could get into the vault. But although I looked for Julia in the backs of closets, I didn't want to visit her jewels in a vault.

Michel said that since I wasn't going to the Courtauld, I should go to the Ecole du Louvre. "Like half the girls you went to school with," he added. I would have preferred to go back to the boutique. Dad wanted me to work with him in the shop.

I slept. I discovered a narcotic cough syrup in the pharmacy, and found that if I drank half a bottle of it I could ride the afternoons to dark, unconscious on the sofa. I tried to dream of Julia. When I felt a dream coming on I steered to the safe sofa to fall face forward on its scratched velvet, and hold the cushions tight into sleep. She was there, waiting on the other side, waiting to explain she wasn't dead at all.

The phone would ring and ring, and I'd get off the sofa and answer it to find it was Michel who said he needed me at the shop with a wrench or a key he'd left at home. At first I fell dumbly back onto the cushions, but after further harassment, I'd call a cab and go to the shop. Which meant that the three of us, Dad, Michel, and I, would walk home in the dark, with me feeling like a dog forced to take its exercise.

One day Michel woke me at nine. "Why?" I asked.

"We need you in the shop, Maud's sick," he said. I did the windows with a bottle of Glassex, and dusted the bronze animals from Egyptian graves and the terracotta Amors from Greek ones. People came and went in the shop, and I answered their questions with haphazard guesses. For the two weeks that I worked there, everything green was Luristan, every figure of a woman was Tanagra, and every piece of pottery was Etruscan. I didn't know the prices: that was Michel's affair, figures listed in a long brown book.

I got up at nine and got used to it. I didn't call my friends: they were studying and being serious, they were in love and being happy, there was nothing we had in common anymore. And I had told them I was leaving, I was gone.

One day in the shop I answered the phone and it was Maud. "Are you better?" I asked.

"I've had a lovely holiday," she said.

"I thought you were ill."

"Ill? I went to England to see my nieces," she answered, "and it was lovely. I wasn't ill, Lord no. Your father gave me a fortnight off."

I stopped going to the shop. They managed to find me a job. Michel mentioned one evening that he knew a photographer who was looking for an assistant. "I don't even know how to load a camera, I couldn't do it," I said.

"Not that kind of assistant, someone to make up the models and pin the dresses. You could do that." Michel made the appointment.

The photographer was called Delaborde; he had a short black beard and thick eyebrows, and wore a thick black cotton jacket, faintly Chinese. "I want someone with energy and imagination," he said; I assured him I had both. "We'll try," he said, adding that he liked the fact I spoke English as well as French. "Most of the models are American, and too stupid to learn French," he said. I would interpret.

I became good at finding stuffed animals, cardboard canoes, false noses, eighteenth century wigs, plaster casts of statues, and artificial plants. I didn't have time to drink cough syrup anymore, but Luc, Delaborde's assistant, taught me how to roll joints, which we smoked in the studio once Delaborde had gone home.

"Delaborde," said my father, "will keep you on your toes."

"Or at least on your feet," said Michel.

Sometimes I called the London number just to see what would happen. She didn't answer.

Dad took me for a walk in the cold, dusty Luxembourg gardens, and down the Seine and along the quays; we talked about love, so as not to talk about Julia. I asked if he and Michel had ever had affairs with others and Dad said, "Of course."

"A woman?"

"No," he said, "various people." Then he tried to reassure me. "Nothing that has ever threatened our life together. Seventeen years together is a lifetime. The physical thing doesn't last that long. Even the greatest passion can only last two and a half years. We've told you that."

"How do you know?" I asked, though I'd heard it said as truth for years.

"Michel can explain. It's his idea, but he's right."

"And my mother?"

"That was different," he said. But that was all he said.

A few weeks later Georgie and Alexis brought a famous American writer to dinner. He was called Fred Gardner, and he lived in London. My ears were alert to Julia's name; I remembered that she knew him. Dad had never met Mr. Gardner, but he admired him unconditionally. I looked at the titles in the bookcase: *A Boy's Body, Very Good Charlie, The Heel of Mercury, The Shoulders of the Ox.* He arrived punctually with Georgie and Alexis, stood back deliberately from the Kouros in the hall and nodded, with a smile. He made his way around the living room at the slow pace of a prospective buyer. "He's looking at everything as if it were for sale," I whispered to Michel.

"Well, it is," said Michel.

Nguyen had made the Vietnamese soup, Fred Gardner drank bourbon and talked about Angkor Wat and Phnom Penh, and said words ending in -*oc* with loud authority. I was, as usual, the only female at the table, and I stared at Mr. Gardner all through dinner. "Such round eyes," he said, looking at me. I wanted to say, "You knew my aunt," but there was nowhere I could fit it in.

After dinner we were back in the living room. Michel pointed to the dark leaves of the magnolias and told Mr. Gardner that they would be flowering in two months, and I installed myself on the sofa and looked at the Buddha's head with its pointed earlobes and waited for the right moment. If he came to sit by me, I thought, then, quietly, I could say Julia's name, and there would be that warmth of her between us. Like love.

But Mr. Gardner took the armchair, and Alexis sat on the sofa next to me and leaned forward to gossip with him. "Help me get the framboise," said Dad in a brisk voice, and I went with him to the pantry and chose the dark cut-glass tumblers, which he said were wrong, so that I had to put them back and get out the little thimbles on stems. And when we came back, Dad with the bottle and me with the right glasses on a tray, I finally heard her name.

Fred Gardner had his head back on the armchair, and was saying to the ceiling in a pleased voice, "Julia was such a fool."

Dad seemed not to have heard, and was putting the bottle down on the coffee table. He motioned me over to him with his hand, made a pile of the catalogues on the table to leave space for the tray.

Georgie and Alexis were laughing along with Fred Gardner. Who went on: "She thought she could get anyone she wanted. She had no idea of her limitations. She even went after the little Cooper boy."

"She was a remarkable woman," said Michel.

I held my breath. My father was silent. The little smile had left his mouth. I knew he would throw Mr. Gardner out if he said another word.

"The Cooper boy is irresistible," Dad said very quietly, "after all."

"He's a whore," said Georgie. "I knew him in Capri, and he's a whore."

"He has talent," said Alexis, "if he'd only work at it."

"It seems confined," said Fred Gardner, "to the ability to attract others. Magnetism more than talent, although to use a word more commonly attributed to politicians and healers seems somehow a little too substantial."

"Irresistible," said my father once again, under his breath. I wondered who the boy was. Not one I'd met.

"Women who have been great beauties imagine they are allowed to get away with anything," continued Fred Gardner, peering at the transparent framboise.

"That cushion was hers," I said, pointing to the needlepoint behind Alexis' elbow.

"She always liked pretty boys," said Alexis.

"Trevor Blake's hideous," I said in her defense.

"So," said Fred Gardner, changing the subject to me, "when do you plan to go to college, and where?"

"Florence isn't the academic type," said Georgie. "She's a working girl."

"You'll regret it," said Fred Gardner.

"Regret it?" I asked. I realized that I was terrified of him.

My father stood up.

"Everyone needs an education," said Fred Gardner, "even girls."

"How about some cherries in brandy?" said my father, making his way out of the room. "They're delicious," he added as he trotted toward the kitchen. He's cooling his temper, I thought.

I got up and went to the yellow silk window seat to wait for his return.

"The Cooper boy," I heard from the sofa. It was Georgie. "I think he affects everyone that way."

"Not me," said Fred Gardner. "I was immune. But of course I'd already been through a few dramas of that kind, though with more compelling people."

"I wouldn't agree that he's common," said Alexis.

"I'd hardly call him an acquired taste," said Georgie. "Reactions tend to be immediate."

"Well, look at Jacob," said Georgie.

"Look at Julia," said Alexis.

I looked around for Michel and realized he was out of the room. I didn't know how long he'd been gone.

"So," Fred Gardner called out to me, "a big girl like you, still living at home?" I looked up to answer but Dad came back with the big glass jar on another tray, and six tiny glass bowls.

"She was rather prim, with it all," continued Fred Gardner.

"The Cooper boy, prim?" asked Georgie.

"Julia."

I sat forward, ready to hear my father defend her. He spoke.

"She got a little that way, recently," he said. "I think it was London that did it to her."

Defend her, I thought. I put a lance in his hand.

"She was afflicted with delusions of adequacy," said Fred Gardner.

"Aren't we all," said Michel, back in the room.

I watched Dad. He was doling out the cherries in brandy, making sure there was an equal number in each bowl.

Show your heart, I thought.

But he wanted to show his discriminating mind.

"She was a little pathetic," he said.

I ran out of the room, and stood in the hall. I wanted revenge on my father, and at once. I called Luc. He was at home. I could hear laughter in the living room, the men.

"Can I come over?" I asked Luc.

I heard him breathing hard into the phone. "Why not?" he said. He was surprised when he opened his door and I stood there with a suitcase.

"It's only for a few nights," I said. "Until I find a place to live."

"You fought with your boyfriend?" he asked, picking up the suitcase.

"No, with my father," I said.

5

Luc had only one bed, and we made love. It seemed the correct thing to do. The next day we had breakfast together in a café, and went to the studio together. A model told me she was leaving her apartment to move in with her fiancé. I had enough sense to know that Luc was not going to be my fiancé, and went back to look at her apartment. Since Luc was busy working, I phoned Nguyen and got him to help me move my things from Dad's place to the tiny two-story room on the Rue du Bac. "Swear you won't tell my father or Michel," I said. Nguyen nodded and gave me some star anise, which he said was good for the digestion.

I had taken only one suitcase of clothes and a few books, and the needlepoint pillows from Julia's house. I wanted to be as smooth and swift as an arrow. Clean, like a spy on a mission. I had to be stealthy, invisible, unencumbered.

I went to the studio and completed my elaborate futile tasks, and came home to eat a deliberately austere dinner of two fried eggs and a plate of grated carrots from the charcuterie downstairs. Do this, I thought, and then do that, and wash the tin plate from China and dry the side of the sink and put the knives away and go to bed. If I adhered to the subtle architecture of my new life, to a strict set of duties and limits, I would be safe. It was a tightrope.

My room was on a narrow part of the street. You went through a doorway between the charcuterie and a pastry shop, up two flights of stairs with thick wooden balustrades, across a corridor tiled in red, and up two more flights, where my front door huddled like a toad beneath a curve of stairs rising to the attic. The room was cunningly cut into a sleeping loft, a standing space that could be a living room if you insisted, a kitchen and a bath. The kitchen was just a narrow recess between the bathroom and the wall; the bathroom was a slim box between the kitchen and the low tunnel that served as my entry, and over all this was the balcony on which lay my mattress, like thick blue frosting. The sleeping balcony was as comfortable as the upper bunk of a second-class sleeper; its principal attraction was the climb up the wide wooden rungs of the short ladder.

The building was scrawny on the outside, and destitute inside. Living there made me, I thought, authentic. I felt I was surrounded by the struggle of life, that behind the lopsided doors lived artists and alcoholics, lost souls. The splintered wood and painted stone and chipped walls seemed irrevocably grim. Until Julia's death I had expected great and wonderful things to happen, because she said so. I had been waiting for my real life to begin, the real life that would be full of great events. Now I knew that it was safer not to want anything at all.

Order would save me. I made my bed in the morning before I went to work. I wrote down every franc I spent. I bought a vacuum cleaner and vacuumed several times a week. I did not want anyone to come to my room, my shell. I did not invite Luc over. If I was going to have an affair, here in my new life, it would be with an extraordinary being, a stranger. I had faith that what I had lost would be returned to me; not Julia but some person whose living weight could cancel out the dead absence. And because I believed suffering was rewarded, I gladly endured, and sought to endure even more, just to make sure.

For Delaborde I did menial things. Carried packages, cleaned the studio floor, took métros to far sides of Paris to look for bulky and ridiculous props. I put the makeup on the models. Delaborde bought me a tall black case that opened out like a toolbox, with tiers of plastic jars of every shade of skin and membrane. I hated carrying packages, loathed the métro, was inept with mop and broom, and I persevered. The first contact of my fingers with a model's face were never pleasant: I didn't like to touch the skin of girls, but once the thick base had obliterated their pores, and once I'd powdered it to the texture of unglazed pottery, each face was reduced to surface and I worked gladly. Delaborde liked the girls to have dead-white faces, red mouths.

I didn't talk much to the models, but eavesdropped on their conversations, stories about boyfriends and plane tickets to Milan. The boyfriends were always giving trouble, appropriating paychecks, leaving town, misbehaving with other girls.

The studio was a place where lank, bulbous human beings labored in a reddish gloom to make a cold perfection in the acid gray starlight given off by the Balcar flash on a set of permanently gray paper. The Balcar, a metal box with a long stem topped by a silver umbrella, gave off clicks that sounded like sparks, while the camera's sound was heavy with metal, rounded, mechanical. There was no music. When Delaborde worked, all the air in the long red room was pulled into the set, and Luc and I labored over the miniature moment from outside the light, with electric fans to make the hair blow and nylon threads to pull at the hems of the dresses to make them fly. I wore garage mechanic's overalls, so that I could wipe my hands on my legs, and crawl fearlessly on the floor.

In the first months at Delaborde's, my actions were uncluttered by will, perfect. I did my work, and he paid me every four weeks. I did my work better, and he gave me a bonus. I applied myself, and the models looked better, more still, more dead. I let Delaborde have the Coca-Cola I was about to drink, and he was in a good mood. I avoided Luc's eyes, and he went after a model. I did something wrong, and I got shouted at. I spent no money and charged him for taxis I hadn't taken, and I never had to write a check.

My fight with my father was the most precious thing I had. The distance between us required the same care and attention as my apartment, so as not to get dusty and ragged. I didn't want to be his daughter anymore. I would be defined by Delaborde. I would be the assistant with the long black hair, that was all. I curled into that small space with ease; it was not a tight fit. As the months went by and the execution of the tasks slid into routine, the routine became my only life.

One day, carrying my two bottles of Evian water up the various flights of stairs that led to my room, I slipped on some vomit at the curve of a landing. It was a tramp, probably, one of the dark huddles who slept on the first landing and used the public toilet that was clamped to the third flight of stairs, a stink of beer and ammonia seeping through its unboltable door. A loud voice inside me said, *You're too young to live like this, you should have some fun.* That evening, a friend of a friend at a table of fourteen in a cheap restaurant took my hand as I reached for the wine, and I went back to his room, in the tiled basement of a run-down hotel near the Coupole. Late in the night he said, "Do you want to stay? My girlfriend doesn't come back until tomorrow afternoon," and I thought how wonderful it was to know such things in advance.

I did not want to be deceived, so I started with deceit. I fled bachelors and unattached men, and sought out those who were married or living with women. As long as I could be sure things were impossible, I felt safe. The models hated married men, and spent their time plotting against rivals. I wanted to be sure my rivals were already in place, that the game was loaded against me. And of course I got my way.

My life began to split in half, so as to appear to me, in high moments, almost double. In the studio I was meek, efficient. Outside, I was something else. I never took a man back to my room. I did not sleep with men at night, but saw them in the afternoon in borrowed apartments, and sometimes between the bed and the floor I managed a short nap, from which I would wake, disoriented, delighted, briefly, at the degradation of a damp unfamiliar towel and strange soap. The character of these encounters accorded with my view of the world—nasty, brutish, and short, exaltingly so.

The only ethical condition I attached to my behavior was that I would not touch any man married to any girl I knew. I proceeded therefore a little like the knight on the chessboard, soliciting and responding always two away and diagonally across from where I sat. I was fond of men at other tables.

As the months went on and my encounters multiplied, I found that my desire was increasing, to become at times incapacitating. The minute I wanted a man, I could not make any sense until I had panicked both of us into bed, though it wasn't always a bed. There was a large building where studios and processing labs were grouped together, called PhoLab, which I had to visit several times a week on errands for Delaborde. There were photographers there, and assistants, and dark projection rooms, and offices with doors that locked.

The two sides of life rarely crossed. If an attractive man wandered into Delaborde's studio, I had no rational way of behaving, and either left or made a fool of myself. One day we photographed an actress. While she was on the set, her boyfriend, a tall Englishman with limpid eyes, waited in the dressing room where I had persuaded Rémi the hairdresser to trim my hair. The Englishman was looking through his address book to let us know he had other places to be, and also he was watching Rémi's scissors on my hair. "Thick black hair, heavy and straight," he said in the tone of someone eating a peach. "Asiatic hair." I felt his gaze like a field of white energy, blinding and warm.

"Thanks, big boy, want another Mai Tai?" I answered in a high-pitched voice. My approximation of what a Chinese bargirl would say. He stood up quickly and left the dressing room.

Another day it was a writer, whose portrait Delaborde was taking for a book cover. It happened that we left the studio together. The door of the studio closed and we were alone in the bright outer hall. The man was neither young nor very attractive, but he stood close to me and I could see the freckles on his cheeks and smell his skin. I wanted to touch my mouth to his. I felt the kiss before it happened, as we stood facing each other, and blushed so hard that it didn't happen. "We'd better separate immediately or they'll catch us," I said, and ran past him to the door. I didn't look back, and never saw him again. The next day, to prove to myself I wasn't a coward, I spent an hour in bed with the husband of a woman who worked for *Elle*, and part of the afternoon in the loft of a photographer who lived near Pigalle.

Friendship did not come far behind sexual adventure in my scale of things. I treated it a little the same, but instead of consummation, I wanted confession. And instead of a multiplicity of strange bodies, I had one friend, and that was Sylvie. I knew as much about her life as she did, and she certainly knew more than she could digest about mine. Sylvie was a nymph. She was rounded and tapered like a doll, and blonde. Old men followed her in the street. She could have modeled, she could have been paid to look the way she looked, but she did nothing. She lived partly with her mother, and partly with a man named Marc. He was forty at the time; Sylvie was seventeen. Where I had adventures, Sylvie had love affairs. She had already had three since she was fifteen. Her mother approved. Her mother was like that too.

Sylvie's mother was a client of my father's. She was called Suzy Ambelic, and she had been married without being married to various rich men. She had a complicated past and a stringent voice. As a child, sitting in the shop, I had listened with alarm and fascination to Madame Ambelic's dissertations on the color of her dining room walls and the pretty things men had given her.

Her voice cracked glass. Michel called her basilisk, which, Dad explained, was a magical snake that lived inside wells and cast spells. I didn't think Madame Ambelic was magical; her print dresses, her potbelly and her gray hair placed her well out of the realm of the temptress. I had always known that she had a daughter, a little younger than me, but we didn't go to the same school and Dad didn't socialize with his female customers.

I met Sylvie just after Julia died, during the last months I lived with Dad. We all had lunch together one day, and Sylvie and I might never have exchanged another word, except that we ran into each other that same night at a place on the Rue Fontaine, which meant we could be friends.

Sylvie listened well. It was one of the two things her mother said were important in a woman. The other was grooming. Sylvie kept her eyes on me while I talked, and never disapproved of anything I did. Her disapproval was reserved for people she hadn't met, so that I could never get her to agree that my father was vile, whereas Delaborde, whom she had never seen, was in her eyes an unremitting pig. I could tell Sylvie my affairs, though for the sake of coherence, I told her in each case that I was, at least a little, in love with the man. So that the man who paid me for my work was an object of our hatred, and the strangers I slept with were worth long hours of attentive speculation. Occasionally, she would say, "I think you have too many people in your life," and I would say, "You are the only person who's ever been to my room, what do you mean?"

I had written to Geraldine, and to Doctor Emery. A letter from Mr. Leon found me at my new address. In it he said that there was money for me, which would be coming from Switzerland. I decided not to allow the fact that I was rich to interfere with my life of poverty, but the sum was not particularly big. He hinted at something larger, for later, and sent me papers which I was supposed to sign and send back within a month. There were old friends of Julia's who came through and found my phone number, although I wasn't listed. They called early in the mornings. "This is the first thing I had to do," they'd say. Geraldine wrote me long letters about her spring garden, her early summer garden, and so on. "I think you'd like to know that the baby is called Julia," she wrote. I shuddered. In the summer she came over, took me to tea at W. H. Smith's, and bought me a book on Bellini which we both knew was something Julia would have wanted.

The Americans were different. There were men who had known Julia as a girl in New York, "Before all the European stuff." There were rich matrons who had gone to school with her, but seemed, with their pale dyed hair and skin-colored shoes, far older than Julia. They stayed at the big hotels and summoned me for drinks. They wanted to cry, and halfway through their first drink, tears would come to their eyes, and then to mine. "Such a waste," they said. A Mrs. Pomerand, who had been best friends with Julia when they were growing up, opened her brown lizard bag and pressed a hundred-dollar bill into my hand. I tried to give it back: "I don't need it," I said.

"I want to do this for Julia," said Mrs. Pomerand. "Buy yourself something nice. Please."

I looked over at the other tables in the hotel bar: there were sleek prostitutes with their hair swept back and good clothes sitting with bald gentlemen in bold ties. Mrs. Pomerand touched a handkerchief to her eyes. I was crying too. I put the money in my pocket. A hundred dollars for my tears. What the prostitutes were doing seemed a cleaner and less painful transaction. I was weeping, demolished by Mrs. Pomerand's grief. It would be so much simpler to be a call girl than to cry on cue for this stranger, for the other strangers from Julia's past. I liked the idea of being beautiful enough to be bought. But I would have to be bought by a connoisseur, not by a mere lonely consumer on a ten-day trip.

The Americans came in numbers in the late spring and at the end of summer; they asked me how she had died, and what Trevor Blake had done, what had happened to the house. They asked about my father and I said he was fine, and they looked knowing and wise and skeptical. I got another hundred-dollar bill from a couple who lived in Florida, and mourning began to seem unpleasantly lucrative. "Your aunt loved London," they said, "but she should have come home."

I went home from these visits drained, and hugged the cushions that had come from Julia's house to Dad's apartment to my room.

6

A WEEK BEFORE THE anniversary of Julia's death I sent a personal ad and a money order to the London *Times*. J.E., In Loving Memory. That was all I dared insert, and no signature. I wanted to call attention to her, and not to me. If any of her friends were reading that day, they would understand, and perhaps wonder who had remembered before them. The twenty-seventh of January was a dead dark hole of a day, with bad fog at the airport. The papers did not arrive from London. The first newsstand yielded the first disappointment. Maybe in the afternoon, the woman said, looking up at the sky.

I had to spend the day looking for props for the couture dresses we would be photographing that night. It was collection time, when Delaborde worked from six until dawn, the only time we could get the dresses. This time he wanted animals: "Wild animals, big ones, and pretty ones, life size, real ones, dead," was how he put it.

I spent the day between taxidermists and paper stands, collecting a dik-dik and a baby zebra, with a brief exchange about what a baby zebra could die of: "These animals do not die of old age," the taxidermist told me. Then I got a bear and a tiger, and a pair of mothy leopards with red felt collars, one of which was missing an eye. Luc drove the van, which was filled with beasts. I made him stop at every paper stand. "Are you in the paper?" he asked, and I said no. The studio was in the old Jewish quarter. When we got back the shopkeepers came out to watch Luc unload the dead menagerie.

"No rouge," said Delaborde, standing at the dressing room door. The models that night had pale hair and light eyes the color of tap water. He wanted them *"effacées,"* rubbed out, erased, almost invisible. Bits of Julia came to me as I worked. I stopped to blow my nose, and saw the model draw back when I started on her lips with the brush. "It's okay," I said, "I haven't got a cold."

The dresses were printed to look like tigers and leopards and snakes. I got Delaborde's point, and stood in a corner of the studio thinking how clever he was, as I watched the live dresses and the dead animals.

I got home at five-thirty and was up at eleven. The London *Times* was at the newsstand, yesterday's paper. I bought two copies just in case, and carried them back to the café on the corner of my street. I sat at a table, so that I could open out the paper without getting it wet on the counter. My heart beat hard.

J.E., in bold print. IN LOVING MEMORY. My fringe felt wet. I read it again; the words seemed closer to me than the rest of the page. I forgot that I had paid to put them there. They were a message to me, more than a message from me. It was so big, so unmistakable. Everyone in London must have seen it. I wondered who. I hoped Trevor Blake had cried. I wanted to show it to someone. I called Sylvie.

Sylvie said an hour later, in a different, more elegant bar, "I don't think you should do this." She was wearing an old coat of her mother's, with a fur collar. We drank hot chocolate.

"Look," I said, showing her the paper, "it's as if she were talking to me."

Sylvie made a face. "It's not good," she said.

"What?"

"This, playing with these things about Julia. It's not healthy."

"She's not healthy, she's dead," I answered.

Sylvie gave a sigh. "It would be healthier for you to go see a person who could let you, you know, contact her. You don't put ads in the paper to speak to your own family. Even if they are dead."

"I have to go to a clairvoyant? I don't think that's any better. And what's wrong with an in-memoriam, anyway? It's a perfectly normal thing to do." I was getting angry, because if she hadn't exactly understood, suddenly neither did I. The effort of explaining made me see how little I knew what I was doing. I tried to build up my argument. "In England, it's perfectly common, it's what's done, a year after someone dies. It marks a date."

"We're not in England, you're not English, and neither was your aunt," said Sylvie.

"*Merde*, Sylvie," I hissed over the dregs of my chocolate. I hated her crude simplicity.

She took my hand; she wore a ring on every finger, as did I. "Go see Rosa, please. She's someone my mother believes in absolutely. She's a genius. She'll give you messages from Julia, and she'll tell you what is going to happen to you."

"I don't want to know about the future," I said.

"You miss your aunt, it's natural, she was like your mother. I'd miss mine too if she were dead."

I didn't like Julia being compared to the raucous Madame Ambelic.

"What if it's bad news?" I asked. "I don't want to hear anything bad."

"It won't be bad, I promise," said Sylvie, taking my hand. "It will be wonderful."

And I wanted to believe her. "Maybe," I said. Maybe. "Sylvie, I'll go. Today. Where is she?"

"I'll have to get the number from my mother. I don't know it. I'll ask her later."

I didn't want to wait. "Call your mother now," I said, and gave Sylvie a *jeton*. She dragged herself up from the table. While she called I decided I would ask Rosa about my aunt. I would ask Rosa about love. I would ask Rosa about the meaning of life.

I hadn't really thought about all these things before.

"She can't see you until next week, and my mother has to set it up," said Sylvie, returning. Which meant I had to have lunch with Madame Ambelic. She liked involving herself in people's lives.

I went on Sunday, the maid's day off so that Madame Ambelic cooked herself. We ate quiche with thick pastry crusts and runny centers, which, Madame Ambelic informed me, was Tadzio's favorite dish. Sylvie sighed slightly at the name. Her mother's talk was a long rush of memories, names of places and names of men running together in a bulky travelogue. At last we came to Rosa.

"I thought it was over with Jean-Pierre. We had been together for a year, yes and no and here and there, and I was ready to give up. I loved him so, but he made me eat dirt. I thought it was over and would never get anywhere. Someone gave me Rosa's name, I wish I could remember who it was. Anyway, she read my cards, she was young then—well, so was I—and she told me that within one week he would declare himself. And he did. We married! And all because of Rosa. It didn't last, of course. Nothing does. But she was right, and she's been right about everything since then."

She got up to make coffee, and I asked Sylvie who Jean-Pierre was.

"My father," she said.

This gave Rosa's predictions some body: without Rosa there might have been no Sylvie.

Suzy Ambelic returned with a tray. "When you go see her," she said, "I want you to be very honest about what you want to know. Rosa can see things no one else can, but if you are critical while she's trying to concentrate, it's disturbing for her."

I promised. I would be good. Sylvie announced she wanted to go too, and her mother had a moment's hesitation—"Are you sure? Why?" during which I wondered why Rosa was unfit for Sylvie.

"I'll ask her about Marc," said Sylvie.

"Oh, if that's what it is, it's fine," said Suzy Ambelic, adding, "Are you sure it's not too early?"

"I've been with him almost six months!" protested Sylvie.

Madame Ambelic nodded her head and turned to me. "Florence," she said, "I know you don't have much money, and I want this to be my gift, and I don't want to hear another word about it."

I wasn't going to remind her that I received an allowance. In the last year I hadn't been given anything that I had not worked for, except for the hundred-dollar bills, and this gift, although I could neither wear it nor spend it, and had not yet received it, made me feel unexpectedly loved. A slow warmth spread through me. Oh God, I said under my breath. "Thank you," I murmured.

"You're blushing," said Sylvie.

A gift felt very much like sex.

Sylvie and I had to go sit in the Flore after lunch. We had not yet been seen that day, and we needed to be looked at while we talked.

Before Rosa we were already looking for signs, but for signs in reality. Sylvie wanted to know what I thought about the fact that Marc was taking her to dinner with friends of his. It was important, she said, because he usually saw her alone, which she took to mean that she was not fit for adult company. "He likes me in bed, I don't see why I'd be any different in a restaurant with his friends," she said. I agreed it was an important change. But did I really understand how important? she asked me. I nodded. Sylvie's hunger for reassurance was boundless. I thought of her Marc, a rounded man with an apartment near the Etoile, a car, men friends, a smooth and modern and expensive life, not unlike a leather desk set. Compared to him, my stolen husbands seemed insubstantial. "You wouldn't understand," said Sylvie, "you're only interested in sex." I liked the idea of being a fearless nymphomaniac. I gave a smile that was deliberately embarrassed. She went on: "You see, I love Marc, I really love him. And I want to marry him."

"But you have everything to live for!" I said. "You're only seventeen!"

"This is true love. I don't even care if he sleeps with other women, I want to be his wife."

Sa femme, she said. The French word for wife and the only word for adult female, wife and woman are one. Both signified defeat for me, the end of perpetual emotion. "You're mad," I said, "my mother did it once, and she died."

"I'm not going to marry a homosexual," she said, "that is the maddest thing any woman can do to herself."

"She was in love," I said. That's what I imagined. That was all I knew about my mother, that and the photograph of her on his dresser. We never saw her family. My father said there was no reason to. Elise, my mysterious mother who died in childbirth.

I was nervous on my way to Rosa's a week later. I hoped my nerves would not fake her reading. It was like heartbeats that started just before the doctor's annual visit at school; I was always shaking, and sure that any diagnostic he made in those conditions would be false. I wanted a diagnostic from Rosa, an accurate gauge of my deeper truth. Everything I did seemed to be entirely without consequences, once I stepped beyond the careful boundaries I had set myself—and in carrying my past and present to a seer, I think I hoped to hear about some grand order that would make all the parts have sense.

Rosa lived on the Avenue Bosquet. There was a normal concierge downstairs, a regular elevator, an anonymous front door. No clues. A tall woman answered the door. Her gray hair was cut short, she was overweight, she had an air at once composed and lonely. She wore a sweater with stripes, and a shawl, the winter afternoon shawl of someone who occasionally knits. There were burls and knots in the deep red wool. She did not look like a witch. She looked like the slow person who stands in front of you at the grocer's.

"Florence Ellis," she enunciated, "protégée of Suzy Ambelic." She had an ironic smile, as if to let me in on the joke of her calling. Her face was square, serene.

Inside she sat with her back to the window, at a table covered with a deep magenta cloth. On the walls were representations of the ineffable, paintings of sunrise and birds in flight. My father's lessons in taste had left me with a disdain for art that used shorthand sentiment: sunsets, dawns, birds, children, rainbows. He liked the beautiful only if it was in a dead, unknown, or forgotten language. He couldn't bear to read the words Joy, or Beauty, or Sorrow, or Happiness, or Soul, or God, and snickered at anyone who used them. The Kouros in the front hall was acceptable. His smile, my father said, was Attic. I wanted that smile to be mysterious, holy, sexual. The dictionary said Attic was a dialect of Greek, and that as an adjective it was marked by purity, simplicity, and refinement. It seemed a cold way to describe a smile. "We Jews were forbidden to name God," my father told me, during my religious mania. "And it is in bad taste to try to represent him."

"What about all the gods in the shop?" I asked.

"They're not gods, they're pretty things," he'd said. "Don't get the two mixed up."

I sat sneering at the inferior art that tried to name beauty and soul, waiting for Rosa to tell me the beauty of my soul. The table was littered with her tools. A crystal ball, which I expected. A wax model of a hand, fetid pale. A blue candle on my left in a dish. As I watched she lit it with a match. "What's that for?" I asked.

"Shhh," she said, and then in a distracted voice, "it brings the good spirits."

She joined her hands in prayer. They were perfectly conical, the palms curved in like the simple petal of a calla lily. Behind her and through the window, it was raining.

Her eyelids were arched, hooded, graceful. Pale gray eyes. She breathed on her hands and placed them facedown on the table. "So," she said, "what was it you wanted to know?"

I opened my own hands, struck by how small and square the palms were next to hers. I didn't want to talk to Julia as much as I had the week before. I didn't know what I wanted. The generosity of the beyond left me speechless.

"Money?" she asked. "Work, health, family, lost objects, return of love, legal problems, contact with the dead?"

She'd mentioned it. The only reason I was there. I nodded.

"The dead then," she said, and changing her tone, she began a fast chant—"The dead, the dead, your grandmother, no, your father, your mother, your mother, yes. I'm getting your mother, she's on the other side, isn't she?"

Don't tell her, I thought. But a tear was already running down my cheek. I knew she could see it. I wanted her to. Paying in tears. Julia would be my mother. Julia counted as my mother.

She took my hand. Hers was cold, like the washcloth my father used to put on my forehead, soaked with tap water and cologne.

She gripped. I was trembling.

"She went quickly," she said. "She knew nothing. She felt no pain. She was in a car."

I nodded again.

"She was driving. It was very early. She should not have been there, she should not have been doing what she was doing. She was stubborn. The man next to her is alive. She forgives him."

"The man? He wasn't next to her, he was in the house."

"He was next to her," she said. "He is young, he is handsome, he is very sad. You should talk with him."

"I don't know him," I said. "She was alone. There wasn't anyone with her." I wished she would get back to the truth.

"He ran away," she went on, "he was scared. It wasn't right for him to be there. He ran away." Here she shut her eyes tight.

I wondered what the beyond considered "right." Did sin apply in the same way as in a church? I was annoyed by this intruder and the problem he brought with him. Julia had said, used to say, that love was never a sin. It couldn't have been a lover. Did Rosa mean something Julia would have felt was a sin, or something that was a public sin? It certainly wasn't Trevor Blake, young and handsome, never.

"What's his name?" I asked, reluctantly, because I was sure he didn't exist.

"Happy Sin," she said, in a low voice like a reverie.

"That's a name?" I murmured back. I felt something else was happening to her, and I didn't want to disturb her. But Happy Sin was no kind of name. Maybe she was answering the question I hadn't asked: it was a happy sin. At that moment I began to think that Rosa was very special, to answer an unasked question. I waited for more proof of her power.

"She wants you to know she did not suffer. She is with you always. She wants you to be kind to your father. She says he is not to blame. She loves you."

So she knew. Reproach from the other side. I had to make it up with Dad. "Do I have to?" I whispered, without bothering to specify, since Rosa could read my thoughts.

"You must, but remember this: do not be too curious. Let well enough alone."

One message of love and two bits of sharp advice. How very much Julia. I felt like a bad child. "Tell her I'm sorry about the cologne and the beads . . ." I began.

"Shhh," said Rosa. Her hands were folded in prayer again. Rosa let out a deep sigh. "You don't need me," she said, in a slower voice, more hers, "you have the gift. Just learn to listen."

My heart stopped beating. So she knew about the voice. I felt something like warm oil being poured on me. I wanted to hug Julia. Rosa's words had made clouds and mists of Julia in the room. I shut my eyes and saw Julia's face, solemn, impassive, no postcard smile. My arms went forward to hug her. I opened my eyes and saw she was not there. I saw Rosa, and the window behind her, and the table with its instruments to receive other worlds. There was nothing that had a shape or a color I could recognize as Julia, or even a part of Julia, or a token from Julia, a flower petal, a drifting feather. I looked over at the paintings: The enthusiastic evocation of dawn beckoned, started to pull me in. I longed to be in that pink and blue unreachable sky. Then I looked back at Rosa, stared at her gray eyes, saw how little they were brown or like Julia's. I wanted to ask about my real mother, about Elise, but Rosa said, "Now, about you."

"Is that all she has to tell me?" I felt irrelevant at that moment, my future dispensable.

Rosa reached behind her chair with a practiced hand and gave me a Kleenex. I blew my nose several times; she gave me another.

"Now," she said. She shuffled a deck of long cards. I had seen Tarots before. I knew a girl, a hairdresser, who did her cards every morning: her pack was brown around the edges, dank and sticky to the touch. These were cleaner. Rosa asked me to cut three times.

"Lay them out, left to right."

The pictures were gloomy, emphatic. An unintelligible, urgent whisper. I didn't like looking at the wide arc of images, because I have a sharp recall of the deep magenta cloth beneath them.

"What a nice spread!" she said. I thought to make up for the tears.

I was tired from what had come before. The cards were laid out in a cross, people by a river and a woman alone in a church, and children waving at the sun, and dogs baying at the moon, and I was ready to believe each picture was the story of my life, but there were so many that they canceled each other out. I looked at her face instead of the pictures, and then at her hands, and then again at the pink and pale mauve dawn on the wall. I heard her tell me that I should make it up with my father, who really loved me, and that there would be an enemy around me, and that I couldn't trust anyone but myself. And then just as I was getting bored, she told me I was going to meet the love of my life.

"When?" I asked. That'll show Sylvie, I thought.

"Soon," she said.

"Will I be happy?" I asked. Not the kind of question I thought I had in me. Happiness was for the innocent, happiness was for the mob. The words Good and Bad and Should and Ought were pushing things into categories inside my head. Good, good, Bad, bad. Sad, happy. I hadn't given these names to anything since I had taken the picture of Jesus off the wall. Not since I was a child on the linoleum squares. Now I was forced to do some formal thinking. Good, bad, happy, sad. The notions came in cubes that fell like dice.

"Happy?" she asked, and smiled. She didn't answer. Maybe she was cynical after all.

"Is he rich?" If I couldn't be happy, I would have to be rich. Madame Ambelic always said it was better to cry in a Rolls-Royce than in the métro. I didn't believe she'd cried in either. But a lover would be rich and single if he were to fit into a clairvoyant's vision.

"He isn't rich, and you probably won't marry him, but he is part of your life." She turned over a card. I remember that picture: a young man walking toward a precipice, his head held high. He can't see where he's going, he's going to fall.

"The Fool," she said, "the most innocent and powerful card in the great Arcana."

Arcana was not a word I knew. "What's the zero underneath him for?" I asked.

"It's nothing," she said. Yes, of course it's nothing. "And everything. The beginning and the end of all things."

"Will it last?" I asked.

"Nothing ever ends," she said. She folded the cards back together and shook them into line on the table. "I hope I helped," she said, with a ceremonial little modesty.

I thanked her. I stood up. We shook hands, an oddly social thing to do with hands after having used them to gather in Julia's spirit. "Does she know I love her?" I asked.

"Don't worry," she said. I wanted more, but the curtain had dropped.

Outside, in the freezing rain of the Avenue Bosquet, I held tight to the hour I had just spent. I had to go home to remember it all from the beginning, but the flavor of it was good. I would make sure her words came true. I would prove I was the mistress of my destiny. I would show fate that I was a willing pupil, follow Rosa's instructions, and then my wishes would come true. I would live happily ever after.

Like Julia. Unlike Julia . . . I wanted to know who the man in the car was. I wanted to know more. The panic of not knowing where to go to find her stunned me, and then I remembered one place where her things were gathered, and went to the bank on the Rue Cambon. The bank was about to close, but I cried at the gate so the guard let me in. A bald man in a gray suit led me downstairs, and made me wait while he checked my signature and went behind a door. "Are you sure you don't have a key?" he asked, and sounded angry. After minutes he placed me in a small cubicle, and deposited a long pale beige metal box in front of me. I unhooked the painted wire catch, and raised the lid. The emeralds were in there, in little suede pouches, and the pearl bracelets, and her earrings, all for pierced ears. I turned them over in my hands and remembered them on the dressing table and saw her bottle of Mitsouko and her three-sided mirror glinting just beyond my vision. I closed my eyes to see better, but it didn't help; holding the smooth stones and sharp chains in my hot palms didn't help. I put everything back in the suede pouches and called the man to come and lock them up again. I didn't take anything, I didn't want to wear anything of hers.

At home I lit an incense stick and put the water on to boil for tea and sat down on my cushions to think about Rosa's words. There was too much promise and too much contradiction to hold on to all alone; I had to call Sylvie.

"Yes, Rosa's great, I saw her this morning," she said.

"Why didn't you tell me? What did she tell you?"

"She said I was made for love, so I'm not so sure I want to get married after all."

I wished I had been told the same thing.

"She told me I was about to meet the love of my life," I said.

"Me too," said Sylvie.

"No, a real one, the big one," I said, to elbow her out of my destiny.

"That'll make a change," she said, giggling.

"Sylvie, be serious. I feel so much better." I lowered my voice, in case of a crossed line. "Julia talked to me."

"What did she say?" Sylvie asked.

I didn't have the words for what I had felt while Julia spoke through Rosa, and though I wanted to tell Sylvie about looking for Julia in the painting I knew she would laugh. "She said wonderful things," I managed at last. "It was really her."

"Bravo!" said Sylvie, as if I had won a prize.

"Thank you for sending me, and thank your mother. I just feel so much better, I feel happy."

"Yes," said Sylvie, "she's cheering, isn't she? My mother says an hour with Rosa is better than an afternoon at Elizabeth Arden's."

THAT EVENING I TOOK out the Roman ring and looked carefully at the incised image of Leda and the swan. This is what I want, I thought. It was a wish. He would have wings, he would be a god in disguise. Now that I had been told he would come, it was safe to wish; like asking for the sun to rise.

A few days later I dreamt that I had cut my hair. It was a vivid dream, so vivid that the next day at the studio I kept looking at the hairdresser's scissors. I looked at myself in the mirror, and I looked. I held my hair out on either side of me, the long black curtain that was me. That made me look, from the back, Bolivian or Japanese. That got stuck in my coat collar in the winter, and jammed under my arms in bed. That men loved. That took an hour to dry with the blower.

I waited a day. We worked with Rémi, again. I asked him to do it. "Like a boy," I said. In the dream I had looked like a boy. The dream had felt so good. My neck was cold when Rémi finished. I saw that my ears were slightly pointed. I saw that I was, maybe, beautiful. "You look better as a boy," said Rémi.

That night I went to the Coupole with my new neck and my good looks of a boy. I felt so light, as if there were half of me, and what was left concentrated everything that had been dispersed on the long tips of my hair.

I went to the Coupole almost every night. No one was supposed to call me at the studio. I needed the Coupole to see who was around, who was alive. If I was invited for dinner I tried to make sure it was at the Coupole, so that I could see as many people as possible. If I had no invitation, I went around nine, to see who was there; it was a rare night that I wasn't asked to sit down at one table or another. And when dinner elsewhere yielded no romance, I went on to the Coupole, alone, to see who was still lingering, and to give myself the secret pleasure of seeing my lovers with their wives.

So long as I knew, I was in control.

Julia would have called it undignified, my father would have called it cruising, and Sylvie said it was pure masochism. To me, it was the most reliable of thrills.

There were various approaches. The right-hand door led straight into the tablecloth section, where the people with money ate. That door had to be taken at high speed, with the pretense of a purpose. It was best taken late, because the people at the cloth tables were less likely to ask me to sit down than those at the paper tables. It was dangerous, because the headwaiter here was not a friend, and people who sit at cloth tables are not all friendly. The only advantage it had was that the main aisle led straight to the toilet and the telephones, so that if I lost my nerve all I had to do was keep walking in a straight line to be in the safety of the cloakroom, where I could plan the rest of my itinerary while buying a package of cigarettes or making a phone call.

The left-hand door led to the bar and the paper tablecloths. It was more like home; the headwaiter knew me, Delaborde ate there often, Luc and Nancy ate there. These tables always had friendly faces. It was humbler than the other side. And, comfortable as I felt being humble, I didn't always want to acknowledge my comfort. This was the side where I had dinner. This was the side from which young models, sitting with a large group of us, departed to eat oysters with famous photographers at the linen tables. And we cheered and said, "Good for her," and watched her clothes get more sober and her makeup subtler as the months went by, until she disappeared to live in Milan or New York, or grew a fat stomach and went to be a real person in the country and have a real baby.

In those days enough rich and successful people went to the Coupole for us on the paper side to imagine that opportunity was always at hand. And enough sad and sour people for us to know that failure was as present as success, but, this being Paris, no less attractive.

There was so much life in the Coupole that I thought I wasn't living if I was kept away from it, and to be there allowed me to think better. What I called thinking then was no more logical a process than being drowned in impressions and grabbing the largest one I could find.

It was eleven when I got there. I came in from the artists' door, the left-hand door. Sallow men in shaggy white coats sat on the terrace with thin women and big dogs. I pushed past the people crowding out of the bar, backing up in the wait for a table. The lights were terribly bright. I had never been there with my short hair. The movable landmarks of familiar faces were not enough. Something special was going to happen. I had made a dream come true, and even if it was the unsolicited composition of sleep, rather than a wish, it was still a dream. I anticipated the presence of someone, but I didn't know who.

At first I couldn't focus. I was too aware of my new head to allow my eyes to rest on anyone. I looked at the floor to steady myself, and the mosaics danced, ocher and navy and yellow and white. I stood up straight, pulled my rib cage up the way I had been taught to in ballet class, and walked past the tables. Would they know that I was me? I raised my hand to feel the space behind my ears, the indentation at the nape.

I was in the paper side. A high tide of blond hair, turtleneck sweaters, paste brooches, lipstick, haggard chins, pursed mouths, oyster trays on stilts, wine bottles, arms reaching for bread, couples leaning into each other, couples tensed apart, talkers waving hands, elderly men sitting well back to be erect, dogs opening their little jaws for tiny pieces of meat held by big fingers, coatcheck girls hugging thick wads of coats, headwaiters in bow ties and suits with shiny lapels manning the intersections of the aisles, dour and responsible, holding little pads in their hands on which were names.

Names. Delaborde with his wife, or ex-wife, Agnes. Nelly Fink and one of her painters. Sylvie's cousin Emmanuelle Cattin, Nancy and Luc. Luc and Delaborde waved. They were the only two who recognized me; they'd seen me that day.

I went down the aisle past the fountain. There was one of my men, with his girlfriend. He looked up, gave a vague smile, then frowned and mouthed, "Florence?" I nodded. My heart beat faster, so that I had to look down again to steady myself. I turned left toward the toilets, made a brief run in to the cigarette stand, and came out again. It didn't make much sense to do this unless they could recognize me. If every man had to frown and mouth my name at me, the subtle charge was lost. I made for the linen exit, realizing that I would have to impress my new face on everyone before I tried this again.

At the crossing of two aisles I saw my father and Michel. They never came to the Coupole. There they were.

They were looking at their menus.

I looked away quickly so as not to be seen. There was a third person with them, a man with long dark hair, facing them, his back to me. He was on a chair, they had a banquette: he was in the subservient position. I was briefly aware of broad shoulders and a green jacket before I wheeled to the right and made for the bar. I no longer looked like me and they had not seen me. My back felt hot as if there were eyes on it, and at the bar I made a sharp left and went out the door, and once out I ran to the taxi stand in the middle of the street.

I had seen them, they hadn't seen me, and even if they had, they couldn't be sure it was me. The idea was irresistible. I knew I had to call Dad and start being his daughter again. There was no challenge left in hiding from him.

I called him the next morning. He was in the shop.

"Dad."

A closed, prissy tone when he answered. A Jacob I was not used to. I thought I might hang up immediately, pretend I'd never called. If only I'd said Jacob. Dad was irreparably from me.

"Dad," he said, "and who would that be?"

"I'm sorry. I mean, I'm back. I never went away. Hi."

I had no feelings in the matter of making it up with him. I could have been honest and said, "A fortune teller told me I would meet the love of my life once I made it up with you, so let's make up because I want to fall in love." I could have said, "I went to a woman who put me in contact with Julia and she wants us to be friends again." I could have said, "I've cut my hair, so if you see me in the street you won't even know it's me, which is why you might as well see what I look like now, and by the way you'll be pleased because I look like a boy."

There was nothing I could say.

"Hi, Florence. I'm glad you called." The words were open, warm.

"How are you?"

"We're fine, we're fine. I had to let you make the first move, you know? You understand, don't you?"

I'm not making the first move, I thought. I'm just trying to get destiny going.

"We knew where you were, and what you're up to. We're both very proud of you," he said.

"Proud?"

"That you've still got that job, that you're working hard. Routine is the hardest thing for people like us."

"How's Michel?"

"He's better. He's fine. So am I. So, this means we'll be seeing you."

"Yes." I could see it. Dinner Chez Georges. Dinner at home. Nguyen, beaming crooked teeth at me. And then in the middle of feeling cold and clever on my end of the phone, I found I wanted him to be the way I remembered him.

"Are you well? Are you? I'm sorry."

"There's nothing to apologize about. Tonight we've got to go to the country and see Michel's aunt, she's about to die. What about tomorrow night? We can have a cozy evening, just the three of us. I'd ask you to run over here now and throw your arms around me, but since we've been in the same city for the whole time it would seem a little dramatic, don't you think?"

He was always very particular about schedules. I would have liked him to drop everything. Michel's dying aunt! "Dad, Dad . . ."

"There's a sucker at the door eyeing my best piece. I'd better go."

I wanted to say something.

"I've missed you," he said. And we hung up.

When I got to the studio I heard a great slamming of doors; Delaborde was shouting at Luc. Luc pulled at two rolls of paper, screamed at Delaborde, who threw a bottle of Evian at him. The paper rolls, jammed by the metal bar from which they hung, began to pitch forward, and fell on the floor, clanging metal under the thick paper, which tore as Luc pulled at them. Delaborde stamped his foot. I made myself very small by the front door. It would be too risky to try to get over to the dressing room. Delaborde screamed, *"Petit con,"* Luc shouted, *"Salaud."* Luc pulled his foot back to kick the Balcar, and then stopped himself. He wasn't going to injure a delicate machine.

The studio became silent. Delaborde came toward me. "Call André Routière," he said, "and tell him I'd like him to start work this afternoon." I opened the big studio address book. I didn't want to lose Luc, but there was no way to save him. Through the corner of my eye I saw him pull his big green army bag up over his shoulder. He walked past me as I dialed, and whispered, "See you at the café in five minutes." We made faces at each other as he passed.

André Routière's number rang a long time before anyone answered. A sleepy man's voice. *"Allô?"* It wasn't André, but he put him on.

"He wants me to work for him? Permanently?" André's voice was strangled with joy. "Really? Delaborde? Who's calling?"

"Florence Ellis. I'm his assistant. We've worked together. Last week, when you helped me out with the lights. The week before. You know me."

"I'll be there," said André, who showed little interest in remembering me. I hung up. I hated him already.

At the café Luc and I put our arms around each other. "What will I do without you?" I asked.

"You won't have anyone to talk to," said Luc, looking at his coffee.

We held hands. He was going to call PhoLab and see if they needed a roving assistant for the moment. "We can still see each other," he said, "when Nancy's away." He gave my waist a squeeze and I thought, Yes, now that we don't work together anymore we can go to bed again.

"I don't like André," I told him.

"Well that's because you know that he doesn't like girls. He's a *pédé*," he said.

Pédé. A word I had grown up with. It was a chorus that followed Dad and Michel. In the summers when we went to Michel's house in Provence, and their friends came with us—Georgie, who skied in the winter and dealt in Persian miniatures, Arthur, who'd inherited a firm that made automatic labels, and who did nothing much besides shopping, and Alexis, who was older and had lived a lot, and told stories about everyone he had ever known. Alexis brought along young men who were, he said, wildly talented if only they could settle down. And we'd all go down to the market to buy food, because food was important. I loved being with so many men, and their tight white trousers and pastel sweaters didn't mean anything to me except that they were dressed for spring, for summer. They giggled and were careful about cheese and knew how to smell cantaloupes. And when one of them or Dad, or Michel, said that the change was wrong, or that last week's tomatoes had been mealy, the word would come out, just as we all turned to go. Spat out the side of a vendor's mouth, "*sale pédé*," dirty faggot. It was the same at the terraces of the bars on the port, where we sat before going home for lunch; when there was a silence some woman at another table would be impelled to identify our table, "*des pédés*," as if to explain the laughter and the bright colors.

Luc and I hugged in the street, and I went back to work. That afternoon, André Routière arrived, spindly and blond with a pointed nose. Delaborde showed him where the cables and attachments for the Balcars were kept, and watched him set up various lights.

André was handsome, despite his pointed nose. When he went into the darkroom, I followed him. I didn't believe Luc's theory. I waited for him to put his hands on my waist or brush his arms against my breast, and he did neither. Some models came to show their books that afternoon, and André stood behind Delaborde, peering over his shoulder at the photographs, a slight sneer on his face. Whatever Delaborde said, André followed with a quick "yes, yes." "A little too much of the jungle," he said of a black girl after she had left. It was the kind of remark Georgie and Arthur and Alexis made. In the middle of the afternoon the phone rang; it was a man, for André.

"Delaborde does not like anyone getting phone calls here," I whispered to André as I handed him the phone.

"Don't phone me here," I heard him say. "I'll meet you in an hour, at Goldenberg's."

I was busy preparing for the next day's work, a large advertising shoot. I was making hats to cheer the dresses up, because the dresses were the subjects of the campaign and they were awful. I had feathers and half birds from a theatrical costumer's, and spangles and ribbons. It was elementary fun; it gave me time to think about Rosa, and the message from Julia, and what had been promised. Delaborde interrupted me to ask me to go to PhoLab. I put on my coat and went out.

A man standing on the corner caught my eye. He was wearing a cape, which swung in the chill wind. He was tall, with dark curling hair that reminded me of something. I lingered, to see where he was going. He was standing in front of Goldenberg's, the only delicatessen in Paris. He turned toward me, and began to walk my way. I was looking at him and he was looking at me.

He had arched cheekbones, almost winged, and heavy lids over curiously pale eyes. He was older than me but not old, maybe twenty-seven or thirty. He was not French: there was nothing pinched, nothing disciplined about the way he looked. I stepped off the sidewalk and started toward him. He stood still. His skin was slightly tanned, bronzed. Not winter skin. He began to walk toward me, opened his soft triangular mouth and gave me a smile. And with the smile, he sent something over to me. I stopped, and so did he. I thought he was the most beautiful man I'd ever seen, this man in the street. We were stalking each other. I had to walk on. I was still blushing when I boarded the bus.

When I came back an hour later, I looked into the windows of the café to see if he wasn't inside. I was right, he wasn't. *Bad news* came into my head, and I modified it to mean, "Bad news he isn't here." Then I went back to Delaborde's.

"I sent her out. That's the difference. We don't take breaks here unless I say we can take them. Florence runs errands. You are to stay here and take care of the studio," said Delaborde, his beard moving like a cluster of cockroaches on his chin. "What a day," he said to me as I handed him the contacts I'd gone to get. "Thank God you're not a boy."

8

ON THE WAY HOME that evening I bought a blue candle like the one Rosa had. I lit it while I ate dinner sitting on the floor. I didn't want to go out: I could feel something gathering.

Just before I woke the following morning I felt someone next to me, his shoulder touching mine, a muddled voice murmuring incoherent love in my ear. I tried to keep the sure stillness of the dream with me as I sat up and climbed down the ladder. I ran my bath slowly so that the rush of water would not frighten the feeling away. By the time I had dressed the dream was beginning to fade and I stood still a few moments to hold it, the certainty. Even the way the towel was bunched over the bath seemed to be part of a definite scheme of things. My hand on my door keys felt correct. I went downstairs to have breakfast at the corner bar with the full feeling that everything I did was right.

The street had just been washed, and the wet tarmac reflected bright into my eyes. I walked up the street to the corner and before I was even in the bar I saw him, just the way I had wanted to see him through the window the day before.

The stranger. He had his nose in a coffee cup, but he was leaning against the counter, his back to it, and when he had swallowed, his eyes came up and he was looking at me. I stood still at the door. He gave me that smile again. I walked toward him. "Hello," I said in English.

He answered in English. "Didn't I see you yesterday?"

I nodded. My throat was too tight for me to speak. The barman began to make my café crème. I looked over at the stranger. My coffee was put on the counter. "But it wasn't around here," he said.

"No, in the Marais," I said, and added, "I live just up the street here."

His skin was almost the color of apricots, his eyebrows faint strokes above his eyes, the eyes a cloudy sky. It could be just another man, not the one. He was looking at me. "Are you French or American?" he asked.

"That's sort of like when I was a child and people asked if I was a girl or a boy," I said.

"I could have asked that too," he said with a smile and I reached back and touched my head and said, "Oh, my hair."

"So what are you?" he asked again.

"Girl," I said, "American and French."

"And you?"

He laughed. "Too long to explain," he said.

I ordered another coffee. His hand grazed mine as he handed me the cup, intercepting the barman. An electric shock went through me, from my hand to my feet. He had felt it too: his eyes opened quickly, he pulled his hand back, and rested it on the counter as if to steady himself.

I felt the heat reverberate in my body. I had to make him stay there. I looked at him and he saw, he understood.

"We could have dinner tonight," he said, a miracle—"if you're free."

"Yes," I said, much too fast, but it didn't matter.

His eyes full of mischief. He said, "Let's meet here then, at eight, or is that too early?"

"No, it's not too early," I said. I'd never get out of the studio in time. Eight. I looked at my watch. I had to prove that I was capable of looking at something other than him.

"I must run," I said. He laughed, and he took my hand. The shock went through us both again. We looked down at our hands, witnesses to the voltage. We smiled at the same moment, and then I let go of him and tried to walk out the door. I wanted to run, and I desperately wanted to stay. It was so warm near him.

I didn't go to the studio, I went home and called Rosa. I begged her to see me at once, that day, today. Please please please. "Fine," she said, "if you get here before eleven. It's obviously an emergency." I took five hundred francs from the envelope of bills I kept under my sweaters and took the bus over to the Avenue Bosquet. I had to make sure.

"I've found him," I said once we were seated at her table.

"Who?" she asked.

"The man you told me about."

"I'm sorry," said Rosa, she still seemed a little sleepy—"I can never remember anything about the future. You must remind me."

"The man who was going to be the great love of my life. I want to make sure it's the right one."

"Fine," she said, "that's good. Tell me his birthdate, so I can compare your charts."

"I don't know."

"Well, find out. It takes time, but it's the best way. Do you want to call him to ask?"

"I can't," I said.

"Then give me his full name, so I can do his numerology with yours."

"I can't give you that either." She looked annoyed. "You don't understand, I've seen him, we've met, but I want to make sure before it goes any further."

"You may have reached the limits of my powers," she said. She shook her head. "What makes you think this is the man?"

"Electricity," I said.

"Electricity accounts for a great many things, including storms," she told me, "but I'm not sure it's a good indicator of love."

"Tell me it's him!" I said.

"But I'm not in a trance, I don't know," said Rosa. "I haven't started yet. What do you want me to do?"

"Tell me if I've met my great love. The one you predicted last time."

"I'll do the cards," she said, and started shuffling the pack. She told me there was a reunion. I nodded, delighted. She told me there was an evil young man, newly around me. André, of course. Then the card with the young man walking toward the cliff turned up again. "The Fool," she said, "there he is."

"How can I make him love me?" I asked.

Rosa put down the cards. "I may be able to see things, predict events, but there is nothing you or I can do to make things happen."

"But I want to make sure that things work out," I said.

"Destiny works in mysterious ways," she said. "One must always accept what it gives us."

"But I want it to give me what I want," I went on.

"You can't. You can't force things."

"Why not?"

"It's wrong. If you try to influence things, they turn against you."

I felt helpless, cheated.

"Look, if this is the man, you'll see him again. Do you have any plans to see him?" she asked gently.

"Yes, tonight," I said.

"You see?" she said. "Tonight. Everything will be fine, you'll see."

She wouldn't let me pay her. "It's hardly a full consultation," she said, "just some advice. Good luck."

"So, today it's your turn to behave like a jerk," said Delaborde as I walked in. "You're two hours late. What's the matter with young people these days?" Two models were waiting in the dressing room for me to apply their bee-stung lips. Once the models were on the set, in dresses and my hats, I started doing things to my face, to see how I would look best that night. I remembered something else I was supposed to do that night. My father and Michel. Our reconciliation. I called the shop, got Maud, left Delaborde's number and the message to call me. When the phone rang, I was on the floor, pulling strategic nylon threads. André picked it up. "No, she's working," I heard him say, and then he said, "Oh!" in a delighted voice, and "It's André, André Routière," and he gave a little laugh, and I was listening so hard I forgot to tug at the nylon thread and Delaborde screamed at me.

When Delaborde's camera had clicked to a stop, and the models had untwined themselves from a posture both graceful and improbable, André came over to me and said, "That was Michel Dupuy." Michel's last name was rarely used; for him to be Michel Dupuy meant André was an outsider, who for some reason looked up to him. I went to call Michel.

"So, we see you tonight," said Michel, his voice enveloping, relaxed.

"I have to work very late," I lied. "That's why I called. Can we do it tomorrow? I'm really sorry this happened, but I can't get out of it."

A small silence. "I'm sure Jacob will understand," he said very slowly. "What a pity. He was very excited, and so am I, relieved that this game is ending."

"Me too," I said. "It was stupid. Tomorrow night, is that all right? Chez Georges?"

"Fine, I'll tell Jacob," said Michel. Before he hung up, he added, "By the way, you've got a young friend of ours working there, André Routière."

Shit. Inevitable. My silence.

"He's very talented, I hear," said Michel.

"He's a friend of Alexis's?"

"How did you guess, Florence?"

It wasn't that difficult. We said fond, if straitened, goodbyes, and said we'd meet the next night at nine Chez Georges.

By seven o'clock I had darted to the door maybe five times, with my coat on. Delaborde seemed to be preparing to work all night. At seven-fifteen I had my coat on again. Delaborde was still on the set with a model. André was holding the electric fan in his hands, directing wind at her hair. He gave me a nasty look.

"I have to go," I said, and before anyone could stop me, I left.

I stopped on the way home to buy two gigantic cups. Breakfast, I thought. I bought some milk at a place near me, and ran up the stairs. I poured half a bottle of perfume into my bath. I was trembling so hard when I stepped in that the water slapped the sides, like waves.

I changed three times before I was ready to go out, and threw the rejected clothes into the back of my closet. I lit a sandalwood stick and pulled a scarf over the lamp on the floor, and went down.

Trembling. I was late.

He was at the bar, just as he had been that morning. As if he had nothing better to do, nowhere else to be. He didn't look at his watch as I came through the door, he smiled. I walked over to his lips, our mouths touched. "How nice," he said, *"que c'est bien."*

He smelled of cedarwood, something sepia, foreign. A patch of corduroy jacket showed where his coat was open. The electricity of the morning stung briefly at my lips. I stopped it. I didn't want it to begin. Not yet.

"What's your name?" I asked.

"Felix," he said. "Felix Kulpar." He said it with a thick, strange accent.

"What a funny name," I said.

"Yours?" he asked. His accent in French was good enough. Slow vowels, quick consonants. "What's your name?" he asked again.

No, said the loud voice inside me, *no no no.* I paused. No, not to have this dinner with him, or No, not to give him my name? No answer? I chose the less painful of the two.

"Elise," I said.

"Elise Beethoven?" he asked, with a laugh. I didn't get the joke, but laughed a little too.

"No, Elise Radford," I said. My father's, my aunt's lost chances reborn.

We walked down toward the river. Elise Radford, I kept repeating to myself, Elise Radford, Elise Radford. For my real mother, for Julia. They would watch over me. We came to the boulevard. He took my arm, and I felt his elbow on my hip through our coats, and another shudder went through me.

"I didn't eat today," he said, and I asked "Why" and he shrugged a little and said, "Things got in the way."

What things? I wanted to ask. The other men, the afternoon men, all had jobs and families and frowns and datebooks, and reasons to be places and things to do. The less Felix looked and sounded like the others with their real lives, the easier it was for him to be destiny. Real life was a slow crawl along a gravel path, destiny was a sudden upward draft to a golden beam. The walk to the restaurant was a golden beam.

I was aware of every move he made. When his elbow touched the side of the banquette, I could feel the hard bounce of the stuffed hide under my own arm. He heaved off his coat and helped me off with mine. The menus were in front of us. I stared at him and he stared at me. I was flying. He took my chin in his palm and kissed me again, the mouth.

"How strange," I said, when he stopped, "how strange to meet someone just like that, and . . . then . . ." It was my lie.

He gave me a menu, purple scrawls. I couldn't read it. When the food came, I couldn't eat. I watched his fingers on the tablecloth and imagined them inside me. There was a glow around both of us. I couldn't breathe, but I didn't need to breathe.

We talked about Paris. We could have talked about ourselves if we had been different people. But I was Elise Radford, and she was so new she didn't have much to say. And Paris was there with us, the monument in which we both lived, worthy of comment. How cold it was, how bad the heating was, and what spring was like, when it came. And sunset through the roof of the Grand Palais, and crossing the Pont des Arts. A tightrope of common places, stretched over what would come next. I felt very naked under my clothes, as if everything I wore had risen slightly to allow a draft of Felix to touch me already. I felt I was bathing in light.

I wanted to ask about the accent, his life, and I also wanted him to remain a pure product of fate, with no details to bind him. Instead, I filled out Elise. Elise had always lived in Paris, I decided. Her father was a professor of art history, her mother a housewife. A French housewife. No deaths, no antique shop, no Michel.

"Are you married?" I allowed myself to ask at last, to check if he resembled the others at all, to see if he was really something new.

"No," he said, and my heart stopped. "I used to live with a woman, now I'm alone."

We were having coffee.

A woman. *Une femme*. Therefore, not a girl. An impression of broad hips and a lined forehead, someone older, responsible, perhaps sad. I had asked what he did, earlier. And he'd said, "I have projects," and left it at that. On the word projects the accent had become oily again, foreign.

I looked into the bottom of my coffee cup and wondered if he knew how much I wanted him. Whoever he was.

"Shall we go?" he asked, and threw some notes onto the bill by his wineglass.

"I live up the street," I said. Maybe, unmarried, unattached, he wouldn't follow me home. He would have somewhere else to go.

He took my arm. We went back up the street, and then up to my room. The sandalwood incense had made a stringy pile of dust on the carpet. The light from the lamp was maroon and the scarf had a hole in it where it touched the bulb. We stood facing each other. He took my hands. The whole room was electric. It went through us both and it brought the walls nearer.

We climbed the ladder. There all night we wound in and out of each other. Sometimes I passed out, and woke to see his profile horizontal against the light from the street, and then my body went to him and we started again.

Just before I woke I remembered the previous day's dream, and knew that it had come true. I climbed down the ladder carefully so as not to wake him. He was the first man in my room, and he was the first man in my life. Felix. I put the water on to boil for coffee, glad that there were specific daylight actions. I placed both of the oversized cups on the platform. From above me, he opened his eyes.

"Do you have tea?" he asked. "I prefer tea."

I made a pot of tea and climbed up to drink my coffee next to him.

He took my phone number before he left. He wrote it down in a red notebook with thin blue pages. The E of Elise was big, with a sort of Z through it. He glanced up at me before closing the book.

"It's nothing personal," he said with a smile, and then he laughed to let me know it was a joke.

I was in love.

I knew nothing about him except his name and his skin, that he had projects and had once lived with a woman. He was as smooth as polished stone, as smooth as the Kouros in Dad's front hall. The statue, with its sweet idiot grin, its Attic smile, was not as dashing as Felix, but they had the same stone skin. He was maybe more like Morpheus. My fingers had slid along the chest of the Kouros every day since I was tall enough to reach, and I had slept under the picture of Morpheus for years. Half my life of familiarity with smooth stone and a closed, perfect smile. The living Felix, once in the street, twice in a bar, once in a restaurant and all night in my bed, was less a person than an event. A coming true, a color to the time. Almost a god.

So that when he said, "It's nothing personal," I knew that he understood things beyond the reach of normal people.

9

THE PRESSURE OF LAST night's grace, still in my body, stretched my limbs and filled me with a strict comfort. When I joined my father and Michel for dinner it was as if Felix were still with me, and always would be.

They sat facing a banquette left empty for me. From a distance, they could have been brothers, if not twins. Two men of the same height and weight and style, Dad's color a little higher, his face a little rounder than Michel's waxy aristocratic mask.

They turned as I came to the table. Dad rose, and Michel watched his progress before looking at me. I saw Dad's hand grasp the back of Michel's chair to help himself up, and I thought he might be ill. He was only nervous; I was so full of Felix that I had no nerves at all.

With Dad and Michel things were always light. Not so tonight. "My darling," said my father, "you've had enough of being an orphan. I'm so glad. Boy, am I glad." I saw tears in his eyes, and thought how inelegant the expression "boy" was.

"I like my family," I said, and gave Michel a hug too. I'd forgotten how easy it was to be with them.

"What a family, a pair of aging twins and a wayward child," said Dad. His hair, just washed, fell across his forehead, and he looked more than ever like a little boy. He was talking to the mirror behind me.

"Let me look at you," said Dad. And he looked. He made me turn my head. He smiled. He asked Michel what he thought.

"A surprise," said Michel. "I would never have known you."

"You look like a little boy," said Dad. "Is that the point?"

"I was tired of being a Chinese orphan," I said.

"The boys must love it," said Dad, "it's so confusing. It's wonderful. Turn your head again."

I was not going to tell them about Felix.

"So tell us," said Michel, "are you in love?"

"She's broken every heart in Paris," said Dad before I could answer. "Haven't you heard what havoc my daughter wreaks?"

If only, I thought. I loved the idea, and so did he. The seducer, the wild one. Don Juan, the conqueror, not the whore.

"Are you breaking hearts?" asked Michel.

I played with my rings. "I make them send jewels and flowers," I said, "and furs for the winter and fans for the summer."

"And why have none of them proposed to take you off my hands?" asked Dad.

"They all propose," I said, "but none of them are good enough."

"Watch it," said Michel, "she's got a father fixation."

Only they talked like that. Figure skating over thin ice, black Freudian waters beneath, faster, faster, so as not to fall. "I do," I said, "but come on, Michel, how can I help it? Look at him. With a father like Jacob, wouldn't you?"

I could go as fast as they did.

They told me how Trevor Blake had come to Paris and visited the shop; as Michel talked I saw Dad's eyes riveted on the mirror behind me.

He was looking at the young couple behind him who were sitting at a table across the aisle. Then Michel's eyes locked onto the mirror behind me too, and he stopped talking.

"What?" I said. "What is it?" I was looking straight at the couple; they were tall and young, he was handsome with blond hair to his collar and a knotted antique market scarf around his neck, and she was a little round in the face but beautiful.

"Just admiring the bone structure," said Michel.

Dad said more. "If there is the least bit of the incubus in you, you end up wishing you could be each one to love the other, no?"

Michel didn't answer. I looked across the aisle again, stared. He was not as good as Felix, but if you didn't know Felix, then maybe you could wish to be her to love him. As for wanting to be him to love her, her face was really rather fat. I didn't understand. "So what about Trevor Blake?" I asked.

"Basically," said Dad, returning with great difficulty to my face, to our side of the room, "I think he wanted me, and you, to put Julia's money into his company."

"Rapacious, the English," said Michel.

"How horrible!" I said. It sounded like theft. "What money?"

"From the sale of the house, and other things. She left us a good amount, and you're going to be a very rich woman one day," said Dad.

That again. Much as I despised Trevor Blake I still didn't like hearing those words.

"Why not give it to him?" I asked.

"There's better things to do with the money," said my father.

"Anyway, Jacob wasn't there," said Michel. "I had to deal with him."

"Why weren't you there?" I asked.

"Seeing a restorer. Aubiot," said Dad.

"That's what you say," said Michel.

"You're impossible," said Dad.

"What's the matter?" I asked.

"Nothing," said Dad.

"Well, who's Aubiot?"

"He restores, mainly Erghi's things. And there's something wonderful in the air."

"What's that?" I asked. My father's lower lip was trembling a little in his smile.

"Oh, really, Jacob," said Michel, "really, this is not the time."

"She's my daughter," said Dad.

"That has nothing to do with it. It's too early."

Dad was already reaching into his jacket pocket, the one over his heart.

"No," said Michel.

Dad pulled out an envelope. I knew what he would pull out: a black and white Polaroid of some piece, a picture streaky where

Erghi had wiped the pink varnish carelessly across the surface, so that the image came already ruined. But it was a postcard. A man and a woman lying on a draped couch, his arm around hers, her fingers moving as if she were playing an instrument. She wore a rounded hat with a flat brim, like an American sailor's cap; he had a black beard.

"A pair of dead adulterers," said Michel.

"A married couple, one of those happy couples," said my father.

"It's not the legitimacy of their union we're worried about," said Michel.

"There were only two in the world. This is the third," said Dad.

She had long dark braids that came from behind her ears and fell down the front of her dress, and laced-up pointed shoes. He was barefoot. A star-shaped cushion supported her elbow, his left hand disappeared behind her arm. Under her cloak, he could have been holding her breast.

"They're beautiful," I said. "Where are they from?"

"They're about twenty-five hundred years old," said Michel, which was not an answer.

"None of your business," said Dad, and he put the picture, the postcard, back in the envelope.

"Is it Erghi's?" I asked.

They both burst out laughing. Dad wiped his mouth with his napkin. Michel said, "I wish it were, if only . . ."

Dad glared at him. "This is the best piece I have ever had the opportunity to buy. There has never been anything of that quality on the market. The finest example of its kind, better than anything at the Villa Giulia. This is the most exciting thing that has happened to me since I began."

"Would you trade the Kouros for them?" I asked.

"No." He said it very quickly.

"You might have to," said Michel.

"No," said Dad, "he was my first good piece. He will always be with me. I can afford them. There are just a few adjustments, that's all. I may have to sell some pieces. But I'll manage."

He had his hand inside his jacket, and his mouth was pursed, his eyes were distant.

"It's mad," Michel murmured at me, and then he shook his head, as if to dispel the people on the postcard.

"If they're on a card, they must have been in a museum. Were they stolen?" I asked brightly, trying to be part of the plot, in on their game.

"Stolen!" said Dad. "Where have you been living? I don't deal in stolen goods, I never have. Florence, I'm astounded . . ."

"I have been living at Seventy-Four, Rue du Bac," I said, "since you ask."

"Oh, we knew that," said Dad—and I was pleased to see how easily I could divert him from his outrage.

"We didn't want to bother you," he went on. The expression seemed so humble. "Nguyen told us where you were, and we had your phone number, and we knew you were at Delaborde's."

"You had to do it, it's perfectly natural for young people to do that," said Michel. "Jacob even checked with Doctor Emery."

"I wasn't sick," I said.

"I know. That's what Doctor Emery explained. Grief and pain, he said, which sounded very American of him. You had disappeared in a terrible huff, but Doctor Emery said that if you had been serious, you would have gone to London to see Geraldine, or even gone to America."

"Why would I go to America?" I asked.

"Well, there's money there," said Dad. I wasn't sure what he meant. "He said that since you'd taken an apartment some seven hundred yards from where we live, you were playing hide and seek with us, and it was the same as a kid leaving home with a satin quilt and a chocolate bar. That you'd come back when you were bored with hiding."

"I meant it," I said.

"That's why we didn't come after you. We had to leave you the dignity of your decision," said Michel.

Why are you taking it away now? I thought. I don't want to see the cogs and wheels of your behavior. Then Michel became fey, and it was inappropriate, embarrassing. "When children flee the nest," he said, "the parents discover each other all over again."

"Well, it doesn't seem to have done you much good," I said, being bold, and I noticed that Dad flinched.

"You're right," said Michel, "but that's life. One nail chases another."

"What nail?" I asked.

"Nothing," said my father. "I don't like the turn this is taking. How's your dinner? I bet you haven't had a decent meal in a year."

"Really, Jacob, how vulgar," said Michel, and I was glad he'd said it. Dad was looking at himself in the mirror. Just himself.

"About your money," said Dad, now launched, "you have to get in touch with Mr. Leon. It's important, there are papers to sign. You're going to be a rich woman one day."

"I'm twenty-one now," I said.

"No, later. Twenty-one is young," said Dad.

"Thank you for not coming after me," I said.

"Oh," said Dad, "we were away a lot, Thailand and Turkey and Greece. There was a dig in Anatolia, with some of my friends in the crew. And Michel was in Provence, and I went to the Eastern countries a bit."

"India?" I asked.

"He means Prague, actually he means Vienna," said Michel.

"Was Nguyen spying on me?" I asked.

"Not spying," said Dad, "keeping an eye out. He's been working for me ever since Bertha left, that's fifteen years, that's a long time. He's loyal."

When I was a child Nguyen came to collect me at school when everyone else in my class took the bus home. And Dad . . . he made phone calls to the parents of the boys I went dancing with. He waited up, reading his catalogues in the living room when I came in at two or three, his voice jolly—"Florence, honey, that you?" His nauseating care. "Are his parents rich? What do they do? How do they feel about Jews? You can't be too careful in France." But, Dad, I don't want to marry this boy, I just want to go dancing. And maybe go to bed with him before I come home. Anyway, Ellis isn't a Jewish name. Not anymore. Not since Olivia changed it.

Yet he was proud of the number of boys who were after me. I wondered if he could know how I had really spent the last year. Do you know how many men I've had, Dad? And now I have Felix.

"Florence!" Michel had his hand around my arm. "Come back. Where were you?"

"Right here, on the Rue du Bac," I said.

"We must come and visit you one day," said Michel.

"No, please. You'll hate it. The stairs are killers. Please don't, please."

Dad laughed. "We know when we're not wanted. Oh, Florence, I'm so glad to see you."

"So am I," I said.

"I missed you," he said.

"I missed you."

"And I want you to know that I would never do anything that could upset you."

"Like what?"

"Get rid of Julia's things," he said.

"I wasn't thinking about that," I said.

"Well, it's just that you get so upset about her that I want to make sure that you know. All her stuff is yours."

"I'm not thinking about that, I've never thought about that," I repeated.

"My how we've changed, in a year," said Michel.

It wasn't Julia's things, I thought, it was her good name. Michel was better at things than at ideas. Michel was not one of us.

"Tell us what it's like working with André Routière," said Dad. "We only know him as an ornamental object."

"He's only been there two days," I said, and told them about Delaborde's temper, and Luc, and the fight. They wanted to hear more, so I told them what I could about André, and tried to make him sound interesting. I wanted to say he was a nasty little faggot, but not in front of them. "He's good," I said, and then had to qualify it, he seemed to have taste, he was graceful, he concentrated very well, the Balcar never hiccuped and gave out the way it used to with Luc. Then I had to explain what a Balcar was, although I'd been through that when I started with Delaborde, while I was still at home. I talked on and thought about Felix. He should have called. Must have called. Might call later. I knew he would. He had to.

"We knew him through Alexis, of course," said my father. "He went around with him for a while. I think André wanted to be a painter."

"Something that needs talent, in any case," said Michel. "He seemed devoted to Alexis, and then Alexis replaced him with . . ."

My father said, "Shut up." He banged his glass down on the table. "Shut up" was not his usual way of dealing with unpleasant things. I held my breath.

Michel and Dad were staring at each other, two animals about to fight. "André is really very, very good," I said, in a bland, loose voice, to distract them.

"Give him my best," said Michel.

The argument was going on in silence, subterranean.

"So," said Dad, joining his hands, making an effort, leaning toward me, "what are your plans?"

"I have to get to bed early, I have to get up at six," I said.

Michel laughed. "Real plans," he said.

And again their eyes were fixed on the mirror, on either side of me. The couple were kissing. "I really must get home," I said. "It's been wonderful. I'm so glad."

"We could spend Easter together," said Dad. "I've set it up with Alexis. Venice."

I glanced at my watch. I had to get back. I could hear the phone ringing from here. "I have to go now, I really have to go." I slid along the banquette.

"Your boyfriend's waiting," said Michel.

"Work," I said.

"That man must be a real slave driver. What are you doing at six?" he asked.

"The props are arriving at seven, and I have to be there to supervise."

My father put his arms up around my shoulders. "We're a pair of nasty old queens and you don't want to be anywhere near us," he said. "I understand."

"Jacob, your masochism is showing," said Michel.

"I love you," I whispered in my father's ear, pulled down over him. "I just have to go home. You understand, don't you?"

"I do," he whispered back, "and I'm so glad to have a daughter again that I don't mind who you're running home to fuck."

"It's not true," I said, and pulled back up. I kissed Michel on the cheek. "Remember, Venice," said Michel. "We'll call you tomorrow."

"It's not for two months," I said. "How can you plan so far in advance?"

Michel pulled at my hair as I turned and left.

Felix, I thought all the way home. Felix. I drew the curtains and lit another incense stick. I brushed my teeth with Vademecum, which I liked to think of as a powerful invocation. I put on a striped oriental robe and sat on the floor, arranged myself around an anthology of English poetry that I had bought one day in a romantic mood, and never yet opened. The aftertaste of the evening was unpleasant, Dad's gluttonous affection, Michel's sly allusions to my greed, their bickering.

I stood up and tried to feel his arms around me, tried to conjure him into being there. This was the test: if he phoned, if he came, it was an affair, if he didn't, it was just strangers. I put my hand to my mouth and tried to feel the shape of his, there. I went to the bathroom mirror and looked at my mouth. It had a good shape, perhaps not as good as his, but good. I pursed my lips, opened wide. The bulb over the sink threw just enough light to prevent excesses of rouge. By that bulb I saw that with my short hair I looked like my father. The strong short nose, the wide eyes the color of satinwood, the round mouth. On me the features were like decals on a firm surface of undecided youth. I was not ugly, I was not a beauty. I looked like I might grow up to be beautiful. Every day I compared myself to the models in the studio. But now I was looking for Felix in the mirror, in my mouth, and what I saw was Jacob. His eyes on himself all evening. Would I look at myself in the mirror like that too when I was old?

I did not look like my mother. She had left no traces on me. The face I saw in the photograph had been wiped out by Jacob's superior genes. I was not French, I was not delicate. I was like the Ellis family, the mirror said it. Behind Dad, Julia, and behind them both my grandmother Olivia.

Once, a long time ago, Michel asked Olivia what she would have done differently if she could relive her life. She looked at the milky domed sapphire on her finger and said, "I would have been exactly the same, but fast."

Fast, I was being fast for her. She was not fast. She was faithful to a man who didn't love her, and she was slow. She had married young, and married well—there was a time when my grandfather was still called Lipschitz and he had money, before she changed it to Ellis and spent the cash—and then she had slowed down, so that inertia piled weight on her body, making her helpless. My grandfather didn't pay as much attention to her as to the slim young women he met on his travels, and though she had a mind inclined to revenge, her body was becalmed by the silt of accumulated flesh. She lost her husband young. My grandfather died in 1935, on a train between Chicago and New York. Of a heart attack. There was a woman in his compartment. Olivia, rich and proud and fat, did not look for another husband. She traveled.

Twice a year she thought she might find her old body again, if she went and starved in Europe. She found it easier to diet in Italian mountain towns where the water had properties known to the ancients. She went to the flat Belgian sea resorts where water therapy and massage cost more than the food she was not allowed to eat. She took her children with her. It was during a summer spent waiting for her to lose pounds that Jacob, at fourteen, discovered the use of boys. If my grandmother had not been fat, Jacob once told me, he would have been a man like other men. As if it were her fault.

My father came to antiquities via the Circus Maximus and dark Roman porticoes where unnamed things happened between nameless men. Olivia was delighted that her son had such high regard for ancient culture. Jacob had never gone to college, nor did he fight in the war. He was sickly, Olivia said, too weak to be drafted at eighteen or nineteen or twenty.

After the war he went to Europe with his mother and Julia and got the education he wanted. Erghi taught him everything. When they met, Erghi was already paying grave robbers for their pots and their slivers. The summer Olivia brought Dad and Julia to Europe, she took her two hundred and fifty pounds to the Terme di Monte Balneario. Julia went to Rome with Jacob.

A few years later, Dad started selling heads and brooches from an apartment in Paris. Which turned into Jacob Ellis et Compagnie, on the corner of the Rue Jacob, a long façade that grew longer with the years and then crept around the corner, until it seemed to be the biggest shop on the Rue Jacob. Erghi came up from Rome, empty-handed, always, to tell my father about the things he had in his back room. He never carried photographs, did not trust the telephone, and he couldn't risk leaving Italy with things on him.

Dad used to go down to Rome, with his sister at first, then with Michel. They'd come back with things wrapped in blankets in the back of the car, Julia driving, then Michel. That was how it worked. Dad loved the danger as much as he loved his treasures, loved having to hide what he would later show off.

He'd never had a couple on a coffin lid before. They didn't exist outside of museums.

I wrapped a scarf around my head, with the two ends hanging over my ears like the thick Etruscan braids. I tried to make that smile in the mirror, but I didn't have the mouth for it. I put on the Roman ring.

It was twelve-thirty. The night was drawing close to the dead time when no one calls. I thought I could hear him breathing in the room. It was one o'clock. The cars grew rarer in the street, and with them the chances of his coming.

I heard a noise on the stairs. It wasn't he; I didn't yet know his step, but sensed it wasn't his. A little later I stood up, suddenly, without looking at the clock, and went to the door. I opened it. He was there.

"But I didn't knock yet!" he said.

"I know," I said, proud of myself, and I put my arms up to him.

"How did you know I'd come back?" he asked, pulling a little away from me.

"How did you know I wouldn't be asleep, or out, or in bed with another man?" I asked, and we both laughed.

He leaned down and I put my hands to his cheekbones, the bold curves sharp with cold. I considered cheekbones the noblest part of a body. "What's that?" he said, as my ring rubbed along his face.

"Nothing. A Roman ring," I said. I wanted to say: you.

My hands rested on his arms in bed and felt him through the tips of my fingers and inside me. There was no effort, it was so simple and so good, bucking waves in a warm sea, an undertow that shook us both. I had a terrible sensation that I had to pay attention to the now, that it would have to last me a long time.

Later I was on my stomach beside him, and told him in my sleep that I was cold, so he pulled up the sheets—my sheets, I had forgotten this was my bed—and I slipped under them, and he moved his warm legs in beside me, and we slept.

I did not want to lose one moment of consciousness while he was there, but we slept.

Then it was day again, there were uneven strips of light surrounding the curtains. He was still there. It was the first thing I knew before waking.

While I made tea for both of us he picked up his boots from the floor, cowboy boots with worn heels. I wanted to watch him dress, to keep that sight forever. He took his shirt off the back of the chair and put his arms through it. "What time do you have to be at work?" he asked.

I busied myself toward the bathroom, and shouted back, "Ten." I could do without the bath and leave with him. He was about to leave. The bath was filling up. I saw my face. Olivia would have been proud: I looked fast.

"Where do you have to go?" I shouted over the water. I was still in my robe. I heard a mumbled answer, and came out of the bathroom. "Where?" I asked.

"I have to be somewhere," he said.

I longed to ask what he did. "I'm going over to the Marais, is that your direction?" I asked.

"Sort of, not really," he said. "I'd better go."

He had all his clothes on. "Isn't your bath going to run over?" he asked.

"No," I said, and went back to the bathroom to turn off the taps.

Stranded in the bathroom with my task accomplished, I wondered what to do next. *Go out,* said the voice inside me. Where? I asked. *Out,* said the voice. Yes, but out the door with him, wearing my robe, down the stairs and into the cold in my robe, or just out into the room? Which? *Out,* said the voice.

"I'll see you out," I said, and took his arm. I preceded him down the stairs, and in the dark hall where the mailboxes were, I turned, and kissed him on the cheek.

"Tonight?" I said.

"Maybe," he answered, "if I can. But late. Don't wait up for me."

10

THE SMALL INSTRUMENTS OF everyday life became important with passion. The phone was invented so that he could call me. If anyone else should call, they were trespassing. The mail was there for him to send me cards, which he did. The name Elise Radford went up on my mailbox, the proper receptor. If anything arrived for Florence Ellis, bills, letters from London, they were intruders, and the postman left them on the ledge.

When Felix put a can of shaving cream by my sink and hung a torn chambray shirt on the doorknob of the bathroom I felt consecrated. They guaranteed his return, without specifying time. I told Sylvie about the telephone, the mail, and the repetition of return. What could not be told was the shock of silver in the veins, the way the skin inside my arms disappeared to let him in. His returns were his constancy.

Waiting for Felix was also a way of spending time with him. His absence was as personal as his presence. He existed in my flesh when he was there and in my head when he was not. He came and went, unpredictable, unseizable, and always silent when questioned directly. Often when he phoned one could hear the jumbled voices of a café behind him, the clangor of street traffic. He had a home, somewhere, for his shirts were always clean, his trousers pressed, and his skin smelled good. But where he went when he left and what he did there and where he kept his clothes and who ironed them were mysteries.

The time when I wasn't with him didn't count. My hours at Delaborde's were parentheses, large transparent bags full of shapes and incidents that had no bearing on what I loved. I rushed home every evening, sometimes by cab if I sensed he would call early, and when I was back in my room I was free to wait. The expanse of carpet that ran between the ladder and the window became a picnic ground, a sitting room, the inside of a tent. Some days those few square feet stretched to infinity. I constructed a nest in which to receive him, and filled it with things that expanded the hints he had dropped about his travels, his tastes.

He had been to Afghanistan, and told a story in which he passed out in a hut after eating too much hashish. I went to the Indian store and bought a bedspread that I tacked on the big white wall, and the next time he came in he said, "A tent," and we played at being nomads. He had been to the desert and told me about the intense cold of the desert night, the sound of his blood in his ears, magnified across an endless expanse of nothing but stones. I went to the Luxembourg and picked up smooth round stones and placed them in a dish by the lamp, so he'd recognize the desert.

He carried relics of adventures on his body, as clothes: the cowboy boots were from San Antonio, Texas, the cape, from a village in the Appenines, where he had friends who were painters. The word friend in Felix's mouth covered a multitude of sins. They had given him things: a necklace of sliced stones from New Mexico, thin gold bangles, from Southeast Asia, that rang together when he moved his hand.

The bracelets, the long hair, the slow eyes and the quiet voice. Felix gave no orders and voiced few opinions. He wound around me, but it was I who reached for him, who felt the heat first and turned the moment to lust, and I who climbed on top of him for sex. He was there for my pleasure and for his. The rest of him, everything else, was left outside.

When he talked about himself there was sometimes a kind of surprised regret, an astonishment that time had passed in his life. The sadness made me want to make things better for him, and made me respect him, too. He didn't talk much, and not in long sentences; details had to be pulled out, and his reluctance to name the people in his life seemed the discretion of someone who had been privy to secrets. He never said where he had been, where he had just come from. He talked about the far past. "I went back to the village where I was a child," he said one night. "I got out of the car, and there was the water pump, and a cart stranded next to it, and the last snow on top of the mountain. I wasn't far from my mother's house, but I was looking away from it, and it was the same mountain and the same road I saw every day when I was a child. And then a man came up the road to me, and he looked at me in an odd way, because it's not the kind of place where people come, there's no skiing. And he asked if I was lost, and I said no, but that I hadn't been there for twenty years. And when I said it I felt strange, because to remember twenty years ago means you're old."

"You're not old," I said.

"I won't live long," he said quickly, and I let him say it. He went on, "The man, he was a man. He had wrinkles, he had a red face. He was old. He looked at me and said, 'Felix?' and I recognized him. He was in school with me. We were the same age."

Some of his stories had no point, or the point was how pink the light had been one dawn in Greece. He had a huge collection of names and places. "Cape Sounion," he'd say, "when you pass it at dusk, the columns seem to be leaning with the wind, as if they were about to fall."

What kind of boat, Felix, where were you going, who were you with, when was it, all the things I didn't ask. The naming of places had to be enough. I was grateful when it was Greece or Italy, places I could picture, places I could remember from objects my father had. They seemed almost classical references, and if I had paid attention to my Virgil in school I could have quoted words back at him for his places. I wanted to ask him if he knew the shop but if he said yes, how could I go on pretending not to be its daughter?

Questions didn't help.

"Do you know Vienna?" he asked, and I said, "No, why?"

"It's beautiful, you should go there."

"Do you go back often?"

"To see my friends, yes, sometimes. I studied there."

"What?"

"Architecture. But the mathematics were too much. So I studied art instead."

"Where?"

"At a school called the Slade."

"But that's in London."

"Yes."

"Were you good?"

"I still am."

"Was it painting, or sculpture?"

"Painting."

"Do you still paint?"

"No."

"Why not?"

"Questions, questions."

"New Mexico," he said one time, "did you ever go?"

"No."

"I played pool with the Indians in Albuquerque. Downtown Albuquerque. Pueblo Indians. They can't drink, it makes them crazy, and they keep drinking. That's how the white men took their land."

"How's their pool?"

"Bad players, I always won. I practiced in Vienna."

I went on to the English bookshop on the Rue de Rivoli and bought a book on New Mexico, a guidebook. There were no pool halls in it, but there were names. "Did you ever go to Taos?" I asked Felix a few days later.

He sat up on the cushions. "Yes, how did you know?"

"Taos," I said, "is an art colony. The Pueblo was built in the thirteenth century. New Mexico was explored by Francisco Vásquez de Coronado."

"Book knowledge," he said with a derisive wave, and I blushed in case he'd seen the book, although I'd hidden it. He showed me some photographs of Vienna, blurred trees and a statue in a summer park. Faces of people who, he said, were friends. "Fountains everywhere," he said, "in every square; in the winter they are covered with wooden lids, and in the summer they play." The way he said, "they play," it sounded as if they played games, or music. He gave me the names of pastry shops.

"You eat cakes?" I asked. Cakes were for old ladies.

"Everyone eats pastries in Vienna," he said, "except for intellectuals. They eat little sandwiches with fish, and they drink coffee." I bought another book on Viennese pastries, but it was a recipe book. I had no oven. I put it in the back of the closet.

It seemed that everything beyond the senses was taboo, too complicated for us to approach together. What we could share was silent: The intensity of drugs, the taste of fruit, the feeling of each other's bodies.

I looked for things to touch and feel and eat and smell, so that my room could be a holy place, an extension of our pleasure. I found plates so thin they were almost transparent, with a border of shining red. Knives with handles shaped like bulbs, hollow, thin silver, that balanced oddly in the palm and seemed to have something inside them that made them roll off the plates. Fish forks, for their trident tines, curved and switchbacked, with scaled mother of pearl fish as their bases. Goblets with processions of tiny leaves on them, which held the white wine high above clear stems, twisted like running water, which made the wine into an offering.

I touched fabrics with my eyes closed in the great central hall of the Bon Marché, until I'd found a panné velvet that was like his skin, a suede that was like the soles of his feet, and a satin that I knew from a dream.

The dream was of a battleship, an immense cliff of raw gray metal, which had to be turned into a handful of pale blue satin, a sample of excruciating softness that my dream self grasped in her right hand. The task was to rub the battleship long enough so that it would become as sleek and tender as that satin.

I made the fabrics into covers for cushions that I piled against the wall on the floor. We listened to American tapes, songs about rainy days and wild worlds, words that blurred in the smoke of bitter hashish.

The moments seemed made of enamel, bright colors on a surface that was hard and thin and would chip and break if I tried to bend it to know it better. There was so much color then. There were colors that Felix had brought back from the world, the colors that began to burst out on everything. He came to see me in an almond suit on the first warm day, in a purple shirt and a red scarf with yellow birds printed on it. He said he wanted to go to China, and I shed the cold blue garageman's overalls for Tibetan robes from a refugee shop, and Chinese jackets of slick fake silk with embroidery like handwriting crawling along the white margins of the hems.

I bought flowers for their color, found the peonies with the widest petals, the most generous expanses of red and pink. I wanted to paint the air for him, to make it glow.

Incense burned in the ashtrays, foreign smoke to weigh down the air so that we could gather it about us. Jasmine and gardenia and narcissus and sandalwood. The smell of a clean peony opening its face in a little blue vase I'd found at the flea market, the smell of oily concoctions from San Francisco labeled Spirit and Dream, which smelled of burnt honey and artificial raspberry. The smell of tarragon in a little mustard glass above the tiny refrigerator where I stored the food for Felix. I was taming a special creature, who could not be asked to eat what French people ate in restaurants. I discovered mangoes for him, and Cape gooseberries, and hazelnuts in their pointed wings, papayas and the earliest kiwis, because I did not want to give him apples and common pears. I cut passion fruit in half and we ate them with tiny silver spoons.

He brought things to add to this, his own oriental swag. A rug from Algeria, a tapestry of bright red and faded yellow, with shining fringe, which I tacked to the wall.

He brought the wine, white wine from the Rhine, thick Austrian wine, and Muscadet. Only white. He brought one bottle at a time, and we shared it, and finished it together. I bought more white myself, so as to drink without him, too. I collected his presents as carefully as I dried the petals of the flowers on the windowsill. He gave me three postcards: a group of black people in the bush, gathered around a hill of cloves, and one of the Cathedral of Reims, and a picture of the Virgin of Elche, a Spanish madonna with a headdress made of bent boulders. He gave me a blue tin box with a phoenix on it.

The nights when I went out were terrible because they were one less chance to see him. When I had dinner with Dad and Michel, they said, "Bring your boyfriend." I'd say, "Maybe." I knew that I never would, because they were supposed to be a normal couple who lived in Neuilly, and their name was Radford and mine was Elise. On the nights I saw them I invariably came home to find a little note against my door, "Where are you?" and often a Toblerone bar with it. I picked up the long beige triangles and put them carefully in the back of my closet. I didn't dare eat them because they were proof that he had missed me, and although that meant he had wanted to see me, it also meant I had failed to be there. I didn't know which of the two I would be absorbing if I ate the chocolate, so it went in the back of the closet with the cards and the box. And the book on Taos.

For two months there was a perfect balance. Love or the time, or both. The curtains stayed drawn. It was February, it was March, it was cold outside and there was no reason to open the window. The thick radiator on casters that lived beneath the ladder gave off enough heat for the whole room. We gave off enough heat for the whole room.

He would come, sometimes, in the middle of the night, a warm body under chill clothes, and put his cold fingers inside me and draw a deep breath.

I liked it when he was cold because he melted so fast.

And then the weather changed, and with it the balance. The room was no longer hot by the radiator and cold by the window, the window became a source of heat and the space under the ladder, once warm, became cold, like a cave. I felt the reversal of heat and cold as a disturbing draft on my skin. Things were changing direction. Dark and light were changing place, and it unnerved me. The balance had to be restored. I went out and bought a second blue candle like Rosa's, and lit it to make sure Felix kept coming.

I barely saw Sylvie anymore, sometimes quickly during the day, for lunch. I did not call her at night, so as to keep my phone free. One evening, while Felix was there, she rang. "I'm not alone," I said.

"So your boyfriend is there. When do I get to meet him?" she asked.

"No," I said. The idea was deeply unpleasant.

"Why not? You know mine."

"It's not the same thing," I said. "Let's talk tomorrow."

"You're mean, I really have to talk to you," she said.

"Good night," I said, and hung up.

Felix had been listening. "You're not very nice to that person," he said.

"It's not important," I said. I hoped he had seen how tough I could be, how cold.

Then he didn't come for five nights in a row.

I lit the candle on the fifth night, and the doorbell rang within half an hour. It worked, but even so, I felt something slipping away. The feeling was no longer the same.

I started trying to memorize him when he was there. The curve of his neck where it joined the shoulders, the hollows above the clavicle, the entrancing flatness of his chest. And the mouth; the upper lip barely indented, drooping slightly at the edges, above the perfect cushion of his lower lip. In the matt dawn light, when the room was indistinct, like blotting paper, I lay still, watching the mouth cleave and renew its symmetry.

I put the picture of Morpheus up above the bed and pointed to it: "Oh," he said, with a delighted smile, "you think that's me?"

I nodded. Maybe I shouldn't have let him know, I thought.

"Elise," he said, "I am not a statue."

I was beginning to be scared.

YOU THINK THAT THINGS can't hurt you because they're not quite real. I knew I could eliminate what I didn't like by pretending it didn't exist. When I had to go to PhoLab, the scene of my various vices, I ignored the receptionist who knew too much, I ignored the photographers who greeted me with winks, and walked quickly past the doors to the locked rooms that I knew too well. Felix had made me respectable, and even if no one knew about Felix, they could see my new dignity, they could hear it, they could do everything but touch it.

I longed to tell Felix my real name; I wanted to take him to the shop, introduce him to Dad and Michel. But I was afraid of Dad's volatile lust as much as of his coarse protection; there was no way to tell if he would start breathing too slowly, his eyes fixed on Felix, or whether he would take him aside and ask him what his intentions were, and how much money he had, and bring out the line about how I'd be a very rich woman one day.

I wanted to be myself with Felix, to be real to him. He had never mentioned taking me home; I still didn't know where he lived, I still didn't know his phone number. Once he had tried to give it to me, and I had refused, saying, "I prefer it this way." Bravado. Showing a little restraint. And that was followed by the immediate fear that I was getting so good at the closed room that we would never get out of it.

Erghi came to town, and Dad invited me to dinner with them, at home. At the door of the apartment, he said, "Don't, whatever you do, don't mention you know what."

"The couple on the coffin lid?" I asked. Dad had his own kind of theatregoing.

"He doesn't know about it," Dad said, his hands tight on my shoulders. "It's a secret. I shouldn't have told you. I want your word now."

"What do you want me to promise?"

"To keep quiet about the coffin," he said. "That's all."

I ran my hands across the chest of the Kouros in the hall. "He's shining tonight," I said. Dad turned me around and pointed up at a bright light above the front door. "I had it installed last week, it's good, isn't it?"

That evening the Kouros looked like he was getting ready to run a race. The stiff arms seemed to swing. The braids on his chest and the curling pink smile were so bright under the light, and the dark blue hallway darker around him.

"Now remember, no Salonika horse," said Dad, giving a little tap on my shoulders.

When I was eight he bought the Salonika horse and it came to the apartment. Except it wasn't called the Salonika horse, it was just a white marble horse's front, head and mane and legs, a slice of sculpted marble that was flat behind, a sculpture that came in a slice like so many of his things. Then after a year it went to America, and not long after that a curator came from Greece and while he sat having drinks with Dad and Michel he handed them a catalogue. Dad opened it to a page where there was a colored picture of the horse, and with a loud and deliberate voice read out, " 'The Salonika Horse; third century B.C., an important recent acquisition.' My, but I'd love to go to New York and take a close look at that."

"That should be in Athens," said the curator.

"I'd like to get a closer look at it," said my father.

"But," I said, looking over their shoulders, "that looks exactly like . . ." and before I could finish Dad had interrupted me with "Your pony. I know, it looks just like Sixpence, doesn't it? Nice horsey," and turning to the man from Greece, he told him I was crazy about horses, a natural phenomenon in a girl my age, but a costly one. And because he was pinching my arm, not hard enough to hurt but hard enough to let me know that I was to shut up, I kept quiet.

At least tonight I'd been warned. I sat on the sofa with deliberate caution, as if any loose movement would be a betrayal, the way I imagined people behaved in church or in court, the way the others had behaved at Julia's funeral. Erghi came in a few minutes later. He wore an open-necked yellow shirt and a bulky watch, which he told me worked hundreds of feet under water. "Do you go diving?" I asked, and he said, grimly, like an undertaker or a murderer, "I go where the work is."

Nguyen brought in the white wings of deep-fried shrimp batter, and I drank Campari to make Erghi feel at home. Dad had opened a bottle of Château Margaux and Erghi drank that.

We ate the Phō in the dining room, moving the meat around the soup with chopsticks. Erghi said he loved French cuisine, and gave us the names of restaurants he had heard about.

Dad and Michel talked about Venice. "Pure holiday," said Dad. Erghi said, "I'm coming up to see you, I don't believe you have pure holidays. I'd like to see what one of them looks like." And they all laughed. He turned to me. "Will you be there too?"

"I may have something else to do," I said. I was hoping Felix would take me away somewhere.

"You'll love Venice," said Erghi.

"She knows it well," said Michel.

"Do you still have the Roman ring?" asked Dad. I nodded.

"Good, don't lose it, it's valuable," said Dad.

"Do you wear jewelry?" asked Erghi.

I held up my hands; snake rings, and the little blue stone ring, the little square amulets from the twenties. "Junk," said Erghi. "Don't you like gold?"

"She's not that kind of girl," said Michel.

"I work with my hands, I don't want to hurt anything good," I said. Dad was watching me carefully, so I tried to be nice. "The little gold sea horses, the earrings Dad has in the case, are they from you?" I asked.

"London," said Dad, and to Erghi, "Sotheby's, from a mixed lot."

"Women travel with lots of jewelry," Erghi said dreamily—"in little printed cotton bags, and suede pouches, you know? Don't you?"

I shrugged. I had my black plastic bangles from the thirties but they just went in a side of my suitcase. I didn't know what he meant.

After dinner we moved back to the living room, and while Michel and Erghi were talking about, I think, rhododendrons—Erghi had a big garden in Rome, full of rhododendrons—my father took me aside, again. "About Julia's money," he said. Oh God, I thought, leave me alone with this money.

"I don't want any more money," I said.

"You have to be responsible," said Dad. How ugly, I thought, how low.

But the next day I called Mr. Leon in London from the studio while Delaborde was out. "My dear little girl," he said, "I've been waiting for those papers for weeks. Are you going to sign them and send them back to me?"

"That's why I'm calling. Is that what I have to do? I'm not very good at this stuff."

"The artistic type, just like your father," said Mr. Leon. "Falling to pieces at the sight of a dotted line. Just sign where I put your initials, and send them back to me, will you? I can't leave Julia's affairs lying around like this."

I promised, and forgot all about it. I was so pleased at having used Delaborde's phone to call London that the purpose of the call vanished in the glow of my little feat.

André was reading a horoscope magazine. It did not please me that we had this in common. I didn't ask what sign he was, I didn't want him to have a sign; I wanted him to be an orphan of the zodiac, loose in outer space. I waited until he put it down, to grab it and look up my sign. "Do not confide in enemies," it said, "weigh all your acts. Take advice from someone you work with." I put down the magazine and watched André move around the studio, his blond hair swinging across his shoulders. The task was obviously to get advice from him without confiding in him.

"You believe in that stuff?" I asked, pointing to the horoscope magazine.

"Why not?" he said. "It's dumb, but it's funny."

"So what do you believe in?" I asked.

He stopped to look at me. "What do I believe in? You mean do I go to church?" He laughed at me. "Do I believe in the Virgin?"

Weigh all your acts. "No, that's not what I mean. Do you believe in magic?"

I had to be careful not to sound like a witch.

"Some people I know do," he said. "I don't let anyone tell me what to do."

"Nor do I," I hastened to agree. "But don't you want to know?"

"A gypsy came up to me on the street the other day," said André, "and she gave me her card. I kept it because I thought I might take her portrait, she was the ugliest woman I've ever seen. Maybe she'll do you some good."

He went to get the card. It was the first thing he had ever given me, and I felt odd when I put it in my pocket. But since the horoscope had said to take advice from someone you work with I tacked the card to the lowest beam in my room when I got home.

The next day I thought that perhaps the horoscope should be interpreted as taking advice from my father, since I used to work with him. I didn't feel in any particular need of advice, since Felix was almost every night in my bed, but something was shifting. Delaborde was away, and I was free to do what I pleased. I walked over to the shop.

There was a moving van outside, and two men in blue had just set down a crate on the sidewalk. I paused and waited for them to pick it up again and carry it into the shop, but they put it in the van instead. Michel sat inside signing papers at the desk. A green candle burned in a glass, exuding the calm smell of pine.

The coconut matting on the floor and the brass strips holding it down and the warm spotlights on the objects were comforting and peaceful. In the windows, facing out, were a slice of a god on a slab of polished stone, a pharaoh's mask, a portion of a tall, twisted girl in a billowing dress. There was the torso of a man on a pedestal in the middle of the shop, one arm by his side and the other gone, beyond a raised shoulder. David holding up the head of Goliath, maybe, or Perseus holding up the Medusa's head, or maybe

Dionysus with a bunch of grapes, although the body was too good for the god of wine and debauch. I delighted myself with speculation. These were things I knew about.

Glass shelves along the wall behind the desk held the small pieces, the cosmetic pots and the glass beads which, if you looked carefully, revealed faces that ran right through them, the same on both sides. The jewelry was under the glass of a locked table: bracelets, earrings, necklaces, torques.

The only interesting job I ever had in the shop was emptying the vacuum cleaner onto a large sieve in the back room. The sieve caught little pieces of gold or glass, little pieces of ancient garbage, missing links from chains, drops and curls of bronze, illegible metal twitters that Dad kept together in flat wooden trays. Sometimes one of the restorers brought handfuls of these bits, which Dad carefully stored. I'd seen them at Sotheby's, and they were always in the lots I could afford but didn't want. Dad kept everything in case something broke, but the things that broke were always those that could not be repaired. A statue went from masterpiece to curiosity in one second when its nose broke off, while the small bronze pins and thick little pots carried on unharmed, safe in their lack of distinction, the silt layer of inexpensive remnants. From which I gleaned the notion that the beautiful is doomed and the common survives.

"Florence!" Maud came out of the back room.

"Where's Dad?"

"He's in London," said Michel, rising to give me a kiss. "He'll be back tonight."

I sat down in one of the armchairs, the one behind the desk. "Tea time?" said Maud to Michel, who said, "Of course."

There were art magazines on the desk, and I flipped through them while Michel took care of a man who had come in. I found a full-page ad from Jacob Ellis et Compagnie. The caption read, "Roman marble relief of hermaphrodite in 'restless sleep.' Circa 1st century A.D. Price on demand." Michel was showing the man the little wooden statue of an Egyptian housewife, which had been in the shop for years. The man held it up, turned it around, ran his fingers on her painted wig, and said, "*Merci*." He handed it back to Michel and left.

"What's 'restless sleep'?" I asked.

Michel stacked the magazines so we'd have somewhere for the tea tray. "You've never had restless sleep?"

"Is that to do with sex?" I asked.

"Usually lack of it. It's just a description. If you were a hermaphrodite, you'd have trouble sleeping too."

Maud brought us tea in cups that didn't match and Michel said, "Maud, *vraiment*," and she said, "She's family, it doesn't matter." We dipped our cookies—Bourbon biscuits from London—in our tea the way Maud hated, and Michel put his hand over mine and asked if I was coming to Venice. "I still don't know," I said. I held the magazine open at the picture of the hermaphrodite. "Where is he? She?" I asked.

Michel waved his hand toward the front door. "Not here."

"Erghi?" I asked.

"Maybe. Don't be so curious. When will you know if you're coming?"

"I don't like Erghi. Does he want me to smuggle things out, is that all the talk about jewelry?"

"Nothing very big," said Michel, "you've done it before."

I remembered my first handbag, from Rome, with the bottom full of tissue paper.

"Is there anything here that I carried back?"

Michel didn't look up. "Not anymore, all that was gone years ago."

I got up to look inside the locked cases. I was good at dumb questions; as a child I'd asked what the English word for apple was. "Is everything real?" I asked casually.

Michel was filing his nails, his ankle resting on his knee. He didn't look up and he didn't answer. I came back to the desk. "Well, is it?"

"You have an eye, you were brought up with this stuff," he said, looking at his cuticles.

"But I never studied it," I said. "All I've ever known is what's in the shop."

"You've been to the Louvre," he said.

"I hate the Louvre, it smells of dirty hair and wet coats and school,"
I said. "Come on, Michel, is everything real?"

"Is it that important?" he asked under his breath, and I felt the
draft of an open door.

He shouted for Maud, and when she appeared he told her she
had to go to the post office. "Today?" she asked.

"It would be better if you could go today," he said. She looked
out the window and went to get her raincoat from the closet.

"You won't need it," I said, "it's nice out."

"You never know," she answered. Michel handed her a stack of
envelopes from the desk drawer.

When she was gone he took my wrists and pulled me over to the
window. He pointed down the row of pieces on display. "The third
one along, and the horseman, and the pharaoh's head on the wall.
They're real."

"And the rest?" I asked. There was no answer. Michel proceeded
by silences. I looked up at him.

"Nothing else?" I asked again. Silence.

"But this is the best shop in Paris," I said. "It's always been the
best."

"I think your father has been making some mistakes," said Michel,
"and I don't know how to stop him." This last was so unexpected
that it was worse than what had gone before. He's making it up, I
thought. He's making it up, or he's being disloyal. I tried to be adult:
"Have you told Dad what you think?"

"He won't listen. I wouldn't be telling you this if he listened."

I was proud that he trusted me. I despised him for betraying Dad.
And I didn't know what to say, because I wasn't sure what any of
it meant. We both walked back to the desk, as if the window had
said enough. I pointed to the black ceramic pots on the glass shelves
behind Michel. "That's all real Bucchero," I declared, naming it.
Jacob had taught me all about Bucchero, its strange lightness, its
unrelieved blackness.

"Bucchero," said Michel, smiling. "What do you know about Bucchero?"

I was delighted to be asked. I pointed at a black jug. "Seventh century B.C.,'' I said. "Etruscan, and it's a kind of clay that is very thin and black all the way through." I stopped and smiled at Michel, who nodded. I loved this test, and went on: "It was so fine that the potters made things that looked like silver, and you can tell seventh-century Bucchero because it's very light, like good porcelain, Dad says. Right?''

Michel nodded. "Very good. Now pick it up."

I reached for the jug. It was heavy. "Oh, then it's later," I said, "the next kind, when it wasn't for rich people anymore, when it was popular."

Michel shook his head. I was reciting now, faster and faster. "Late Bucchero is still black all the way through . . ." I turned the jug over. On the base the label said, BUCCHERO, ETRUSQUE, 7ÈME SIÈCLE AV. JC.

Michel took it from my hand. He swung his arm back and knocked the jug hard against the side of the table. The neck broke. And at the break was a circle of bright pink clay.

I stared at the pink, the color of Roman walls: "How could you do that?''

Michel laughed and slammed the rest of the jug against the table leg; triangular pieces like orange skin fell to the floor. "Plenty more where that comes from," he said in English. He pulled the waste-basket over to him with his foot and dropped in the rest of the jug. He didn't pick the pieces up off the floor.

"What does it mean?" I asked.

"Your father got greedy. Supply and demand. Or he was greedy before but didn't give in to it."

"Greedy?''

He drank some more tea. As if what he was saying wasn't important, was just chat. "I don't know," he said, putting his cup down. "Little things. Now it's big things."

"Isn't it simpler to keep selling whatever Erghi finds," I asked, "the way he always has?''

"Erghi isn't finding things anymore. He has people working for him, making things. There are no new sites, at least not good ones."

"But then why do you keep going to Italy?''

"There are very good artisans in Italy. The restoration schools they started after the flood . . ."

I walked around the shop, staring at the neat lines of thick cord on the floor. "It won't last," I said. "He just got weird after Julia died. So did I."

"Your father has a lot of problems right now," said Michel. He usually said "Jacob."

I reached for a little bronze chariot with seven stubby horses attached to it by thick wires. "This is real," I said, loud, my hands on the cool green metal. "Look at the horses' necks; it's authentic, I can feel it's authentic."

Michel closed his eyes and put his head back, snorting, "Of course it's real, it's a little toy that I picked up at the sales last week for nine hundred francs. It's real, but not particularly interesting."

"Nine hundred francs? Is that all?"

"We sell it for three thousand."

"I thought everything here was priceless," I said.

Michel stood up and came over to me. "Everything that was any good in the shop has gone to pay for those people on the postcard. The Etruscan couple. They're priceless."

"How much?"

"I can't say, I'm not even sure. It's too much for Jacob and it's not enough for what it is, and he shouldn't have gone near it. It's for a museum, that. But he wants the perfect object, the masterpiece."

"I can understand," I said. Thinking of Felix.

"Unfortunately, before he decided to dedicate himself to the sublime, he got greedy. Which means there was very little to sell that was any good. Do you see?"

"The shop does very well," I told Michel firmly. I wanted him to agree with me.

"We used to manage," he said.

"Is something awful going to happen?" I asked.

He put his arms around me and led me back to the big table, and he took a sugar cube out of the bowl on the tray and handed it to me. "Don't make a drama out of all this. There is no tragedy. I thought it was time you knew a little about what goes on, since you asked. And maybe you could talk to Jacob, at some point."

"But what would I say?" I asked.

"You'll know what to say," said Michel.

"I'm not coming to work in the shop," I said. I had to leave. I couldn't wait to get out of there.

Michel was just jealous. All those years devoted to Dad, and leaving his land in Provence so that it was just a place for the holidays. He'd let his life slip into Dad's, he'd been eaten by the shop and by Dad's obsessions, and now he had nothing to do but be bitter behind the bleached white desk. He had to cause trouble, he was mean.

Whatever he was trying to tell me, I wanted no part of it.

Maybe Dad was in love with someone else. It was the most pleasant explanation. Michel tied to the desk while Dad did what he wanted, loved what he wanted, wanted what he loved. We were made of the same stuff, what Olivia called the Oo La La. Rolling her eyes. Oo La La in Gay Paree, and those words used to make me cringe; they sounded the way the ceramic poodle that turned into a lighter on her living room table looked. If only she were still around, she would explain it. "You can't trust these boys," she'd say. "Michel is just a jealous pansy." Jacob, of course, was not a pansy.

Julia would say, Julia would say . . . nothing. I tried to make her shape in front of me. I tried to see her face, but that only came in dreams.

Julia would say, "He should work harder."

I walked toward the street market on Rue de Buci. I would buy green grapes and blue cheese, spinach and celery. I bought cornflowers from the street stall, for the blue. I wanted cool colors, sky colors. He had come two nights ago. But he would return.

The tingling was steady and increased through the evening. My body was more accurate than my mind. The light faded; I made a salad with the blue cheese, the spinach and the celery. I put the green grapes in a purple bowl. At ten-thirty the doorbell rang.

It was Felix. I laid my palms flat on his arms and then his chest and his face and the back of his head. We made love on the floor and I felt his wet hair, our sweat. I thought, This is real, this counts, this means something. This is true.

"Elise," he said, "Elise Elise Elise."

He put his hands behind my neck, to hold it still while he kissed me.

I wished it were my real name.

We lay there on the cushions. He pulled one toward him to rest his head, and it was one of Julia's petits points from London, a garden of blue flowers with a yellow trellis around it. He followed the petals of an azalea with his finger. "Pretty," he said before he laid his head down.

"It was my aunt's, in London," I said.

His body relaxed into the beginning of sleep. "Whose?" he asked, in a drowsy murmur.

"My aunt, in London, no one you know," I said.

I felt his body grow rigid, and then he gave a heave and his arm came over me again and we slept.

12

BUT NONE OF THIS was fast enough for me. I asked Rosa how to make the affair progress; she dealt her cards and gave me short sentences about being discreet, not forcing. I bought a book on astrology, read up everything about my sign, and all the other signs because he wouldn't tell me when his birthdate was. I had an astroflash done in the Arcades du Lido. It said I was inclined to dark and obscure events in my love life. I bought a book on astrological houses, and figured out my own chart. I saw that the house of love affairs was opposed, always, to the house of friends and hopes and dreams. I told myself I was content to have him in my bed when he came, and I filled in the hole he made in my life by asking Rosa and Sylvie what to do. Like spiderwebs in the cracks, a bridge between the beams and the wall, trying to fill in with other people's words what wasn't there.

Sylvie's advice was sound and inelegant. It came from the world of women who get what they want, and consisted of sly methods for obtaining position, money, social advantages. I thought my calculations were pure because I only wanted his body, more of his body. I had told her what was necessary: that he was young and handsome and strange; I had also told her that we loved each other. Sylvie was, for all her wisdom, prudish. Maybe I was. I did not tell her what I felt like in bed with Felix. There didn't seem to be any words, and it was mine. Flesh to flesh melting of the flesh, silver in the veins. So I said we loved each other, because together with no clothes we were one body, even without touching.

I had not given her his name, because I was afraid that by naming him I would cause him to disappear. "He's married since you won't tell me his name," she said.

"No, I'm through with all that," I said. "This is real, this isn't poaching."

I did tell her how we'd met, because that was one piece of magic that I could share: it was public. If she had been in the street with me that day she would have seen it.

She was amazed. "You picked a man up in the street and he asked you to dinner? That never happens. That's so dangerous. I would never dare do that," she said. I was alarmed to realize that she envied my courage.

"It's only because I knew inside me that he was right," I said.

"You mean Rosa told you," she answered.

"No, no, I knew the moment I looked at him that he was the one," I said, passing over my visit to Rosa the next day.

I didn't like to be envied. It was difficult to share something extraordinary with her without making her envious. I heard the little signs: she'd say, "I haven't met the love of my life yet, I wish it would hurry up and happen," and it was clear that she felt I'd won the race. To dull the lustre, I tried to point out that it wasn't easy, that I hated leaving my apartment during the hours when I was supposed to be home, in case he called or he came. Sylvie disapproved of that: "You have to go out, you absolutely must let him know he's not the only man in your life."

"But he is the only man in my life, he's the only man I love," I said.

"You didn't tell him that, did you? You fool. The most you can ever say to a man is maybe fifteen seconds while you're making love, as if you'd lost your head with passion, and then never mention it again. That's the last thing in the world you should say."

"But I love him," I said, remembering as faults the times I had slipped an "I love you, Felix," into his ear as he left.

"No, no, no," said Sylvie. "Keep him interested. Don't ever put a man on the spot. They hate that, they think it means they have to marry you."

"But I don't want to marry anyone," I said.

I didn't tell her that I was Elise Radford. If she should ever meet him, he wouldn't be able to tell her about me. If he ever left me, it would be Elise Radford he humiliated, not me. Bless Elise. She was my sole defense.

Sylvie had spent several uncomfortable weekends with Marc at a hotel in Deauville, where he played poker and gin with his men friends, and she was allowed to watch. I told her she was lucky, and thought to myself that crass strategies brought crass rewards. Which she sensed: "What I've got with Marc, you know, it's not passion, it's not what you're living." Another time she said, "Marc is so predictable," as I was telling her that I had waited three nights running for a phone call from Felix, a visit, a sign.

I told her about the chocolate bars he left for me. "How romantic," she said. I pointed to the chain around her neck, from which hung a round little gold heart.

"Marc gives you real presents," I said. I despised gold. I might not have despised it if Felix had ever tried to give it to me.

Marc was renting a house in Portofino for Easter. Sylvie showed me the photographs Marc had received from the agent. It was on top of a cliff, a house with balconies and flowers, a house in the shape of a funnel. I waited to be invited. "How many bedrooms?" I asked casually.

"Oh, six or seven, lots," she said. I imagined her saying, "Why don't you and your mysterious man come down and spend a week with us?" I imagined Felix and me on a train, or a plane . . .

"How are you getting there?" I asked.

"I think Marc's renting a car from Milan. We have to fly to Milan." Milan, where the models went. March wore on, and April began, and still she didn't ask me. Easter was late that year. She wouldn't ask me. "It's not my house," she said one day. "You understand."

When I couldn't ask Rosa and I couldn't ask Sylvie I could always ask the voice. It was unsteady, and needed to be summoned by rigid disciplines beforehand. When I wanted anything too badly, when I lay on the floor of my room with cold palpitations because Felix hadn't called, when I felt my face boiling because he had sounded cool on the telephone, the voice was nowhere around. Only in those rare moments walking down the street when I was content, or when

I was working hard in the studio and not thinking about Felix, then the voice came. Sober, modulated. It said things such as, *Go home now,* or *A call will come tonight.* It was always right. It existed like a jagged railway line along my life, invisible and then present, reliable, distant.

I began to work more with other photographers. Luc hired me for two days, when Delaborde was away taking a water cure with his ex-wife. It was a small job, but the idea that Luc was now signing his pictures, and able to pay me for my work, made me feel that we were growing up to become important people. We joked about Delaborde's manias. The models were listening, and they laughed. A few days later, I was putting the makeup away in the dressing room when Delaborde came in.

"So we're moonlighting?" he said.

"You told me I could work for others," I said.

"Others, yes. A former assistant, no. I don't need that kind of flattery."

I didn't answer.

"If André hadn't shown me those pictures, I wouldn't have known. At least there's someone around here who's on my side," he said, and went out.

André. That little shit. I heard the front door bang back and forth on its one good hinge. I got up and went to the darkroom to find André.

"Listen, you horrible creep," I began, opening the door wide.

"The light! The light! You're out of your mind! Shut it!"

I pulled the door shut. That day's black and white pictures were in the bath.

He had his back to me.

"Listen," I began again, as if I didn't have his attention . . . "I hate you," was the best I could come up with.

"You're not the only one," he said, still bent over the square vats.

"Others do too?" I asked, startled at his answer. In a way it was delightful. If he was going to put his weapons down I was prepared to listen.

"Yes?" I said, to get him to talk.

"You think you're the only one, and you're not," he said.

I crossed my arms and leaned against the side of the door.

"Just because you look like a little boy doesn't mean you can have who you want," he said.

"I'm talking about Luc's pictures," I said.

"I'm not," he said.

A sudden wash of cold came over me. I turned and felt the heels of my boots dig into the soft linoleum of the floor. But I had to stay and speak: "André, you're not a good friend. I spend my time telling my father and Michel, Michel Dupuy, how talented you are and how clever you are, and you're really just a spy."

"That's when you're not with Felix," he said.

The noise of hands and paper in water stopped. In the red light I saw him coming toward me. His chin was thrust forward. "You think you're the only one, don't you? Well, you're not. I was there first. And what's more, he prefers boys."

I couldn't move. I stood there, the door handle turning curiously warm and wet in my hand, my heart pounding against every inch of my body. No one but me said that name. I wanted to throw something at André, and I wanted to disappear. I tried to close my hand over the knob, to turn it and open the door, but my hand kept slipping. I was trapped there in the red. I pulled my scarf off and put it over the handle, and got out.

I had to cross the studio to get my bag from the dressing room. My datebook was in my bag, with its signs and secrets, and my money, and my keys. I had to get them away from him. His hands would be everywhere. My enemy. I ran.

I ran. At home, I found the unbearable cold of not knowing what to do. I might call the studio and confront André. "Tell me his last name," I'd say. And he would say some other name, and it wouldn't be my Felix at all, and everything would be all right again.

But I couldn't pull at a loose thread of the wrong name and unravel the pattern people had been knitting behind my back.

Felix in the street the first day, Felix outside Goldenberg's. Felix waiting for André. Felix part of someone else's life, not fate. Not my divine being.

I couldn't think any further. *Sylvie,* I heard in my head. *Sylvie.* The voice was saying it, not I. I looked at my watch: seven forty-five. I could ask her over. She had not come to my room since it began with Felix. Felix, the possibility of Felix, was an iron curtain over my door, a stone block barring access. I wanted to call her, I didn't call her in case Felix called during the time I was on the phone to Sylvie.

I couldn't think any further than the name Felix in André's mouth. The name had been soiled. That name in that mouth was filth. The only way to think would be to talk to someone. I dialed Rosa.

"I'm with a client," she said.

"Please please please. It's so urgent I can't wait," I begged.

"It's always urgent. I'm sure you'll hear from him before the night is out. That's all I can tell you now," she said, and hung up before I could tell her any more.

I wished I had some means at my disposal for reading the future. Alexis used to bring the *I Ching* with him on holidays, and would roll the coins and tell my father what to do. There was my friend with the tarots, but I hadn't seen her in ages. I couldn't call and inveigle her into reading my cards over the phone. And what could the cards tell anyone who didn't know the situation?

Sylvie, I heard in my head again. Her advice, if crass, was sensible. And even if she wanted to come over, the truth was he wouldn't be here before eleven, if he came.

"My darling," she said, "I'm so glad you called. Marc has gone to Geneva."

I asked her to come over. "I really need to talk to you," I said.

"I'll bring some food," she said.

"I have food," I told her.

"Will your man be there?"

"No," I said.

It was still light. The window was open, and I had a peony in the little vase. "We haven't had a girl evening like this in months," she said, settling onto my floor, gathering my cushions around her.

"Do you want something to drink?" I asked, and I could hear how reluctant I sounded. She had barely arrived and I was pushing her away. I didn't want a girl evening. I wanted to slap André and kill Felix. I didn't want to watch Sylvie settle into Felix's territory, using her sunglasses and her bag and her cigarettes to colonize my room.

"What's up?" she asked, and without waiting for me to answer she went into a story about Marc's trip to Geneva. The pillows made a soft nest around her. "So where's my drink?" she asked. I opened a bottle of white wine, the white wine I kept for Felix. I handed her the glass and reclaimed one of the needlepoint pillows. Marc this, Marc that, Marc said. I stopped her.

"Sylvie."

"Yes?"

"I have to talk."

"Your married man."

"He's not married."

"Well, whatever he is, he's giving you problems."

"Yes."

"Well, what are they?"

I burst into tears.

"Oh my God," she said, "he's left you for someone else."

"I don't think so, something like that."

Sylvie sat up. "What? What? What is it?"

"Somebody told me today that I wasn't the only one."

"Darling, you expected to be the only one? No one is ever the only one in somebody's life. It isn't possible. Life isn't made like that."

"Don't you believe in love?" I asked, appalled.

"I try to take things intelligently," she said. What that mother must have told her, over eighteen years. "You have to be really installed in someone's life before you can be sure, and even then . . . there's always the phone booth on the corner, you know. You can never be sure."

"Sylvie," I said. A habit of mine, to use people's names even when there was no one else in the room. To make sure, maybe, that I had their full attention. "You sound like a cynical old cocotte. It's not your generation. It's not mine. There is love. It can happen when two people exist only for each other."

"How often do you see him?" she asked, suddenly pointed.

I was about to tell her that I'd seen him sixteen times. But to be too precise would betray an unhealthy amount of time spent counting. "A lot, most nights," I said.

"Where is he the rest of the time?" she asked.

"I don't know," I said.

"What does his wife say?"

"He doesn't have a wife, how many times do I have to tell you that?"

"He has someone," she said. "Have you been to where he lives?"

I shook my head.

"Do you call him at home? Do you see his friends? See! He's married. Or he's living with someone."

Sylvie only wanted to hear things she could understand. "I think he has a double life," was the cleanest way I could say it.

She was pulling at the threads of one of Julia's pillows.

"Sylvie, pay attention. I think he's a homosexual."

A silence.

"Not you too," she said.

"Who else?" I asked, alarmed in case she knew who I was talking about.

"It runs in your family. Your mother . . ." said Sylvie.

"No," I said very quickly. This was nothing to do with my mother.

"What do you mean, no? What about your father?" said Sylvie.

I shook my head. It wasn't the same thing, not at all. Couldn't apply.

"What would you do?" I asked.

"I wouldn't go near that vipers' nest in the first place," she said, rising from the cushions to put an end to a discussion that had nothing to hook her. "What's for dinner?"

I had my Felix food in the kitchen. Exotic fruits, dried meat, peasant cheese, and tomatoes. "I'll just have a tomato," he'd say and then devour all the smoked and sliced things from the waxed paper packages. Sylvie turned over the kiwis in their tin bowl, the mango, the papaya—"What's this one?" she asked—and opened the refrigerator and turned over the packages. "What's this?" and "What's that?" and "How old is this?" Every one of her fingers on Felix's food was a violation. I felt helpless in front of her breathing hungry distracted presence in my sliver of kitchen. She seemed to me an animal, a large puppy, loose in my room, fouling my privacy with incontinent giggles and inapposite concerns. But I'd invited her in. It was my fault.

We sat on the floor and ate off paper plates. Sylvie said it was a pity I didn't have a television. Sylvie finished the meat and the cheese and the bottle of wine. Sylvie said that if a man loved you, he wanted you to live with him, unless he wanted you to be a mistress in which case he wants to keep you at a certain distance so that the intensity is allowed to grow. All this came out in neat aphorisms, like lessons learned. "The daily routine destroys love," she said. I wondered if that meant it was bad to make his tea in the morning. I knew nothing. The more Sylvie talked the more she remembered what she'd been told. "The strongest kind of love affair is the one that cannot be fully realized. If you want daily life with someone, you have to have tastes and friends in common, and if you want a mad passion you have to be happy with whatever you get."

"It sounds so strict," I said. "Isn't there any other way?"

"I want both. I'm beginning to see that Marc is becoming sort of everyday, and that I'm becoming everyday for him. I'd like a mad passion too."

"But I never know when I'll see him again," I said, to push her away from wanting too much of my life.

"That's wonderful, it's the element of surprise. You've got what everyone wants, you should be happy."

I knew I had to tarnish it for her, prove how unhappy I was. But there was pride, and there was vanity, and the urge to make it shine by telling, and all that was stronger than the urge I had to make it dark and vile so she wouldn't want what I had.

"Fifteen years from now, or twenty, when I'm old, I'll remember this as the greatest love of my life," I said.

Sylvie sighed. "Is he a good lover?" she asked.

I hadn't thought of him in terms of general consumption. And since each return provoked such energetic gratitude in me, I had not really had the chance to find out what he would do of his own accord. The moment he was in the room, something else took over. I couldn't describe the something else, the heat, the confidence of being wanted.

"Yes," I said.

Another ready-made came out. "Good lovers practice, my mother always says so. It's like playing the piano. They have to do it every day. And they can't always play the same piece." She sighed, and asked: "Do you have any cake, any chocolate?" I got up to look in the kitchen, and came back with some petit-beurres. "Is that all?" she asked. I nodded. "What about the chocolate he brings you, can't we have some of that?"

"No," I said, and sat down, determined to bring her back to what interested me. "I want him to love me," I said. As if she could do something about it.

"He does," she said, helping herself to a petit-beurre.

"Look at me when you say that."

"Okay, I'm looking at you. He loves you."

"But how do I know? Oh, Sylvie, can't you do the cards, or something? Isn't there some other way of knowing?"

"You certainly can't ask him. There's nothing a man hates more than that."

"I know, so what can I do?"

There on my floor I listened to Sylvie's truisms as if they applied to me and Felix. The advice seemed impossible to follow: take, be silent, disappear, be mysterious, never show anything, and you will be loved. Imitate Daphne, skitter through the woods, peer from behind trees, vanish, ululate in the night, turn into a tree if caught. Impossible. How could you do that with two feet in clogs and a garageman's uniform and a telephone number and a job?

There was no comfort in the advice, but it had a certain sedative quality. As if love had a structure, a set of rules, a shape which, if studied, could reveal instructions for use. But Sylvie couldn't know the things that passed between me and Felix. And I would lose the goodwill of the other side if I stooped to schemes. That I knew. I looked at my watch: it was ten-thirty. I stood up, releasing crumbs all over the carpet. "He's coming soon," I said. Sylvie put her hands behind her head and lay back, flat on the floor.

"Maybe I'd better see this animal," she said. I felt my back go stiff. She continued: "How many times have I invited you to dinner with me and Marc? I've shown you mine, it's time for you to show me yours."

"Yours," I said, "is part of everyday life, you said so yourself. Common friends, common interests. Mine is special and secret. You can't ask me for that."

She rolled over on her belly and addressed the carpet. "Just you wait till I have a nice big secret in my life, and you start begging me to share it with you, and I won't. I'll keep him all to myself, I won't even tell you it's happened."

Don't cross her, said the voice. Why not? I thought, she's being a pig. Anyway, you told me to bring her here. I remembered the voice had said *Sylvie*. Not *Call Sylvie*. I checked to see where she had left her bag, her sunglasses, so that I could assemble Sylvie in a minute and a half and get her out the door. My breath was coming irregularly. He would be here soon. They would meet. It couldn't happen.

"Please go."

"All right," she said from the floor, "tell me you want to throw me out after everything I've done for you. Who sent you to Rosa?"

"Your mother!" I screamed—"I know! Please get up, Sylvie."

She sat on her crossed legs and slowly stood up, pretending to be old. "My knees," she said. "Ouch, my rheumatism. Oh dear. Up we go. Now, I'm up. Happy?"

Where does she think she gets this power from? I wondered. Who does she think she is to do this to me? Then it came to me: I gave it to her, I listened to her.

"I am a very good friend of yours," she said, putting her arms slowly and languidly on my shoulders. "Don't you ever forget that."

I kissed her on both cheeks, and firmly handed her her bag and her sunglasses.

"Will you see me out?" she asked. "I'm afraid of those tramps on your stairs."

"They aren't dangerous," I said. "Were there any when you came up?"

"No," she said.

"You can go, Sylvie, it's safe, no one is going to assault you on the stairs. I swear it on my father's life."

I pushed her toward the door. Felix's door.

"Call me tomorrow and tell me how it went, and whatever you

do, don't confront him," she said. I closed the door behind her, and then opened it again to shout "Thank you!" for her advice.

I tried to reclaim the room. To clean it so that no trace of the evening remained. I didn't want him to sense anything other than us. I threw away the paper plates and the empty wine bottle and tied the plastic garbage bag tight so that no smell came out, and emptied the ashtray and lit two incense sticks and then a third, all jasmine, and threw the maroon scarf over the lamp on the floor. I washed the glasses, and ran a bath and filled it with the smell of gardenia, and put on a transparent Indian shirt. Then I looked at the room.

Despite the threads of incense smoke and the maroon stain of light, it looked garish, public, common. I put a few drops of narcissus oil on a wedge of cotton and put it on the bulb, where it sizzled and turned brown under the maroon scarf. And to wait, I made a new nest of the cushions on the floor and curled into it. I did not want to go up to bed. That would be to admit that the night was over, that the night had been nothing but Sylvie talking, intruding. If I went up to bed I would be showing a lack of faith. He had to come. The night had to become his.

And I waited. And he didn't come.

13

I WOKE FEELING I had lost everything during my sleep. I was on the cushions, on the floor, my winter coat pulled over me. It was a bright morning, and hot. My coat was too warm and so was the radiator. The lamp was a glowing stain behind me. I lay still until something could come to me, the ring of the telephone, reassurance.

It's all over, said the voice.

I stood up knowing that I had to phone Felix. To stop its being over. To bring him back. I tried to hear the voice again. I seemed to know that something was in the street. *In the street*, I heard. I pulled off my useless pretty shirt and put on some jeans. I didn't need a bath, I'd bathed enough the night before. I ran down the stairs. On the right the charcuterie, on the left the baker's. I was listening. Instructions were bound to come. *Here*, I heard, *right here.* I looked down at my feet and saw an illegible surface of gray asphalt that I consulted like a telephone book, squinting. A little further up, toward the Rue de Grenelle, maybe ten yards away from me, I saw a piece of paper. I went toward it, and saw that it was a little gray-green slip from the P.T.T., something to do with a long-distance call. There was a telephone number on it. I picked it up. The paper had been rained on in the night, it was soft and cold. I looked at the seven digits and knew this had to be Felix's number. I turned around and went back up to my room.

I dialed the number. It had to be his. He would answer. He had to.

"*Allô?*" A deep voice, male, or older. Not Felix's.

"*C'est Elise,*" I said. "I want to speak with Felix."

"Never heard of him," the voice said, and the phone was hung up. Motionless on the floor, I kept the receiver in my hand. "Never heard of him." That was what thieves said in films when you confronted them with the name of their accomplice. That was what resistance members said when the Gestapo asked if they knew Marcel. "Never heard of him" was the proof of something to hide. A normal answer would be, "Who?" or "Wrong number." Never heard of him. I started to dial again, and put the receiver back instead. I would wait until the person had gone to work, and call again. This time Felix would answer.

I went down to the café for my breakfast. I might see him in the street. He could be at my café, though I had never seen him there again after that first morning. If I walked slowly, right foot first, right foot first, he would be there. Anything was possible.

Few people in the café. It was still only a quarter to eight. Clean morning counter, clean chins and ears. Jackets thinning for spring. A group of Algerian workers came in. A slap on my nose after the jasmine and gardenia of my room. A smell I seem to be the only one to recognize, a fascinating smell. Piss-fermented sting of sweat, a stone, that smell, ripened gestures petrified into odor. The pants drawn on, no underwear, stale piss on the top of the leg front of the thigh, same clothes every day. Whistling drops of white sweat alit on curls, the curls on the body, all dark, tighter curls, ammonia, and back to work, two fingers on the cock inside the pocket, an enlightened scratching, hand goes over the nose across the eyebrows, the smell travels, coats the whole body, seeps into the shoes, lands on the hair, is blown on the wind the doors make, in winter, closing tight, just a crack of ice air through the side, nailed by a pair of silver bars.

But it was a spring morning, and warm despite the hour. The smell was free to roam, mix with the warm butter smell of the new croissants in the plastic tray by my elbow. Two gay boys drank tea in a corner, wearing sunglasses. It was too early for gay boys.

I paid and went outside, inhaled the fresh yeast near the métro entrance, breath spray and mouthwash in neat passing mouths. I couldn't go home after my defeat. It was too early to go to the studio,

I didn't want to be there alone with André. I would go late. My body was sluggish from the waiting sleep, each joint and each muscle ready all night to jump up at the sound of my bell. If I had given him a key he never would have come.

If I went up Felix might call.

I walked past my front door and up the street, where only the cheese shop was open, and kept walking. It was absurd to know that the number was his, but then so was everything.

I came to a stoplight. The meaning of red. I couldn't even call Rosa till ten. Out in the street with nowhere to go. No home. I started toward my father's apartment. Toward home.

Nguyen let me in. "You are here for breakfast?" he asked. I said I might as well be, and asked for coffee. Michel, he said, was in the bath, and my father was having coffee in bed. I paused by the Kouros in the hall, ran my palm over his chest.

I went to his room, knocked on the half-open door. I could see the end of his red velvet bed, a thin mohair blanket crumpled at his feet. What used to be so familiar now looked luxurious beyond my experience. The clean edges of his morning were intimidating. The *Herald Tribune* open before him. His hair splayed over the square white pillows behind him.

"Florence." A purr. He made a space next to him on the bed, an automatic curl back into the side nearest the telephone. His bifocals in his hand, an affectation of age: he only needed the reading part. I climbed next to him. The smell of sleep still on him, chaste cotton sleep, a bowl of white flowers on his bedside table. Michel's room was down the corridor. The pajama top was open, gaping blue cotton edged in darker blue, the buttons pearly gray plastic, round with an unpleasant straight sheen.

"I don't like your buttons," I said. He squinted through his small glasses. "Oh, no. This pair's from London. They're not very pretty, are they? I must get Nguyen to change them for me. Mother of pearl?"

"Plain white plastic. Matt, with a little raised edge, you know the kind?" I said.

"Like on workmen's jackets, I know exactly. What's up, Florence?"

"I was in the street and it's too early to go to work and I thought it might be nice to come and see you. You're happy I'm here, aren't you?"

"Is everything okay? Do you need money?"

"No." I pulled at the holes in the mohair blanket. It didn't occur to me that I must have had more, then, more than he did. "I just wanted to see you. Are you okay?"

"More or less. What's the matter, darling?"

I sighed. If I could tell him everything. I could have told Julia. "Dad," I said, "I'm in love."

"At last," he said, and put his paper down. "Do we know him?"

"Of course not, how would you know him?" I asked.

"That's what fathers say. Who is this young man, where does he live, what does he do, how much does he earn, what are his prospects, who are his parents, all that. I have to be a serious father."

"I never said I wanted to marry him, I said I was in love. It isn't the same thing, you know that."

"You're quite sure we're talking about a boy, now?" He looked like a bird professor in a child's book. I laughed.

"Of course."

"Heterosexuals," he said, "are put on this earth to make human beings. It's easier to make human beings if you have a private company founded for that express purpose, and the company goes by the name of marriage. If you are in love it means that your DNA is all excited over his DNA. You will make decent babies. That's what it's about. If you're in love you have to get married."

"How can you be so old-fashioned?"

'I'm not old-fashioned, I'm realistic."

"What about love affairs, you've had love affairs, you've told me! Come on."

"Love affairs are what you have when your purpose isn't to make more human beings. Love affairs are what you do when the essential has been taken care of."

"What's the essential?"

"You."

I took it personally. I was flattered. "Me?"

"You. I've reproduced. You don't know how important that is. If you love someone, if you really love them, you want a baby with them. It's the only purpose to love. That's love. The rest is affairs. If you are in love, you should have a baby."

"There's plenty of time for that," I said, lying on my back in his bed. I put my feet on his shins under the covers. "That's for ordinary girls. I'll have a baby later."

I thought of Felix. I thought I had not yet had my period. I thought it was possible. I would come back here in two months, with a fat belly, and say, "Dad, I listened to you."

"No, you should do it now. Like that when you're thirty-five you can have a teenage child and be a young mother. The baby will be healthier and stronger and live longer. Babies are about the human race. We have to make strong people. The master race."

"Babies are for Nazis?"

"Babies are like armies, or industry. They're essential but not amusing. Romance is something else. Romance is art. Romance is a boy dead three thousand years ago who turns up, in effigy, smiling that smile. Maybe that smile didn't bring him anything in life. But I can look at him and think, You knew, You knew, You had it. And that can help me look at someone else and think he has it too."

"What's the it? It, what?"

"It. The other thing. The better, the divine, the incomprehensible. The graceful. Bliss and love. The thing that you feel in the first kiss and then spend the rest of your time begging for, and the more you beg the more it refuses to come back."

I knew. And he knew too. I wiped a tear with my knuckle. "We are sort of the same, aren't we?" I said, and rolled over until I was body to body with him. A faint smell of sandalwood came from somewhere in the bed. "Go on, please, I love this," I said.

"Do you like sex?" he asked, his eyes on the newspaper. How could he say that with me in bed next to him?

"Sure I do," I said, feeling bold and a little chilled.

"It's the bait. It feels so good so that people will reproduce. It's like the rats in a maze, give them a reward, they'll keep doing whatever gives them the reward. Simple. God thought of it first. All he wanted to do was populate the planet."

"I didn't know you believed in God," I said.

"I may not believe, but I pay attention to him," he said.

A streak of yellow light blazed across the carpet, over the pink velvet armchair where my father's checked Charvet robe, orange and green like an old game box, was thrown. I'd like to give Felix a robe like that. I'd like to give Felix a shirt, a pair of cuff links, a watch, a ring.

Maybe I can, I thought, maybe there's still time.

My father looked up. "Someone planned it. Let's call him God."

"So what about love?"

"Love is here, or there, to make babies, and dreams. Once you've made your babies you can have your dreams."

"But dreams lead to something, don't they? I mean, wanting something and dreaming of it, you get it, don't you?"

"Dreams are just there. They are no more than themselves. An ideal of what might be always falls into cheap imitations of the everyday you already know. Move in with the man you love and you'll see the dried egg on his chin and smell the onions on his breath."

"But that's terrible!"

"That's why you have to make babies. They have enough stuff dribbling out of them the whole time to take your mind off the egg on your husband's chin."

"That's a cartoon. Dad, tell me love isn't just that."

"Now that we're having an exhausting conversation, you can pay attention. That's how it is. There is the stuff we will never, ever attain, that will always stay just beyond our grasp, and there's the stuff we can have. The stuff we can have will always end up looking like it came from the five and ten."

"Is that why you want the Etruscan couple?"

"That's why I want perfection and end up selling pieces of gods," he said.

And Nguyen came in with coffee for me, and raisin toast. Dad's tone became suddenly formal. "Excuse me," he said, "I have to make a phone call." He got up from the bed. I buttered my toast, waiting for him to come back with a phone number and sit on the bed. He left the room: I wondered why. I pulled my legs up under me and started to look at the comics.

The toast and the *Herald Tribune*. My shoes on the floor. As if I had never moved away.

Michel came in, dressed. *"Bonjour,"* he said. "Is this a new habit?"

"I'm not really back, I'm just visiting," I said.

"Stay, the more the merrier," he said, and he bent down to kiss me. "What's Jacob got to say for himself this morning?"

"We had philosophy. Lots of philosophy. About love."

"He's been like that for a while. I think it's age. Was it the impossibility of love?"

"How did you know? Michel!"

"He's been like that for a while. I told you. Where's the *Figaro?*"

"I don't know, I don't live here. Since when?"

Michel sat down next to me. "Your father's been like that since . . . since . . ." Suddenly his eyes were wet.

"Since Julia died?"

Michel looked down at the floor. "That's not the only thing that happened, Florence. Yes, around then."

A secret. *Don't ask*, said the voice. "Michel," I said, "you've got to tell me. I'm a grown-up girl and you have to tell me." I pulled him down next to me and tried to tickle under his arms.

"Very grown up," he said, sitting up and brushing back his hair. "What a nice piece of sunshine, right there, look at it."

I whispered in his ear. "I want to know, come on, please."

"Nothing. You know, a little passing fancy."

"A boy?"

"It happens to all of us, once in a while. It's called something to pass the time."

"He fell in love? With a boy?"

Michel said nothing.

If he can do it at almost fifty, I'll be able to as well, I thought.

"Let's talk about something else," said Michel. "Where is he, anyway?"

I realized why Dad had left the room. "I don't know," I said. Then I pulled on Michel's arm. "I'm in love, Michel," I said. "It's awful."

"Is it a boy or a girl?" he asked.

"Dad asked that too. What makes you both think it's a girl?"

Michel ran his hand over my head. "It's normal. Girls usually fall in love with girls at some point."

"It's a man," I said. "Sorry."

"Old?" asked Michel.

"Almost thirty. Almost oldish. But I don't know if he loves me."

"You never do," he said, "until it's too late."

"I think it's over," I said.

"That's usually when it begins," said Michel. "I have to go to work," he added, rising.

"Is that true?" I asked. "Don't go!" I felt like Sylvie, cajoling, languid, bored, lazy. Pretty. I saw myself in the mirror.

"Do you think I'm pretty?" I asked.

"If I were almost thirty I'd be wildly in love with you," he said, and kissed me on the ear. "Come to the shop if you have nothing to do. I could use some help with the plate glass."

I stuck my tongue out at him.

"In a few weeks you can see the Etruscan couple."

"I thought you didn't approve of them," I said.

"It's very effective, whatever it is. I just hope Jacob keeps out of prison."

I laughed.

When Michel left, the room became different. I took the piece of paper out of my pocket. The phone sat there like a large animal waiting to be stroked. I crawled along the bed on my knees and picked up the receiver. "Where were you?" I heard my father say, and an intake of breath from someone on the other end, which somehow chilled me, and I knew I shouldn't listen and I knew I would, and my father knew too because I heard, "Florence, did you just pick up the phone? Please wait until I've finished talking."

"Oh," I said, hoping to hear the other voice.

"So get off the line," said Dad.

"Sorry," I said, and my fingers pushed down the metal bars.

It couldn't be his number anyway. How stupid. I looked at the ragged P.T.T. slip and put it back in my pocket. You never knew. My father came back into the room. I put up my hand. "I swear I wasn't trying to hear," I said. He looked tired, more tired than when he'd gotten out of bed. "Just as well, I don't like little spies," he said.

"Nor do I," I said, and I was about to tell him about André. But then I'd have to tell the whole thing and I couldn't do that. Not yet.

He gazed down at his robe on the chair, and picked it up to put it on, as if he were going to spend the day lying around the house. He put it down again and padded into the bathroom. I heard him turn on the water. He came out and asked, "Don't you have a job where you're paid to turn up and do things?" he asked. I didn't move from his bed. "I'm not throwing you out, but shouldn't you be there?" he went on. I pulled the sheets up over me. He picked up the phone. "Here," he said, "call, and tell them you had to see your sick father and then go to work. I have to get to the shop."

It was André who answered, with an unexpectedly nice voice.

"Ah, Florence," he said.

"My father's sick, I had to go see him," I said. Family crisis, take that you little worm.

"Jacob's sick? Please give him my regards. I hope he's not really ill," said André, and I thought, shit, these people all know each other. There was something terribly wrong about my father's name in his mouth. I assured him Dad was all right, just a touch of food poisoning. "Your friend Sylvie called four times already," said André. "Maybe you should call her back. And we start at eleven."

I tried Sylvie at Marc's; there was no answer. I reached her at her mother's. "Thank God," she said when she heard my voice, "I have to speak to you. Something incredible's happened."

I told her I was with Dad. "Food poisoning, nothing bad," I said. She hadn't asked. She repeated, "I have to see you."

"I can't," I said. "I'm already late for work." I'd had enough of Sylvie for twenty-four hours.

"I can't wait," she said. "I have to leave on Monday. I've got to see you today."

I weighed my power. It felt heavy and good, like being in an expensive car. Was this what I was supposed to do with Felix, say no, and hear him beg? "No, Sylvie," I said, practicing. "Not today," and I hung up.

My father came out of the bathroom and opened the closet door. I stood behind him while he looked over the greens and the browns and the pale blues of his Harris tweed jackets. He dressed like a rainy day on a Scottish moor. Except for the sweaters, orange and vermilion and violet and canary. "How's Sylvie?" he asked.

"I adore her, but it's odd. Every time I see her, something goes wrong. As if she brought bad luck."

"Nice girl," said my father, closing his hand over a tweed jacket the color of oatmeal. "Her mother's a nightmare, but Sylvie's all right."

"Do you know what I mean, though?"

He had said so much before his bath and now he wasn't listening. I took my bag and kissed him on both cheeks. "Come to dinner tonight?" he asked. I said I couldn't. I had to go home and wait for Felix.

I took care not to step in any cracks on the way to the bus stop, and counted in multiples of five until the bus arrived. When I found a seat I slapped it before I sat down, to destroy the aura of whoever had been sitting there before. I listened for the voice. I thought I heard it say, *Just do everything right,* but the advice was so sound, though vague, that I knew it wasn't the voice, it was more common sense. But the "right" was a problem. At the studio door I knocked the doorjamb five times before pushing it open. André was standing near the door. He gave me the first smile of his life. You are doing things right, I told myself. "Did you speak to Sylvie?" he asked.

"Yes, yes," I said. He moved to bar my way, his eyebrows raised in imitation of Delaborde, but with an expectant grin on his face. "What do you want, André?" I asked.

He answered after too long a time. "Did you give Jacob my regards?"

There was a plaster moon in the center of the set, about eight feet high. It had come out brown, like a chocolate truffle. Delaborde was giving instructions to two men mixing paint. "Chalky," he was saying, "pale, greenish beige, almost white, more white." André stood behind him, nodding. "Yes, yes," he said. Delaborde gave him the first pot of the right color. "Fast," he said. André climbed a ladder to the side of the moon and began to paint.

I crept to the phone. "Rosa," I whispered, "I absolutely have to see you. Today. When can I come?"

"I don't know what's going on in the stars, but you girls are all crazed today," she said. "Sylvie Ambelic just called me, and I'm seeing her at noon. That was the one free moment I had. Then I've got clients all day, I can't fit you in. If Sylvie hadn't called, of course. What's the matter?"

"I think something dreadful's happened, and I'm not sure what it is," I said.

"You're too sensitive. I'm sure everything is all right. Didn't you hear from him yesterday?"

"No," I said.

"Well, you're sure to see him today. I'm looking at your chart and you'll have news today. Whatever you do, don't get into a fight."

We worked fast that day, despite the problem with the color of the moon. The models came and I made their faces lunar; Delaborde had André turn the moon so that only the new, pale part, showed. André went out to get lunch, and gave me such a smile on his way out that I didn't touch the sandwich he brought back for me in case he had poisoned it. At four I said I had to get some cold cream and went to the baker's to get a petit pain au chocolat. I was careful on the way back—sticking to the right side of the street, beginning each step with the right foot, crossing only between blue and white cars, never between two red. When I came in I saw Sylvie inside the studio, making herself small by the door.

Delaborde was bent over his Hasselblad, André was moving the umbrella shade over the light. The three women from the ad agency stood in a concerned knot, watching the model on top of her moon truffle. "What are you doing here?" I asked Sylvie. "I'm never supposed to have visitors."

"I had to come," she said. She had a plastic bag in her hand, the kind you get in a grocery shop. She looked exhausted but her eyes were shining, as if she had just done an afternoon of ballet. "I've got to talk to you."

"Not here, I've just gone out, I can't go out again."

"What about back there?" she asked, pointing beyond the set to the dressing room.

"No," I said. I thought of the darkroom. The films weren't in the bath yet, André never did that until the end of the day. Anyway, today was color, and color went to PhoLab. I pulled her in and closed the door behind us. The tap dripped into the plastic vat in the sink.

"I met someone," she said. "I think I met him."

"Him?"

"The man Rosa predicted. Florence, I think I'm in love. He's so mysterious and so magical."

"Since last night and this morning you've met someone and fallen in love? When? What time did it happen?"

"I was leaving your place. Last night. About, whatever time it was—" As if I really needed to know the time. As if I didn't now see with my heart in my stomach that I should have seen her out, my God, I needed to know the time to stop her being so happy, to make her think of a number, to take her brain away from being happy—"Whenever you threw me out. I walked to the corner. There was the most beautiful man I've ever seen standing there."

"You picked up a stranger? You never do things like that!"

"He picked me up," she said, proudly. Her fingers reached for the corner of a piece of paper protruding from one of the big yellow envelopes stacked on the filing cabinet.

"Stop that. Don't touch," I snapped. "Go on. You're mad."

"I wanted to do something brave, like you did. Be adventurous. He looked at me and smiled, and I smiled back, and then . . ."

"Then?"

"A taxi came by and we both hailed it at the same time. At least I think that's what happened, I'm not sure. He said he'd been waiting for a cab there."

So it couldn't be Felix.

"And it turned out he was going in the same direction I was. At least, near my mother's. So I didn't go to Marc's, I went home. She's away too. I told him he could ride with me, and in the taxi he was really charming. He told me about the Indians in the South of America, and he asked me to have lunch with him today."

"You've just had lunch with him?" I asked. I was choking. My ears buzzed. The Indians. She blushed, she giggled.

The puppy.

"I had to tell you, because you're the only person in the world who can appreciate it. I've never done this before. I took him home with me. I felt safe doing it. I wanted a mad adventure, like you have. I'm bored with Marc, bored, bored, bored."

"Tell me what he's called, right now," I said.

"Felix," she said. "Felix something."

My hand hit her in the chest as I pushed past her and ran out of the darkroom to the toilet, where I barely had time to close the door.

Afterward I brushed my teeth with one of the toothbrushes we kept there, and ran water on my wrists and splashed my face. And once that was done, there was no reason to stay in the toilet, but coming out had to be done as if nothing had happened, as a triumph. I opened the door slowly and peered around it. Sylvie was standing uncertainly in the doorway of the darkroom. Everyone else was still on the set. I'd only been in there a short time. Sylvie saw me and held up the plastic bag. I crossed over to her. "Are you okay?" she asked.

"Yes."

"I don't like it in there, it smells bad."

"I can't go out," I said. "So, when are you seeing him again?"

"I went to see Rosa today."

"I know. I mean, of course you would. Yes?"

"Rosa said I had to be careful. I had lunch with him. Oh, Florence, he's wonderful. And I've done the most insane thing. I wanted to ask you about it. It's the kind of thing you'd do."

"What would I do?" I was several paces behind myself. The tone I had was metallic, cold. Maybe this was another Felix. Maybe there was another Florence. Thank God, there was. She was called Elise.

"I've invited him to Portofino," Sylvie said. "With me and Marc. What do you think?" My stomach gave another cramp. Not again. There was nothing left.

"I know I should have invited you," she said, "but it wasn't practical with Marc. But I have to invite him, I'll die if I can't see him for another week."

Die, I thought. Just die.

"Why are you looking at me like that?"

"Nothing," I said. "Why don't you just move in with him?"

"I can't," she said, "he lives with someone else."

Hah. "A wife?"

"This is the worst of it. Florence, he lives with a man! Someone called André. In the morning I heard him call André to say why he hadn't been home."

"Florence!" André was calling my name from the outer studio.

"You have to go now," I said, "and I think it's mad to invite your new lover to spend Easter with you and your Marc."

"I'll tell Marc he's queer, Marc won't mind," she said.

"Florence!" It was André again.

She handed me the plastic bag. "Anyway," she said, "I bought you this, because I ate all your food last night. It's only fair."

14

THE TREES WERE POLLINATING, and the air that evening was full of little white wisps, tickling throats, blurring shapes. The pavement was never quite where I expected to find it. Strange tides rose and fell inside me. At home the spring heat swelled at the open window. I took a bath and lit the candle.

Then I took out the Roman ring. Slipped my finger through it. I was surprised to find that it felt the same.

The doorbell rang. It was too early for Felix. I stood up and crossed the desert to the door. It was him.

"Hi," leaning against the top of the door, his smile across my eyes.

I looked down at the ring. "What's that?" he asked, taking my hand. I put my thumb over the seal so he couldn't see.

"Nothing," I said. I turned my back to him and opened the big closet and pulled the ring off inside the middle shelf, and pushed it to the back. Behind my sweaters.

"I thought I'd come early today," he said, lying down on the cushions. I looked at his cowboy boots. His long legs. He patted the carpet next to him. "Come," he said.

I crossed the few feet and lay by his side. He put his arm around me. "It's so beautiful today," he said, "don't you think?" I made a vague hum. "We should go away," he said.

Sylvie didn't exist.

His hand gave my shoulder a squeeze. "What do you think? You like the idea?"

"Where?" I whispered.

"The country. Somewhere fresh and green. I miss the country."

I had my head against his heart. I could feel pounding inside his body, against the ridged barrier of his chest. That thing was melting between us again. I tried to think that I hated him and that he had betrayed me but the slow sun was growing between us, that heat where we touched and the pressure of the air pushing us together. I could stop breathing, it was breathing for us. I put my hand up to his neck, to the smooth tender part beneath his earlobe, and turned my mouth to him. The strange prickling above my eyes was happening again.

If he stops me, came the blade in my head, he loves Sylvie. If he lets me, we are all right.

Throwing the condition onto the knife edge that will separate everything's fine from it's all over.

Free will. He rolled over, releasing me, dropping me to the floor like an insect off a piece of paper.

He faced the wall. The soft cotton billowed a little under his breath. "What are you looking at?" I asked.

I shouldn't have set that condition. It doesn't mean anything. "Nothing," he said. And he turned to me and took my face and kissed me.

"I waited for you last night," I said.

"I couldn't come."

"You didn't come." I could have killed him.

This might be the time to say I love you. To pull all his presents out of the back of the closet. To make him see how he counted.

Not that.

Or to tell him I could lie too. "I can lie too. You don't even know my real name. I'm not Elise. I won't tell you who I really am." Did it matter, though? Did who I was make any difference to what he'd done?

Don't confront him. Be light and evasive, luminous and compelling. My body could, under the right conditions of heat and confidence.

I put my hand flat against his chest and pulled myself up to him, the way you swim to the edge of a pool and pull your body flat against the tiles on the wall, so the mortar scrapes your thighs.

The body would save me. I didn't have anything in my head but my body, curled up, folded inside my skull, heaving.

When I was a child, during a holiday that I spent in London, something happened. I was twelve. It was a warm day. I had gone out for an ice cream bar, around the corner from the house. I was walking back, watching the perfect chocolate corner of the ice cream emerge from the silver wrapping paper. A car drew up silently along-side me. The driver was on my side, on the French side, the left instead of the right, where English drivers sat. I think that's what made him so familiar. The window was open; I smiled at him. We were both wearing short-sleeved polo shirts. The soft cotton on my chest. On where my breasts were beginning. My stripes were a paler blue than his. I looked at his stripes since he was looking at mine. He was swarthy, with a round face and square ridged patent hair. Dark glasses. He smiled at me. I listened.

"Hello," he said. He had an accent, which made him one of us in not being English. But he was too dark and rounded to be French. "Do you want to come home and see my cock?"

The moment swayed. I knew, and didn't know, what he meant. He didn't touch me. The silent car and the slow words did it. A dark hole opened in the car window, just a few inches away from me. Murdered, I thought first. It was death and it was that other thing, too. They were the same. It would be so simple to walk around the car and open the door and never be seen alive again.

And also: it's happening. What they warned me about. I held the moment as long as I could, to judge its weight and see the filaments coming off it. I could change my life forever if I went. I tried to know what would happen if I went. I couldn't peer around the corner of what I had to do, get in the car, go, to see what would be done to me. There was only one way to find out. I tried to detain him.

"I didn't know you could keep a cock in London," I said. I didn't move.

He gave a short nod with his head and changed the position of the large brown arm folded over the windowsill.

Why can't I do both, I thought, go and find out and still be here, safe, untouched. While I was thinking the car gathered noise and the man drove away.

That's what happened and didn't happen.

The idea that I could choose prevented me from thinking. I could believe Felix, I could believe Sylvie. I held my breath. It would take over. The thing that pushed us together. But nothing came. It was too light in the room, the windows were open, the curtains not drawn. The outline of Felix's arms and legs was sharp, unequivocal, normal. There was no magic.

I had to beg. "Can we really go somewhere?"

"Why not?" he asked.

No reason why not, I could forget that Sylvie had said he was going to Portofino with her. That was part of another world, where nothing really happened.

I asked if we could go to Vienna. He twisted around on the cushions. "Not country," he said. I saw fields and flowers and long low walls, and dogs jumping through the high grass.

I asked him if he was hungry. He wasn't hungry.

I tried to grab something of ours. The little bracelet ashtray was right there, but it didn't look like us anymore, it just looked foolish. The Algerian rug was hidden by Felix's body. And there was no white wine left.

"Do you love me, Felix?" I asked. The words were like stones in my mouth, the wrong shape, too big, and even more wrong and bigger once they were out. They hung like gigantic ungainly balloons between us. At least I'd found the worst thing I could say, and I was glad of it.

He turned his wide face to me and looked into my eyes.

"Yes," he said.

His eyes were steady and the heat came back. I closed the curtains and we went up the ladder. There was only a body inside my head, and we were violent on that mattress. I passed out. When I woke the alarm showed eleven o'clock and he was gone. It was night. I made myself a cup of tea and I was happy.

My father woke me in the morning. I had forgotten to take the telephone onto the platform and it rang a long time before I answered. "It's such a beautiful day that we're going to have lunch on the terrace, why don't you come?" He added that Alexis was coming over. "I don't think I can come," I said. "He's bringing the *I Ching*," Dad added. "I had a question to ask."

The *I Ching* was called upon only in moments of great stress. "What's wrong?" I asked.

"Nothing, nothing," said Dad. "Are you coming? I have to tell Nguyen."

I said I'd come. I might have to talk about André, but I'd get Alexis to tell me my future, or my present, or whatever the book did. I didn't mind what price I had to pay. I'd say André was a genius and my lover, if I had to.

Alexis was sitting on the terrace, tall and shaky in a checked shirt with a scribble of Indian silk at his neck. He looked pale. I kissed his cheek and asked him where the book was.

"What book?" he asked, his voice in the register of three countries.

"The *I Ching*," I said, sitting down on one of the iron chairs.

"It's not for little girls," said Michel, "or old men either."

Alexis glanced into the living room. "I brought it for Jacob," he said. "It's really not a party trick."

"I have a serious question," I said. "A crisis."

Michel looked up from the salad he was carefully tossing. Dad hadn't heard. The thick green leaves of the magnolia rattled slightly in the little gusts of wind that found their way onto the terrace.

"I have to do Jacob first, then I'll do you," said Alexis, kindly, and he added, inevitably—"How's André getting on?"

I paid in advance. "He's great," I said. "He's doing better and better."

"I'm so glad," said Alexis. "Give him my regards if you see him."

Dad said he had booked the tickets to Venice. "We're going Tuesday, are you coming or not? I had the agent take you a seat, but I'd really like to know today."

If I believed Felix, I couldn't go. He would be taking me away, he would just show up with the tickets he'd bought, and take me.

If I believed Sylvie I might as well go with Dad and Michel.

"I can't go," I said. "I have plans."

"That's the crisis?" asked Michel.

We ate the pretty salad and drank the bullshots that Alexis had made. They had all been to see a play that lasted seven hours and they talked about that while I drifted slightly. Michel invited me to go to the Louvre to look at something with him, and I said no. Dad handed me a big book on Art Nouveau and I stayed in the garden while he went to the living room with Alexis. I looked at the pictures of curls on everything and waited. It was good to know that Dad also had doubts enough to ask the *I Ching*.

I heard their voices indistinctly through the window. When they were finished, they called me in. "I'll leave you two to it," said Dad, withdrawing graciously.

Alexis patted the sofa next to him, and when I was about to sit down he said, "No, take the far corner." The central cushion was between us. He bounced three Chinese coins up and down in his palm.

"Remember," he said, "you can only ask one question, and you must be absolutely sincere."

Sincere. Like André. Like Felix. And then it came to me, and it never had before, that if Alexis knew André he also knew Felix.

"So what's your question?" asked Alexis.

"Do I have to tell you?"

"The usual method is to write it down on a piece of paper," he said, as if he were explaining something to someone very dumb.

Which of course I was.

He slid a big pad across the sofa to me. Words were written along the top, but it wasn't Dad's writing and I couldn't read it. In the center of the page was drawn a neat little group of sticks that looked like an elevator stuck between floors. I bent my head to take a closer look, and Alexis's long pleated hand came down and tore the page off, crumpled it, and handed me a pen.

"I have to write the question?" I asked. I would write Does Felix Love Me and he would see it.

"There's only one question you can ask," said Alexis.

I looked up quickly. He could know everything, they could all have been laughing at me for months. Even Dad.

"You silly girl you've dropped the pen on the floor," said Alexis. "Now pick it up. I hope it hasn't made a mess, it leaks."

"What's the question?" I asked with the pen in my hand.

"The only question is, What is my situation at present and how must I behave?"

"Is that all?"

He made his oyster eyes stern. "That's all there ever is to know, what's really going on," he said.

I obediently wrote down "What Is My Situation At Present And How Must I Behave?"

"Wasn't it you who wrote Dad's question?" I asked.

"It doesn't make any difference," he said, and handed me the coins. "Throw them six times," he said, "and concentrate."

The first time I threw them, the coins rolled off the taut silk of the sofa and ran on the floor. Alexis sighed. "Less enthusiasm, more concentration."

"Will it tell me the truth?" I asked.

He gave an irritated sigh. "Of course it will, so long as you don't mess around with it. Now throw again. Properly this time."

"What did Dad want to know?" I asked, the coins in my hand. I didn't want to look entirely selfish.

"That's none of your business," said Alexis, "now throw."

I threw the coins, and he drew stick lines on the pad. My pattern looked like the towers of Notre Dame with a bridge in between. He picked up the book and found my page: the title was The Marrying Maiden. I was delighted. Alexis clicked his teeth at me. "You think it means one thing," he said, "and it doesn't."

"Dad wants me to get married," I said.

"But that's not what the book is telling you. Listen." And he read: "The marrying maiden. Undertakings bring misfortune, nothing that would further."

And he read on: "A girl who is taken into the family, but not as the chief wife, must behave with special caution and reserve. She must not take it upon herself to supplant the mistress of the house, for that would mean disorder and lead to untenable relationships."

He took a deep breath. I had never liked Alexis before, but now I was willing to consider him the wisest and kindest man on earth.

He read on, after a pause: "Relationships based on personal inclination depend in the long run entirely on tactful reserve."

"I have to be tactful and reserved?" I asked.

"We don't know yet," he said, pulling the book nearer to him. He raised one finger: "The superior man understands the transitory in the light of the eternity of the end."

"What's ending?"

"It means you have to be sure what you want," said Alexis, and he read on further: "Six in the third place."

"Six what?"

"It's what you threw, a six. Never mind, just listen to me: The marrying maiden as slave. She marries as a concubine."

I took a cigarette from the silver tumbler on the table. I didn't understand a word anymore, but I didn't want Alexis to know that. I went "Um, hum," once I'd lit the cigarette.

"Here is the explanation," said Alexis, and he read on: "This pictures a situation of a person who longs too much for joys that cannot be obtained in the usual way. He enters—it means you, so I'll say She—enters upon a situation not altogether compatible with self-esteem. Neither judgment nor warning is added to this line; it merely lays bare the actual situation, so that everyone may draw a lesson from it."

"What lesson?" I asked, as casually as I could.

Alexis placed the book back on the coffee table, next to the Buddha's head, which he stroked lightly on the cheek. "I forgot," he said, and picked up the book again, and riffled through to the last page, which folded out, and turned to another oracle. He read it without telling me, and then said, "Do not tread upon paths that do not accord with the established order." He shut the book again and started to get up.

"But what does it mean?" I asked.

"Timing, it's all a question of timing," he said. "Now where's Jacob?"

I stood up too. "Alexis," I said, "you can't leave me with just that. I don't understand what it means. All you did was read out of the book."

"Your father understands when I do it for him, and all I do is read out of the book. There's no way to explain what it says. All the wisdom of the Chinese is contained in that book, you can't expect it to be clear."

"But it meant something. I'm just not very sure what, that's all. Please, Alexis, please tell me some more."

The sleeve of his shirt was in my hand. I was begging. "Oh my dear," he said pulling away, "you're obviously involved with some man you should never have met. And it's not a very flattering situation for you, whatever it is. If I were you, I'd get out of it at once, before it gets any worse for you. But I really don't like to talk about love, it doesn't suit me. So that's all. Now where's Jacob got to?"

Alexis went to Dad's room, and I pulled my legs up onto the couch and picked up the book from the table and sat with my problem. Get out of it. As if Felix were a place, a well, a hole that could be climbed out of. A place. If I went to another country, perhaps. The only other country I could think of was Vienna, a city not a country. Which was more Felix. I was puzzled by the idea of longing for joys that could not be obtained in the usual way. I could fathom joys, and longing I knew by heart. But what were they, specifically?

Vague perversions twined through my mind, none of them appealing. The usual way I supposed to be marriage. But was it me who longed for these joys, or was it Felix? I opened the book and after a while managed to find the page again.

"Not entirely compatible with self-esteem." The sentence was there in the book, with its peculiar, elegant turn. I had thought it was a bit of Alexis, it sounded so cynical and cosmopolitan. So the book knew I was abasing myself. I read through everything else that came under the title The Marrying Maiden, and as I read I lost sight of whether I was the marrying maiden or my situation—"not entirely compatible with self-esteem"—was the marrying maiden. I even entertained the idea that Felix was the marrying maiden, or perhaps Sylvie. The more I read the less sense I had of what the words said. Each word branched into two directions, each with good and bad at the end. I grew dizzy and finally put the book down and went to find Dad.

They were still in the bedroom, Dad on the bed with a pile of catalogues and Alexis in an armchair he had drawn up to the bed, his legs on the quilt, his toes sticking up in orange socks like the flowers of a rare and brutish plant. Alexis was talking, using his hands. So was my father. His hands went on moving after I came in and they both stopped talking at once.

"You all right, darling?" asked Dad with a crinkling of his eyes, as if to see me better.

"Fine," I said, and came nearer to him. The catalogues slipped in slate-gray piles all around him. I thanked Alexis with a formal bow. It felt odd to be grateful to someone I disliked, and I wasn't sure what I was grateful for.

"Darling," said Dad, pushing papers around on the bed with one hand, "did you write to the lawyer—Mr. Leon?"

"Oh God, not yet," I said.

I expected him to scold me. I waited for the "how many times do I have to tell you," but it didn't come. Instead, his hand held up a thin white sheet of paper. The knuckles of his other hand curled around a pen, on the bed. Oddly, the cap was already off; I saw the gold band glinting on the bedside table. It's Alexis's pen, I thought, why isn't Dad taking more care that it doesn't leak and stain the sheets?

"Here," he said, waving the paper as if to prove how insubstantial it was. "Here."

Alexis stood up and gave me his place, the armchair. I shook my head, but Alexis motioned me to sit down and he left the room.

"Like this you won't have to bother since you're so bad at the mail and stuff, you won't have to bother," said Dad. "Just sign this."

I took the pen from him. His hand trembled slightly. With the other one he pushed a bound catalogue over to me, *The Year at Sotheby's*. The piece of paper covered the book. "Where?" I asked. His finger pointed to a line of dashes near the bottom of the page.

Florence Ellis, I wrote, and just signing my name seemed a victory over Felix. That's who I am, I thought, this is me, and you'll never know.

"Good," said Dad, and the paper was whisked away, and the pen retrieved.

"Is that it?"

"You don't have to worry about anything from now on," he said, screwing the cap back on the pen.

"Well," I said, "I'm going to go now."

"What are you doing?" he asked. Casual.

"Shopping," I said.

He asked if I had enough money, again. I assured him that I did and gave him a kiss. Alexis came in again, and I left. I wasn't going shopping. I just wanted to get out of that apartment. It was a day to be with Julia, in London, a day to be a girl with Sylvie, and alone all I knew how to do was mess it up. I had spent two months vacuuming my apartment on Saturdays, making it pretty for Felix. Now everything was vague, he loved her but he said he loved me, and there seemed to be no reason to make my room pretty. There seemed, even, to be a reason to let it be dusty and full of crumbs, so that he could know something about me, something that wasn't an attempt at perfection turned toward him.

I waited for him that evening in my deliberately scruffy room, but he neither called nor came. The next day Luc and Nancy invited me to lunch at her apartment, which was in a small street behind the Comédie-Française. Her living room was dark, with painted walls where cherubs chased arrows above the doors and a wall of windowpanes separated the bedroom from the living room. I went to the window and looked out; a fountain gave off a high plume of foam. Men sat writing and sketching in little chairs; women pushed strollers with babies in them. Three stories down it was like a toy village, sand and arcades. I longed for Felix to see it with me, and ate lunch without feeling the food in my mouth. Nancy had an answering machine, and we listened every time the phone rang. It was just like playing hide and seek, watching someone open the door to the closet where you're hiding to peer into your dark and then shaking his head, and closing the door again. I wanted to have a machine like hers: to hear every time anyone tried to get me, without having to let them know I knew. A sublime invention.

But then it was Sunday night and I waited for Felix again, and he didn't come, and the next day was Monday, the day Sylvie and Marc were going to Portofino without me, with Felix, and the fact that he'd said he loved me shredded in my hands as the hours passed and he didn't call.

On Monday Delaborde announced we wouldn't work from Tuesday until the following Thursday, and that he was going to Brittany. Paris seemed to be emptying like a tub after a bath, and I could see myself rattling alone in the streets, a lost ball, an orphan, a marble. I called my father and said I'd go to Venice.

"Don't you think it's a little late?" he asked. But I went.

15

I FLEW DOWN TO Venice the next day, with my father and Michel and Alexis. Before I left I wrote a note in careful block capitals, and pinned it to my door, for Felix. I put down the name and number of the hotel, and two words: Join me. I didn't sign it. It didn't matter if he asked for Elise Radford, I would tell the hotel that name too. I didn't mind if he met Dad and Michel, it didn't matter if he knew Alexis already. He would come looking for me, tear the envelope off the door, open it, and call Venice. He would fly down, cross the canal from the airport, walk across the water, why not, and find me at the hotel. He would ask my father if he could marry me, as in all fairy tales, and we would live happily ever after.

"Ah, God, home," said Dad as the hotel launch came into the Grand Canal. For him, Venice made up for what life lacked. It had the opposite effect on me. I was never sure when I was in Venice that I was really there. The rise of colored marble from the soft water always seemed to be the punch line of a lecture, a slide projected on a wall to prove something, illuminated to force the idea in, and about to disappear. I had enough illusions of my own, the shimmering lake town only confused me more. Buildings on water, and shoe stores.

Michel took Venice with a little more humor than Dad, a little more greed. He wanted gigantic black mirrors encrusted with pieces of dark red stone, he wanted curved chairs with torn silk backs and small landscapes of stone squares. He remembered stories he had heard from Alexis and from others, and he told them as we walked.

I followed them through the stone streets, through gulleys and arches where the names of old duchesses and famous cuckolds eddied about us, through descriptions of rooms Alexis had once been invited to see, to restaurants where very small crawling things were served deep-fried and barely dead.

And more walks, Venice absorbed by foot. We'd come upon the vista of a square where the buildings seemed to draw back from the flat center, and my jaw would drop too. The height and mass of the church of San Moïse almost managed to convince me that I was there, but its color, all black and white and gray, proved that it was just a monstrous engraving.

I told the concierge at the hotel that Elise Radford was another name for me, and he winked. I wrote it down for him. "*Sì, sì,*" he said. Alexis was buying the London *Telegraph*, and glanced down at the paper on the counter.

"What are you doing?" he asked.

"Nothing," I said. He came over and took a closer look. I tried to push the paper over to the concierge, so Alexis couldn't read it.

"You're expecting a girlfriend?" he asked.

"No," I said, "it's me. I have another name."

"I knew we did things like that," he said, "but women don't normally take on pseudonyms." He didn't catch the meaning of the names.

I spent Venice thinking about Portofino, which I had never seen, and which in any case was composed of close-ups of Felix and Sylvie. If he didn't come to get me in Venice, he was there, the shape of real love took him there, and my will had no power to influence anything. Maybe it was all the water in Venice, interfering with what Rosa called the Fluids. There was a sign in her front hall that said, SMOKING FORBIDDEN: SMOKE INTERFERES WITH THE FLUIDS. Maybe water did as well, too much of the same thing.

I asked the concierge how long it would take to get to Portofino, and he offered to book me a room in the Splendido hotel, because he had influence. "It's very full at Easter," he said. I knew what he meant. I asked him if it was pretty. "Rocky, high, beautiful, with a famous piazza," he said. I tried to think of rocks and the piazza to remove Sylvie from my head. Stones, rocks, and Felix.

I was told not to sulk. They dragged me to dinner out in the countryside, for which we had to take the water bus to the parking lot, where a car driven by a butler in a striped jacket met us and drove us into what Dad kept calling "Palladio land," a dark landscape that was entirely flat. We ate in a Palladian villa owned by an American lady. By the time we got home at midnight they were drunk on decoration and Veneto wine, and I had resolved to go back to Paris. It didn't make any sense to be waiting here anymore.

There were no vaporetti to be seen, and Alexis went to look for a water taxi. It was cold by the canal. Dad and Michel were talking in low voices about the woman we had visited. "But she never bought it, she just borrowed it," said Michel.

"He gave it to her," said Dad. I moved away so as not to hear. A lone speedboat, a Riva, came down the canal, too fast, hitting the water. The man driving it stood very straight, black and white like San Moïse because he was wearing a dinner jacket. Dad and Michel were watching him too. "That's the kind of man I'd like to see you with, someone with a private income and a house in Venice," said Dad. Michel gave a little laugh, approbation.

I put my fingers in my mouth and whistled. The man in the Riva turned the boat around without turning his head, and came toward the dock where we stood, letting out white wings of foam on the black water. "What is she doing?" asked Michel, and Dad laughed. We, the seducers.

"Taxi?" said the man in the boat, rocking on his own wake.

I went as close to the water as I could. He held a hand up to me and I stepped into the boat. He was tall, broad, with thick hair and dark eyes, not bad looking. Young, maybe ten years older than I. I was thrilled at my own theatrical boldness. He put his hand on the ignition. "Wait," I said, "there's my father and Michel." As if he knew who they were. As if he were an intimate of ours, already. "Of course," he said. In English.

The two of them were peering over the dock at us. "Come on," I said, "get in." Alexis appeared behind them. "That's Alexis," I said. "He's with us too. You don't mind?" The man shook his head.

My father gave me a proud pat on the back as he stepped into the boat; Michel fixed on the canal ahead, embarrassed, I think. Alexis leaned into the man's face and said, "Alexis Perrin, what's your name?" "Massimo Della Croce," said the man, and they shook hands.

The moon was bright on the Grand Canal and I was happy. I had effected a pickup that did not separate me from my father, I had used whatever it was I had for the good of our little society, I had summoned and been answered. I knew I should stand next to the stranger, my hands on the edge of the windshield, my nose in the air. But there were Dad and Michel and Alexis. It was too early to do that.

"So, where to?" asked the man. He was heading straight down the Grand Canal.

"I think we should go to the Danieli," I said.

"We?" he asked.

"Well, they're at the Danieli," I said.

He nodded. His satin revers shone in the reflection of the light on the front of his boat. On either side of us, walls rose like teeth, a little cracked on top, yellow and gray. "My God, how beautiful," said Dad.

"Della Croce," said Alexis. "So you're the grandson of Emilia Del Mezzo."

"Nephew," said our driver.

Alexis moved nearer. "I knew her in 1934, on Ischia. Then of course when she had the house near Nice, I used to see her a lot. How is she?"

"Not dead yet," said our driver, and I laughed.

"Do give her my regards," said Alexis.

The boat took on a curve, an angle, and we all fell a little to the left. Massimo pulled over to the Danieli dock from the center of the canal, cut the motor, and floated gently toward the stairs. Alexis shook Massimo's hand again and pulled himself out, cursing the slippery steps. Michel followed, without looking at me or saying a word. Dad hesitated an instant: "Well, I suppose you kids want to go for a drive, so I'll see you later," he said, and threw one leg out of the boat to get onto the stairs in a quick movement.

I was embarrassed and delighted. "Bring us back a palazzo," shouted

Dad from the shore, as the boat pulled into the center of the canal. I was clutching the windshield the way I knew one should. The boat slapped the water a few times, and then he stopped the motor.

"Now, where do you live?"

"At the Danieli," I said, and we both laughed.

"With those men? Why?"

"Those men are my family," I said.

He pursed his lips. Alone under the moon he looked less handsome than he had when the boat was full. I knew I should move closer to him and we should kiss, because this was the Grand Canal, and Massimo Della Croce was exactly what my father wanted me to have. "Do you have a palazzo?" I asked, to get it over with. "Yes," he said, "do you want to see it?" I nodded, and he kissed me. The kiss was no more compelling than the moonlight on the water or the speed of the boat, but I told myself that perhaps the best settings diluted things. He turned the key in the ignition again and turned the boat around, while I watched the great white wave of foam that we sliced out of the water, and he proceeded back up the Grand Canal.

I knew how to seduce; I knew how to do the things I'd seen Dad and Michel and their friends do. I knew how to act with a stranger whom I desired, but there seemed to be other rules for a palazzo. The houses along the canal shivered like curtains as we passed, and the noise of the motor filled the air. Massimo Della Croce once more cut the engine and swung the boat over to a wooden pier that jutted out from a wide dark palazzo. I grabbed one of the tall posts and pulled myself up onto the wooden boards. He was busy with a rope, tying it to a post. I walked along the pier until I came to the door, and there, just before Massimo caught up with me, I dropped my bag in the shallow water that covered the old steps.

"What are you looking at?" he asked.

"My bag's in the water," I said.

His hand went into the water and held out the bag to me.

"Isn't it dangerous," I asked, "the water?"

He laughed. "You think your evening bag has typhoid? I can throw it back if you want me to."

I had money in the bag, two thousand francs I had brought with me for shopping or running away, and I hadn't spent any of it, and I hadn't wanted to leave it in the hotel room. "I have money in it," I said. I wanted him to know I was rich, too, since he had a palazzo.

"Money?" he said.

"Nothing," I said. "Throw it back. I don't want to get poisoned."

He heaved the bag out into the canal, where it fell on the water and then was lost. He put his arm around me and led me to the front door, which he opened with a big key from his breast pocket.

"Welcome," he said, allowing me to precede him indoors. The room was an empty hall, vast and damp, and dark. A lantern hung low from a high ceiling, on a long chain. "Come," he said after I had looked around, and he led the way up the stairs.

The stairs were patterned in stars and circles and lozenges made of marble, green and white and black and red. At the first landing I stopped, but he called down, "That's only the ballroom, come on," and I followed him, up the staircase that rose through landings that grew gradually narrower until we were high up and in front of a shiny door made of highly varnished wood. He pulled out another key, a small gold one, and pushed the door open.

I saw a modern living room, sliding gently down from the left to the right: leather sofas and a steel table, everything listing slightly. Behind was a wall of arches, windows and a door. He took me through a door to the terrace, where we leaned over the parapet. The Grand Canal came at us from the left and went out toward the right: we were in the exact center of the curve. "This is where I watch the regatta," he said, his eyes shining. I didn't know if it was seduction or tourism, but a Venetian with a palazzo combined the two. "You must love Venice very much," I said, feeling a fool. I thought it was time for him to jump on me.

He had a strange face, fleshy and long at the same time, with big, confused brown eyes, like an animal. I felt a certain family pressure to move closer to him and make love with the palazzo. Just before he took me by the hand to his bedroom it crossed my mind that he might simply have rented the top floor. I hoped he hadn't; I was doing this for Dad and Michel, I didn't want us all to be cheated.

In the morning he was in a hurry to get up; the phone rang several times, people were making a commotion in the living room. "I have to get to the factory," he said. He gave me a wet kiss before he left, and told me how to get out onto the street side. Everything about him had been disgusting. He was nothing like Felix, and that was my punishment. His girth, his weight, his grunts, and worst of all, the lack of hum in the air while he did it had made me feel wrong and bad and stupid.

Back at the hotel the concierge gave me a wink and handed me my key with a little too much ceremony, considering the morning and my evening clothes. I took a bath with some dark blue stuff from a package by the tub. I had to wash him off me. I dressed and went to my father's room. He and Michel were up, reading the Rome *Daily American,* a copy each, at the wheeled breakfast table.

"I'm going back to Paris," I said.

"How was the palazzo?" asked Dad.

"Big and empty," I said.

"How's Massimo?" asked Michel.

"Big and empty," I said—"you remember his name?"

"Alexis told us about his family. Remarkable, really. When are you seeing him again?"

"I'm going back to Paris, I just told you."

"Are you sure, darling?" asked Dad. "He seemed so nice. We have tickets for La Fenice, he could come with us."

"Tell us about the palazzo," said Michel, again.

"I'm sure he'll show you the palazzo if you ask him," I said. "May I have my plane ticket?"

"The girl's in love," said Dad, getting up from his chair, "but I'm afraid it's not with the palazzo."

I flew back to Paris that afternoon. You travel to forget, I told myself on the plane. Maybe four days weren't enough. I left my bag on the second landing so that I could run up the next two flights to see what was on my door. If I had given him the key to the room he'd be inside. He'd be sitting on the floor with one leg folded up, sitting in the path of the sun. Smiling, waiting for me. "Where were you, I tried to find you . . . What note? My darling, I'm so glad you're back, let's get married right now, I never have missed anyone so much." And rising, he takes me in his arms and hugs me so tight that I am part of him, between his hands and his chest, I am enfolded.

There was an envelope on the door. I pulled it off carefully, so as not to harm it. FELIX was written on the front but I didn't recognize the writing as mine. Just like him to put his own name on the front. Hotel Danieli, I read, 041 293 45, Join me.

How strange that the hotel in Portofino had the same name, is what went through my mind. So he was there, alone, waiting for me. I was so happy that I pushed the key into the door wrong, and had to rattle the lock to get it opened. I left the door open and sat on the floor next to the telephone, trembling so hard I could hardly dial. Only as I touched the numbers did they seem familiar, but I paid no attention to that. "Danieli Royal Excelsior," I heard the operator say.

"What town are you in?" I asked.

"*Prego?*"

"Are you in Portofino?"

"No, here in Venice," said the operator.

"Wrong number," I said, and hung up fast.

Then I looked at the piece of paper and finally saw that it was my own writing.

And then I was in a rage.

He had not come and he didn't care. I was betrayed. Once, years ago, a doll betrayed me. I had put her alone on a shelf and I found her later sitting with two plush bears. The evidence of her betrayal gave me rage and a blunt strength that allowed me to hurl her hard across the room, so that her celluloid head shattered. I was so glad to hear that crack and so scared afterward of what I'd done. I ran to where she was lying, broken, and knelt on the floor and wept and begged to be forgiven. But there's no forgiveness from a doll.

Alone in my room I had that rage and there was no one to hurt. I started to call Rosa, but Rosa would be wise and quiet and tell me there was nothing to do. I wanted action, I wanted fire, I had to do something. I had to hurt something. I started to go down for my bag when I saw, pinned to the beam where I had left it a month ago, the little card for the gypsy that André had given me. *Magie en toutes sortes*, it said. The address was out in the eastern suburbs.

There was no phone number. I took the key out of the door where I had left it and ran downstairs. Two flights down my bag rested against the wall. Later, I thought. No one will want it.

The métro station was called Liberté. The street wasn't far. The woman was young, with long dirty black hair and a flowered dress. She had pimples on her face, untouched. I wondered at her patience. A baby cried in the next room.

She sold me a black candle that she said worked miracles when you have been betrayed. "If you are really sure that you hate him," she said. I told her I was.

I took the candle home. On the way up the stairs I noticed something odd, something out of place, missing. Once I was in the room I put the candle on the kitchen counter and got out a little saucer that I put in the middle of the room. I set the candle upright in its center and lit it.

"I wish Felix was dead," I said.

The candle flame grew tall and bright, then small and sharp and mean.

Oh my God, I thought, what have I done?

I blew quickly. And again and again.

It wouldn't go out.

And then I had to blow harder. As if the room were on fire.

I lay on the floor next to it, panting. When I opened my eyes, it was dark. Something had happened. I lay there telling myself it was okay, and then slowly my heart began to thump like an animal's tail hitting the floor. Mud in my veins. I stood up, trying to keep calm, and turned on the lamp.

The whole front of my chest was moving in and out in a strange rhythm.

My bag, I suddenly remembered my bag. That was it, my bag. I took the key and ran out. Two flights down I saw that the bag wasn't there. I ran up the stairs, happy that it was only theft.

The candle looked small and deadly in its saucer on the floor.

I wrapped it in a newspaper I had taken from the hotel, and went down to the garbage can to throw it away. But the entrance of my building didn't seem far away enough once I was down there, so I walked up the Rue du Bac, and on and on, until I got to the square in front of the Bon Marché. There I found a tall wastebasket with strangers' trash in it, and threw the candle in. I crossed the fingers on both hands and walked home, counting backward from eleven, the way Bertha had taught me, to remedy the evil eye.

Five days I was alone in Paris. Delaborde was away, Luc and Nancy were away, Dad and Michel were away, and Sylvie, of course, and Felix. I tried not to think of them. I went to every movie playing on the Left Bank and finished off my hashish. I had bad dreams, I ate little, and I was afraid of the dark.

After five days Dad and Michel came back. Michel called me. They'd seen Massimo several times, and he was looking for me. They had messages. He'd even sent a present, a round paperweight with sections of glass inside to look like drowned flowers. "You were a success, you're learning," said Michel. He went on with stories about Alexis and the contessas who had invited them for dinner and for tea. I asked how Dad was.

"Not very well," said Michel, "he's had some bad news about a friend of his. Of ours, really."

Some old goat's croaked, I thought. "Who?" I asked, to be polite.

"No one you know. Young man, fell off a cliff. In Portofino. It's a horrible story, there's no need to go into it. They haven't found the body yet, and if they do I don't know what they'd do with Felix's body."

"Felix?" I asked. "Felix?"

"No one you know. So listen, come and have dinner with us tonight, cheer Jacob up. By the way, how's your love affair?"

My bright burning hatred on the black candle flame killed him. I had wished him into my life, and now I had wished him dead. Express trains raced through my head, speed and accidents, furious will.

"You can have anything you want," Julia had said. My love kills. I promise never to wish again.

PART TWO

1

IT WAS AFTER I'D moved back to Dad's, back to my old room, just a few days after Nguyen helped me down the stairs at the Rue du Bac with all my cushions and ashtrays and lampshades. I stood by the chest of drawers, my hand on its mass of wood, and in the other the pills and a glass of water, a dark feeling around my legs because I had already swallowed some of them. A few more, and it was dark and unbreathable in front of me, the foretaste of never being able to breathe again, and more pills and I let the darkness rise and come into me. And just when I was most willing to go, a nervous worm along my backbone gave a start and said, *No*. The next day I was still alive, but with the memory of how close that darkness had been, and how warm the taste of that finality.

Michel woke me. I heard him say he found it original of me to have chosen to sleep on the floor, and while I tried to find words that might explain, he kept talking. "Your father's sick, and I have to go back to the shop, and Nguyen has other things to do. You have to go to the pharmacy." I waited until he was out of the room to try and get up; my bathroom seemed to have moved far away from my room. The clock by my bed said four. Swimming through cotton I made my way to Dad's room, where he lay in bed with a yellow face.

"Jaundice," he said in a weak voice.

Michel stood by his bed, and registered my eyes for the first time. "You look like hell, what happened?" and turning to Dad, told him he'd found me on the floor.

"The fall of the house of Usher," said Dad, and then gave a little laugh that ended with him retching. Michel held forward an enamel bowl.

"A bad oyster," said Michel across the bed to me.

"How did you get on the floor?" asked Dad, looking up from the enamel pan. I looked away.

Michel handed me a slip of paper. "He'll stop that when you get this," he said. "Go."

I went to the door.

When I brought back the prescriptions, Michel had left. Nguyen put a finger over his mouth and took the little boxes from me. "I can do that," I said, but Nguyen shook his head. I started toward the door of Dad's bedroom. "Sleeping," called Nguyen after me in a loud whisper.

He slept in his room and I slept in mine that afternoon. Nguyen brought him consommé, but he threw it across the room. I cut a pineapple into tiny squares: he left the plate untouched on his tray. Michel brought home Lucozade, from an English friend who had a stock. Dad lost ten pounds in three days, and he was always furious when he was awake. "It's part of the illness," said Michel. I wanted to laugh because it was so funny to see Dad's angry yellow face, but when I laughed no one else did.

I couldn't sleep at night. The pills had dimmed me, but now I was afraid to sleep. I stayed awake so that Felix couldn't hurt me. He might be vengeful, there, on the other side. Once Michel was asleep in his room, and Dad's door closed and Nguyen had gone upstairs to his room, where Bertha had once lived with her blue and purple Jesus, I read and looked at old magazines, and when it was really night, two or three, I went into the living room and dialed at random, and tried the old number in London, which never answered though the house had been bought long ago. When light unfolded on the terrace of the garden and it was safe to sleep, I pulled a coat on over my wrinkled t-shirt and went out into the streets and walked until people began their real days. The air was clean and warm, and because I wore slippers instead of high heels distances seemed much shorter. I found myself often at the Louvre, long before it opened, and twice waited for nine o'clock to go in to stare at the winged armless Victory. One day I somehow got mixed in with a group of people who were donating a picture to the museum; there were *légions d'honneur* in lapels, and guards, and a minister, and old sisters hanging together with canes. People shook hands and said, *"ma très chère,"* and *"ravie."* I nodded politely at everyone, too sleepless stunned to be embarrassed by my unwashed face and my dirty hair and the pajama bottoms under my raincoat.

Once I pushed as far as the Marais, a distance I had never walked when I had to go there. I found myself at the door of Delaborde's studio at eight in the morning, with the Jewish shopkeepers sweeping their front steps and clean water running in the gutters and the sound of twig brooms like hairbrushes on the stone. I looked toward the corner where Felix had been the first time I saw him, his cape swirling around him, winding windblown metal curls and the smile of Morpheus, God of Sleep, on the pale skin of his mouth, and I was scared that something had come true, though not ever in the way I wanted it.

And on one of those mornings when I was like a ghost in other people's lives, a simple and Christian solution came to me. Since Dad had fallen ill at the very moment I tried to kill myself, I had been spared in order to take care of him. The idea that I had taken just enough pills for a bad hangover did not apply; providence had shown its hand, and I was to devote myself to my father. I would do its will.

Nguyen taught me how to skim the fat off broth as the bones boil, and how to cut scallions so they looked like trees. I bought tray cloths, took a flower from the garden every morning to put in the little iridescent vase that I brought into him with his weak jasmine tea. I washed the dishes in case that helped. I called Doctor Emery in London, who said jaundice took three weeks, and there was a pill I should take, and these days it was called hepatitis and what sort was it? The French doctor gave me a list of *tisanes* and I brewed Dad special teas in the afternoon. He no longer threw food across the room, but sometimes I found his reading glasses by the door, and the newspaper crumpled by his bed, which could have been merely sloth.

"Don't you have anything better to do?" asked Dad now and then, but with a smile. I loved it.

I slept often on the chaise longue in his room, on the pretext that he might need me in the night. "I'm better," he said, to keep me away. I used the checked throw and took naps in the dark. As long as I didn't use sheets and nightgowns, I wasn't really sleeping.

He wasn't up to conversation. It was enough that Julia was there between us, and now Felix. When he took long baths that I had filled with herbs said to be restorative, I went through his dresser drawers to find a picture, a note, anything that would be a link to Felix. I found three Austrian schillings and wondered if they had been in Vienna together. And what had been so much mine until Sylvie took it away and I destroyed it, what had been my whole existence at the Rue du Bac, became, back in that apartment, the untouchable property of my father.

One day Nguyen brought in an envelope that had been left outside the front door. I was out of the room while Dad opened it, and by the time I came back he had torn up a large black and white photograph into little pieces that littered his quilt. "What was that?" I asked.

"Garbage," he said. I saw that there were tears at the corners of his eyes. I picked the pieces off the bed and went to the kitchen to throw them away, with some idea of hiding in my room to piece the picture together. But Nguyen was in the hall and he took the shreds of paper from my hand as if he'd been waiting. The paper had the thick touch of gallery-quality prints. When I got back to Dad's room, the bed was empty and the bathroom door closed. I sat on the bed and saw a little slip of paper on the floor. Typed on it were the words: "This little bird thought he could fly. But he sank."

I could have made up my mind that I knew then, but it was my father's secret as it had been my own, and his private property. So I didn't know. Anything was possible. I went and lit a candle at Saint Sulpice, and when I came home I threw away the popular astrology book I had bought, and crossed Rosa's name out of my address book.

Sylvie called. I told Nguyen I didn't want to talk to her, and then one day she got to me. "I have so much to tell you," she said, "oh my God."

But I dreaded hearing whatever she had to say more than I had ever dreaded anything, and I told her I didn't want to know. I felt I had managed a great sacrifice. A few days later, she called again, and Dad, who was by now better, took the call. "Sylvie wants you to know she's pregnant," he said.

You won, I thought, you're the one who won.

My FATHER DEALS IN fakes and reproductions; after the shop on the Rue Jacob closed, he said the only way to survive was to make small objects on a big scale. When Michel moved to Provence he invited us to come down and see him whenever we wanted, but all three of us knew he didn't mean it.

As I packed up things in the apartment for the move, I found the urn containing Julia's ashes; it was in a thick cardboard box at the side of a cupboard where Nguyen put the good glasses. I took two suitcases of clothes and a box of books; the urn I put in a weekend bag that I'd left for last-minute sundries. We moved out of the apartment four years after Julia's death. Dad and I had dinner at the Coupole that night, although he hadn't been to a restaurant in years, by then; he hated going out, he was afraid of running into people he knew. But there was no food in the house and I thought it would cheer us up.

On the way out that evening I made sure to blow out the one scented candle I had burning in the living room; there were a few inches of green left inside the glass, and it was no use wasting it. The strain of carrying boxes and moving furniture had made my neck ache, and outside the damp made the back of my hands hurt. We waited outside the door for a cab, neither of us talking, because it was the last time we would wait outside that door. The new address seemed unreal, an invention; and yet everything was packed and ready to go. I was willing to believe that we had lost everything, while my father believed only that there had been some mistake. I'd abandoned ambition for a happy life; those hopes were for whores. I hadn't been out of Paris in two years, not since Michel left and we stopped traveling. After my move back to my father's, my life constricted, first with my will, to an artful concentration on the management of objects and food, and then imperceptibly, out of control, tinier and tinier, until now the only concern was survival.

A man next to us ordered oysters; we were eating fried whiting, the cheapest thing on the menu. "The pearls look nice," said my father. I touched my neck; I wasn't afraid to wear her jewels anymore, what was left of them. The emeralds had gone a few years before, just after the fines and the legal fees swallowed up everything left in the shop. For a year every time I opened a can of tunafish and toasted some bread, every time I bought washing powder, every time I used the expensive soft toilet paper, I was struck with the variety of ways one can consume emeralds. Then the emeralds were used up, and we consumed two diamond brooches, the amethyst necklace—a poor investment, it only lasted us two months—and the sapphire rings. That was when I let Nguyen go.

We drank Beaujolais, while Dad complained. "We could have a Romanée-Conti," he said, dreamily, his eyes inquiring. Behind him, coming up the aisle, I saw Bleulot, whose shop thrived on the Quai Voltaire. Bleulot was Dad's enemy at Drouot; he always got what he wanted. His expensive overcoat stood behind Dad; the woman with him, a squinting brunette with a black and white fur, was exchanging greetings with the people at the table next to ours. Bleulot caught my eye; I gave him a smile, and he said, "*Alors, Florence, ça va?*" Dad's mouth turned up, and he had bared his teeth into a smile before he twisted his shoulders around. "*Salut,*" he shouted at Bleulot, who recoiled a little. It was very loud. Bleulot hit him gently on the shoulder, "*Alors, ça va?*" he asked. Dad nodded, the teeth now hidden, the smile stretched to its fullest. "Join us for a drink," said Dad, and to me, "Where are they with that champagne? God, the service is getting bad here." I waited to see what Bleulot would do; if he sat down I would have to get up and find the waiter and order a bottle of Dom Pérignon, at four hundred and twenty francs, so that Dad could pretend everything was fine. The sharp woman in the furs shook Dad's hand and nodded at me, and took Bleulot's arm. "We have to go, another time," said Bleulot, in English.

"You don't have to do that," I said when they had gone.

"Why not, he's a nice guy," said Dad.

"You hate him," I said.

"Florence, why do you always try to interfere?" he asked, and put down the forkful of watercress that he had just picked up. He squeezed his fists together. The smile was gone.

"We can't afford it, that's why," I said.

"I never took one penny of yours," he said, "not one penny."

"I promise not to interfere with your friends," I said, low.

"You think I blew it all, that's why you give yourself the right to behave like a policeman. But I never took a penny of yours," he went on.

"If the kitchen is dark blue, don't you think it will be too dark?" I asked.

I had learned to throw other ideas at him when he got like this; he'd catch anything on the fly and answer it.

"Well, you're the one who offered to paint it. Maybe light green would be better."

And it was okay again, for a while.

I tipped the coat girl five francs when she came back with our coats; ten was customary, but ten would eat into cab money, and it was too cold to walk home. My father's coat was elegantly beige and green, prosperous looking; it was one that Michel had left behind. Dad wore whatever Michel had forgotten in the closets, and soon I was doing the same thing. All I spent money on was tights, because I was proud of my legs; tights and shoes, and now and then a skirt. There was pleasure in men's clothes, the wide cashmere sweaters with timid V-necks, the soft, roomy shirts with cuffs where the stripes had worn away to show the cotton batten underneath. Pleasure and protection.

No man had touched me since the Venetian. I preferred to think that no man had touched me since Felix, and told myself the tale that my life had stopped with Felix's. But the Venetian's misspent hands and mouth came back, an impertinent memory that made my faith heretic.

After a while you forget what it was like. I'd see people in movie lines—as the years went on, I found them surprisingly young—and wonder if saliva was as sticky as it looked. There was one such couple kissing at a table in our path out of the restaurant. I must have slowed to watch them, because my father was far ahead of me when the waiter caught my arm and said, *"Monsieur!"* I turned, annoyed at his banal misunderstanding of what I like to consider my style, so as not to call it my necessity. He handed me Dad's umbrella.

"Erghi gets out of prison soon," Dad said in the cab. He said it in French, so that the driver would understand, and with a little growl, as if to show that he was a convict type himself.

"Will he be free to travel?" I asked. Dad shrugged his shoulders. "Please don't give him the new address," I said.

Dad laughed: "What if I need him?"

"You don't need him. The last thing you need is to see him, or be seen with him."

"I may call him," he said, under his breath.

I reminded him about the new phone. "You'd have to go through the operator, and that's not a good idea. I'm sure they've got his number on a list."

"Why did you have the phone installed that way?" he asked. "It will make calling abroad almost impossible."

"That's what it's supposed to do," I said.

"I think the move is a good idea," he said after a while, as I was getting my change purse out of the coat pocket. He said it as if we had chosen to move on a whim.

He stood in the front hall facing the Kouros; we could not afford an art packer, so the Kouros stood there, his long body in an acid circle of chalky light, ready to be wrapped in blankets the next day and carried like a body, in a cab, by the two of us. Everything else had gone to the sale room and to former colleagues to pay the bills. All of the money was gone.

"We love him, don't we?" said my father.

I was at the door to the living room, looking at the boxes standing across the floor, with the dim light of the garden thrusting faintly through the window.

"The little bastard," he said.

The new apartment was over in the 17th, on a long gray boulevard with more than its share of buses. "You can see where you're going in a bus," my father said, standing at the window, looking down at people in the buses looking up at him. "You just have to turn your head a little. You actually get to see how pretty the city is."

His filing cabinets came with us. There were four of them, side by side in the hall. He didn't want to put them in his bedroom, he said, because they were too ugly; and for the same reason I didn't want them in the living room. Everything was in those cabinets, he said. What hadn't been seized for evidence. While I painted the kitchen he sat on a chair in the hall, peering into the filing drawers, piles of paper around him.

It was a tiny apartment. We each had a bedroom, there was one bathroom, and a small living room. The Kouros, without the luxury of space around him, without a spotlight and without dark walls to set him off, looked like a big doll made out of bread. His motionless walk, with one foot forward, suddenly gave him a dangerously intrusive bearing. If he could have walked he would have crashed his shins into the coffee table, stone on glass.

The Buddha was gone. "A good deal, that," said Dad. We had enough money to last us another year, maybe more since the rent was so much less. I wanted to work in one of the Left Bank shops, Au Beau Passé, for instance, which had a stock not unlike Dad's, torsos and heads and iridescent Egyptian vases. Dad agreed it was a good idea, but when we went down the list of who he didn't mind having as my employer, there was not one who won his approval. This one, he said, was a crook, and that one had nothing good, and that one he knew too well and this one too little.

I didn't want to leave him alone all day. He set up the long table from the dining room in the kitchen, and unpacked all the art books, leaving them in piles on the floor, so that he could find the ones on sculpture; these lay open on the long table. "Master molds," he said, his glasses pushed up on his forehead, his shirt open and his fingers stuck in every page. "Scaled down. It's amazing what they can do with new materials these days. Nothing complicated; round shapes better than things with too much detail." He made notes. He drew; fine academic drawings, heads and figures from his memory. He showed me a sketch of Rodin's *Thinker*, with wings coming out of his back.

"I don't think so," I said.

"It was just a joke," he said, tearing it up.

He talked incessantly about the molds. "Tanagra women in shifting dresses, Amors from the tombs of haetarae, the more rounded the better." They couldn't be museum reproductions, since the museums, he said, were already in that racket. They couldn't be reproductions of pieces in private collections, because no one would give their consent; "Or worse, they'd ask for money," he explained.

"But what exactly are you going to make, and who are you going to sell it to?" I asked.

"You'll see," he said. The sketches piled on one side of the table, a cup of coffee forgotten by his elbow. I washed the cup and saucer, and brought him another cup of coffee. As I put it down next to him, the coffee spilled out of the cup and onto one of his books. "You've ruined everything," he yelled, mopping the coffee with his shirtsleeve. He turned and looked up at me with such hatred in his eyes that I went and locked myself in my room. When I came out he was bent over his table, crying. "I'm sorry, Florence," he said. But I knew that I had ruined everything. He was right.

"All I need is one idea, one thing that will sell a million," he said the next day, "then everything will be okay." I put on my coat with an inviting smile and said, "There's a few archaeology lots coming up at Drouot, do you want to come with me?"

"The lousy bastards," he said. "I don't want to see them."

"We don't have to talk to anyone, it's just the viewing, it's not the sale. Come on, it'll be interesting."

"I know more than all of them put together," he muttered.

"We don't have to talk to anyone, it's just to look at the lots. Don't you want to come with me? Come on."

"I have work to do," he said, pointing at the table. He had stopped going to Drouot just after all the trouble, and he was sullen at the suggestion. "Look at all this. I have to make sense of all this."

"Can't a lawyer do it?" I asked.

"No one else would understand."

"Maybe you could get Maud to help you," I said. Maud had sent us a little English card, with robins on it, that said, "Welcome to your new home."

"Maud loves you."

"No, not Maud," he said. "She's a good soul. I don't want her here."

"Why not?"

"Because it's none of her business. It's mine, it's mine!"

For a while I thought it was because he had a secret, and then I realized it was because the four filing cabinets were all he had left.

I never really knew what was in them. I assumed invoices on thin paper, with the heading Jacob Ellis et Cie in fine letters; sales slips, bills, letters, insurance forms, value-added-tax forms, receipts, the crinkling dross of commerce.

I went out to Drouot. When the sale rooms pair ethnology and archaeology there's never anything very good for sale. I had gone because I wanted my father to go; standing on the sad rug in the auction room, I felt lonely and incurious.

A hush of absolute indifference reigned in the room. A few dealers and a considerable number of working housewives on lunch break moved with ritual slowness past the objects, eyes riveted on the unshapely forms set before them by the death and bankruptcy of strangers.

There was nothing to buy. I walked down the Rue de la Grange Batelière and peered in the window of a restaurant. The menu displayed on the outside was Italian, and I wanted to eat lunch there, but if I started having lunch in restaurants just because I happened to be in the streets at lunchtime, what we had to live on wouldn't last six months. The Etruscan couple had eaten everything we had.

The Etruscan couple on the coffin lid had been in my father's possession for a little over a week when my father invited an expert from London to visit. He was so proud of the couple that he even invited the concierge in to take a look at them, something he had never done before. "Do you think this is wise?" asked Michel, standing by me at the door as Dad made the concierge walk around the piece, which was set in the middle of the living room. He didn't want the concierge's opinion, but her admiration; what he got was a muttered, "*Bravo, très bien, Monsieur, vous l'avez fait quand?*"

"You see," said Michel, "she thinks your father made it."

"What does she know, she's a concierge," I answered.

The Etruscan couple was the best piece in the living room. The frieze, the horse, the bronze cats and ivory Hathor and seated Isis and crouching Ibis and flying Victory had all gone to pay for the dead couple, and so had the terracotta Naiads riding sidesaddle on the prancing waves, the wiry votive soldiers, the squatting scribe.

"I like the minimal look," Alexis had said when he saw how bare the room was.

"Aha," said the man from the British Museum, going straight for the Buddha head on the coffee table. "How nice to see him again." Dad stood by his Etruscan couple, turning his head from the Buddha to the coffin as if it were a tennis match. Then the expert, Mr. Smith-Jones, in a tweed suit dank with age and untouched by dry cleaning, circled the coffin a few times before returning to the sofa without a word. "Oh God," said Michel, who was standing by the door with me, "let's get out of here," and we repaired to the kitchen, where he made English tea sandwiches and I made tea, as if offerings could ward off fate. By then I'd been working for Dad long enough to know how bad a bad opinion could be. When we came back into the living room, with the tea tray and the smiles of children at Christmas, Dad too was sitting on the sofa, his hands limp like gloves at the end of his red sleeves. Neither he nor the man from the British Museum said a word while I was in the room, so I left, followed by Michel.

"I think it's bad," he said, and gave my shoulder a hug. I knew then how stupid I had been not to trust him, and with it came the sour, irrevocable knowledge that my father was going to have to pay for his folly.

"He's not trying to sell it, so does it matter all that much?" I asked.

"It matters," said Michel.

And it did. From then on Dad began to make phone calls, to

London, to California, to Greece, to Turkey, to Liechtenstein and to Basel. "You're not thinking of selling it, after all that?" Michel asked one night at dinner. By now we were accomplices in the pretense that everything was all right.

"Oh," said Dad, "once you own something, it's not the same. The real excitement was in getting hold of it. Now that I've got it, how much more can it be mine?"

"No," said Dad at dinner. "I think I can't keep it; it has to move on."

"You're right," said Michel. I could tell he was relieved.

"After all," said Dad, "no object should stay put in the hands of one person. A collection is just a financial cushion for bad times. And the only way to really possess this, or anything, would be to smash it to pieces."

How right he was.

"There isn't much time," Michel said later, to Dad. "Word travels fast."

"Don't be silly," said Dad, "don't get hysterical."

There were letters and telegrams. People came to visit it. Many wanted the Kouros in the hall. Some days there were two, three visits. Finally a small American museum bought it, and less than a month after the Etruscan couple arrived, the art packers came to take it away again.

Dad and Michel were so relieved that we all went to the Club Méditerranée at Agadir for two weeks.

My father sunbathed on a curved terrace that wound around the swimming pool, surrounded by French couples doing the same thing. Michel and I sat at the curved bar behind the undulating walls of windows. We wore beads to pay for the drinks and the camel rides on the beach. "What are we doing here?" I asked.

"Jacob wanted a rest," said Michel, "and some sun."

"But we know so many people with nice houses, what are we doing here with these strangers?"

"Jacob wanted a change," said Michel. He didn't tell me then that Dad had borrowed money from every person we knew who had a nice house. "It's more relaxing to be among strangers," added Michel.

"This doesn't look like Morocco, it doesn't feel like Morocco, it doesn't taste like Morocco," I said.

"Just wait till tonight," said Michel. "I hear they're barbecueing sheep in tents on the beach."

Dad had sold the piece to the wrong people. The small museum in America sprouted a three-headed academic who knew someone at the British Museum. We found all this out later; at the time it only seemed like bad luck.

He could have gone to prison for fraud; he didn't. He wrote a check for the amount he had received from the small American museum. Papers were seized; there were meetings with "*maîtres*" in their "*cabinets*" (masters in their toilets, Dad said, on his way to one of them). The piece, we heard later, was smashed to pieces in a ceremony at the small American museum. The event was covered by the press. The small museum's curator and the two North American experts in Etruscan and archaeological pottery officiated.

Unfortunately, it got into the papers. The man who wrote about sale rooms for the *International Herald Tribune* wrote an article entitled "Fakery Still Alive." Michel was worried about the honor of his name. "Who cares about Dupuy?" I asked. "Dad's the one who's in trouble."

Dad came to me one day and told me that Julia's money had gone to buy the piece. "You needed that, too?" I asked. The price, he said, had been high.

"How could you have thought it was good?" I asked Dad when we were living in the small apartment.

"Sometimes you want something so badly that you don't even pay attention to what you really know," he said.

PART THREE

SUMMER. SHE IS OUT buying food for dinner when the sky turns icy blue and flesh pink at once, something rears up behind the colors but does not yet roar, and the air smells metallic, smooth with ozone. Tides of garbage have left crushed white shapes, flimsy geometries, stuck to the gutter corners where street becomes avenue. People rising from the subway in accidental pairs move in stillness. In her hand the plastic strap of the evening's vegetables is hot and tight; if her legs were shorter, the belly of the bag would graze the ground. Black boys in shorts, looking the other way, walking backward, contrive to kick and spin the bag, dull thud against her calves. She buys food every evening; hers is a reasonable and ordered life. The weight of food is part of being down to earth, but what she knew as earth was never this sequence of asphalt squares bright with flattened pink chewing gum, subsided sections of paving patched with temporary fillings of white mortar. Why, she wonders, is this street so much like the inside of her own mouth?

She is normal now, she is almost American. She has lived with Ben for ten years, and for eight of those they have been in New York. "Go," her father said, "you are American." The passport had always been American; gray-green, with raised medallions on it at first, and then smooth navy blue, and then suddenly a smaller version, because, as the woman at the consulate explained, the kids kept losing them and the smaller model fit exactly into the back pocket of a pair of jeans.

"Go," Jacob had said, "go home. I'll stay here." To let her know he was brave and self-sufficient; as if there were danger in Europe, as if again a war were coalescing out of innumerable small events, devaluations, deployments, strikes, migrant workers, the sudden ornery behavior of ministries. As if he wanted to be alone.

She had watched over him, a nervous guardian. In the first two years at the new apartment he had gained weight, refused to speak French or answer the phone. His forehead beaded with sweat at the recollection of each mistake, and he had to be persuaded to take pills so that he would sleep more than two hours a night. When they finally had to sell the Kouros, Jacob seemed to recover; once the statue had been crated and sent to Lausanne, he was himself again. He traveled, he spoke to Michel on the phone, he went to Italy with Alexis. He was fine and she had nothing left to do.

"You should have your own life," he said. It was with alarm that she watched his distress recede. It left her with no vow to keep. When she met Ben she found someone worldly and a little chilled. Safe.

Ben agreed with Jacob. "It's time to grow up, to go home," he said. He had spent twenty years in Europe, he had almost forgotten America, and she had never known it.

The tools for reclaiming America were no more noble than the screws and wrenches, precut curtain rods, nails, and plugs hanging in plastic bags on curved hooks at the hardware store. And principally, numbers. Checks to a real estate agent with bouncing eyes, checks to a landlord with a dirty office, checks to cleaning companies and cable companies. Answers to the telephone company, the grocery store, the dry cleaner, the insurance company: how much did they earn, how long had they been where they were, how soon did they want the service to begin. The questions made Ben feel he was being pushed against a sharp metal grid, the flesh of his back sliced into neat squares. But she enjoyed them. They were a form of attention, a call to order. Ben was astonished at her compulsion to be registered, to get a Social Security card, to have a number, as many numbers as she could get, and to send away for more. "I haven't paid American tax in years," he said, running his hand through what was left of his hair, "not since I got out of school."

"Well, I've never paid any tax, and I want to," she said. He told her she didn't earn anything, but there was the income. The income.

From the way she had talked in Paris, he thought she would be rich. "There's money in America, I get it when I turn thirty," she said, often. When she hadn't said it for a while, Jacob said it: "Don't forget, there's money in America. You'll be a rich woman."

On her thirtieth birthday the first check arrived. It was for six hundred dollars. Ben laughed. "There'll be another check tomorrow," he said, to reassure her. She went out and spent it all on a duffle coat for Ben, and there was no check the next day. So now, he thought, when all the forms began arriving in the apartment in New York, we are going to pay tax on her seven thousand dollars a year.

New York attacked them when they arrived, attacked their bodies from the inside. They developed rheumatic pains in their arms, sore joints, burning wrists. His skin was allergic to something the Chinese laundry used on their sheets, and she was poisoned regularly, after veal chops or mayonnaise or tunafish from the deli. They had cable TV installed so that a young actress playing a child possessed by the devil could vomit green bile at them as they lay in bed. Ben had a toothache and went to the dentist, who prescribed something she had never heard of, root canal; and for the next five weeks Ben went to have a hole drilled into the bone of his jaw and came home swooning on pills, and for that they paid a thousand dollars. One morning she rose and went to stand by the window, her heart beating hard. They would both become ill and helpless in this pitiless place, and then they would die.

There seemed to be nothing but bills for what was wrong with them, no praise for what was right. "You get no prizes for just living, you have to succeed," said one of Ben's friends, and she thought how cruel and stupid it was to think like that. When they went to the insurance man he asked if they had any dependents; they shook their heads and said no, and then she said, a question, "My father?" and the insurance man asked if they took care of her father financially, and she said no, and he said, "Well, he's not a dependent, then." And told them that they didn't need life insurance if both of them worked and they had no dependents. And their lives, which in Paris had been people and meals and work and weather, changed character. There was a purpose to earning money for Ben, there was a purpose to cooking dinner for Florence: success and healthy survival. And the filaments of inclination, of affection, of languid preference, which clung to all their actions so that even without much money they had lived in luxury, gave way to an abstract discipline.

They hadn't noticed they were getting older in Paris. They hadn't noticed they weren't rich in Paris, because they had the cupola of the Institut de France outside their living room window and their friends didn't mind climbing the stairs. Ben sold his designs to sheet companies and to fabric jobbers, she helped her father with his catalogue and did small translations from French into English.

"There's money in America," said Ben, and she shook her head: "You know it's not that much."

He pursed his lips and said, "For me, not for you." The market was bigger in America. They would have a house in the country and a car. Now they have medical insurance and a bank loan. They are older, but they are not old. They seem to have no age, because they have none of the markers of age. No children, no car, no wall-to-wall carpet, not even a kilim made yesterday in India, with bright blue and pale pink hatchet squares. Bare floors and drafty windows. They are still starting out.

Ben has two tables in his workroom: one where he spreads out his sheets of paper and sticks them to the pale green surface with masking tape, and one where the bills and forms are arranged in piles. He spends more time puzzling out the bills than making his drawings of repeated ibexes leaping over gold fronds, repeated flowers and leaves, repeated fruits and bees. The essential has become to stay in line, to keep abreast, to stay afloat. He moved here to be a success, to make money; and he finds himself hanging in the wave of debt and opportunity, like plankton, like krill, rising and falling gently with the market, matter that doesn't matter.

Ben has his private opinion about most things, an opinion that he refuses to share. It is his only way of knowing he has not given up. He was beautiful until he was twenty-five, handsome until he was thirty. An innocent face and soft blond hair, a profile drawn as if by a fine pen with great skill, slim wrists and limpid eyes. When he studied in Vienna the girls were mad for him. He posed naked with one of them in his arms for a Perseus and Andromeda by a famous painter who lived above the Graben and whose paintings were sold as post-cards in all the art shops. As he aged his features lost their definition, but by then he was in Paris. He had been, briefly, social: light and witty in a company of mixed languages and equal fortunes. His parents were quiet people, art teachers in California; when they answered the letters he wrote them on thin hotel paper with heavy shining crests they made it clear they thought he was wasting his life. He knew that he was winging it, but at times he felt almost able to fly. He lived with a succession of rich women, he was used to other people paying for things, he thought there was nothing wrong in having a good time. His friends were critical of the wrong shoes or bad haircuts, but never of each other's lives. Each moment, each meal, was so complete that the only need it called up was for more of the same, the next meal, the next moment. There was no question of striving; for what?

With Nina he had stayed at all the best places, he had attended the weddings of her friends, and he had flirted with these other girls, and often consummated the flirtations at some risk to the peace of his daily life.

He sat at dinners where he knew every woman a little too well, and he considered this proof of his exceptional charm. But as the years went on he realized that every other man knew the same women in the same way, and what he had taken for personal triumph was simply proof of a generalized casual attitude toward love.

And then he stayed too long. The strange sensation of losing began to come upon him, first as a hangover: evanescent, unpleasant, with no definite source. He waited for the attention he was used to, and it didn't come; eyes skipped over his face when before they had lingered, waiting for an invitation. Then Nina went on a trip without him, and didn't come back, stayed in India too long, prolonged her stay in Kashmir. He thought she was being merely whimsical until the bailiffs came to say the rent was unpaid and would he pay or leave, and because he couldn't afford her twenty-two-foot ceilings and gilt address, he left.

As his waistband became tight and his cheeks loose, he understood he could no longer simply be, he had to produce. It took him years to stop thinking it was foolish to be hard on himself.

He returned to Vienna, he collected documents for his prints, he exhumed his student portfolio, he phoned people who made fabric. Grunting slightly, he told himself he was paying at last for the good years he'd had. He was so used to other people paying for things that often in the first years of working he'd stop at his table and put down his brush and wait to be rescued.

He missed his moment, it passed while he was sleeping, reading a magazine in an airport lounge, thinking of the next meal. It's gone. And now he is an ordinary person, but still he has flashes of what his life should be: a leather diary on a bedside table at the Ritz; a wedding in a castle, and the guests arrive by helicopter; headwaiters presenting Cuban cigars for his approval, his taste for art turned to good use with the advised and repeated purchases of major works, Paris at his feet.

But he's not in Paris, he's in New York. He's at his table with brushes and pens, his ruler and his scalpel, which he uses to cut out his mistakes. The bottles of ink are lined up two deep, seventeen across. He doesn't have thirty-four colors, he has some doubles: buttercup yellow, two cobalts, and three viridians. He just finished a tropical series, twenty-four sheets, four variations on six drawings each, palm trees, toucans, mangoes and pineapples on a ground of surf and beach. Not his best work. He used to care that his colors should be reproduced faultlessly on smooth silk. Now he's happy if the blurred acetate has sold well to the mail order customers. He is forty-eight years old and he has given up.

He and Florence have that in common. They shared it before they met and it keeps them together, this certainty of a chance missed, of something broken in the past that the future will not mend. The night they met he was eloquent about missed chances, it was one of his party tricks. He saw a strange girl in men's clothes, who wore no makeup and stared out from behind her fringe like an animal locked in a cage of good sense, lashed to small actions and good behavior. "I would like to be very old, but in good health, and curious and dignified," she said.

"Why?" he asked, though he knew what she meant.

"Because then you're not waiting for anything anymore," she said.

"What are you waiting for?" he asked.

"Nothing," she said, "that's why it would be so much easier to be old."

She smiled at him with sad eyes, and the eyes made the smile honest. Something he could trust, the resignation.

Their regrets matched; they were assumed to have fallen in love.

She liked his look of a wrinkled child, an overused doll. She had been handling statues for so long that a doll was almost easy. Ancient and broken things were familiar; crusts and omissions had become the only lens through which she could see what had been, not what was. She liked his nervous hands, the catch in his throat, his American accent. They talked about handmade shoes, walking sticks, and spas. A few days later, they left together for Vichy, where they stayed in a large white hotel and took the waters—pungent sulfur in tin cups, hot from gilt taps manned by women with white caps— they also lay on a big white bed and touched each other's bodies slowly and carefully. Without clothes they both looked younger. His skin and hers were smooth, and with the curtains drawn and no trace of haste they went about each other like curious children, like fingertips in a dream.

It had been a long time, she said. His touch was so light and unhurried she imagined that it must be like that with a woman. His way, their way, was a laconic indifference to passion, a quiet toying with each other's bodies, naked with the sheets pulled off, cool from the air. So composed, so calm, that the heat and the longing called up by palms and quiet lips withdrew to a secret sphere inside the solar plexus, into a round silver ball, that received from the whole body, his and hers.

For him the indifference was practiced, sly. When he was young and beautiful, he had been invaded, solicited, pulled at by women, and most of all in bed; holding back had been a measure of his grace, then, and now it was his art. She subsided to his idle pace, she welcomed it. She would not let him enter her. Everything but that.

"Does it hurt?" he whispered to her, as his body covered hers.

"No," she said, "but it will make me cry. Don't."

He let it go. It didn't matter. The tension in itself was pleasure enough.

They have been together ten years and he has never been inside her. She has cried in his arms in the middle of the night, but because of nightmares which she has not told. They have held hands in planes, thinking of death. They have signed forms together and they have lied to others together, they are a couple. For the last five years or so they have given up even touching in bed, where she wears flannel and he wears an old t-shirt. They share food and money, they share a life, their destinies are indissoluble. They each once considered the normal mediocre, and now they do their best to be normal. He has his flashes of the smooth leather diary on the marble bedside table in the good hotel, and he keeps it back, he doesn't share it. If he talked about the wisps of remembered luxury, he would lose even that. He has not given up completely, but he won't call his memories dreams, because he once lived them.

And she still has Felix, who has been dead for fifteen years.

12

THE WINTERS IN NEW YORK are full of sun; February passes no faster, but the light belies the hibernation. From the first year she was amazed by the sugar festivals: the orange and yellow and white teeth of corn candy at Halloween, the marshmallows at Thanksgiving, the pale chocolate trees at Christmas, and the chocolate hearts on Valentine's Day, and then the chocolate eggs at Easter. Every time the pace gets a little slow, she learned, you go out and buy candy.

Valentine's Day. Deborah is on the phone; Florence holds the phone between her shoulder and her jaw, stirring something in a pan. She is making a sweet dessert.

"Not even a flower!" says Deborah.

"Well, you haven't known him that long," says Florence, who puts down the pan and opens the refrigerator door.

"The shit, I could kill him," says Deborah.

"It's only four o'clock," says Florence. "Maybe they'll be at home when you get there, a huge bunch waiting for you, roses."

"I have given that man head every time we've been to bed together, and do you think he's been down on me once?" asks Deborah, her voice shrill.

Florence clamps her lips together. She doesn't like to hear about that. "Let's get back to the flowers," she says. "I'm sure it will be fine. You'll see."

"Last year I got flowers from three different men," says Deborah, "so I wish I knew what I was doing wrong this year. Christ, last year I wasn't even going to a gym!" Florence inspects her upper arm with index and thumb. It sags a little. She went to a gym for a while, a few years back, but the boredom was worse than the effort. That and the forced community with women she did not admire, women like Deborah.

"You're okay," says Deborah. "You can eat everything you want and not gain an ounce."

"Um," says Florence.

"It's because you're so tall. But we all have to watch out for our flab," adds Deborah. "There's nothing a man hates more than to feel something soft under his hand."

Florence is stirring again, watching the sugar and the butter join, liquefy . . .

"Of course Ben isn't going to start looking around, he's not the type," says Deborah. This isn't a compliment.

"Oh, but he does," Florence could say, or "he has." To slice at Deborah's assumption, her arrogance. Deborah adds, "He just wouldn't do that to you," and now Florence has nowhere to go. "He has a girlfriend," she wants to tell Deborah, just to shut her up, and she could add, "He's all man, my dear, he's all man." She knows that Deborah lives in a world of wild animals and brushfires, that she admires blood and lust.

"My shrink says I shouldn't be so ready to accept defeat," says Deborah.

"I don't think you are being defeated," says Florence.

"No flowers on Valentine's Day!" Deborah is shouting now, and Florence wonders what Deborah's secretary thinks of all this.

"Do you realize what an insult that is?" Deborah goes on, "after everything I've given up for this guy? He doesn't know how lucky he is. . . . Do you realize I could be in Sun Valley, right now, with that Italian who owns the restaurant on Amsterdam Avenue?"

"Why aren't you?" asks Florence, as she opens up the book. She has to check the proportions again. She thought she knew how to make it, she must have forgotten.

"Because of him! I figured out if I stayed in New York, we'd be together on Valentine's Day. Look at all the emotional energy I've wasted on this jerk, Florence, it's a crime!"

"You haven't known him that long," says Florence. "A week?"

She's counting, twelve, sixteen ounces, and then the butter, damn, she's used too much butter, and now she has to go out and buy more.

"Two weeks! Not one week, what do you think I am, desperate? Two weeks! That's a lot of time, in New York!"

Ben is sensitive to weather. His blood pressure drops when it is very cold. The radiator is hot; the green plastic panel in the center of his worktable feels sticky under his hand, it's buckling. He likes to face the window although there is nothing to see outside except other windows, a thousand of them. This happens every winter; wearily he gets up and pulls the table to the center of the room. He doesn't know where to put it anymore, he's exhausted all the possibilities, the corner, the window, the left wall, the right wall, even, for three months one spring, facing the closet door, where their summer clothes rotted in the old damp of seaside weekends.

Florence comes in in her coat and puts her arms around him, and he rubs his cheeks on the rough tweed of her sleeves. "This is my coat," he says, which is family ritual, because she's been wearing it for three years now.

"I'm going out for food, do you want anything?" she asks.

"I don't know," he says.

"Do you want to come with me and see?" she asks. When the table is in the middle of the room Ben needs to be taken for walks, taken to the movies. So that he won't start drinking.

Ben closes his eyes. With his eyes closed he can see the room no, he opens them, it isn't the same, he's moved, he forgot. "Deli or grocer?" he asks. He knows she wouldn't invite him to the supermarket, the supermarket is like the toilet, never mentioned in polite company.

The deli has a pale yellow floor, a neon ceiling, noodle salads behind bulletproof glass edged with bright chrome. There are rows of boxes with pictures on them, pictures of: wheat sheafs, bunches of raisins, clusters of barley, tomatoes, apples, pears, ears of corn, honeybees in formation and red barns alone, all of them rendered in a process between the photographic and the merely graphic, and placed in compositions with happy children, farmers, founding fathers, and black women. White women are confined to the large boxes of soap flakes and bottles of detergent. On the cereal boxes there is almost always a picture of the sun. The soap boxes show clouds, white wisps. There are angels on the toilet paper, and birds. Ben is confused by the deli. The pictures send his mind off far away from food, and the smell of burnt pork with sugar, of rotting eggs, stale pimentos, and Lysol, do nothing to call it back.

The grocer is different. The grocer endorses the real. The sugar and the mustard, the salt and the flour stocked there have stripes on their plain paper bags; there is a barrel of nuts with a little shovel in it, a scoop. There are costly but authentic vegetables in wooden bins, and if it weren't for the prices Ben would think the grocer was a deliberate replica of an older and more dignified America. Something he likes to think he remembers from his California childhood, but all that comes back to him is a vision of huge grapefruit and skinny Necco wafers.

He doesn't like this neighborhood, and there's nothing he can do to get out of it. What do his A.A. friends tell him? "God give me the strength to change what I can and the wisdom to endure what I can't"?

"Let's go out tonight," he says.

So he isn't coming. She is planning, after the butter is bought, to buy a magazine and sit in the coffee shop for half an hour. So as not to be home. She has enough quarters she's collected from around the house to buy a four-dollar magazine, so that it won't count as expensive. Using change is a form of saving.

"I thought pasta," she says.

"You used to call it spaghetti," he says.

"We used to call it *pâtes*, don't give me that. *You* used to call it spaghetti, maybe."

Outside, a winter sky the color of uniforms. There are hearts in every shop window, the man in the paper shop wishes her a happy Valentine's Day through his emphysema, her hands are cold but she's come out with only one glove. She stops in front of the drugstore; there are heart-shaped soaps strung up in a garland, and she considers buying Ben a present.

A reward. He's still there, after all.

Small rewards to keep going.

Ben turns on the radio. There's the end of a concert by Pogorelich, Chopin. He lets himself go on the notes until the music ends. "This is the radio station of the *New York Times*," says a hearty woman's voice, as if announcing good news. A man's voice takes over: "Stravinsky . . . Shostakovich . . . Rimsky-Korsakov . . . Borodin . . . Berlioz . . . Gounod . . . Tchaikovsky . . . ballet!" He turns off the radio and begins to pace around the table. He is saved by the phone.

Katy would like them to come to dinner, tonight. "I just threw it together," she says. Ben is relieved.

"Can we bring anything? I think Florence is making some kind of dessert."

"Great," says Katy.

He forgot to ask how many people there would be.

"How could you?" says Florence, unwinding her scarf, her face contracted from the cold. "I've only made enough for us, and for tomorrow's lunch. If there are six people it will look ridiculous to have a tiny pie like that. Call her back."

There are five people at Katy's. The apartment is in a new building in the Village; the walls seem thick, the parquet floor is laid in a checkerboard system of parallel paillettes, which resonate. There is Ed, who publishes a small democratic newsletter, and Phyllis, who paints; Frank, who works with silk makers in China, and Gloria, who works in the mayor's office. Katy is alone.

She's made a molded salad to begin with, in the shape of a heart. It is cold and tastes either of tomatoes or cranberries, Florence isn't sure; there are regular squares of white vegetable inside the aspic, and little yellow grains of corn, and dashes of red peppers. Ben and Ed and Phyllis and Frank and Gloria and Katy all remember when their mothers made molded aspics; dates and seasons of previous aspics are brought up, there is much screaming, "God, yes!" and "What about when . . ." Florence withdraws, there at the table, which is travertine marble from Bloomingdale's, covered in Filipino rush mats, with small squares of bright pink napkins. A pair of

Pierrots, made of felt and nylon, with silver stars on their cheeks, embrace in the middle of the table, surrounded by pink foil candy hearts.

Ed and Phyllis have been married for four and a half years; they lived together for a year before they married. Ed is handsome, tall, blond, bearded. Phyllis was married before and has a six-year-old child; she says that now she has found happiness. Frank is not the type to settle down, but he has lived with Gloria for twelve years. Gloria has affairs, which Florence knows about, because Gloria tells her. They are with younger men, boys, assistants from the mayor's office, young men from Brooklyn, married boys from Queens. Gloria wears an ankle bracelet and never goes out without makeup. Katy is divorced. Her only passion is hating her husband, Robert, whose money allows her to live. It's a generous alimony, but as Katy said to Florence, "I don't care how much it is, I thought I'd be married for the rest of my life, and the money can't make up for that."

Phyllis put Ed on a diet recently, more than a diet, "a new approach to food," she says. Ed is proud of the six pounds he has already lost, and proud of what he calls his new awareness. Florence is not drinking; she asks for a Coca-Cola. Katy can't find the right glass, "I don't mind, I'll drink it from the can," shouts Florence, and as she raises the cool metal to her lips Ed puts out a hand to stop her.

"That's very dangerous," he says.

"I won't cut myself," says Florence.

"That's not what I mean," says Ed.

"What, in case it's dirty?" asks Florence—"I'm sure Katy wouldn't allow a dirty can in her house, I know it's clean," she goes on, and then takes a gulp.

"It's been proven that aluminum causes cancer," says Ed. He has everyone's attention.

"I always thought it was aluminium," says Gloria.

"Trace elements," says Ed. "Carcinogenic. Like dishwashing soap."

"I always wash my dishes very carefully," says Phyllis.

"I think the dishwashers rinse all that stuff out," says Katy.

"You can't be too careful," says Ed. "I come from a long line of cancer victims. You just try to eliminate the risks, one by one."

"Did you see the *New York Times*?" asks Gloria, to change the subject. It could be something to do with the mayor, with the weather, with politics or even with design. But it's Tuesday.

"Whipple's syndrome?" asks Frank. Everyone leans forward; they all nod eagerly. They've all seen it. The roast baby veal is forgotten. They could be talking about politics or love, since it's Valentine's Day, but it's easier to talk about what they can each consider a personal matter. Memories of aspic cannot compete with the condition of the body. The Tuesday health column in the *New York Times* identifies each week a new enemy of the body, locates its provenance, logs its successes. The body count reads variously as a cell count, as the slow singular atrophy of unsuspected muscles. Benign clues gather into a pattern, incontrovertible evidence, a map of approaching death; all the tragedies of life are lived within one's single body, war, famine, exile, shame, loss. Even survival. Every week, something new to be aware of, to be afraid of . . .

"She thought she was going to be cured of colitis, and instead they cut off her leg," says Phyllis, who's seen a few in her time.

Frank knows about a young girl whose brain swelled during an operation: "The doctor scooped out some of the brain matter and threw it against the wall."

"Why did he do that?" asks Ben.

"I don't know," Frank says rapidly, and continues his story: family, lawsuits, slow rehabilitation, and she learned to play the piano again.

"Why did he do that?" asks Ben.

No one bothers to answer, to consider the question. Fate is blind, fate is stupid, the agents of change have no reason, they are dumb.

"So what's Whipple's syndrome?" asks Florence.

"Oh," says Gloria, "it's terrible, it's amazing."

Phyllis cuts in: "Worse for men, for once."

"Come on, Phyllis," says Gloria.

Phyllis turns to her:

"All the bad stuff usually happens to women. This one's an exception. That's all I meant."

"What does it do? Will somebody please explain it?" asks Florence. "I didn't read the paper today."

"Well," says Frank, pulling back from the table so that he will have to raise his voice a little, "I don't think you can say all the bad stuff happens to women."

Florence turns to Ed. "What is it? Is it bad?"

"Let me see," says Ed, "Whipple's syndrome affects males between the ages of twenty-eight and forty. It's a gradual decrease of tactile control, of mobility, of sexual interest. It's an urge to sleep later and later all the time, and a lack of appetite, and headaches, and loss of rational thought . . ."

"You mean they turn into women?" asks Florence. Gloria gives a loud laugh, Phyllis looks appalled.

"No, it's more serious than that," says Ed, determined to be solemn. "It leads to infantilism, premature dementia, and death."

"What can be done about it?" asks Florence.

"They've found a pill, haven't they," says Katy, leaning forward. "I read that, there's a pill."

"It sounds like life," says Ben.

"You're way beyond the danger age, that's why you're being cynical," says Phyllis.

"Thanks," says Ben.

"Yes," continues Katy, "there's a pill, but it has side effects, doesn't it? I forgot what they are."

"Hair loss, principally," says Ed. "Weight gain, failing eyesight, and it does something bad to the arches of the feet."

Ben laughs out loud. "See, it's nothing. There are worse things."

"Exactly," says Ed, pulling back the way Frank did. "I'm working on the Central America project."

Gloria leans forward, eager to join in, to help.

"Before we can do anything, we need to raise a half a million dollars," says Ed.

"As usual," says Gloria knowingly.

Florence offers to help clear the table with Katy, who doesn't answer but gets up and starts to collect the dirty plates. In the kitchen she asks Florence if she's all right. "You look a little depressed, how's he treating you?" she says.

"Who?" asks Florence.

"Ben," says Katy.

"Oh, fine," says Florence, rinsing the silver.

"Just leave that," says Katy. "I have to tell you what happened. Robert called today."

"What did he want?" asks Florence.

"Today? You know, today. Isn't that sweet of him?"

"Today," says Florence, dully.

"Valentine's Day," says Katy, "you know what that means."

"Good things?" asks Florence with a smile. Katy turns on her toes, a remnant of ballet in her. "So what did he say?" asks Florence.

"Oh, he just wanted to talk about when I wanted the house on the island, which weeks in July and which weeks in August. And something to do with the medical insurance. Nothing important." She's still on her toes, still beaming.

"What else?" asks Florence.

"Well, what else would he say, the shit?"

"But you said he was sweet. Was he sweet?" Florence is being strictly logical; it's something her friends don't like in her, a cold condition. It's the only way Florence can be sure she is acting normal. Katy comes down on her heels.

"It's not anything he said, it's just the fact he called today. I think it means something."

And so that she won't have to explain herself any further, she hands a pile of dishes to Florence and puts Florence's pie on a tray. Florence returns to the living room.

"I'm just not interested," Ben is saying. Phyllis turns to him. "Why not?" she asks; it's not a question, but a baited challenge.

Ben puts his hands up. "No interest. Maybe I've got Whipple's syndrome."

Phyllis's lower teeth jut out as she speaks; she holds her elbows in her arms and thrusts her neck at him. "Because of your art, Ben? That's it, your art takes up too much of your time?"

"I don't do art, Phyllis. I leave that to the women."

Phyllis's hand comes across the table at him, finger pointed. "Cheap shot," she says. "You should be painting, instead of wasting your time on little patterns for sheets. You know what I mean."

"I don't want to paint," says Ben.

"Wait a minute," says Gloria, "wait a minute. You can do whatever you want with your life, so long as you go on caring about the world. I don't think the issue here is Ben's career. It's caring."

"I don't have a career," says Ben.

"Exactly," says Phyllis.

"Stop it," says Gloria. "He only said that to get sympathy."

"I only said that to be funny," says Ben.

"Call that funny?" says Frank.

"You see, you're doing that charming European bit again," says Phyllis. "It doesn't work."

"That is not the issue," says Gloria.

"I think charming European is great," shouts Katy from the kitchen.

"Wait a minute," says Gloria. "People are dying."

"People are meant to die. It's the way life ends," says Ben.

"Don't say that," says Phyllis.

"It's the truth. People here think life is one eternal race to progress. Promotion. Success."

"Until illness interferes, or tragedy," says Frank. "Don't forget that."

"Cancer, murder, accidents," says Phyllis.

"That's just personal tragedy," says Gloria. "But then there's war. Famine. Collective, social tragedy. We don't have that here."

"No," says Ed, "we just have our genes. No matter what happens, we're what our parents were. Blood can trip us up when we least expect it."

"There's nothing you can do to change the past," says Phyllis, "and it gets bigger every day."

"You can lie," says Frank. "Lots of people do."

"Makes no difference," says Ed. "Lies are just for others. Lying makes no difference to what's in store for you."

"Nothing makes any difference," says Ben, "to you or to others."

"You mean nothing makes any difference to you," says Phyllis. "Stop pretending that you don't have feelings, that you don't have something going on under that fake European facade."

"I can see," says Gloria. "I can see why you're just not interested in anything. You just don't give."

"You cut yourself off from America when you left,"—it's Phyllis now, disgusted—"when you went off on your fancy life. You forgot who you were and where you came from."

"Pomona?" asks Ben, with a little smile. He can't take any of this too seriously while it's happening.

"Paris this and Vienna that, you know what we're talking about. You're in America now." Phyllis rests her case.

Florence is still standing up, her hands full of plates.

And what does that mean, you're in America now? It means you have to care. She knows that. You have to think there is such a thing as a future. You have to care about Central America because it's near and Africa is too far, and Vietnam and Bangladesh no longer exist. But you're not supposed to care about Paris or Vienna.

You have to care even if you wake up every morning wondering whether you have cancer. You have to pretend you want to be alive. Poor Ben, she loves him because he's as little convinced of life on earth as she is. As lucid, she thinks. In a way it's easier for them both in New York, where every day is so bluntly about bare survival that the small graces are testaments of victory. Medals. She opens her mouth to defend him, and all she can say is—"Pie?"

"You've been back for five years," says Ed. "Isn't it time you opened your eyes?"

"Eight," says Ben, "and what am I supposed to do? Find a cure, stop wars, save the world? Come on. I know there's not a single thing I can do or say that will make one bit of dif-ference."

Ed shakes his head. "There's so much to do. To begin with, we have to raise half a million dollars just to get the Central American Concerned Citizen project going." He checks his pulse, a new habit, as he speaks.

Gloria turns the discussion practical. "We can have fund-raisers, art sales, direct mail solicitations, a group affiliation—maybe you could design a badge, Ben?"

"I'll do the badge," says Phyllis.

"Would you?" Ed turns to her with a grin—"I didn't want to ask you earlier."

"You see?" says Ben. "You don't need me. It all can go on just fine without me."

"Your pie is delicious," Gloria tells Florence.

"We all care about something," says Katy, her little fists on the table. "We all have something we hold on to, Ben. You must too."

"What do you care about, Ben?" asks Ed, who's shuffling the papers he had put on the table. He's written BADGE across the top of the budget breakdown.

Ben lights one of Florence's cigarettes.

"I just try to get by," he says. "I don't have any pretensions about my effectiveness in the world."

"You shouldn't smoke," says Ed.

Florence takes one of her cigarettes and lights it, deliberately, slowly.

"I know that Ben cares, deep down inside. He just won't show it," says Katy.

"The problem is, you were away too long. You haven't participated in America, you're as much of a stranger here as you were in Paris." It's Frank talking. "I bet you don't even vote."

"Coffee?" asks Katy. She is greeted with a chorus of nos, in which Ed's voice, solo, stands out: "Decaffeinated?"

Florence feels Ben's foot against her leg, the insistent signal to leave. Florence stands up. "We must leave," she says.

"We should go too," says Phyllis. "I'm bushed. These confrontations just kill me, but they do open up the way to a real dialogue."

"Everything is hard work," says Ed, to his wife, and then gets up. "I promised myself I'd get around the reservoir twice before work tomorrow morning, so we'd better go too."

"Don't all leave me," says Katy, her voice higher still than when she's being polite. "I don't want to be alone." They see her eyes slide over to the Pierrots kissing in the middle of the table.

"We'll stay," says Gloria. "We can watch the eleven o'clock news here, see what the governor said."

"Sure," says Frank.

"I never want to go back there," says Florence.

Ben puts his arm around her.

"They can't forgive you for Paris," she says. "As if it gave you something they can't get at."

"Well I suppose it did," he says.

She squeezes his arm.

"Let's go home," he says. They walk down the cold street, where there are antique shops. They look at columns and tufted sofas, a directoire bed, a console with sphinxes, and a tall iron railing thick with acanthus leaves, a gate displayed as a screen.

"Dad used to have one like that," she says, pointing at the daybed.

He's looking at the railing. It's a twin to the one that guarded the courtyard at Nina's apartment on the Rue Auguste Vacquerie. "How much do you think . . ." she begins, but she stops.

Their past is all in shop windows, and they can't afford to buy it back.

"I think," says Ben, as they walk on, "that we've got something wrong. I think we have to get rid of our nostalgia if we are to make it here."

But the past is all I have, thinks Florence, it's all I ever had. "You're right," she says. And later, as the new black and silver buildings on Third Avenue roll past the cab window, she asks: "Did we come here to make it? Is that why we came here?"

"I don't remember why we came back," says Ben. Everything he knew before he left has been replaced by a picture, a photograph, a slogan.

We're lost, thinks Florence.

BEN IS OUT THAT night in bars. He's been downtown to a place where his artist friends drink, he's been midtown to a dive with plaster hams on the ceiling and ornate menus framed on the walls, and now he's with Sam way up on the West Side. Sam is a poet. Sam is a barman. His legs ache from standing all night, and he wears sandals with shaped wooden soles. Ben sits on a Thonet stool that's a little too high and too fine for comfort. "Watch it, they keep falling off," says Sam, as he hands Ben his fourth bourbon. He means the customers, but Ben pushes the bourbon away from the rolled edge of the bar with his index finger. Ben wanted slivovitz, but Goldy's doesn't have slivovitz. He remembers the bottles of Cynar in Rome, he wants to taste liquor made of artichoke and fennel, surprise on the tongue. He wants the raspberries of Himbeergeist, he wants Marillen Schnapps with the taste of tiny yellow plums.

"So?" asks Sam when he comes over. Ben shakes his head. Sam has such compassion that Ben feels his troubles are insufficient. His old loden coat hangs over his shoulders, a scarf is knotted at his neck. Sam thinks Ben is elegant. He wishes he had that frail, rattled aristocratic manner, and wonders how he could get it. Sam is earnest and reformed, and will always be young.

"I haven't seen you up here this late, ever," says Sam.

"It was hell getting here," says Ben. He knows windstorms and earthquakes, mud slides, and flash floods, but the steam at the street corners in winter still alarms him. He is afraid that if he walked into the center of one of those round metal lids he would disappear.

202

"You should get used to the subway," says Sam, a street fighter.

"Never," says Ben. "Life is too short."

Sam comes back a few minutes later. "C'mon," he says, "it's better if you get it out."

Ben acquiesces into his glass. "Anything you say," he tells the end of the bourbon. Then he looks up. "No. It doesn't have words."

"I thought you'd stopped drinking," says Sam.

"You never stop doing something you used to do. Once you've done it, that's it, that's what you do," says Ben.

"That's not true," says Sam, shaking his head. "I used to do drugs, I stopped. I used to live with Sasha, I stopped. I used to steal cars, I stopped. Man is perfectible."

"Where did you get that idea?" asks Ben.

"Self-analysis. It was the only choice I had. Life can be good, you just have to work at it."

"I'm older than you," says Ben, "and nothing works. Let me tell you, you're wrong."

"Bullshit," says Sam. He's hunched over slightly, defending his safety.

"Are you happier now than when you were twenty?" asks Ben, slowly.

"Hell, yes. When I was twenty I was in a reform home."

"You're happy now, serving drinks?" asks Ben.

"Unfair," says Sam. "Who are you to judge? I'm working on a book when I can, which is when I want to, which has become the same thing."

"And you're happy like that?" asks Ben.

"No, there's a lot more I want. But I'm a lucid, rational adult. I can't be happy. But at least I'm not crazy. For me that's a lot."

"She's crazy," says Ben, under his breath. Sam hasn't heard; he goes on, afraid that he seems to have said he's satisfied with his lot. "And anyway, things aren't always going to be like this."

"She's crazy," says Ben, a little louder. He might as well be heard.

"She is?" asks Sam, gratified that a confession is finally being offered for his compassion to fasten on to. He leans forward, passive and sympathetic: "Yeah?"

"Florence," says Ben.

"I figured," says Sam.

"Not anything I can describe. She's closed off."

"When did she start changing?" asks Sam in a low voice.

"Oh, she's always been like that," says Ben. "That's what I like about her."

"If that's why you chose her," says Sam, "maybe you're the one who's changing. Have you thought of that?"

Ben looks up, startled. "No," he says.

"Life is change," says Sam, with passionate respect for the words that helped him through. "Growth and change."

"No," says Ben, again. "Not after a while. After a while everything stops."

"You're wrong," says Sam. "Maybe you just need something new. You don't realize it yet. If you change your point of view, just a little, you'll see . . ."

"I don't think like that," says Ben.

"Hey, nothing lasts forever," says Sam. "Not anything." He puts his fist down to make the point. "If only people would realize that, they'd be a lot less unhappy."

"I happen to like my past," says Ben. "It was nice."

"You can't hold on to anything. If you love someone, let them go," says Sam.

Ben cannot be polite. "That's the stupidest idea I've heard in my life. Now what does that mean?"

"If things are bad between you and Florence, maybe it's time to end it, that's all I'm saying," says Sam, producing a cloth with which he wipes the bar; a few careful strokes, busy, and he whisks it away.

Ben sits on his stool and thinks.

"Maybe you should try to see someone," says Sam, who is back, with a beer for himself.

See someone, thinks Ben, what does that mean? "See another woman, have an affair?" he asks.

"No, see someone to talk to."

"Another woman to talk to, but not to sleep with?" asks Ben.

Sam gets impatient. "A doctor, someone who could help."

"But there's nothing wrong with me," says Ben.

"There's something wrong with everyone," says Sam with conviction.

"Oh, yeah? So what's wrong with me?" risks Ben. He can make up the list himself and faster than Sam. Old, failed, a eunuch, unattractive. In the European measure, he is no longer what he used to be, and that's a pity. In the American measure, he never became anything, and that's the sin. Caught between two ways of failing.

"Florence, I'd say. She's holding you back," says Sam.

"But I'm not going anywhere." Ben raises his voice. The assumption of progress makes him itch every time.

"You might be," says Sam, knowingly.

"Get a better wife, trade in the old model on your way up the ladder? That's too California for me," says Ben. "I left home to get away from that. I'm not . . ."

"You act as if you owe her something," says Sam, "like a debt of honor, is that it?" He's trying to provoke. If only people would take on less responsibility for others and more for themselves. His group, the group he goes to each week, is all about personal responsibility. Taking charge of your own life. "Listen, listen," he says. "I'm sure she can take care of herself. She existed before she met you and she'll exist after you."

"Long after me," says Ben. "I'm twelve years older than she is."

"It's you you should be worrying about," says Sam. He wants so badly for Ben to be like him, since they're friends. Be a little more like him. Exactly like him.

"I don't want to worry about me," says Ben. "I don't want to worry about anything."

At home Florence is having a dream. A family picnics in a forest clearing. The mother is blonde, the father dark, they are happy smiling people like the families on food packages. Two little boys in striped polo shirts and shorts run around the checkered cloth spread out on the grass. One of them opens the basket and begins unpacking thick sandwiches wrapped in wax paper. Two dinosaurs, genus Tyrannosaurus Rex, come out of the woods, attracted by the smell of roast beef sandwiches. They are bigger than the trees, higher than houses. They move fast on their enormous curved haunches as they make for the picnic cloth. The parents scatter into the woods. The dinosaurs reach for the sandwiches with ugly hands that end in pointed claws, and eat the children.

She wakes screaming, and reaches for Ben. He's not there. The light coming through the thin blinds makes the room fuzzy, white blue. There seem to be strange fibrillating hairs on the table at the foot of the bed, on the chair against the wall, on the television set, on everything. The room is a pale palpitating tapestry, present and loud with a question she cannot make out.

A few days later Jacob calls. At five in the morning. Florence picks up the phone. *"Bonjour, ma petite chérie,"* she hears. Ben winces next to her.

"Dad," she says and sits up in bed, an old reflex. Ben groans and jerks the sheets over to his side. At this hour the heating hasn't started up, it's cold. Florence considers taking the call in the kitchen, but that would mean asking Ben to hold the receiver and then hang up. Too much for a sleeping man. She whispers instead.

"Are you asleep?" Jacob asks.

"No," she says, "are you?"

"I can call back later," says Jacob.

"No, no, it's fine," she lies, "what is it?" She remembers the catalogues in the closet for months that she swore she would distribute. The duties undone.

"Nothing," he says. "How are you? How's Ben?"

"Maybe you could call later?" she asks. "It's early."

"Oh Christ, I thought it was afternoon there. Evening. I got the time mixed up."

"It's all right, Dad. What's going on?"

"I just felt like talking. Nothing. Oh, by the way, Sylvie called. She wanted to know how to find you."

Sylvie. For an instant, Florence doesn't know who he means. "Who?" she asks.

"Sylvie, Sylvie Ambelic. Suzy Ambelic's daughter. Your friend."

"Sylvie," says Florence. She gathers her nightgown into a knot over her chest, fist clenched.

Jacob's voice wavers, an effect, she thinks, of the waves over the underwater cable—no, it's satellite now, space. "She's moving to New York. I gave her your number, it was a while ago."

"I wish you hadn't," says Florence.

"You and Ben should have her to dinner. I told her you were a great cook, she didn't believe me."

"I wish you hadn't," says Florence again, and loud. Ben hisses out a "Shhh!", grabs her pillow and holds it over his head.

"What would you do?" asks Florence. "It's Dad." And once again into the phone, "I don't want to see her."

"Well, do whatever you want. I'll call soon. Go back to sleep." Jacob's voice, now meek, withdraws. Florence hangs up, full of regret. She's been mean to him and now he's hurt.

"Are you finished?" asks Ben from beneath the pillows. The hunched back is mean.

"You heard me hang up," she says.

"You woke me up," he mumbles. "What time is it? The middle of the night. Why is he calling in the middle of the night?"

"He got the hour wrong. Please don't be like that. He's getting old." Poor Jacob, he must be so alone.

"I'm getting old and people won't let me sleep," from Ben. He scratches in the covers, like a dog, to get deeper.

She pulls at the sheets. Pig, she thinks. But she can't fall back into sleep. Sylvie, what is Sylvie doing here in this bed?

Florence hasn't seen Sylvie in fifteen years.

In the next few days Florence scares herself with the thought of Sylvie. She thinks she sees her on Madison Avenue, a thin girl with blonde hair and a fur coat, and brown boots. She follows the strange woman for a few blocks to make sure, and walks past her rapidly, her head turned to see the face. Not Sylvie. She dreads seeing Sylvie and she can't wait for her to call. She considers calling her father for Sylvie's number. She wants to know what Sylvie has become and she wants to see through Sylvie to what she has become. But she connects Sylvie with bad luck, and she senses that if she saw Sylvie, everything she has built would fall apart. Everything; her safety, and Ben. The earth will crack open and this time the fires will get her.

She comes home one day, carrying food, and Ben says, "Sylvie called." Florence doesn't answer. He pushes the piece of paper at her over the table where they are eating dinner. She puts the carrot dish on top of it. Later that night he says, "Who is this Sylvie, anyway?"

"Just someone I don't want to see," she says.

He goes out later that night, and ends up with Sam again, uptown. "It would be good for her to see her old friends," says Sam in the middle of his lecture at Goldy's. Florence has taken on the character of a problem child, someone for whom one considers the possibilities. When Ben gets home Florence is still awake, reading a book about Vienna. He looks at the cover.

"I didn't know that interested you," he says.

"There are lots of things that interest me that you don't know about," she answers. He thinks Vienna has something to do with him.

The weather improves. Outside their living room, on a spindly tree that would go by the name of twig in any other place, small green boils have appeared. She is crossing the street one day, at Park. While she waits for the traffic light to turn she senses someone looking at her, and turns to see where the heat comes from. A man is in a car, a dark man. A shape to the bones that she recognizes but can't name. The lights change and the car drives off.

Sylvie calls again. Florence submits to circumstance and takes the phone from Ben.

"Do you think we'll recognize each other?" asks Sylvie.

"I hope so," says Florence. They will meet for lunch.

"I'm sorry I haven't called before, I've been getting this apartment and having to meet decorators and I've been so busy, and the life here! How do you stand the pace?"

"We manage," says Florence.

Sylvie is talking English. No matter how many French words Florence uses, Sylvie won't talk French. Her accent is Italian.

"Where have you been living all these years?" asks Florence, drawling now, to sound more American.

"Monte Carlo, and Geneva, which is deadly. So, tomorrow? I'll book at L'Arnaque, one o'clock. See you then."

L'Arnaque is the first French word Sylvie has used. Florence has no idea what L'Arnaque is and has to look it up in the phone book. It isn't there. She thinks she is having a bad dream, another one. She goes in to Ben and says: "The person I haven't seen in fifteen years and don't want to see has just given me a lunch date at a restaurant that doesn't exist." She is in a cold sweat.

"Call information," he says.

It's a new number, Sixtieth Street. How can Sylvie be so familiar with things here? Florence wonders, as she dresses the next day. She stops as she's pulling one of Ben's sweaters over her head. Maybe she shouldn't go at all. That other world will jar.

4

Sylvie sits at the portion of banquette that has become her territory in the three weeks she has been in New York. Sylvie conquers. The restaurant is staffed by young Italians and frequented by slightly older Italians. Her fox coat surrounds her; bristling gold and brown animal hairs outline her shoulders like a halo. She isn't cold, but she keeps her coat around her. Her blonde hair, which has taken on the variegated hues of a rich pelt, mingles with the fur in a way that makes men dream. They have told her so. Her sunglasses are red, and so is her lipstick, and she wears emerald earrings with gold shields dangling beneath the stones. A heavy gold chain culminates in a sapphire at her collarbone; a gold sports watch hangs loose on her wrist, under a profusion of gold bangles. The rest of her is pale-beige cashmere. The colors attract the eye, the red, the blue, the green, the gold. She doesn't return casual glances. If the men know her they come to her table, they call her name. There is no need to make an effort toward strangers.

She powders her nose often. Always a little aware of the shine, the flaw that could discredit her. You can't be too careful what people see, since there's nothing you can do about what they'll say. For Sylvie, thirty-five is a tragedy, and it's just around the corner. The spring born. She moves the mirror sideways, checks the angle and alacrity of her hair. When she was younger she was a girl who wanted to get around, and now she's a girl who's been around. Fifteen years with Marc, a miracle. It's never the man who leaves, always the woman, and she's had the good sense to keep that in mind, and stay with Marc no matter how in love she was elsewhere. Because, as her mother pointed out and still reminds her, once you're past twenty-five all the best men are taken. And the only way to poach with dignity is to have land of your own with signs that say NO TRESPASSING.

What time . . . a shake of the wrist informs her that the date is almost broken. Florence is late. She never used to be, that's not the kind of girl she was. Is? Was? Sylvie is annoyed. She is doing Florence a favor, looking her up when she has no need of her. Sylvie has dutifully kept track of every change of address over the years, relayed by Suzy Ambelic with little sighs and groans as to the fortunes of Jacob and his daughter. If she never called it wasn't from lack of fidelity; it was a faint strange boredom at the sight of the name, a lassitude that followed on every determination to keep in touch. Some kind of ancient obligation that it was no longer her duty to honor. The fact that she bothered to look up Florence shows Sylvie what a good person she still is.

One-thirty. Another Campari soda, a different red to put against her beige. "Sylvie," she hears—the *i* short, the French way—and looks up. A tall woman stands in front of her, in a man's coat. With a bare face and chopped short hair. She had forgotten how tall Florence was. And before she says hello, before she reaches up her arms for her old friend, she knows that Florence looks ten years younger than she does, as if time for her had never passed, had never been.

Florence sees the colored jewels and the fur, like walls around a face she used to know.

"We were so young," says Sylvie once Florence sits down.

As if to make another wall between then and now, to pile up the differences between them.

"I don't drink," says Florence, when the waiter asks what color wine she'll have.

"I find just a little white at lunch makes the afternoon pass like a dream," says Sylvie.

"I don't like what drink does to me," says Florence. She orders pâté and spaghetti with meat sauce. Sylvie says she must have the carpaccio. Florence doesn't know what carpaccio is, so Sylvie has to explain that it is thin slices of raw beef. "I don't think I'll like it," says Florence, "I really want spaghetti." Sylvie takes in the bitten nails with dried blood at the corners, the frayed edge of the man's sweater, the perfect, shining skin. Florence's hands tremble a little as she holds the menu. Sylvie manages to knock over her own bag, so that the contents pour out onto the floor; a wallet and an address book, a datebook, a list of dry cleaners, a bundle of silk swatches in shades of peach, sunglasses in their case, keys and hotel keys, boxes of pills, and a clutter of lipsticks and combs and little compacts lie on the composition marble floor. Florence, who sits on the outside, gets on her knees to pick everything up, because Sylvie is wedged on her banquette. "And here!" says Florence, handing things onto the table with her long arms. "I'm so sorry," says Sylvie, as to a stranger. Florence straightens up and sits down again without brushing the dust off her skirt.

"So much stuff," says Sylvie, blushing. "Between the apartment and the hotel and the school for Claudia and trying to get organized. It's so complicated."

Florence is still holding the swatches in her hand. She has never bought so much as a carpet, and these thick silks the color of cosmetics remind her of the way Jacob used to go about his walls. Her fingers take in the slub and the weave of the silks, and then her eyes take in her own fingers, hideously unfinished. Quickly she puts the swatches down. Her hands are not as good as Sylvie's walls.

"You look wonderful," says Sylvie.

"So do you," says Florence, "the fur, the jewels, you're a *grande dame.*"

"It's just accumulated," she says. "It didn't happen all at once." She looks for some corresponding thing to compliment on Florence, and can find none. Not even a watch. "Tell me about you," she says.

"Where do I start?" asks Florence. "I moved here with Ben eight years ago, you never met Ben. He was long after . . ."

"After all that," says Sylvie.

"Yes, yes. He designs printed fabrics, I translate things from the French, sometimes into French as well. We have a quiet life."

"A quiet life? Here? You mean it's possible?" asks Sylvie.

"Of course it's possible," says Florence. A congress of furs eddies around her, kisses and greetings are exchanged over her head. She turns a little, notices that the people around her are more dressed, more ably presented than they ever were in Paris.

"I'm not used to this at all," says Florence.

"So you live removed from all this, how wonderful," says Sylvie. "Do you have a place in the country?"

"We spend weekends in the country, in the summer, like everyone else," says Florence.

"Oh, where?" asks Sylvie. "I don't know which is better, East Hampton or Southampton. God, that's another thing I have got to get organized."

"Wherever our friends have houses," says Florence, "that's where we go." No house, thinks Sylvie. No jewels, no house.

"Did you know people when you came here?" asks Sylvie.

"Ben did. He went to college here, but he's from California. He has friends here."

"Do they like you?" asks Sylvie, and Florence remembers how important it was for her to be liked by Marc's friends.

"They're okay. How's Marc?"

"Fifteen years, we've been together fifteen years, can you imagine? My life is too complicated," says Sylvie. A couple is waving to her from across the restaurant. She nods, waves back, puts her hand to her ear, she'll call. "The Grants, do you know them?" she asks. Florence shakes her head. Sylvie brings out more names, people in the restaurant, people Florence has never heard of, or whose names she has read in the columns of the tabloids while sitting in a coffee shop. Strangers dressed in newsprint. "No, no," she says, "that's not my world at all."

"What is your world?" asks Sylvie, with honest curiosity.

"I don't have one," says Florence.

Careful, thinks Sylvie. No jewels, no house, no world. She has figured out that Florence is no longer rich. But from that to being completely dispossessed . . .

Florence has sensed it and gathers some achievement around her. "Ben is wonderful," she says. "He's kind. He's good."

"I don't know a single kind man," says Sylvie. "I sometimes wish I did. I just don't think kind men are very sexy. Oh God, I'm probably wrong about your man, but you know what I mean. In general."

"I don't really think about that anymore," says Florence. Sex fades after a time, she thinks. You can manage not to think about it for years. Men no longer have skin and bodies, they have faces and voices and hands, and that's it. Hands on tables.

"What are you thinking?" asks Sylvie.

"That sex fades," says Florence.

"You're so right!" Sylvie nods, welcoming. "After a few years with someone, it's just not the same anymore. There comes a point when it's just not sexy . . ."

They are speaking French, but the word stands out in English, a neon sign. Florence remembers a bar she used to see in Paris, Le Sexy.

Sylvie thoughtfully adjusts a bra strap under the beige cashmere, and goes on. Contracting her wishes to make Florence feel good. "I would love to have something simple and real, with just one person, like you do with Ben . . ."

Florence gives a little wave of her hand that means please don't think it's so great. Their eyes meet and they laugh.

"Fifteen years," says Sylvie. "It becomes a tightrope."

"A tightrope?"

"Yes, you know, a circus act. Juggling on a tightrope, throwing spangles in their eyes." And Sylvie picks up her bread roll and throws it in the air, tries to catch it, and misses; her hand shoots forward to catch the roll as it falls into her waterglass.

Florence laughs. Sylvie does too, and they both feel better.

"See," says Sylvie, "it's not easy!"

"I'm glad to see you, really," says Florence. Now she is smiling, now she is less guarded, now she is at ease.

Sylvie feels a warm impulse to tell her everything. Real friends are so rare. There are almost tears in her eyes, she has made Florence laugh, she loves her. She leans forward. "I moved here because I'm in love," she says, releasing her secret in short little breaths, and Florence suddenly sees the old Sylvie, Sylvie from before the time of Felix.

"An American?" asks Florence.

"No. Swiss. But he's here most of the time, and like this I can be near him."

"What does Marc say?"

"He agrees that Europe is going downhill, that it's essential to have a place in New York, and that we were fools not to do it earlier. Of course, he stays in Geneva!" And she lets out a hoot of laughter.

"You managed to do that?"

"I have to be discreet, but if you play your cards right you can get what you want," says Sylvie.

Florence had forgotten there were winners. For so long she has thought that hiding is the only way.

"You can?" asks Florence, low.

"It's not easy, but there are ways," says Sylvie.

A man comes to the table. He stands, legs apart, next to Florence, telling Sylvie a story about a boat, in French. It is a long time since Florence has heard a man speak French and she is enchanted. Sylvie introduces her as "my best, oldest friend," and Florence hears conviction in her voice, believes it. He shakes her hand, keeps it a little longer than he needs to, while asking Sylvie where Marc is. When he leaves, Florence can still feel the warmth of his fingers.

"He's all right," says Sylvie, "he's good. The two of you would get on."

The day begins to sparkle with possibility, the room spins slightly. "I don't need anyone," says Florence, but she is less prim, and the words sound futile to her.

"That's the best time," says Sylvie. "In fact you should come out to dinner with me and Thierry some night."

"But how did you do it?" asks Florence.

"What? Oh, moving here? God, why are you so interested in that? That's minor. The real problem will be to see the man I love here, and keep Marc happy, and the others." She won't say his name.

"Others? Other lovers?" asks Florence; she uses the New York word, the bold word for unafraid seductresses.

"*Amants*? Nobody in Paris says *amants* anymore. Someone is in your life or he isn't."

Ah. In your life. Florence wants to know: "You have others, too? How do you do it?" It sounds confusing, too busy.

"You used to have plenty of people in your life. You and your married men, your married man," says Sylvie.

Florence doesn't want Sylvie to remember anything. "He wasn't married," she says.

Sylvie sees that Florence's face has gone stony, somber, that her eyes are on the tablecloth. She thinks Florence disapproves of her.

Florence is searching, wildly, silently, for something to say. He is all around them, gigantic, looming. Felix. Change the subject, get away from this huge shadow. She can find nothing to say. The years of burying Felix under silence have left nothing but silence.

Sylvie can feel herself flush, as if she had done something wrong. "I know I must sound fickle," she says, taking Florence's hand, "but if I were happy with Marc, it would be different."

Florence lets her hand rest in Sylvie's. It is as if Sylvie's hand could save her from drowning, from fear. If she listens she won't have to talk.

"It's just that I need love to live," says Sylvie.

Florence begins to cry. She grasps Sylvie's hand harder. Sylvie's eyes are tender, despite the gold around her face.

"Me too," says Florence. "But I . . ." This can't turn into sobs. She won't let it. She pulls her hand away, smiles at Sylvie, reaches back toward her again. Sylvie has lit a cigarette.

"And you never came back to Paris?" asks Sylvie, rubbing the corner of her eye.

"No," says Florence, "there was no reason. Dad comes here sometimes."

"My mother told me everything. It must have been horrible."

"There's nothing left."

"It's all gone? Even that big statue in the entry?"

"The Kouros? He's gone."

"Your father had such beautiful things, so many beautiful things."

"It's over." On the firm ground of her father's failure, Florence can be confident. She tells Sylvie about the Etruscan couple, swears her to secrecy.

The warmth of Sylvie's hand and of her eyes makes her feel she might be saved.

When she gets home from the lunch Ben asks, "Well, how was it?"

"I got through," says Florence. "It wasn't bad at all."

5

SYLVIE HAS NO CLEAR plan. Until she phoned Florence, and for the first time in her life, she felt stranded. She was lonely in New York. Bruno does not arrive in New York as often as he used to leave for New York. He explains the discrepancy by saying, "There are places in between." She wonders whose places. It's too late to move back to Geneva; she's bought this apartment with Marc's money, she's hired the decorator, the contractor, she's chosen the paint, the wallpaper, the furniture. She has to stay until the apartment is finished.

Sylvie has friends here, but not real friends. Women with big apartments like hers, who sit on ballet committees. The women are hospitable but wary. They have noticed how ready Sylvie is to have private understandings with men, and the men are their husbands. These are rich women who travel, who know all the right gossip, and they know that Sylvie and Marc are not married, even if there is a child. They are decent Americans for whom the written word counts, and this lack of legality moderates any feeling they might have for Sylvie. Leads them to ask each other on the phone who she is, and whether she has any money of her own. God protect us from indigent immigrants, and pretty ones at that. Pretty ones who know how to smile too close to our husband's mouths. That's the kind of thing they do in Europe, where no one ever gets a divorce. In New York men are less afraid to change their lives, and quickly. Sylvie could be dangerous.

When Sylvie is with Florence, she feels she is herself again. As if her real self existed only when she was eighteen, and what she inhabits today is no more than a worn postscript.

Sylvie situates her moment of reality before she started having to tell lies, before the birth of Claudia. The essential date is the same for Florence.

"Don't you ever miss Paris?" asks Sylvie, as she and Florence hunt for new clothes in the boutiques of Madison Avenue.

"Sure, I'm homesick, but where would I go?" asks Florence in return. Sylvie can't answer.

Since Sylvie came back into her life Florence has started dreaming of the apartment in Paris, the first one, the real one. The dark green sitting room and the long wide halls. The ridged oval knobs on the windows, the moldings on the thin elaborate doors, the tiny brass light switches. Volume, color, details, are stronger memories than the various pieces, which moved so fast and never stayed the same. Only the Kouros is in her dreams, and he talks, he mutters an incoherent stream of words without moving his painted smile.

Florence wants to get back to before Julia died, to before Felix, to before the Etruscan couple, to before Michel left, to before. She is looking forward to her own past. She cannot conceive of a future better than what she has already known. Before she ruined it all.

The part of her, good taste, that is offended by Sylvie is not as strong as her desire for home, for past. She is having trouble believing her recent construct of a life with Ben.

"I have a wonderful psychic here," says Sylvie one day.

"Oh, no," says Florence, thinking: Not again. That is one trap I will not fall into.

"She's better than a fortune teller, she's more scientific. She's a lot better than Rosa."

"I don't want to go," says Florence; then: "What did she tell you about your move to New York?"

"She said it was dangerous but necessary. And that I would learn a lot."

Florence thinks it brave of Sylvie to do something that promises no more than danger and instruction.

Florence tries on knit dresses, and Sylvie notices that Florence's long legs are firm at the thighs, that her ass is small and tight, still. The eyes of one woman on another, cool and critical and a little afraid of finding perfection.

Sylvie watches her own face in the mirrors of the shops; her makeup runs after a few hours, she keeps repowdering her nose, her hair goes limp, the set of her collar is dislodged by her shoulder bag. She is younger than Florence but she looks older; and while she wants to bring Florence out of her willed drab shell, while she feels she has the power to turn her old friend into a beauty, she doesn't want it to go too far. But is there any way to control the consequences of one's best impulses?

So Sylvie generously tells Florence about the people who tend her in Geneva and Monte Carlo: the woman whose fingers can find the most ancient knots in the sinews along her spine, the man who knows just what gradations of color to put in her hair. She misses them dreadfully, she says. They are hers. When she talks about the men to whom she gave that tended body she is less proprietary; she could never call them hers. She gives Florence a few names, and names of places; to Florence it sounds a little like Madame Ambelic, except that Sylvie does not go into such details about the hotels.

Sylvie thinks of herself as what her mother called "*une grande nature*"—her appetites are big. Sometimes she tells herself there is too much of her for just one man, that she has been cursed with an excess of passion. On the few occasions she's been caught out, Marc has managed to suggest that she lacks common sense, decency, discretion, respect for others. He has never accused her of failing in some obscure moral duty to be faithful. To what? He has other women. He doesn't want his schedule upset, that's all. They stay together for dinners and holidays, for trips and parties, for Claudia. It is a life.

"And you?" she asks Florence.

"I'm faithful, and that's it," says Florence.

She is not going to tell Sylvie that she has not had a man inside her for fifteen years.

Chastity is her atonement. She wished Felix dead. Without her wish she would have had an ordinary life, children, love. She wished herself into cold, safe perdition. Passion will not be brought up again. If she lets those powers gain on her, she will die or kill. Felix's name hangs over her, a sweet transparent cloud. Poison. Eternal death.

She is silent; she appears to be discreet. Sylvie begins to think that Florence was perhaps never really wild, that she was just responding to the times when she was young. There is something bare and clean about Florence, something that strikes Sylvie as nunlike. Perhaps she can make Florence beautiful with the right clothes, perhaps she can make her desirable so that she will get away from that dreadful, sad Ben.

Finally Florence asks the question she dreads the most, the question that waits in her head every time she sees Sylvie: "So where's the baby?"

"When Claudia's school is out she'll come over. At Easter. I don't know whether to enroll her here for the third term, or let it go until next year. And I have to find a house for the summer. Really, it's all so much work."

And Florence lets her breath out, relieved. If the child, if Claudia, is just school terms and a house for the summer, if she can be reduced to Sylvie's rich woman's chores, there is nothing threatening about her. There is no Felix about her; she might even be Marc's child. But that she can't ask. She wants to believe the best; she is becoming a little giddy.

She still translates her little texts, she has even taken on more work because she is spending money fast, but the lunches and the spendthrift afternoons have changed the shape of her days. It makes her dizzy to write checks on the account she shares with Ben, but she likes that dizziness. She feels all this a preparation for another step, for good times. She feels new and eager, brittle and untaught.

Handsome men seem to be materializing all over Manhattan, wherever they go. A tall Greek stops them as they walk up Fifth—"Sylvie! The beautiful French girls are here!"—and the plural on girls, the plural on beautiful, makes Florence blush under the powder that she has started to wear, and her ears turn red.

"Do you like him?" asks Sylvie, when he is gone. "We could have dinner with him one night."

"No, no," says Florence.

"You have to take me to antique shops," says Sylvie. "I need things to make the apartment look lived in."

The apartment is cavernous rooms with a staircase that curves in an unsure oval up from the entrance hall, which is being inlaid with mosaic tile. Florence tries to show Sylvie the things she knows best, old daybeds, tall statues, eight-panel screens, heads of Buddhas, but Sylvie responds only to the instant collections, two or three of the same thing. Pillars and cones, pyramids and spheres, things to line up on a useless table against the light of a window that will never be opened. Sylvie's hands always go to the folded piles of paisley shawls that the best antique dealers keep on a chair by the door, to tempt the European immigrants.

Where Florence is attracted by wreckage, Sylvie likes things that are smooth to the touch, simple shapes without confusion. In the old, Sylvie seeks the new, ennobled by age. Florence knows that Sylvie would love the dreadful knickknacks of her father's catalogues, but she does not want to take advantage of Sylvie's poor taste and endless money. She would like to elevate her instead, educate her a little.

Florence is above wanting the kind of rewards that Sylvie's life offers, the stones on her neck and the gold on her wrists and the large collection of real leather handbags. But when she sees the lingering hands and glances of these myriad men on Sylvie, she knows she wants that, and badly.

What the well-married women of New York see in Sylvie, Florence also sees. That automatic current of intimacy with every man, mouth-to-ear stories and clasped hands and languid lids for all of them.

"Is he in your life too?" asks Florence, as another one departs from their table, this time in a Japanese restaurant frequented mainly by the French.

"No," says Sylvie, "not anymore, but there's no reason to alienate anyone."

It strikes Florence that her penitence may be too severe; it occurs to her that modesty and caution might have run their course, that there could be another way to live.

"Don't you want to really fall in love?" asks Sylvie.

"I'm too old for that," says Florence.

"Don't be stupid. You're obviously not happy with Ben, not really happy. I'd so like to see you fulfilled, don't you want a child?"

"It's too late," says Florence.

"Women have children at forty, at forty-five! What are you talking about. It's as if your life were over!" says Sylvie. "And I don't like to hear that."

Florence doesn't want a match made for her. She is just a spectator in Sylvie's life. She cannot be like her, she cannot ever sleep with anyone again, or tragedies will happen.

"You'll see, I'll find you someone," says Sylvie.

"No, really, I don't want anyone. I'm very happy as I am," says Florence.

It takes weeks and even months for Sylvie's heady atmosphere of luxury and excess to work its change on Florence, who at first thinks, "What waste," and later begins to think, "What generosity." If she looks down on Sylvie at first, she later realizes that Sylvie is what she wants to be.

Florence remembers the women in the hotel whose bodies were for sale, while she sold her tears and longed to have her body bought. It suddenly seems possible that Florence could change tables, that she could sell herself instead of her tears. A miracle could be happening. These are not just frivolous lunches and senseless spendthrift afternoons. There is sunshine and luck about them too.

"I have to be very, very careful about Marc," says Sylvie, who has explained Bruno to Florence.

"But if he has other women does it matter that you have other men?"

"Yes. It didn't matter about the other ones, but Bruno"—she lowers her voice when she says the name—"is important to me."

"But if you love him why didn't you leave Marc and go live with Bruno?" asks Florence.

"I couldn't do that." Sylvie is shocked. "Not yet. Everything has to be in place. I have to think of Claudia."

She thinks it a little strange that Florence has not asked to see photographs of Claudia, nor betrayed any other interest in the child. She decides it must be because Florence has never had a child.

Florence doesn't want to see who the child looks like.

"She's old enough to take it, if you separate from Marc, isn't she?" asks Florence. To Sylvie, this sounds a little cruel.

"It hurt me when my parents divorced," says Sylvie.

"Well, I never had a mother," says Florence. "So, what's going to happen with Bruno?"

"I really don't know, but God how I love him!" says Sylvie.

"Is there really any danger of Marc finding out?" asks Florence.

"You have to be careful. He's very cunning, old Marc. He asks questions and you don't even know what he's putting together in his head until you understand he's got it all worked out. You can't be too careful with Marc."

Florence swears to protect Sylvie from Marc. It makes her feel noble, as if she were in the Resistance.

"People are so mean," says Sylvie. "You have to be careful."

"Not in New York," says Florence. "In New York they're honest, and they're always confessing." She's thinking of Katy, of Gloria.

"They're mean in New York, too," says Sylvie. She's thinking of the wives on Park. And some husbands.

Sylvie buys Florence a watch; it's a new Italian model, in bronze that looks old. "So much more you than silver, or gold," says Sylvie.

Florence is delighted. "I haven't bothered about the time in years," she says.

"Maybe that's why you haven't aged," says Sylvie.

"Oh God, maybe I'd better take it off at once," says Florence, looking at the watch. "I have to get home, Ben will want dinner." They are in Sylvie's unfinished living room, surrounded by painters.

"Stay," says Sylvie. "We can go back to the hotel and have a lovely tea."

"I can't," says Florence, "I have to go buy the food for dinner."

Sylvie shows her a place that stays open late and sells ready-made dishes, salads with beef in them, cold chicken curries. Florence gradually stops cooking for Ben. The first time she unpacks the little plastic bowls with lids, he asks, sternly: "Are we having a party?"

"For a change," says Florence. They eat facing each other,

Ben with his nose in a book. The apartment looks sallow and dull; so does Ben. She imagines Sylvie out at a restaurant that is part of a nightclub, surrounded by adoring foreign men. Or in bed with Bruno, curtains closed, room service caviar waiting on the table.

"Why don't I get to meet this Sylvie, since she's such a good friend of yours?" asks Ben.

Florence hesitates.

A dinner is arranged. Sylvie is alone; Bruno has just left town. She is glowing, she wears a new Italian suit with shaped shoulder pads that make her torso look perpetually thrust forward, on offer, ready for sex. Her hair dangles around her face, her earrings tangle in her hair, and she tries to be nice to Ben, who claims he can't hear her over the din of the restaurant. Worse, she takes the check and pays with a platinum American Express card. Florence hails a cab for Sylvie outside the restaurant; she and Ben walk home. Florence doesn't ask what he thinks of Sylvie, but it is out before they are home:

"She's a whore," he says. "What are you doing hanging around with a whore?"

So that when Marc Grandieu arrives in town and Sylvie asks them both to dinner, Ben says, "I don't want to see her, you go."

Florence arranges for Katy to ask Ben over to dinner that night, and she buys a new dress that costs as much as a ticket to Paris. She sneaks it into the apartment in a D'Agostino bag to hide it from Ben. He goes out before she does, calling, "Have a great time," in a sour voice.

She takes the dress out of the D'Agostino bag and hangs it on the shower rail while she takes her bath, so that the wrinkles can drop out in the steam. It's thick black grain-de-poudre, a coat dress, severe and bare.

She wears nothing underneath it except for a pair of tights, and she powders her face carefully so that no powder falls on the satin lapels. She does not recognize herself in the mirror, she sees an austere and powerful woman, someone who looks neither like Jacob nor like Elise, she sees a new self.

Just before she goes out she puts on the new watch, which might be a bit clunky with the dress, but it is new and Sylvie will be glad to see she's wearing it. And since it is bronze, she goes into the back of her closet and takes out a small box, and in the small box she finds the ring. The Roman ring. She slips it on her finger and its touch, its weight, are an ancient, intimate memory.

THE RESTAURANT IS SMALL and pink, and Marc's table is the biggest
one there. Sylvie, wearing gold sequins, waves to her as she stands
by the maitre d'hôtel, clutching a small black velvet pouch.

Florence is introduced to people with long names and tight faces,
placed between an aged ambassador and Marc, which is an honor.

"So nice to see you again," says Marc, in an accent that, like
Sylvie's, floats between European capitals. His hands are large and
tanned, with clean nails. His face has begun to resemble that of a
turtle, the eyes diagonal slits, the nose pointed, the mouth small
and turned down. He must be fifty-six, fifty-seven, now, she thinks,
and I'm almost the age he was when he was a dirty old man running
after Sylvie. Marc asks her to tell him about her life.

"Oh," says Florence, "tell me about yours." She doesn't want to
talk about Ben and translations.

"Your father shut his shop, didn't he?" says Marc. "It's a pity, I
really liked that place. He always had such nice things."

Don't talk about my father, please, thinks Florence. She gives a
smile. "Yes, shut it over ten years ago, longer."

"So what does he . . ." continues Marc.

"Please tell me about Geneva, I've always longed to hear about
Geneva," she says, to stop him.

He doesn't want to discuss Geneva. "So what do you think about
this place Sylvie's found for me here?" he asks.

Me, Florence hears, what about saying "us." This must be what
Sylvie means. Careful. "You'll both be very happy there," she says.

"I think Sylvie's doing a remarkable job. American contractors are so difficult to deal with."

"Do you really think so?" asks Marc.

"It's a full-time job just making sure the decorator knows what he's doing," Florence assures him.

"I assume you've had the same problems," says Marc.

"Not really," says Florence, "but friends of mine have."

She feels strange in her new dress, she sits up straight, she watches her hands as she eats and she tries to take small, elegant bites. The ring slows the movement of her left hand. Halfway through the first course she notices that her dress gapes open, and that the ambassador on her left has his eyes fixed on her bare skin, where her breast pushes against the silk lining. She brings her right hand to her ribs, to keep the dress closed.

"Oh, don't do that," whispers the old man in French. "You were so charming."

She turns to him and sees stained skin, a pair of intense eyes full of old lust, paralyzing.

The ambassador leans into her and says, "It's rare, a woman so unspoiled." She blushes. "I was right," he says.

"Do you live here most of the time?" he asks.

"Yes, most of the time," she says.

"I am surprised we haven't met," he says. "I have been here for eighteen years."

His eyes focused on her skin at the silk, on her bare chest.

"Oh, yes," she answers, "but New York is big."

"I've found it very small, so you are a charming surprise. Tell me, who did you say your husband was?"

"I didn't," says Florence.

"I thought you were the woman who married della Valle," he says.

"No, no," she says, "not della Valle. Who is della Valle?" she continues, trying to be charming and light.

"The Argentine ambassador," he says, "to the UN, of course. Polo player."

"Of course," says Florence, which seems to her the most amenable alignment of words. "Is he here tonight?"

"I don't think so," says the ambassador.

He seems very old. Gnarled fingers, ridged hands, a habit of turning the head slightly to present the better ear. Seventy? Eighty? Ancient. Old enough to die.

"So, how have you been?" asks Marc, coming back to her. As she turns to him she feels the sudden shock to flesh along the back of her left hand; the ambassador's paw grating against her skin, a promise of further familiarity.

Florence looks over to Sylvie for advice, for encouragement, for disapproval. What does she do now? Her hand is stuck to the ambassador's, and Marc has asked a question and she can't remember what it is. Around her the old eyes in the tight faces are suspicious, judging. She should have done something to her nails.

"Oh, yes," she says to Marc. "Thank you."

Hand-sewn clothes in red and green, with matching jewels.

"What are you doing these days?" asks Marc.

Florence tries to think of something amusing yet innocuous to say. Marc helps her with suggestions: "Any trips, amusing holidays?"

"No," says Florence. "I see a lot of Sylvie. That's wonderful. The whole time." This last in case Sylvie needs an extra alibi.

"It must bring back good times," says Marc.

"Of course it does," says Florence, emphatic in banality.

"But then," adds Marc, "I'm not sure if the past is always a good thing."

Florence is surprised to hear Marc express a misgiving.

She looks over at Sylvie, whose shoulders in gold sequins swivel beneath her bouncing hair. She is talking about treasures with the men on each side of her, with the woman across from her. The man on her left just sold a Braque, the man on her right just bought a Picasso, and the woman across from her missed a Tiepolo that her decorator forgot to tell her was coming up at Christie's. The tone and method of the conversation are familiar to Florence, even if the paintings themselves are not, and she begins to fall in with them; she talks about her father's possessions as if she still had them.

Sylvie hears Florence say, "My Kouros," and thinks maybe she heard wrong all these weeks, that Florence still has beautiful things stashed away somewhere, that the bare apartment she shares with

Ben is a pretense. Sylvie cannot conceive that Florence, straight and solemn Florence, whose life she is going to magically transform, could possibly lie.

The prattle is blinding. Breughels traded for Fragonards, up and up through enormous prices and world-famous former owners.

Florence rides the conversation, is in turn awed, impressed, disdainful, amused. The ambassador's leg aligns with her, and her thigh muscle contracts, beyond her will.

Sylvie throws back her head and laughs, her eyes directed into those of a fox-faced man next to her, a sinuous being with oddly spatulated fingers. Florence watches her the way she used to watch her dancing teacher, to see what to do. She tries for a careless laugh of her own, and while her head is thrown back the ambassador's fingers reach up to catch her nape.

She finds his touch is warm, and leans back to feel it more. A message, brute blood, is carried over to her; he is an old man with a bald head, and she shudders with pleasure. The fox-faced man asks to see Sylvie's bracelet, a new gift from Marc, and Sylvie puts her hand out and rests her wrist in his, her topaz and her diamonds shining like sin. Florence sees the fox fingers close in around Sylvie's wrist, as the ambassador's leg begins to insinuate itself beneath her own thigh.

And now the ambassador's hand reaches for Sylvie's bracelet, for Sylvie's hand, and Florence finds herself thinking keep away, he's mine. He inclines the stones toward Florence.

"Do you like jewelry?" he asks.

"I used to eat emeralds," she says, telling the strict truth.

"*Une croqueuse de diamants*," he says. "Do you eat men too?"

"Ah, yes," says Florence. She lets her dress waft away from her body a little.

"Ah! The food!" says the ambassador. "I hope you're hungry."

The food is cured and marinated, sliced, filleted, wrapped upon itself around a mousse of its betters. Sprigs of thyme from turbans of tomatoes, and the sauces come in two colors, drawn into a pattern like the Bulgarian ceramics Georgie used to collect.

"*C'est pas mal*," says the fox-face.

"It's almost as good as Paris," says an old woman in red with a Texas accent.

Marc turns to Florence and confides: "They are learning here."

"Oh, yes," says Florence. "New York has become very international recently." The words pebbles on her tongue.

Her body is sliding toward the left, toward the old man.

"We're all coming here now," says Marc. "Europe is finished."

"Of course," says Florence.

"I'm glad you agree," says Marc.

An undulation in her nerves is taking all her attention. The leg is determined, and a hand has reached around the lower part of her back, where the layers of grain-de-poudre, a dignified fabric, dull sensation but allow something else in, desire.

Sylvie winks at her. Florence thinks she sees a nod in the direction of the ambassador. Surely not.

"Tell me, my dear," says the ambassador, "do you have a father complex?"

"I love older men," she says, drawn along unfamiliar rails. This must be the thing to say, the thing to do. Cheap, she thinks, cheap, cheap, cheap. The table comes into focus as a concatenation of whores and financiers, worshipers of cash and goods, everything she despises. She looks again at Sylvie; a man's hand is on her shoulder, its fingers inside her golden spangles, on her skin; Marc is talking with the woman on his right, he pays no attention to the fate of Sylvie's body. The man whose hand is on Sylvie is not the fox-face, it's the other one, with a German name. But Sylvie loves Bruno, her secret, so what is she doing with this German, and in front of Marc? And what is the use of Florence's proud loyalty? It all seems so wasteful, so incorrect. Cheap, cheap, cheap.

And cheap, she thinks, later, lying on the couch in the living room of the ambassador, her mouth around his cock for no reason at all other than he made her blood move at dinner and now she is grateful. And now she wants to be as cheap and irrelevant as Sylvie, she wants to be chattel, a whore.

He holds her face in his hands when she is finished, her eyes are half closed so as not to see him, and his voice low, resonant, he says: "You have a mouth for this." And she pulls her lower lip beneath her teeth to taste his tired sperm and opens her eyes to look at his old face, and then she rises and unbuttons the dress that she had not wanted to take off, and with her breasts suddenly pointed in the cool room, she rubs her hands on her body down to her ribs and to her waist, where she rests her hands so that her index fingers meet, and she looks at him and opens her mouth.

"Take off those stupid things," he says, pointing to her tights.

She hooks her thumbs under the elastic and pulls them down.

"The gesture was so much prettier before," he says, with memories of women long dead. "From now on, you wear stockings."

Suddenly she is embarrassed, there, naked in his sitting room. "Come here," he says, "now," an order, and she moves the few feet to the couch, and he raises an old hand and takes her pubic hair in his fingers and pulls. And then with slow careful fingers he separates it, to open her, and pulls her close to his mouth, and grips her buttocks in strong hands while his tongue darts, precise and a little cruel. She bends her knees and sighs, loud, the way she thinks she is supposed to.

"No theatre," he says, pulling away. "Don't pretend." She waits, naked, by his mouth, for him to begin again. The hands tighten around her again, this time the fingers pinch, one hard pinch. She lets out a cry. "Shhh," he says, another order.

A hand comes up on her body, pinches one nipple, withdraws. She stays silent.

"You are very beautiful," he says. She looks down at him. "Close your eyes!" she hears. She shuts them. "Good," he says.

And his mouth returns to her, where it is hot, where his tongue is sharp and then soft, piercing, pervasive.

She begins to tremble. "Stop it," he says. "Control yourself." She can't stop; her legs knock together.

A hand slaps her on the thigh. And returns to her buttocks, where it grips her tight. And he pulls her now toward him, he raises his mouth still on her sex, he pulls her forward and with brute authority he uses the back of his hands to separate her thighs, and pushes his tongue into her. A sob slides out of her. And he pulls her further to him, and with his hands pushes her down to the couch and pulls her hips to its edge. Shoulders force her legs to open. The palms of his hands pull her open and he eats her there like a fig, kneeling between her legs, short intent strokes of his tongue on her closed center.

She keeps her eyes shut.

A hand pushes her so that she falls back, and he raises her legs and sucks on her, like a baby at teat.

Her head is hot; she moans. This time he does not hear. Sweat is coming off his skull, running over his ears. Breathing short, breath heavy.

Waves inside her longing to crash, to rise, to crash.

And his tongue in her.

And then below, where she thinks it is dirty, where she does not want him to go. She tries to pull away, to wriggle away.

"Don't," he says.

His hand encircles her waist, compresses her.

A light begins to spread in her chest, a rise of everything inside her.

"Don't," he says. Hands now tight on her upper arms. Her ears are burning.

"You little whore," he says. "What do you want? What do you want? Tell me."

Not that. She can't ask for that.

"Say it." His voice a growl, cool iron, hard.

That is sacred to the memory of Felix. His tomb.

"Say it," he says.

She has to protect Felix. No one can come in. No one will. And then, from long ago, the voice inside her.

You little whore, it says. *You little whore, you know you want it. Ask for it. Ask for it.*

She bites her lips.

You little whore, says the voice again. *You know you want his cock. It's all you want.*

She raises her left hand to her breasts; when she rests it at the division of her ribs, the ring is blazing hot.

"I want your cock," she says. "I want it inside me."

"Don't tell me what to do," he says. "Beg for it."

You little whore, says the voice.

She raises her open hips to him, her shoulders back in the soft cushions of the sofa, her arms loose behind her. Her tongue lolls out of her mouth. The front of her body is burning.

"Please," she says on a shudder.

He ties his wet shirt around her head so that she cannot see, so that her eyes are hidden.

"Put your hands behind your head," he says. She feels her wrists taken in his hands, tied with something, bound. Ritual abandon. She gives in. But Felix. . . .

The voice again: *This is what you want.*

His cock grazes against her cheek, and her mouth opens for it again, but instead his mouth is on hers. It tastes of woman. It tastes of the smell of her own cunt. His tongue large in her mouth, he kisses her for the first time that night. He is soft inside her mouth, and sharp, and wide and thick and long, to the inner edges of her teeth. Smothered from inside. She breathes it in, and he withdraws.

She waits for what will happen.

The skin inside her thighs is stroked, and then once more, pinched. She does not let out a sound.

Beneath the edge of the shirt that binds her eyes she can see that he is about to kneel. His weight on the couch, between her legs, the soft sigh of the cushions.

He pulls her hips to him, grips her from behind. Something soft tries to get in. And tries again. She pushes her hips forward, she wants it. He holds her open with his thumbs, and pushes once more. Something soft collapses there.

It would be worse now if it didn't happen.

He puts a finger inside her; it invests and invades her, all sensation inside her now, around his finger. A second finger comes in, together inside they explore her, distend her. Not enough. They withdraw.

And then. She feels something long and straight inside her, smooth and cool, narrow but hard. It goes in smoothly, so high that it hurts, a punch from the inside, and still he pushes. "No," she says. She can tell that it isn't human. Her wrists hurt where they are tied. She rubs her forehead against her shoulder to move the blindfold, and at last she can see what he holds in his hands, what is being pushed into her.

A candle.

She sees his cock grown soft and small dangle from his old gray hairs.

She raises her body to protest, but he pushes her back.

This is right, says the voice.

The candle is pushed further into her.

"To keep you open," he says. He is watching it go into her slowly, and out again. And from beneath the band across her eyes she sees him grow hard, his cock rises, he pulls the candle out, glistening and wet, places it carefully on the table.

He does not need to use his knees to force her legs to open. And then he is inside her, inside the silent crypt of sex, Felix's last sanctuary. Pissing tallow on the idol.

She cries because Felix is gone. She forgot years ago that there was someone else there after him.

The ambassador follows a strange Venetian.

His rhythm is irregular, the act is brief. While she cries he shudders.

Later, he gives her a handkerchief for her face and asks her if she wants to spend the night. She hopes she will be paid. She would like to go lower than she is now, she would like to be a real whore.

She is happy.

On the way home in the cab—a fifty-dollar bill in her fist, a visiting card in her little black velvet pouch, and how she's glad—she runs her hands along the slick plastic cover of the seat.

"So where were you?" asks Ben. He is lying on their bed, smoking a cigarette in the dark. "And where did you get that dress?"

"We went dancing," she says, an excuse that was good fifteen years ago. She puts down the little velvet pouch.

"I don't believe you," he says.

"Well, you don't have to, because it's a lie," she says.

He doesn't ask her what she really did. Maybe he doesn't want to know.

In the dumb cold light of the bathroom she takes off her makeup.

The expensive dress lies on the floor. There are white crusts on its lapel. She looks at her body in the mirror, and is glad to see that there are small bruises on her long legs, and that her ass, when she turns, is small and tight.

She almost expects to see blood between her legs.

By the time she comes out of the bathroom Ben is simulating sleep, while slow combustion edges along a cigarette in the ashtray next to him.

AND WHAT SHOULD SHE do now? In the night the gigantic metal teeth of the garbage trucks keep her awake, crunching couches and refrigerators, their generators whirring at high pitch, to grind deeper. The slamming of metal jaws reverberate against the suddenly glassy walls of the bedroom.

And she lies there trying to fit what happened into some meaning. Like Cinderella she thinks of her dress hanging hidden behind the robes on the back of the bathroom door, of the visiting card in her bag. Promise of romance, waltzes, sugarwater hope. But no prince this one.

Just her own filth, maybe. An exorcism she's waited for. To release her, to permit her to go on. No, that would be too neat.

Mediocre, she thinks, feeling the polyester sheets and looking at Ben's back. His only crime loving a lesser her. Maybe everyone will die if she goes further.

She will be good. Devote herself to Ben.

She makes porridge for breakfast. It seems the safest thing to do. Irish porridge that comes in a white tin and takes three-quarters of an hour on the double boiler. Last night will not leak out and stain her life. She starts to boil the water for coffee, and then remembers the real thing, and hauls the stepladder from behind the stove and reaches up above the old jars and broken candlesticks for the espresso pot. It has been closed for so long that a sour violent smell is released as she unscrews it. She finds half a tin of Italian coffee, and shakes it messily into the funnel; a crunching black spill falls on the counter.

237

She sets out the bowls, the linen napkins, and butter in a dish, and a little plate of raisins to sprinkle on the porridge. Rich, sweet, soft baby food.

She smiles at Ben when he comes back from the paper shop with the *Times*. "Porridge," he says, "and real coffee. What a treat." She smiles again. She is wearing an old beige toweling robe, and Sylvie's bronze watch. Not the ring.

They both sit down. Ben pours maple syrup into the center of his bowl, takes a handful of raisins, a big wedge of butter. He mixes it all together and takes a spoonful. "Good," he says.

Florence is glad. She reaches for the raisins. Her hand over the plate, her fingers stroke the little brown objects, close in on some five or six of them. As she raises her hand she hears the voice.

Nothing good can happen if you take that one, it says.

Obedient, she stills her hand. In this cluster is one bad one. Which one? She puts them down on the table, and puts her index on one. This one? she asks in her head. The voice is silent. That must mean approval.

"So how were the fat cats?" asks Ben.

She does not answer. "This one?" she is asking in her head, for each. On the sixth the voice says, *That one. Not that one.*

She has five raisins on the table in a little cluster, and the sixth is near the plate, exiled. It looks like all the others. That is the bad one, the one not to take. Fine. She gathers up the rest and drops them on the soft gravel of the cereal.

"What's the matter?" asks Ben. "Are you okay?"

She is wondering what to do with the bad raisin. Throw it away so that Ben doesn't eat it by accident? Or is it only bad for her?

"Have some maple syrup," he says, as he pushes the bottle over to her.

She reaches for it. *Nothing good can happen if you have that*, says the voice.

Florence wants the maple syrup. She keeps her hand on the bottle. Maybe the voice made a mistake. It meant the raisin.

Nothing bad can happen unless you have the maple syrup, says the voice.

This maple syrup, or any maple syrup? asks Florence in her head.

No answer. She releases her grip on the bottle.

Ben has put the paper down and is watching her carefully. He's never seen her be a picky eater before. "Butter, then?" he asks. "What about some butter?"

Florence cuts a slice of cold butter off a corner of the slab and pushes it into her bowl.

"Are you feeling all right?" asks Ben.

"Yes," says Florence. The salty porridge goes into her mouth. She longs for sugar, for maple syrup. This tastes like wood, pleasant wood, but wood.

"You must've overdone it last night," says Ben.

Florence doesn't answer.

He doesn't want to ask, he doesn't. He knows those people are bad, frivolous, stupid and wasteful. He knows stories about Marc Grandieu that would choke an ox. He thinks Sylvie is trash. He had a difficult time downtown last night at Katy's; in the end it was just the two of them, and she cried on his shoulder as he sat next to her on the couch and then she grabbed for his fly and said, "You can't imagine how long it's been." He was appalled; he took a cab home fast. He was waiting for Florence so he could tell her, and then she walked in looking peculiar.

He reaches in the pocket of his jeans for the envelopes.

"Mail," he says, loud, to catch her attention.

A wad of expensive cream envelopes, with windows. Florence barely glances at them.

Ben fans them out, like playing cards. He reads out the names printed on the upper left-hand corners of the envelopes.

"Mobilization for Survival . . . Madre . . . O'Donnelly for Congress . . . March of Dimes . . . Cancer Society . . . Abortion Rights . . ." He glances up at her. "Nothing personal," he says.

"Never is," she says.

He slices an envelope open with the butter knife. "Thirty dollars," he says.

"They always want thirty dollars," she says. "Why?"

"I think it's the smallest amount they can ask for where you still get a tax deduction. Or I do."

He shouldn't have done that, he shouldn't have reminded her. But once launched into sensitive territory, there is no way for Ben to get out. He tries to change the subject.

"So, are you seeing her today?" he asks.

"Who?" asks Florence, her lower lip tight.

"Sylvie, of course."

"I don't know," she says. She is eating slowly, she is listening for the voice. Maybe it will have a message about Sylvie.

"I thought you had a translation to hand in."

"I do," says Florence, "for the tourist office."

"You'd better get it in on time," says Ben.

"I'm never late."

"No, I mean, don't be late this time."

"I know how to do my work," says Florence.

"That kind of world," says Ben, "it destroys you before you know what's happened. Be careful." Irresistible. Couldn't help it.

"I don't know what you mean," says Florence.

"I've been through it all, don't forget, I know that world. You're not equipped for that kind of life."

"Life," says Florence, standing up. "Life, world, what are you talking about? All I did was go out to dinner with my old friend and some friends of hers. What's so dramatic about that?"

If only you knew, she thinks. *If only he knew*, says the voice inside her head.

Ben thinks she is taking a shower, her usual shower. But then he doesn't hear the stream of water on the tiles; he listens by the bathroom door, and opens it to see what she's doing.

She's in the bath.

"I've never seen you take a bath before," he says. "You only take showers."

"Today I thought I'd take a bath, any objection?"

How can he object.

She soaps herself carefully. He watches for some thirty long seconds, and then leaves the bathroom, confused.

It is when you don't want that you are the safest, she thinks. How could she want that strange old man, that satyr, want him in her life or want even to see him again? That was enough, what happened was enough. But glittering behind her strange cool distance is a vague and shimmering prospect of being a woman in an immaculate silk dress, receiving an embassy. But no. Not me. I am Florence Ellis and I lead a quiet life with Ben. I am cleaner and simpler than that.

She doesn't want him, how could she want him, the skin of the hands that seems to be gloves two sizes too big, the bones sliding around inside the loose flesh. You can't love that.

But if you don't love, you can't hurt. It is safest not to love. It is safest not to want.

She knows she has to leave Ben. But she will wait and see what happens. There can be no particular plan; when she wants she does not get. She can only proceed by not wanting, by not caring. She dries herself and dresses, and goes to her desk in the living room where she finishes her translation in a few hours.

She cooks a careful lunch for Ben, who asks, "Aren't you going out to see Sylvie today?"

She hasn't even called Sylvie. She doesn't feel she has to, she doesn't even want to. And she cannot imagine fitting her mouth around a formal thanks for the first part of the evening.

"I think I'll take the stuff downtown, since I'm finished," she says to Ben, her head around the door of his study. He nods from his table. "Need anything?" she asks. He shakes his head. She closes the door.

He remembers he needs some more gold paint, and she could stop in at Sam Flax and get it. He goes out into the living room; her bag is by her desk, a folder is ready on the chair. She's not in the bedroom.

"Florence!" he calls.

"I'm here, what is it?" comes her voice, resonant and watery, from behind the bathroom door.

"What are you doing?" he shouts.

"I'm taking a bath, what is it?"

"Nothing," he says; he's forgotten the gold paint, and he returns to his study. Ten minutes later his head snaps up from the intricate fronds he is outlining on black paper with a silver pen. She already took one this morning, it was this morning, wasn't it?

Today she wears lipstick and it is early spring. Men look at her in the street, but the men who are on the streets of New York in the middle of the day are not anyone a girl would want. Puerto Rican delivery boys, small retired men in gray coats, Irish panhandlers with raw necks, male models with long hair, and, doubtless, AIDS. If she were with Sylvie that tall man in an overcoat, paying a cab in front of the Mayfair Regent, would turn and smile and invite her to dinner.

She delivers her translation, and on her way home, she finds herself near the legation of the ambassador's country. Not that he would necessarily be there; not that she wants to see him.

The men in the street. It's as if she knew them all, that one with the checked shirt and the big hands counting his change meekly before the bus arrives, and that one with a roll of paper under his arm, and those two, young ones in bright yellow and green, crossing the street against the light and arguing, bodies as compact and dangerous as medicine balls, all of them, that black man with a shopping bag and a drooping coat, all of them have had their mouths on her, have drunk from her.

She sees a limousine draw up alongside her, slowly. Its windows are dark, she cannot see through the obsidian rectangles of blackened glass. He could be in it. She tries to peer in and remembers that she isn't even sure what he looked like.

Poor Ben. Kind Ben, good Ben, quiet Ben, slow Ben, meek Ben. The more she feels part of the men on the street, the further she feels from Ben. How could he know, understand, accept? Poor Ben, condemned to the light.

She doesn't want to see the ambassador, she doesn't want to see Sylvie; nonetheless, it is six-thirty and buses are roaring up Madison Avenue in a thunder of painful gears, fumes rise, gray-haired women climb the Lenox Hill in tight pumps, and Florence is in front of Sylvie's hotel. It would be particularly mean not to go in, ungrateful just to leave a note.

The lobby of Sylvie's hotel is down a few steps from the street. A tapestry representing a hunting scene is attached to the far wall; men in evening clothes are behind the reception desk. "Miss Ambelic?" the clerk repeats after her, "Oh, Mr. Grandieu's suite. Certainly." He listens into the phone for a few seconds. "She says to come right up."

The elevator is too fast. Florence is always a little surprised that there is no charge for riding the elevators. Fifty cents, thirty dollars, a nominal fee, the lowest . . . The sum of thirty dollars sets something off, and she is angry at Ben. Poor mean Ben. Showing off about his tax deduction.

"Darling!" Sylvie's superlative. The suite is a mess. Two bags stand packed by the sofa; Marc is leaving for California, then Japan.

Marc stands in the corner, on the phone; the spiral cord is drawn almost straight. Sylvie hugs Florence, rests her arm on Florence's shoulder, pulls her into the bedroom.

"Thank God," she says, eyes rolling up in their sockets.

"Wasn't he leaving today anyway?" asks Florence.

"You never know, though. He almost decided to stay another week, and that would have been a disaster. Then he suddenly was told he had to be in Paris tomorrow, and that would have been worse."

Florence doesn't ask why. She sits on the edge of the bed, prim, neat. A pair of tights lies, softly synthetic, on top of the quilted bedspread. Mechanically, she reaches for them to roll them into a ball.

"The maid will do that," says Sylvie. "Leave it. Let's have a drink. Let's have some tea," and, while waiting for room service to answer—"So, did you have fun last night?"

"Oh, yes," says Florence. "Thank you. It was . . ."

"They loved you," Sylvie says. "A bottle of champagne, and tea for two, and potato chips, and—are you hungry?"

Florence nods. She loves the hotel's little sandwiches.

"Me too," says Sylvie. "Sandwiches, and maybe some cakes. Quickly, please."

Marc is at the door of the bedroom. "Nothing I like so much as the sight of two women on a bed," he says.

"Oh, Marc, stop it," says Sylvie. "Come on in. So now what's the plan?"

"I'm definitely not going to Paris. It's just not on my schedule, but someone has to get the—I'm sorry, Florence, it's so nice to see you again. How are you?"

Florence has stood up, so as not to be one of two women on a bed. There is seemliness. They peck each other's cheeks. His skin is firmer than the old man's. He isn't that bad after all. Better a man should grow into a turtle than a bulldog, a basset hound, a vulture.

"So what are you going to do about it?" asks Sylvie, impatient to get all directions and schedules sorted out.

Marc is looking into Florence's eyes. Florence is looking straight back.

Sylvie is in the bathroom, brushing her hair. What is it out there, some sort of showdown? She drops a bottle of perfume on purpose. "Ouch," she shouts, casually.

"Ma chérie," Marc cries out. "Are you all right?"

Sylvie doesn't answer. Two ounces of Joy are spreading out on the floor. Jagged edges of a glass called crystal but that never grew in caves are pointed up at the ceiling. She pushes the debris aside with her foot, comes out, and tells Marc, "You have to ring the maid. Something slipped."

Marc picks up the phone and asks for the maid.

Florence is struck by the spectacle of such uneven rhythms. She folds her hands together and sits down on the bed again. She hopes they might have a fight, she'd love to see a real couple fight. Unless they throw things. That would not be nice. Nor would shouting, no. She waits. If only there were a magazine in here, but the one thing to read seems to be a bound copy of some promotional thing about New York.

"You don't want to go to Paris tomorrow, do you?" asks Marc.

"Paris?" Sylvie's voice is husky, slow. As if she's never heard the word before.

Florence gets up and collects the hardbound tourist magazine from the table where it is displayed, and opens it to a story about the wine cellars of Bordeaux country.

"My!" she says. "I translated this. It's for the French tourist office."

Marc and Sylvie are staring at each other, and Sylvie looks away. Paris indeed.

Marc turns to Florence. "I didn't know you worked," he says.

"I work, of course I work. This is what I do."

"How interesting," says Marc.

"Oh, no, it's really not interesting at all. It's actually garbage, but it . . ." She was going to say it pays the rent, but she doesn't think the word rent comes into a conversation with Marc. He is less menacing now, there is a freedom about daylight; or maybe there is just a freedom since last night.

Sylvie has picked up the phone again. She talks very loud. "You say he's coming tomorrow? Oh, well, then, I absolutely have to be there. With all the fabric? But how wonderful. Yes, I'll be there at ten, waiting for him."

"Who's that?" asks Marc, turning now toward Sylvie.

"The upholsterer. So you see, I can't possibly go to Paris."

"It has to be back there tomorrow, the day after."

"Well, can't you just get a courier to take it? That's what you usually do."

"Not with a Renoir." Marc goes toward the door into the living room again.

"A Renoir?" says Florence. "A Renoir has to go to Paris?"

"Shhh!" says Sylvie.

"Oh, I'm perfectly used to that," says Florence. "What do you think my father had me do all those years, and Michel? Back and forth to Italy, what do you think that was about?"

Marc has paused in his retreat.

"This isn't a fake," says Sylvie. "Marc has it on approval from a gallery. But I don't like it, so it's going back."

Florence catches her breath on the word fake.

Marc leaves the room. "I just have to make one more call," he says.

Sylvie jumps up and puts her arms around Florence. "Darling, I didn't mean it like that, I swear I didn't. Really, you know that. I'm so sorry, please don't take it badly. Your father never did that."

"You're right," says Florence. "He never did. You know it, don't you?"

Sylvie is distraught. The last thing in the world she ever wants to do is hurt her friend. Ever, ever. She brings her back to the bed and sits down beside her.

"Everyone loved you last night, you know? Mirabel White thought you were so beautiful, and Ginny McGrath wants us to all have lunch together . . ."

Florence is listening for a man's name, but it doesn't come.

"The women," she says, with a peculiar little laugh, "the women liked me."

"The women are very important. If they don't like you, they can block you every step of the way. So it's a good thing that they like you. Listen, Mirabel wants you to come to a dinner she's having week after next."

"But she doesn't know me," says Florence. "Was she the one in the red dress?"

"No, the green one."

"Why did she ask me?"

"You want the truth? She needs an attractive extra woman," Sylvie says, with a giggle.

"An extra woman?" asks Florence. It's such an old-fashioned notion.

"*Ma chérie*, it's as good a way to start as any. Better than being with some old toad you can't get rid of."

What does she know? wonders Florence. Sylvie feels her grow rigid. She wants to give her something, make her feel better. "My darling, do you want to go to Paris?" she whispers in Florence's ear.

"Paris?" Florence repeats, as if it were an alien word for her as well.

"Just a quick trip. On the Concorde. Very fast, there and back. Though you can stay as long as you want." And because Sylvie is a diplomat, despite her gaffe, she adds: "It would help me. Otherwise he'll send me with his precious picture, and I'll miss Bruno. Wouldn't you like that?" And she adds: "We'd get you a room at the Ritz. You'll love it."

Let's play this Cinderella shit straight through, thinks Florence. Already she's got a joker in her pocket. Cinderella isn't supposed to fuck the first toad that comes along. She's supposed to wait for the prince.

"The Ritz," she says. "Ben used to love it."

"Oh, no," says Sylvie, "Marc will never pay for two tickets. This is just for you. Your reward."

"Reward?" asks Florence.

"Why," says Sylvie, "for all the bad years you've had."

Marc comes back into the bedroom. "I've just had an idea," he says. "Florence, my dear, would it amuse you to go to Paris for a couple of days?"

"You could see your father," says Sylvie.

Florence stands up, and Marc comes over to her. She prefers that this should be between her and him, a private understanding between them. She has been longing for one of those, and if it has to be with Sylvie's Marc, too bad. Sylvie called her father a forger, and Sylvie has Bruno anyway.

"Come next door, we'll talk about it," he says, his arm around her, and he leads her to the couch in the living room. She knows just what to do on a living room couch now.

"Do you have a place to stay in Paris?" he asks.

No, wait, Sylvie is her fairy godmother, Sylvie said the Ritz.

"Ummm," she says, pulling a little away from him on the couch. "Not really."

Sylvie stands at the door. "I told her, Marc, that we'd put her up at the Ritz. For a couple of days."

Not that she would do anything against Sylvie. Sylvie is her friend.

"There it is," says Marc. In a corner is a wooden rectangle, several feet across and two feet wide. It is thin and shallow like a briefcase, and closed with brass clamps.

"Do you want to see it?" asks Marc.

"Oh, really, no, I don't have to." Florence can be as cool as anyone. Or is it cooler to want to see it? What the hell. The Concorde.

"I'm going to Paris," she tells Ben when she gets home.

"Running away," he says, but it doesn't sound as funny as he meant it to.

"I have to take something over for Marc," she says, making it sound important.

"Errand girl, how chic," he says. "Is Marc providing a wardrobe as well, or just the ticket?"

She doesn't answer that one. When the messenger arrives half an hour later with the ticket from Air France, she hides it. She doesn't want Ben to see that it's the Concorde.

"So when are you going?" he asks. She is sitting on the bed, dialing Paris to tell her father she's arriving.

"Tomorrow," she says. "Any objection?"

He shoves his hands into his pockets. "No, none at all," he says. "When are you coming back?"

"Just a few days, relax, oh . . ."

"What?"

"Don't you think it's exciting? I haven't been for eight years. What do you want from Paris?"

"Where are you staying?" he asks later.

"Sylvie and Marc have arranged some hotel for me. I'll call you from there."

The Ritz would sound too mean.

8

IT HAS BEEN SO long since she was on a plane that Florence doesn't remember if she is afraid of flying. She would like to be sure she will be safe, but she doesn't know who to ask. She looks at the bookshelves as the sun goes down and wishes that Ben had an *I Ching*. Ben is garrisoned in his study, he doesn't want to talk.

Florence begins to pack. Three black sweaters of Ben's, an old tweed skirt . . . and the new dress, hastily pulled from behind the bathrobes and patted flat at the bottom of Ben's old suitcase. What else? She doesn't want to call Sylvie to ask her what to wear to the Ritz, so she phones Deborah, who travels on business.

"I'm going to Paris," says Florence, trying to sound casual.

"My God, you're finally doing it," says Deborah. "I have to tell you that I completely approve. Now is the time to get out."

"Get out? Of New York? Is something about to happen?" Florence is alert to the prospect of disaster: Indian Point melting down, the radioactivity skating down along the smooth pioneer water of the Hudson and into the jagged city. "Has something happened?"

"Maybe you've just woken up, that's all. Although I love Ben, God knows I love him, that was going nowhere. Listen, you never looked better, and, let's face it, you've got a couple of years to get yourself a really good man. Someone who can take good care of you. Now, where are you going to be living?"

"I'm only going for a couple of days, Deborah."

"I thought you said you were leaving."

"I'm going to Paris for three, four days. That's all. It's very unexpected, and since I haven't been in years, I wanted to know . . ."

"Three or four days?" Deborah sounds appalled. Florence thinks she has to reassure her.

"I have to take something to Paris. It's got to do with Sylvie," she says. Her father's training compels her not to mention the Renoir. So she adds, to flesh out the story—"On the Concorde."

"On the Concorde?" says Deborah. "Who's paying?"

"It's business. Sylvie's boyfriend. It's something they want me to do. They're paying."

"Nothing's too good for you these days," says Deborah. The effort to be nice strains her voice. "The Concorde."

Florence tries to be detached: "Sylvie says you can see the curvature of the earth from up there."

"I hear it's real claustrophobic," says Deborah. And she adds, "Have fun. Maybe you'll meet someone up there. Call me when you get home."

Florence leans over the suitcase, to listen for the voice. It usually comes from a little to the right, above her. But there is nothing to hear. Suddenly she is terrified of this flight, of the trip. A plane like a pencil that goes at twice the speed of sound, but it doesn't seem to affect the people who do it all the time, the rich people. But then the rich people are no longer human. Living mutants, weakened by speed and alcohol, unable to fend for themselves, marooned by their money. They require constant care, they're tuned to a pitch so high only dogs can hear their engines. Like Sylvie. She is not one of them.

She is scared. Who can tell her that it won't crash? She stands up. What a way to die, before anything has happened. The degree of fear she feels makes her understand how much she wants again, how very much she wants. Is there any way to know that she will get it?

The phone rings and it's Sylvie. "I wanted to thank you," she says.

"It's nothing," says Florence, with misplaced modesty.

"Marc wants you to come in the morning to collect the picture, and the papers. He's sending a car for you that will take you to the airport after you've come here. It'll be there at ten. Do you need anything?"

"Like what?" she asks, carefully. Sylvie in the role of executive secretary, and her in the role of beneficiary.

"Oh, clothes, the address of my hairdresser, anything like that."

"No, no thanks," says Florence. She remembers the fortune teller, the scientific psychic. "Oh, what about your . . ."

"I have a jacket you can borrow. It will look great on you, it's a little big on me. I'll give it to you tomorrow morning."

"And maybe you could give me the . . ." The name of the fortune teller, the name of the fortune teller. So she can tell me I won't crash. Even though she doesn't want to give in to this weakness, even though she doesn't want to fall for that again. She longs for someone who will tell her she is on the right path. Someone who will wave her on.

"I know, you want the name of the hairdresser. I'll give it to you in the morning. See you about ten-thirty, then?"

Ben is making no noise in the study. She knocks on the door. "Would you like dinner?" she asks.

"Oh, you're still able to cook," he says, head bent over his table.

She keeps her voice light. She is not running away. Nothing will change.

"What do you feel like eating?" she asks.

"I'll just go up and see Sam later, I'm not hungry," he says.

"I'm only going for a few days," she repeats from the doorway, to convince one of them.

She eats two boiled eggs standing up in the kitchen, her feet bare on the cold concrete floor. She thinks of how many times her recent excesses would have paved the kitchen floor, and grows dizzy. Maybe even carpeted the whole apartment. The bank statement hasn't come; when it does, my God, when it does she'd better not be here. The only reason her checks haven't bounced is that Ben keeps all his money in the checking account.

Fear of death is replaced by fear of Ben. He will say "my money," and ask how she can be so irresponsible. When she isn't at all like that, this isn't her character. It's just as well she's going.

But still she wants advice. She washes her egg dish, and dries it and puts it away, so as to leave no trace of her dinner. In the living room she finds herself facing the bookshelves. Her index finger goes out to *The Confessions of Lady Nijo*. She pulls the book, a small paperback, off the shelf, she will take it with her. Confessions and Lady. If only there were someone to tell her what to do, what was going to happen. She carries the book with her into the bedroom, and leaves it on the chest of drawers.

Ben comes in, changes his sweater, pulls the skin of his face tight with his fingers in the mirror, watching her reflection.

"I think it's great you're going," he says. "Will you bring me some Knize Ten? You get it at the American pharmacy on the Rue de Castiglione."

"I remember," she says. If only he weren't sweet it would be easier.

It hits him right in the chest, her remembering. "Do you want to come up and see Sam with me?" he asks.

"Up there on Ninety-fifth Street? You must be joking. No." She wants to say, stay with me, I'm going away tomorrow. But it's only for a few days. But I haven't been on a plane in years. And this isn't even a plane. Help.

"Have fun," she says, and blows him a kiss.

The car that takes her to the airport is upholstered in velvet, and there is a bar by her feet. She wears Sylvie's jacket under the old tweed coat, and it fits her in such a way that she feels held. She didn't take the ring; she left it at home in a drawer. She plays with the knob that controls the radio, and is surprised to find the songs she knows. A velvet car should have an exclusive frequency, the radio station of the rich.

The Renoir, in its plain brown box, some half a million dollars' worth of hundred-year-old paint, is wedged by her feet, taking up the floor space. The papers are in her bag. Everything is in order, but the discrepancies of value and money jar her. She tries to hear the voice but her head is now so full of the rustle of money that the voice is lost. She looks at Sylvie's bronze watch; she is on time. "It's not Sylvie's," she says to herself, "it's mine."

The Concorde has a special lounge for its customers, who are exceptionally well dressed and strangely idle. Florence will not let go of the picture, but hands over her coat. "You get it back in Paris, you don't need it on the plane," says the stewardess, who goes on to collect bags and briefcases from the other passengers.

Florence is given a glass of champagne and shown a seat. In three and a half hours she will be in Paris, eight years ago. How can an all-knowing mind have determined this world? The passengers stand up and walk onto the plane, empty-handed, like the condemned or kings. Only Florence struggles, because she will not let go of the picture.

The plane seems small, and the windows are tiny. She is seated in the first cabin. The painting in its box is taken away from her. She straps herself in and tries to look out the window, but she cannot see through the thick layers of plexiglass. The stewardess hands her another glass of champagne. The plane starts to whine, and goes forward fast, and faster and faster. She remembers taking off at Nice as a child, in a plane that went so fast she cried. This one goes faster. Pushed back against her seat, and then tilted up as the luxurious rocket takes off. Precise, surgical speed: the inconsiderate universe of the very rich. All those dead dinosaurs up the rocket's ass, twisting time backwards. And then the green numbers on the neat black panel in the wall begin to change, hover at 0.97, 0.98, 0.97, before turning into letters: MACH 1. Spacewriting. She cannot hear the sonic boom, that is for the others. She imagines biblical fishermen down below, gripping the sides of open boats on waves turned suddenly vertical by one large crimp in the basic frequency of sound. A lobster appears in front of her, cooked, dressed, claws aloft, waving from a china dish. "Lunch?" inquires the stewardess.

She recoils from the prehistoric snack, but the only gracious thing to do is accept. As she bites into the stringy white meat she finally has the courage to look around; there is no one next to her, and only one woman across the aisle. "Is the plane empty?" she asks the stewardess.

"No, but the flight to Paris is less popular than the flight to New York. Because of the time."

"Why?"

"We land in Paris at ten-thirty at night. In the other direction, it's like magic. We leave Paris at eleven and we get to New York at nine, two hours before we took off. People prefer that. They gain two hours. It's the speed."

Florence has always hated speed, mistrusted its way of crushing time, its casually monstrous way of ingurgitating space. Country roads vanishing under the wheels of sports cars. Julia's young men with the fast green cars. Do young men still have sports cars? Didn't the oil crisis put a stop to that? This is luxury now, this rocket pencil lined in molded off-white plastic, with narrow seats and pointed headrests. This is luxury, this antiseptic fear. The letters on the board have given way to numbers again, and then MACH 2 is spelled out on the board.

Mach 2, that means we're going at twice the speed of sound. Just a guess. If Mach 1 breaks the sound barrier, what does Mach 2 break? The Concorde itself, I suppose. The plane begins to vibrate, and the background noise, already a loud hum, reaches a stuttering pitch. Her feet are boiling, and she reaches beneath her seat to feel startling heat from a hidden furnace. She looks out but there is not even a wing to see, this is a folded piece of paper they are flying in, and the light out there, wherever that may be—everywhere, since they are burning across the planet with their mad speed—the light is fading, it is twilight over the compressed hours that exist only for Concorde travelers, sixty thousand feet up over the Atlantic. Twice the speed of sound and the wax is melting, her wings will fall off. "Stop, Stop!" she wants to scream. "Stop!" Her forehead is cold and wet; the stewardess offers more champagne. "No," says Florence, firmly. If the plane goes down she has to keep a cool head to save the children. But there are no children on the plane. She looks up at the panel again; 1.98 it reads. No more Mach 2. There are no children on the plane, and if the plane goes down everybody dies.

"I'll have some more," she says, holding her glass out to the stewardess, who is coming toward her again.

There is nothing she can do but sit back. To be so helpless is almost comforting.

Florence gets up to pee. Aware of herself in the tight jacket, of the length of her legs, of her hips as they graze the seats that she passes. The stewardess shakes her head; no, it's back there, behind.

Florence turns and goes to the back of the plane. To her left is a thin man sitting with a briefcase open on his knees. Well, at least one of these turkeys works for a living, she thinks. His body seems to be a good shape, his legs as long as hers, longer. How handsome, she thinks. He glances up at her.

An amazing thing happens: he gives a smile, a startling smile. As unexpected as safety. She smiles back but does not modify her progress toward the toilet. And when she comes out, she watches for his head, for his face, and he looks out over and behind his seat to see her coming, so she looks away.

She is not about to be picked up on a plane. Even on a Concorde. She takes the *Confessions of Lady Nijo* out of her bag and opens the book at random, cracking the spine with both hands.

"That kept coming to mind," she reads. "Will I live to cherish." She closes it quickly. The stewardess offers more champagne. What is this machine I am locked into, this narrow seat, this constant drinking, this pretending that everything is fine? She asks for coffee and opens the book again, but because she seems to have hit it right first time, perversely, she does not open it at the first page but darts into the center again, for more instruction. "Away," she reads, "but he told me to remain for a while."

This is an act of faith, but random faith. She reaches out for her fear and cannot find it. What will I do without my fear?

When the plane lands, there are tears in her eyes. Bless God, she thinks. She hasn't felt this way in fifteen years.

The passengers are given their elegant attaché cases and their end-of-winter coats. Florence waits for the Renoir to be returned to her. A small gathering of people at the Concorde's door, eager to get home to their hotels. The tall man walks past her seat, and turns. She stands up and is helped into her coat by several stewardesses. She stands straight, so straight that her head almost touches the ceiling of the plane. The wooden case gripped in her right hand, her shoulder bag over the left shoulder, she walks toward him. He smiles at her again, and wipes his forehead.

"I hate flying," he says. "It absolutely terrifies me." He continues, without a break: "What are you doing tonight?"

"Tonight?" she says.

"It's ten-thirty. Tonight. Do you have plans?" Gentle, a little timid. Blue eyes, how strange, she thinks blue eyes are ordinary, but not these, and hair that is blond, turning gray.

"I have to do something with business," she says, and then pulls her meaning around a little, to let him in. "But I'm free for dinner. Nobody knows I'm here. Except something I have to do at customs."

I am not making sense, she thinks.

"My driver's meeting me," he says. "Can I give you a ride into Paris?"

"I'm being met too," she says. "But it's business." So he'll know there's room for him.

They walk together along the ramp and into the deserted baggage hall. The light is weak, a special subtlety for Concorde passengers or a failure of power. He pushes his silver chariot with both hands.

"You were working hard on the plane," she says. "What do you do?"

"Science," he says, "difficult to explain."

A crouching little nylon bag appears on the conveyor belt, and he reaches for it. Next to it, her initialed suitcase borrowed from Ben. A present from Nina maybe twenty years ago. Rich person's bag. "That's mine," she says, wishing it didn't have to be a lie. "That is the bag of the man I live with whom I don't love anymore, whom I never loved," is too precise.

"Your bag?" asks the stranger.

"More or less," she says. "That one."

He picks it up easily. "So light," he says. "You travel with nothing."

"Well, almost," she says. She is dragging the Renoir in its box next to her.

"Can I help you with that?" he asks. She shakes her head. The few other passengers have collected their bags—big bags, full bags, multiple bags—and are headed for the customs men. She doesn't want the stranger to know what she has to do with the Renoir. She isn't sure herself, she has to take the papers out of her shoulder bag and find the name of the person to ask for. "What's your name?" she asks. She doesn't want to think of this person as the stranger, she thought of Felix as that.

"Paul," he says, and she wants to ask for the rest of it. He seems impatient to get out of the customs hall, he looks at his watch. "You're sure you have a ride?" he asks. She nods. "May I call you in an hour?" he asks.

"Yes," she says, distracted. "I'm at the Ritz."

"I don't have your name," he says with a smile.

"Florence Ellis."

"I'll call you in less than an hour," he says. "There's no traffic at this time of night."

"Good," she says, a little sharp. Why does he want to see her?

Her hands are sweating around the papers Marc gave her, and she feels small palpitations in her chest. Everything is in order, she hopes. The mad idea that Marc and Sylvie may have plotted to get rid of her by laying a trap—no, she doesn't believe that at all. She finds the head of customs, who normally should not be there that late, and shows him the typed forms and notarized identification papers. He signs, nods, leafs through, offers her a cigarette in his prefabricated office that is hinged, at the corners, with dull white metal. He stamps some of the sheets, takes half the papers, and gives her the rest. *Très bien,* he says.

On the far side of the glass wall a man in a cap holds up a piece of board with Florence Allice written on it. She nods at him. The driver takes her suitcase, and leads her to a Mercedes in the concrete parking lot. She keeps the Renoir.

The car drives through the Place de la Concorde. Of course, she thinks.

The first thing that happens at the Ritz is that the concierge hands her a message. "M. Paul will pick you up at eleven-thirty." She looks at Sylvie's watch: it's eleven-fifteen. Not entirely happy about this. She wants to look at her room, which turns out to be high in a corner of the building and so angled that the gray-green column of the Place Vendôme is squarely placed in the center of her window. She wants to run her hands along the satin tapestry that covers the bed, weigh the tassels that end the ropes that hold back the curtains.

This is a room for millionaires. She opens the suitcase, surprised to find in it exactly what she packed at home last night. Takes out a clean silk shirt and some black trousers, takes them into the huge marble bathroom, takes a quick shower, runs her hands through her wet hair, and looks at herself in the mirror.

She should call Jacob. The important thing to do is call Jacob.

The phone rings; the concierge informs her that a gentleman is waiting for her downstairs.

She'll call Jacob tomorrow.

The elevator is mirrored, set with trellis, so as to look like some garden pavilion, a gazebo for lovers; she finds herself hoping that the stranger will be waiting with a bunch of flowers, white and pink flowers; the elevator is made for a girl going to her first ball.

She steps out with an expectant smile on her face and sees only the concierge, his head bent over the telephone.

The concierge looks up, sees her, points to his left, and she follows his hand down the steps to the main lobby, where there is no one but a stocky security man in a gray suit, scrutinizing the darkness of the Place Vendôme through the prism of the revolving door. Florence goes down the few steps and looks out, trying to remember the square. But it was not on her itinerary when she was young, it is part of another geography, a different Paris.

She turns and looks down the wide hall, and there, bent toward one of the illuminated display cases, peering at gold and diamonds, is the tall man from the plane. Paul, that's it, Paul.

It's a quarter to midnight in the Ritz Hotel. He turns and sees her, and smiles, but it's no longer the smile from the plane, it is a practiced, earthbound smile, common commercial currency. He's just a tired businessman out for a good time. She feels a brief disappointment. A businessman in a gray suit with pouches under his eyes. No magic prince. The only magic thing about him, about her and him, is how fast they got to Paris. And that's technology, not magic.

"Well, here we are," he says.

"Did you say you were a scientist?" she asks; maybe that can be his magic.

"And so fast," he says. "Yes, I am."

She comes nearer to him. She is watching his face, watching his skin. She wants to know what he's made of. He steps back under the assault.

"Where do you want to go?" he asks. "Are you hungry?" He is ready for just about anything; he knows it, it's part of his charm.

She is not hungry: A waving lobster and too much champagne. A sudden headache. She reached for her fear in the Concorde and could not find it; now she reaches for the voice, and cannot find that. Everything has been burned off her by speed. Here she is, dressed as an easy companion, cheerfully anonymous in her pants and striped shirt, deliberately unremarkable. She looks like the kind of girl who'd do anything; to her own dismay, she finds there's nothing she wants to do.

The dispassionate, conversational notes of a piano from the bar suggest a solution to this inadmissible lack of fire.

"Let's just go have a drink in there," she says.

And a talk. Get to know each other. She doesn't want to get to know anyone, but since the voice has gone, she will have to listen to the man. She allows him to precede her to the table, and dislikes the cut of his suit.

The bar looks too much like a cigar box and not enough like a boudoir. She needs garlands on the walls, sculpted flowers, a foam of bows and bouquets, cupids blowing on her to heat her up. Instead, there is a dark-brown gravy of male luxury, Prussian blue and polished wood.

They have just sat down in chairs that are too low and too comfortable for dignity when the pianist, with a coded flourish, begins to play a waltz; the stranger's head snaps up. "Did you ever see the film? This is the music. 'Fascination.'"

She hears wrong. "Satisfaction?" she says.

"'Love in the Afternoon,'" he says. She wonders if he would pay her to sleep with him, maybe that's what all this is about. Going lower. "Audrey Hepburn and Gary Cooper, I think," he continues, "and it happened in this hotel. There is some obstacle that keeps them apart."

"There always is," she says.

"And then there's a happy ending. They run away."

She gives a disgusted little snort.

"You don't believe in happy endings?" he asks.

"I believe in substitutes," she says; "I don't think there's ever a real ending, God just changes the subject."

"You mean you do," he says.

"No, no, God," she answers.

"You blame things on God," he says, "that's not fair. Maybe he's got other things to do."

"Why are you taking his side?" she asks. He calls out to the waiter for a bottle of Cristal. "God and champagne," she says. "What a combination."

"What do you have against either of them?" he asks.

"They just sound odd together," she says.

"You mean God is sacrifice, and champagne is money, evil Mammon," he says.

"Well, not sacrifice, but purity. And champagne is sort of a sin." What else is he doing this for but to get some quick sin. It's all she can think about, his money. So she sneers.

"How very young," he says, amazed.

"How old do you think I am?" she asks, trying to see her reflection in the mirror.

"Twenty-nine," he says.

She smiles.

"All women are twenty-nine, once they aren't twenty-nine anymore," he says.

"I thought you were supposed to flatter me. Isn't that what a man does when he picks a woman up?"

"I don't know, I don't usually do this."

"Of course you do," she says.

"Well, do you want to eat dinner, or not? I'm hungry."

His wrists protrude from his cuffs. His arms are really very long. He eats peanuts by the handful.

"Didn't you eat on the plane?" she asks.

"I was working," he says.

She leans back in her chair and their eyes lock. Warmth rises inside her, and with it a kind of giggle.

"You look like a happy person," he says. "Tell me about you."

She is thinking of the hookers in the hotel bars. She puts her shoulders back so she will look a little more like them.

"There is nothing to tell," she says.

"Well, what are you doing here?" he asks.

"Here?" She looks around the bar. "I'm not really sure," she says.

"Well, what brings you to Paris?" he says. It sounds like any one of Sylvie's friends. Travel. Leisure. Expensive distance.

"Pure chance," she says. "I don't know, fate, luck."

"There's no such thing," he says, "only statistical probabilities."

"Well, what are you doing here?" she asks.

"I go back and forth all the time. . . . But tell me about you. What do you do?"

"I don't do anything at all," she says very loud, and repeats it. It sounds so comfortable to be idle. Lazy, languid, attractive. Does he want to sleep with her or not? She's ready to despise his lust, but where is it?

"So what was the business at the airport?" he asks.

"Oh, that. Nothing. A favor for a friend." She wants him to believe she is the kind of woman who lands in the Ritz at regular intervals, she wants him to think all this is hers. An hour in this hotel and already she wants it to be part of her life. Luxury breeds dependence faster than love.

"Where are you staying?" she asks.

"The Plaza," he says. She manages to feel superior to him, because she's staying here. "I think the Ritz is a better hotel," she says. She knows she's being stupid; she can't stop: "My husband," she says— Ben will be her husband, for the purpose of this impersonation of a rich woman—"always stayed here. In the past."

"You're married," he says.

"No," she says quickly, "we're not. I mean I'm not."

He's watching her and smiling. All right, all right, she'll explain:

"It's a painting," she says, "a painting I had to bring over for a friend. A favor."

He nods. "Now that you've done that, what else are you going to do here?"

"Why are you so interested?" she asks.

More peanuts. The backs of his hands are tanned, his fingers are long. If only he looked more like someone she knew, so that she could imagine . . .

"I'm interested in you," he says.

How ridiculous. "You don't know me," she says.

"Maybe that's why."

Two interpretations to that one. Because there's everything to know. Or, if you knew me you wouldn't want to know. Me.

He twists a little in his chair and is suddenly very still, looking at her.

What is he doing? she thinks. Gray-blond hair, pale eyes, what is so different about him? Why is she sitting here with him? His eyes on her, watching her, she knows, even when she turns her head now to look at the other men sown about the bar, any one of them equally adequate companions, why this table and this stranger from the Concorde? There is no reason. She can feel the pressure of his eyes on her, as a radio signal, a vacillating call for an answer.

"You were saying?" she says, turning back to him, with a sharp voice.

But he says nothing, doesn't answer, merely goes on emitting a radiance, pinpricks of light that are questions, she can feel them all over her, like gnats. Calling up something inside her, desire, but she doesn't want to desire him, why bother, and with desire comes its twin, that says keep away, that says—

"I don't dare look back at you," she says, her chin on her chest.

He laughs.

"What's wrong?"

"That's not exactly the kind of thing a woman of the world says."

"I'm not a woman of the world. I never said I was."

"No, I didn't think you were," he says. "That wasn't the attraction."

"So what was?" she asks. It is not possible that all you have to do is get on the Concorde in a borrowed jacket with a painting under your arm.

He leans forward, elbows on his knees. Stop looking so enchanted, she wants to say, you know you're not enchanted, you're just trying to get laid. "Well, for one, you were praying," he says.

"I was scared, it's normal," she says. "Anyway, I stopped after a while. I just gave up."

"Why?" he asks, playfully.

"I don't think He was listening. And there was nothing to do to help the pilot."

"There never is. Unless you're in a private plane."

"No thanks. What a nightmare. You have one of those?"

"Sometimes." He looks at his watch. "It's very late, and I have to get up at dawn. I think I'm ready to forgo dinner."

"In favor of what?" she asks, tensed, defensive.

"Sleep," he says. "As simple as that. May I call you, back in New York?"

She finds herself blushing deeply. "I couldn't give you my number," she says. "We're just two people who met, that's all."

"Just say it once," he says. "I have a perfect memory for numbers. If you only say it once it's not a sin."

He was supposed to wrestle her to a hotel bed, use her, and vanish. That was the way she thought it was supposed to be. She's ready for anything, but not respect, good manners.

"You won't like me one bit if you see me in New York," she says. "I wouldn't bother to call."

"Let me decide, do you mind?" he says.

She decides to be brave. She is not Cinderella and he is not a prince. "All of this is nothing to do with me. I don't belong here. I'm not part of this."

"Of course you're not part of this. What would you be if you were? A potato chip? A piano tune? A cocktail napkin?"

"I don't mean the bar. I mean the whole thing. I'm just running an errand, that's all. You can't possibly be interested in me."

"More and more, I think," he says.

He is rich and blond and handsome and taller than she is; he is intelligent and aware of her, and so oddly anxious to please. There has to be a trick. Or if it is hope, she can't accept it. "Well, Deborah, I met this fabulous man on the Concorde and he wouldn't leave me alone, and now we're . . ."

And anyway she has a painting to attend to upstairs. She has the duty to at least feel the box, make sure it hasn't been opened. She has to get upstairs.

They shake hands by the revolving door. Stay, she wants to say, come upstairs, look at my magical room, let's have a picnic looking at the column. His hand is warm and she wants to keep it in hers. It's the first time they've touched.

"Have fun in Paris," he says.

"Oh, it's just old business," she says. "I'll be home in a few days." What if Ben answers the phone? Well, so what? He won't call anyway.

Alone in the elevator she finds she looks haggard under the neon ceiling. Why didn't I ask him any questions? She knows nothing about him.

She opens the window wide. The stone symmetry of the square is almost like music, with just one jarring cement note rising above the roof on the far side. She climbs down from the terrace and tries to open the box. Maybe if she knew what the picture represented, she'd know what she was doing in Paris. Sylvie had said, "Just flowers." The clasps are locked. She'll never know.

Just as she's going to sleep, the phone rings. It's Paul with no last name. "I just wanted to say goodnight, and sleep well," he says.

"I'm asleep already," she says.

"Take care," he says. "I'll call you in New York."

9

SHE WAKES UNDER LINEN and mohair, enclosed by water-gray silk walls, bounded by tassels and gilt-bronze wall lights. The breakfast tray is of pink linen, the rolls come in a silver basket. She sneaks a quick look at the tray itself, to see what it's made of. Plain wood veneer, a disappointment. Ritz is written on everything, and the word itself becomes a chant inside her. Ritz, Ritz, Ritz, diamonds and rich hermits confining their life to a single room, with services blowing in like crosswinds. The body she puts in her bath seems a better body than the one she used in New York, and she calls for a blow dryer to give her hair some shape. And she puts on new stockings and high-heeled shoes, and Sylvie's tight black jacket over a new short skirt, and then she feels armed enough to call her father.

A young man comes to collect the picture; she hands it over unexamined. She goes downstairs in the bower elevator and steps out into the square. There is sun, and the pale stone of the buildings seems filled with light. She knows that her Paris is across the river, that this square is the shopping version for the happy rich, but who says she can't be one of them? She wanders past windows of watches with roman numerals and crocodile straps, and buys a length of black lace to use as a scarf. Or a mantilla, should she be called upon to attend a state funeral in a Catholic country. Anything is possible for a woman who lives at the Ritz. Sylvie said, "Stay three, four days." She hopes they will change her life.

She crosses the street and goes into a man's tailor, where Jacob and Michel used to buy their shirts. She pushes her hands up to her wrists into cool piles of silk scarves, as if she could wash her hands in the colors, in the foam of soft silk.

She buys five pairs of knotted elastic cuff links, for Ben. A little souvenir to apologize for having to come back here first. Should it be five, should it be six? No, five: the sixth raisin was bad. She goes to the Swann pharmacy and buys a big bottle of Knize Ten for Ben. She unscrews the top and takes a sniff. A wonderful, compelling smell, immemorial sap, comes from the bottle.

By twelve-thirty on her first morning in Paris she has accomplished every errand she has come to do, and she has spent her two hundred dollars. Jacob will be able to give her more money; he has got to be as well kept and prosperous as the Place Vendôme. That is what all of Paris will be, now. It all depends by what door you came in.

She realizes she has cleared her schedule of everything but Jacob; she realizes she wants Paul to call again. She isn't sure if he is staying in Paris or proceeding elsewhere, but just in case, she is free to see him. Whether it was his call or some strange alignment that took place in her sleep, the man she couldn't look at has become the man she is looking forward to.

She is happy. "They've doubled the streetlights," says the cabdriver, and she sees that the Place de la Concorde is now crowded with *réverbères*. They go over the bridge, and the world constricts to the gray buildings she knew so well, to the black trees, the slow walk of retired professors under the budding trees, the little yellow dogs. The driver is Vietnamese, Korean, Chinese—he has never heard of the Café Flore.

"There, there, here, wait, you've passed it," she shouts. Once out of the cab, she stops at the terrace.

The terrace has been arranged in some peculiar way that doesn't fit memory, yet is familiar enough to be sinister in its new configuration. The old single chairs have been turned into little double seats set out facing each other, like booths in a dining car.

She's home, this is her Paris. But the light and hope she felt on the other side of the river have been drained away. This is where she was bad.

The empty seats reassure her, because the caning is still yellow and green plastic, but the full ones are disturbing, because there is not a single face she recognizes.

Deep breath, and she goes into the café itself. It has become smaller and more emphatic, as if someone had drawn thick black lines around the picture in her head. The paneling is bright new wood, and the mirrors on the walls have been resilvered with a heavy hand. We were blurred in those mirrors, she thinks, and now that the real faces are gone, the reflections are too sharp. The seats are still wine-red imitation leather, but the room is definitely smaller. They have added something by the bar, an interference.

A waiter faces her. *"Bonjour, mademoiselle,"* he says. She looks into his eyes to see if he recognizes her. He called her *mademoiselle,* so he might have, since that's what she was when she came here. But she has moved into an age when the waiters say *madame.* Thus if he says *mademoiselle,* he must be using his memory . . .

But his face means nothing to her. He smiles, though. Perhaps he was less fat, perhaps he had more hair, perhaps his eyes were brighter then, when she used to sit waiting for Sylvie. Or maybe, with the smile he's got now on his face, he's new but he knows who she is. Perhaps the Flore possesses a collective memory into which new waiters are plugged when they are hired.

She sits, not at her old table, but facing the door. Suddenly afraid that she won't recognize her father. But no, he was in New York three years ago, nobody changes in three years, and it is her father. She orders a coffee from the waiter she may or may not know, and then from her right she hears an unmistakable electronic beep. The cashier is talking to another waiter, who is manipulating the keys on a terminal that has replaced the old cash register. "It's very practical, you're right," says the waiter, "but I could swear it hurts my eyes." So that's the Flore's memory, blinking green on her right. A brand-new memory, but only for numbers.

He sees her through the glass door. He often forgets how tall his daughter is. He thinks she looks tired. And elegant, which puzzles him. For Jacob his daughter is indolent and depressed, unbathed, given to Indian scarves and plastic brooches. The spare woman with cheekbones at the table is a little forbidding. His own daughter.

His hair is white. He wears a striped shirt, slick like silk, and good beige tweeds. Half season. He takes her hands and holds them tight, and sits down facing her. Too late she remembers the mirror behind her. His eyes have drooped a little, spilling outwards. The face is almost the same, and despite the sad eyes and the white hair she finds him very handsome.

"Your hair's white," she tells him.

"I stopped dyeing it," he says. "It was becoming ludicrous." His head moves a little to the side, so he can see his face in full. She could shift to block his view, they could play at that. His honesty touches her.

"Oh, Dad." Tears at the corners of her eyes.

"Don't cry." He gives an impatient gesture with his hand. "Don't cry."

She could tell him everything. How life seems to be changing, how she suddenly wants to fly. He would understand. Instead, she tells him about Sylvie—"See, aren't you glad I gave her your number now?" he says—and the Concorde and the painting, and room service and three days. The four days.

"But what are you going to do here? Do you have business here?"

Why does everybody ask that?

"I thought I'd see you," she says. "Are you very busy?"

"Well, I'm very flattered you came all the way over here just to see me."

Well, who else is there to see? she wants to ask, Felix is dead and our old life is dead. Am I supposed to look up Delaborde and find Michel? "You're the only person I want to see," she says.

"So how's the Ritz?" he asks.

"Beautiful," she says. And she means it. "You have to come over, we can have dinner in the room and watch TV with one eye and look at the column with the other."

"Taken over by Arabs," he says. "Arab taste."

"No, really, it's not that bad. I never stayed there before, I never knew it before."

"And the painting? What was it?"

"I don't know. The man from the gallery came this morning and took it away."

"You used to be more curious than that," he says.

She wonders what he means. "Not really," she says. "I'm happier not knowing, a lot of the time."

He orders a glass of wine, and takes her hand in his. "Some surprises are good," he says. "They're not always bad."

"Maybe there comes a point when they stop being bad," she says. She wants so much for everything to be good that at first she doesn't register that Jacob's palm is swollen, the fingers fat under tight skin, the whole hand almost round. He's gained a little weight, she tells herself, while she says—"How's business?"

"Very big in Germany," he says. "That was a good surprise, there's a good surprise for you. And the people I have working for me, making things, they're good."

"Good, good," she says, as if repetition of the word could make it true.

"Very good," he says. "By the way, how are you for money?"

"Well"—she gives a little laugh because it is so reckless—"I just spent the last cash I brought. I don't have any."

"That's all right," he says. "Things are really much better. You came on a good day." He pulls a folded wad of bills from his jacket pocket and holds them on the table. He pulls off some six or seven brown notes, and hands them to her.

"How's Erghi?" she asks as she puts the money away in her bag.

"He's in prison again. That whole thing's fallen apart, it did years ago. There's no future in the past."

"But if it's not the past, then it's fakes."

"My catalogue isn't fakes, it's what you in America call collectibles. Objects. Not fakes."

He thinks she's being precious.

She thinks he's betrayed himself, and therefore her. Betrayed his past, the way he brought her up.

"You'd like to be able to talk about my collection," he says. "You'd like to be able to show people the Kouros, you'd like to walk by my shop. It's not possible anymore. All that had to go, and it's just as well. Life must go on. I've survived. Do you know how many pieces I sold in Germany last year? Do you want to know?"

"No. No, Dad. I'm sorry." His hair is awry and his eyes intense. She's never seen this in him, the fury, the justification. He used to be so reasonable, so meek.

"You'll see, I'm going to do a tie-up with a big store, stores across America. A special shop. They're going to bring me over to do personal appearances, to lecture. You'll see."

"What store?" she asks.

"You'll see. I can't talk about it now, but you'll see."

She's scared sitting there facing him. She's scared to be alone with him, for reasons she doesn't understand.

"You look very good," he says, pushing his hair back off his face. "Something must be agreeing with you."

She watches his face carefully and smiles.

He goes on: "I want to take you out to a nice lunch. Where would you like to go? Think of a really nice place."

"I don't know. I don't know if I'm hungry."

"Well, we'll take a walk and you can think about it." He takes out his glasses, peers at the computer check in the old Bakelite plate, and puts some money down. She picks up her bag; he pulls his jacket forward before he stands up, and she follows him out the door.

"So how's Ben?" he asks.

She has her nose up, reaching for the air. "Ben," she says. "Oh, Ben."

He takes her arm. "Maybe that's run its course. It's been a long time, you've been together a long time. Nothing like that really lasts."

"It was never like that," she says.

"Watch it," he says, as they come up to a brown smear on the sidewalk. "Filthy."

"The pavement is so beautiful, though," she says, "the way the stones are cut." She looks up at the apartments with shutters and wrought-iron balconies, and down at the water running in the gutters. "It's so beautiful."

"It doesn't take much to make you happy," he says, "the Ritz and a sidewalk full of dog shit."

"Nature," she says.

"So is there someone else?" he asks as they cross the street; two red cars have stopped to let them go by.

Someone else. If only there were. She wants to tell Jacob about Paul, but the two red cars seem to be a menace of some kind, and what is there to tell? She doesn't answer.

This was where they walked with Julia. Florence tries to see her striding along with them, in her gray leather coat, swinging her old black handbag. In dark tights and low shoes. She takes her father's arm to get to Julia's flesh. "Remember," she says as they walk down the Rue Bonaparte, and he's thinking the same thing.

"She used to like to come over in the spring," he says.

"She used to say you always had to leave something in Paris, so that you always had to come back," adds Florence.

He glances over at his daughter. "You're looking more and more like her," he says. She feels a sudden nervous pounding in her chest. To cover it she asks, "Where are we going?"

She realizes with alarm that he is headed down the Rue Jacob, to where the shop, his shop, used to be. Until she left Paris she spent her time making sure Jacob never went near the old shop. He walks faster; he is determined.

She grabs his arm. "I'd love to see the Place Furstemberg," she says.

"It's the other way," he says.

"Oh, Dad, I really want to see it. It's where Bertha used to take me to play, remember?"

"I don't remember," he says.

She pulls his arm. "It's the one place I want to see. I dream about it at night. Let's go there, please, for me?"

He slows his steps. She feels the strength of his will as she never has before; his whole body leans forward. It's another two blocks to the shop. "Please?" she says again.

He stops walking. "But we have to go to lunch," he says, in a voice as small and pleading as hers.

"We can have lunch afterwards," she says. "Let's go sit on the benches under the trees. I'd love that so much."

She has her arm linked in his, and she is conscious of pulling him. She talks to distract him, talks about New York, about the apartment, about Ben and the table he keeps moving.

"Here we are," says Jacob, sounding weary.

She finds herself calculating how long she can keep him there. They sit down; she is watching him. He's lost the neat finish he used to have. His shirt gapes open a little, the Indian scarf in his breast pocket has a red smear on it. It might be jam. The toes of his shoes are scuffed. "So, how do you like your square?" he asks, and she looks up and around her, and her mouth falls open.

All around them—it looks like Julia's office in London. Every window in the square is twice the size it used to be, and every window displays printed fabric: flowers on watered taffeta, tiny stripes. She is besieged by decorators' showrooms, fabric shops. "What's happened? This used to be all private houses, apartments. Why have they all gone into the same business?"

"The decorators moved here," he says, "probably because it's pretty."

"It looks like Third Avenue," she says.

"Everyone has to make a living," he says.

"But why do they all have to do the same thing?" The flowers and stripes and spots and repeated chinoiseries are so eagerly, so ingratiatingly displayed, where she used to play.

"Come on, we'll have lunch," says Jacob.

They go to a small restaurant full of coffeepots that opened when she was fifteen.

He holds the menu to his chest and says, over it, "I found some letters from Julia the other day . . ."

She is looking at the menu and notices how cheap the dishes are. Maybe he isn't doing as well as he says.

"Letters from Julia," he says again, "where she talks about you. You may want them."

"Yes, I do," she says. She wants to ask: Did she say she loved me? Did she ever say she loved me? It's like reaching into an old photograph, trying to touch the dead face in black and white, to touch the departed, the beloved.

"We used to eat here with her, when she came over," she says. Why can't Julia be here now, why can't Julia never have died? One of them is in exile in the wrong dimension, in the wrong place.

Jacob orders a bottle of champagne and explains to the waiter that he is celebrating his daughter's return. The waiter, who is new, professes surprise that Jacob should have a daughter. Florence thinks that Julia would never shout for champagne and tell waiters what was happening in her life.

"*Oui, en effet, il y a la ressemblance,*" says the waiter.

Go away, thinks Florence. She wants to ask: Did she say she loved me? but she doesn't want to hurt her father's feelings.

"So, what happens after you go home?" he asks as they eat.

"I don't know. The same, translations. Ben."

"I'm going away in a few weeks," says Jacob. "To Turkey."

"Turkey? A dig?"

"I told you, all that is finished. No, it's because, well, you know. It's cleaner."

"Cleaner? Turkey?"

"The boys are clean there." He says it very quickly, eyes on his food. "Not like here, you never know what you're getting these days. Too dangerous."

She tries to slide into the old mode, but she doesn't fit, she can't do it. "You mean you don't want to get mugged"—obviously not the right word, "by some toughs?"

"That's not what I mean. This new thing, this new thing has made one's life more precarious. *Le SIDA.*"

"*SIDA?*" she asks.

He's getting impatient, he doesn't like having to explain it. How can she not have heard . . .

"The gay plague. They call it that here. Wrath of God. The Catholics are delighted."

"Oh, AIDS," she says. Katy had a friend who died of it. But AIDS is part of New York, part of the ugly present in New York. AIDS can't exist in Paris.

"They have it here?" she asks.

"Of course they have it here," he says.

"In America," she says, "in America, a lot of men have just stopped having sex. Stopped completely." She says it with a touch of ugly righteousness.

"They're mad," says her father. "Mad."

Oh God, now she has to save him from that, too. "Maybe it's an idea, though. Restraint. Until they find the vaccine. Just not doing anything at all . . ."

"You'd hate me if I gave you that kind of advice," he says. "Hate me."

"Well, I'm just telling you what people are doing. So you'll know." She's timid now.

"I'm shocking you," he says, and he's petulant, he's rolling the soft white part of his bread roll around on the tablecloth, rolling it into tiny gray balls.

"Oh, no, not you, Dad," she says.

"Just because you get old, you don't stop wanting. But I don't pay for it, I've never paid for it," he says.

She doesn't want to hear this. He had the wine at the Flore, and now a glass, if that, of champagne. He can't be drunk. But what he says keeps rolling off the edge of propriety. Clean boys, it sounds so dirty. Paying for it. Everyone has to make a living. He's saying all the wrong things. He's not the person she wanted to see. There's no wit, no complicity, no charm. He's gone crude and sad.

"I think in America people have a lot of discipline." She looks up at him for approval, and goes on: "You know, they just make up their minds about something and then that's how they live," she says.

"That's because they aren't sensual," says Jacob. "That's because they don't know about temptation. Irresistible temptation."

"Well, they fight it," says Florence, "they fight it because they have a goal that goes beyond that, beyond just pleasure."

"It's not beauty," he says, looking across at her, straight in her eyes. "Some people are irresistible temptation. That's not the same thing as being beautiful. It's something more than that."

He's looking at her so hard that she feels entitled to ask if she has that beauty, if she could be irresistible temptation. But that's not something you ask your father. That's not something you ask your father when he's gone crude and sad.

"Irresistible temptation. It's the only reason to keep going. If you give in to it—and you must—your life falls apart."

"And if you don't?" asks Florence, hoping to present the Puritan argument from the New World. "I mean, there are more things than just flesh."

"If you don't," says her father, "you might as well be dead."

10

FLORENCE WAITS UNTIL SIX to call Ben. After lunch with Jacob she went home to the Ritz—home to the Ritz, she likes the sound of that—to have a nap, and woke to the tea and petits fours she had ordered for five-thirty.

Jacob will come for dinner at nine, downstairs in the restaurant he says is called L'Espadon.

She calls New York.

"Darling!" she says, the *a* very wide, but her voice is tight.

"Where are you?" he asks.

"In Paris."

"I know that. Where are you staying?"

Florence doesn't answer.

"At Sylvie's apartment?"

"She doesn't have an apartment here."

"Well, where? Florence, I was up all night. I'm exhausted. Don't do this to me. Where are you?"

"You were working hard?"

"Yes," he says. "A series I had to finish. My eyes are killing me. Not that you care."

"I'm at the Ritz," she says.

"Really." He feels himself sinking. And then the questions to make it his: "Is Roger still there? And André at the message desk? What floor are you, front or back?"

And she tells him, and can't remember the name of the concierge, and she's having dinner with Jacob tonight at L'Escadron.

"L'Espadon," he says. "L'Espadon."

"Well, I never lived your life, I don't know all those names," she says, impatient.

"You are now, so you'd better learn," and he hangs up, furious.

Jacob waits for her in the hall, looking at the same nuggets and diamond chains that Paul was examining just the night before. She wears the new black ambassador dress, with the black lace scarf so that she won't gape naked at table with her father.

"Where is it?" she asks. He takes her arm and leads her to the back of the lobby, and down a long corridor full of shop windows. She wants to look at all the merchandise as they walk by, but now it's his turn to pull on her arm, to make her walk so fast she barely registers. . . .

Ivory razors, trader beads, flagons of cologne, embroidered sweaters, lizard shoes, leather toilet cases, amber boxes, peach robes, straw hats, fur collars, coral netsukes, lapis bowls, cloisonné dishes . . .

They sit on the far end of the dining room. The chairs are hand-hewn rustic versions of Louis XV armchairs, with little brass hooks on the armrests for ladies to hang their handbags. Jacob is wearing his blazer and a clean white shirt. He scratches at her lapel with his thumbnail: "Something, but it came off," he says. Her hand covers the mark and comes away.

"You look just wonderful," he says.

"Like Julia?" she asks, before she can stop herself.

"Why Julia?" His face goes red. "Yes, like Julia," he says.

"Am I like her?" she asks.

"You'll have a happier life than she did," he says.

"How do you know?" she asks.

"You won't make the same mistakes. You can't," he says.

His forehead is shining with sweat. He seems to want to tell her something, and she waits through the small talk and dinner, but nothing comes. The bill is brought to their table after coffee, and Florence waits for her father to pay.

"You can sign, can't you," he says. "Since you're a client."

She reaches for the bill as if she meant to pay all along. She doesn't know what Marc will make of this, fourteen hundred francs on her bill, she couldn't very well ask them in New York if her treat included extras. Florence Ellis, she signs. She looks around the room and wishes Paul were with her at another table. She is still waiting for him to call.

In the three days in Paris she sees Jacob for lunch and dinner. She picks him up downstairs from the apartment on the Boulevard Malesherbes, but refuses to go up. She does not want to see the rooms they shared for two years. No. She is able to ensure that they limit their movements to the Left Bank and the Ritz Hotel. Drinks and meals are put on the bill; some days he has cash and some days none, and one night he asks her for two hundred francs, cab fare home. She gives it to him from the money he gave her, thinking, It's only fair. He wants to take her to see his workmen, but somehow there's never time, so he gives her one hundred new catalogues that she swears she will scatter around New York, in stores and what he calls gift shops.

One day he takes her to a shop with his kind of merchandise, antiquities. "You'll like this," he says.

"What?" she asks.

He pushes the door and precedes her in. In the back of the shop is a marble form about five feet high. She can't tell what it's supposed to be.

"Look carefully," says Jacob.

"It hasn't got a head, I don't know," she says.

"Try," he says.

The body of a swan against the body of a woman, a headless Leda with the swan clamped tight against her body, and all along her back and on her legs and on the swan's sculpted wings are little hands, stuck like leeches to the marble.

"I don't get it," she says.

"It's an interesting notion," he says, and she's so grateful to hear him talk in the old way, a detached connoisseur, "that neither Leda nor the swan had anything to do with it, and much less Jupiter. The little hands belong to Cupids, and they're the ones who set the whole thing up."

"But why would they do that?" asks Florence.

"Ask the sculptor," says Jacob.

The day before she leaves she goes to the Samaritaine for sheets. If nothing else she is going to bring back a pair of real linen sheets. Even if they are doomed in the Chinese laundry, she will have slept on real linen for a week or two. Only the moment counts, Concorde lesson. Sensuality, Jacob's lesson.

She finds a pair of white sheets in a material called Métis, half-breed, half linen and half cotton. With an edge of little holes. As she stands in line to pay she sees a face she knows.

A stocky man with a beard, dark eyebrows. Short, somehow un-grown.

"*Bonjour,*" she says.

Delaborde looks over at her. "*Oui?*" he says, curt.

"*Je suis Florence Ellis.*"

He pulls his head back just a little, and then: "I didn't recognize you. You've aged well. I would never have thought it."

Aged hits her as an utterly inappropriate insult. Aged, her?

"What are you buying?" she asks.

"Sheets," he says, and holds up packages of pink cotton.

"Me too. I live in New York."

"I haven't seen you in what, ten years?"

"Sixteen," she says. "Sixteen."

"You left. You were ill. There was some drama."

Does he know? she thinks. The five-hundred-franc notes sticky in her hand.

"André's in New York too, do you see him?" says Delaborde as he hands a Visa card to the cashier.

"André," says Florence. "I haven't thought about him in years."

"He never became a photographer," says Delaborde, as if that were a tragedy. "But he sends me postcards."

"You're still working," she says. She means it as a compliment, despite what he said about her looks. But he takes it as an insult.

"Why shouldn't I work? Did you see my exhibition at the Grand Palais?"

"I live in New York," says Florence again.

She pays; he seems to be waiting for her to have finished.

They walk through the department—dust mats, carpets, brooms, oilcloth hung like dead game on sticks.

"Still living off your father's antiquities?" he asks.

"No. I'm married. My husband is a designer," she lies.

They walk down stone stairs, between banisters daubed with gilt paint. And out past stainless steel cutlery, men's perfume, rubber watches.

"So, you're happy," he says. "Life in New York is good?" They are standing on the pavement, where work uniforms are sold from stalls, and felt berets, feather dusters, vacuum cleaner bags.

"Oh, it's okay," she says. "It's very ordinary."

"You were crazy when you were young," he says.

They cross the street toward the Pont-Neuf. She's hugging her sheets and thinking how she used to carry heavy things for him, how that was her job.

"Are you free for lunch?" he asks.

"I'm going to join my father," she says. "I'm here to see him."

"Is he well?" asks Delaborde.

"He's better, thanks," she says, and shakes his hand, and proceeds along the bridge to the Left Bank before he can ask her what was wrong.

Sylvie calls and asks her to collect a bracelet at a jeweler on the Rue de la Paix. "And you should get stuff there," says Sylvie, with sublime indifference to Florence's lack of cash. "Alex will give you good prices, he's a friend."

Florence noticed that Jacob carries his money loose in his pocket. She goes to the jeweler and picks up the bracelet and sees a money clip. "Of course," says Alex, a man her age with a cleft chin and curly hair. "You can pay next time you're in Paris." She has it inscribed that afternoon: J.E.

"Thank you, my darling," says Jacob when she gives it to him, and he shoves it in his pocket and quickly wipes his eye.

They are walking back to the hotel after dinner. This time he paid. She wanted to keep the present till last.

"Have you found Julia's letters yet?" she asks. She wants them.

"Not yet. I swear I saw them a few weeks ago, but I just don't know where they've gotten to."

Out of reach again. He keeps pulling Julia out and then hiding her again.

"I loved her," she says. But the words can't help. "I miss her now. I miss her more here with you. I loved her so much."

"Me too," says Jacob. "She was the only woman in the world."

She tries to conjure up Julia walking with them, Julia, who would be sixty now. That's impossible to believe. Sixty. Would she have put on weight, would her hair be brown or gray or bottle beige? Florence never thinks of Julia in New York, she never saw Julia there. Maybe that's why the city is so flat and empty. Paris waits for her to come back. Here in Paris Florence feels Julia's absence as if it were new. She came here for advice, and Julia would have told her what to do. No one else can.

And then Florence remembers Rosa. She should have gone to see her. It's too late: she should have seen Rosa and had her future told. Then she might have a future again.

Rosa was right, right about everything. Everything except the man in the car with Julia, the mysterious man.

"Did anyone ever find out," she asks, half in her own thoughts, "who was in the car that day, the day she died?" She has forgotten this wasn't public information. She has forgotten it's something Rosa said.

"With Julia?" asks Jacob.

"With Julia, the day she died. In the car with her."

"It was Felix, of course. Felix Cooper," he says.

Silver birds take off along the water, gulls and cormorants, and the sky is so bright even though it's late. The pavement lurches like a wave.

"Watch it, don't fall," he says. Jacob sees his daughter twist on her ankles, wind like a screw. She grabs his shoulder.

"Your heels are too high," he says.

"I have to know. Tell me, please."

Her face is ghastly white.

"Know what?" asks Jacob.

"About them," she says.

"Oh Lord," he says, "it's not important, it's all so long ago."

"He was with her? With Julia?" She doesn't want to say his name. "Did they live together?"

"I don't want to talk about it . . . I've tried to forget it. Don't bring it up now."

"But I have to know. Who was he?"

"Oh, please, Florence, stop this. It's not important."

"Who was it?"

Jacob gives an exasperated sigh. "You're a bully, Florence."

"Who was in the car with Julia? It was years ago, you can tell me that."

He takes a deep breath and looks out over the water.

"He was called Felix Cooper. He was a friend of mine tòo, later."

Friend, a word that covers a multitude of sins.

"He died," says Jacob.

"He died," she says, the words filling the back of her throat. "He died. How did he die?" She's risking it here. But it's time to know.

"Oh, I don't know. There was an accident and that was that."

"Dad . . ."

"They're both dead. It happened a very long time ago."

He has his hands on her shoulders and is looking straight into her eyes. She can't stand it. Don't look at me, don't look at me, you know I killed him. You know.

"I know, I know, darling," he says quietly, comforting her. "I know. Don't cry. Don't cry. There's nothing we can do about it now, it's all so long ago."

She wants to get back to the safety of the blue silk room where she has no past.

"You know?" she says.

"I know he was with Sylvie. Her mother told me about it."

"I have to go home," she says.

In the cab she holds his hand, and leans her head on his shoulder. If she tells him will he hate her, curse her, kill her?

"Dad," she says softly, "I knew him too."

He can't hear her over the car motor and strokes her head. She takes deep breaths. She is carsick. She will tell him in her new room.

The concierge gives her her key and Jacob is careful to tell him that she is leaving early in the morning. "On the Concorde," he adds. "She will want to leave the hotel at nine," says the concierge.

In her room she opens her window to take a last look at the

Vendôme column with Napoleon in a toga turning his back on her, up there, at the top. Jacob sits on the edge of the bed, his hands between his knees.

"Dad," she says, facing him now, "I knew Felix too."

His eyes come up to hers.

"Oh yes?" he says. It's conversational.

"I knew him." Her heart is beating so hard she can hardly get the words out. "I loved him too." She hears the blood loud in her ears.

His mouth relaxes, he seems to be taking a deep breath.

She goes and kneels by him and takes his legs in her arms. She hopes he'll stroke her hair, and he does.

"I was never sure . . ." she begins.

"No one was ever sure about him," he says, "that was his charm."

Charm. So general, functional, social. Too wide for Felix. "More like a spell," she whispers.

"The ones who really fell for him thought he was magic. They had it the worst. *Umerosque Deo similis.*"

She hasn't heard him quote Latin in years. No Latin, please no Latin.

"Oh, Dad, I'm so sorry," she says. She is crying at his feet.

He begins to laugh. She looks up and watches him.

"You want me to forgive you for falling in love with Felix?"

His eyes are wide open, unseeing, and he has tears on his cheek. Did she put her face to his? "How could you help it? You're one of us," he says.

"But I shouldn't have, it was wrong," she says. She shuts her eyes. A thick-hewn frieze of Felix's grinning lovers, male and female, dances inside her lids. Her father keeps talking.

"Remember Fred Gardner? He said Felix was a whore. He probably was. Everyone had him, everyone."

So that's who they were talking about that night.

"But I shouldn't have."

"Why not?" And he gives another laugh. "There was no free choice. No one had free choice around him. That's what irresistible temptation . . ."

She cries on her father's thighs and then he picks her up and carries her like a child to the side of the bed that's turned down, and pushes her stiff body between the bedcover and the blanket without undressing her. She holds on to his shoulders. "Dad, do you believe in atonement? Is there any way to get cured of a sin? I've tried, but I can't make it go away."

"Shhh," he goes as he pulls the silken coverlet up over her, so that she looks as if she's tucked in bed. The mohair scratches her legs.

"Do you forgive me?" she asks. If she can just get him to forgive her, even if he doesn't know what it's for. If he forgives her for loving Felix . . .

"It's not up to me," he says gently. "It's not your fault. You couldn't help it, you didn't do anything bad." He puts his round hand on her forehead. "None of us could help it."

She's wetting the pillow with her tears. She can't get him to say it.

"I'm sorry, I'm sorry . . . I'm so sorry," she mumbles. If he forgives her she'll be healed, even if he doesn't know everything. The candle. "I'm sorry."

"You'll see, I'll have shops in all the stores in America. I'll come over and lecture. They'll write about me in the art magazines. I'll be back on my feet before you know it."

She opens her eyes.

"Everything will be the way it was before . . ." he says.

Before. Before, when Felix was with Jacob? When he was with Julia? When he was with Florence, who loved him so much she killed him with a wish? Before Felix? She runs the past back in her head, and cannot find a perfect time, a time that was clean. Before, before, before . . .

11

THE SUPERSONIC BLADE TAKES her home at twice the speed of sound to land two hours before she took off. The rich and fortunate can turn back the clock when they travel, but only by two hours. Like a wish in a fairy tale, you get more than you asked for, but not as much as you need.

She does the only thing she can: she drinks. Her sleep was immovable and solid, like a paperweight, and now she drinks and puts off tidying what's in her head.

Irresistible temptation. They all gave in. He was nearer to her than she thought. He probably spent more time with Julia than she ever did. Irresistible temptation. And what did they get? Julia died and Jacob ruined himself and she, Florence, wished him dead, and has not lived since. Only Sylvie continued intact, intact but not admirable. If you have no conscience you will not be hurt.

"Champagne," she says to the stewardess, and casts an eye along the aisle to see who might be on the plane this time. Florence Ellis knows that lightning strikes twice. It never stops.

She is thirty-six. She will get her years back now, before it's too late. A rage rises in her, righteous will. She can't go on apologizing to the dead. Everyone sinned and she's paid enough.

A cab takes her home through choppy yellow traffic and turbulent concrete, past barracked holes and under tall cranes with counterweights as big as bunkers. The air is quick; there are no walking dead to clog it with their exhalations. America is new and New York is life and Florence will get her time back. Deborah is not subtle, but Deborah was right. It's time.

She leaves the heavy boxes full of catalogues by the front door and goes straight to Ben's study where she looks at the design taped to the table. She sees the magnolias and fern fronds with lucid eyes, and understands what she didn't know for ten years, that he was just a way of trying to be with Julia, someone who sat at a table painting flowers and stripes.

Then she pushes the bedroom door open. Ben is a tense shape in bed, his back to her. But he's sleeping on her side, near the door, and as she goes around the bed, she sees a woman's dark hair and smells the sex before she sees it's Katy. How dumb, she thinks, how dumb to do it here, and she is grateful for that dumb mistake. She was going to have to explain, and now she can leave without a word.

This immaculate transgression is a gift. A clean excuse. It won't be her fault. Thank you, Ben.

She's afraid they might wake, but her hand goes into her bag to take out the white envelope with the cuff links in it, and she puts it carefully on the little table. Katy stirs slightly, and Florence pulls back on tiptoes and leaves as fast as she can.

She takes the bottle of cologne out of her bag and puts it on the kitchen counter, a little piece of his past as a present, and she leaves the catalogues in their boxes on the floor, a little bit of Jacob's future as a curse. She pulls the door closed quietly behind her. No need to slam.

An empty cab drives by as she emerges from the door downstairs; she whistles to stop it and gives the address of Sylvie's hotel. It doesn't matter who Sylvie is in bed with, this is more important. This is the most important thing she could do. And speed will help her. It already has. Onward.

When the will works, everything works. A bellboy materializes to carry her suitcase; everything is on her side.

Sylvie, patting herself dry with the edges of a toweling robe, opens the door and is almost knocked over by the energy radiating from Florence, who marches in followed by the bellboy, installs herself in an armchair in the suite's living room, and begins to talk. Thanks for the plane tickets, the opportunity to go to Paris, thanks for the blue silk room, the view of the column, dinner at L'Espadon, the man she met on the plane.

"Man?" says Sylvie.

"No one you know." Florence incorporates the answer in her stream of words, and on to her father, he's all right, here's the bracelet—a rustle in her bag and out comes a box covered in pale blue leather, and while Sylvie opens it the thank yous keep coming, the gratitude is so reiterated and so large that it begins to appear to Sylvie almost as a threat. Florence keeps talking, aware that Sylvie is quiet, that when she does speak the words come out slowly, in that indented, rough English she insists on using—"Speak *French*, Sylvie," she says at one point, "French."

"I'm glad you had a good time," says Sylvie. "That trip did you good. You needed it. So when do you see him again? The man?" she asks.

"I don't know, but I will. Now here's what happened since I came back . . ."

"But you just got off the plane."

"I know, but I've already been home, and Ben's in bed with a woman, so I had to leave." Sylvie hears triumph in Florence's voice: this humiliation is being deposited at her feet as some sort of tribute. Sylvie wants to say, "It isn't my fault," and yet Florence seems to be thanking her for it, thanking her.

"You're leaving because of the man you met," says Sylvie, slowly. Florence looks up, irritated.

"Of course not. He's just a stranger, you have to be careful of strangers you meet in public places."

"The Concorde's not a public place, it's more a private club," says Sylvie. As if money made everything safe.

"But you see, I have to leave. I have to." And Florence settles back into the armchair for all of two seconds, and sits forward again. "I have so much to thank you for," she says, again.

Sylvie wants her to slow down. "Maybe you should think about it for a while, there's no reason why it should be the end. Make a scene. Go home and throw something."

"Don't you see? I don't want to go home. I can't." Florence wants to explain to Sylvie that she's been freed, that she has the hunger to go on now, that everything Sylvie has done for her has made her understand—"Life has to be good. Great things are going to happen. You've made it possible."

Sylvie wants to be looking at a woman who's found her man in flagrant betrayal, a woman in tears, but what she sees is someone who is so happy she seems to be growing wings.

"You have to help me. You've done so much already," says Florence. She shows Sylvie her wrist, with the bronze watch. "See, you've given me my time back," she says.

Sylvie stands up and says she has to get her address book from the bedroom, she'll find someone with an empty apartment, "because although I'd love to have you stay here, I can't . . ."

"Bruno, I understand," says Florence.

"No," says Sylvie, stung—she is after all more than just a mistress, she's a mother too, a responsible person—"Claudia arrives in two days, and I'll have to take care of her. I'll find you something though, don't worry," and she proceeds toward the bedroom. "But you think about it too. You know people here."

Florence turns to the phone on the little table at her elbow and dials Deborah. Deborah will understand.

"Paris was great," she announces.

"Sounds like it. When did you get home?"

"Just now. Listen. I need some help. I need a place to stay. For a while. Do you know about an empty apartment?"

Deborah gives a low professional whistle. "Tough one," she says. "How much are you willing to spend?"

"Nothing," says Florence. "I have no money. At all. You know that. I have six hundred dollars a month."

"In this town . . ." says Deborah. There are columns in Deborah's head, columns of achievement headed by her age, and her sex, her place in a society of strivers, her hard-won gains, her trade-offs, her income level, her chances of promotion, her crack at the big time, her apartment, her loan, her car, her houseplants . . . everything she's earned in twenty years. And now this penniless flake wants a place to stay for nothing because she's feeling whimsical and wants to walk out on a perfectly good man. She doesn't know her own luck, this Florence, she's never had to fight for anything . . .

"You're leaving Ben?" asks Deborah, to be sure.

"I have to. It's survival. I'm changing my life." She doesn't say because he was in bed with Katy. Deborah knows Katy. Maybe she knows about it already. And Deborah encouraged her to leave, before she left for Paris.

"I'll think," says Deborah, full of professional gravitas. "Where do I call you back?"

Florence gives her Sylvie's name and hotel number. "If you're with Sylvie, she's rich, can't she help you?" Deborah is sure that some people have an easy life, these kept women, these Eurotrash types from Madison Avenue with the streaked hair and the big jewelry, she's never seen Sylvie but she's heard enough about her from Ben to know she's no good.

"I can't always count on Sylvie, she's done a lot for me already."

"Well, maybe she'll do more," says Deborah, who promises to call her back.

Sylvie comes out of the bedroom with the address book. "I have an idea," she says. "Mrs. Russell."

"Fine," says Florence. No idea who Mrs. Russell is, but great.

"She's been away for months, and I think she's away for a few more weeks. She has a house on Sixty-third Street. She offered it to me, she wanted someone in there because of the thieves. It's very big. Would you be scared?"

Florence isn't scared of anything right now. Bring on the thieves.

Sylvie calls Mrs. Russell in Palm Beach. Florence is in the living room, lights a cigarette. She wants to ingest something, but it's not food, it's not the cigarette. Champagne. She wishes she had the nerve to call room service and order a bottle, but she doesn't want to alarm Sylvie. The cold yellow bubbles, just what she needs to keep her afloat right now.

She's doing the right thing. Isn't she? She listens for the voice. Maybe it will tell her. She thinks she can hear something, but no, it's the chambermaids in the hall. Anyway the voice is gone. All that is over, all that and the rest of the past. Onward.

Sylvie comes back. "It's fine, you can go there today. The maid will be waiting for you. Here's the address." She hands Florence a piece of hotel paper. "And do you want to go see my psychic? She can tell you what's going on."

"No!" She turns to face Sylvie. "No psychic. Thank you. I don't want any of that, ever again."

Sylvie throws up her hands. "I just want you to have all the help you can get. To make sure you know what you're doing."

"I know," says Florence. "I know."

She picks up her bag, gives Sylvie a passing peck on the cheek, and goes out into the hall.

Sylvie watches the door close behind her and wonders what she has wrought.

Sixty-third Street. The best part of town. The house has a little set of stairs, and a trimmed topiary tree on either side of the door. A small woman in a white uniform opens the door and shows her up to a room on the third floor. "Mrs. Russell, she no like her room to be use," says the woman in white, who shows her a bathroom, new pink towels, pink soap, and the telephone, which is big and black. Florence asks for the phone number of the house.

"Mrs. Russell no like give out number," says the woman in white. "Number private."

Florence has some twenty dollars left from the money she changed at the airport this morning. She doesn't want to waste ten on getting her own phone number, and at the same time, since this is where she's going to be living, she'd better smooth her way. She gives ten to the woman, asking gently, "What is your name?"

"Carmen," says the woman, staring at the ten-dollar bill.

It's half of all the money I have in the world, thinks Florence, take it and get it over with.

"I no take money," says Carmen. "You want lunch?"

"No lunch," says Florence. "Phone number."

"I no give," says Carmen. "I go clean now."

She leaves Florence in a room with a big pink ruffled bed, windows that give onto a back garden where a Scots terrier is yapping at a clothesline, and three desolate trees growing like hangnails between paving stones.

Florence unpacks the few clothes she has with her, and takes out the Ritz Hotel ashtrays and felt-tip pens and the washcloths that arrived new every morning, billed as gifts. The little Ritz favors will make this strange room safe, and glamorous the way her life should be.

She sits down on the bed, feet on the floor. She'll have to call Ben and explain, she'll have to borrow money from someone to live, she'll . . . it will all be easy. She lies back on the pillow to think a little with her eyes closed, and wakes up four hours later by the bronze watch.

She puts her feet on the floor, pulls herself up from the bed, and goes to rinse her mouth. Then she goes out to the landing and down the stairs through the gloomy unfamiliar house. From the size and condition of the reception rooms, she guesses that Mrs. Russell is rich and middle-aged, that she is a Republican—there are photographs of the same blonde woman with Eisenhower, Nixon, and Reagan, all over the house. There are three rooms with sofas in them, linked like sausages with tiny knotted vestibules in between. The dining room has fourteen chairs: she is formal. In the center of the dining table a pair of fighting cocks, rendered in handpainted Hungarian ceramics: she gets presents, or came up from nowhere. Handpainted fighting cocks are not something one inherits, thinks Florence. It's something her father would have said, and it's pleasant to think of her unknown hostess as a grasping little parvenue. The books are locked away in glass-fronted cabinets; war memoirs, books about the Communist threat. Titles like *The Domino Alliance* and *Ten Days with Chiang Kai-Chek*. Pools of darkness around the sofa groupings, there must be a central light switch somewhere, but she can't find it. And everywhere, like house gods, in every window of every room, gigantic pale cream plastic air conditioners, twice the size of the ones she has at home, with yellowing plastic louvered grilles and rows of round knobs along the top third. Surrounded by flowered curtains, velvet curtains, striped curtains.

Upstairs she tries the door of Mrs. Russell's bedroom, which is guarded by a doggy basket in checked madras, with a chewed beige blanket folded carefully in its center. By the size, its usual occupant is a Shih Tzu, if not a Pekinese. The door is locked.

But knowing that Mrs. Russell is a short Republican from nowhere with a Pekinese does not help her immediate problem. Night begins to fall; the days are shorter here than in Paris, which is odd. Surely in the present they should be longer than in the past? She has unpacked her clothes, she is free and safe, she is in hiding, and now she has to figure out what to do this coming night.

She has slept four hours, she is starving. She goes down the stairs, past a grandfather clock, and into the kitchen. Carmen is polishing silver. She makes a motion to hide the silver with a cloth when she sees Florence come in.

"Is there food in the refrigerator?" asks Florence.

"I make you," says Carmen, "before I leave."

"You leave?" asks Florence.

"I go home."

"When do you come back?" Behind her she feels the house grow to vast proportions, open and undefended on Sixty-third Street. She wants someone in the house, for thieves.

"I come tomorrow morning, every morning, at eight."

"You mean, I sleep here alone tonight," says Florence, slowly, so that the woman will understand.

"Yes. You, no me," says Carmen. "What you eat?"

She is guarding the refrigerator with her body. Florence wonders what could be in it. "How long Mrs. Russell away?" she asks.

"Two, three months. She go, she come."

"What in refrigerator?"

"Plenty food. What you want?"

Florence is trying to think what could keep over two or three months. "Whatever's there; do you mind if I have a look?"

Much against her will, and with a practiced sigh, Carmen pulls open the refrigerator door. And Florence sees that it is a deep-freeze, stacked with white boxes, labeled in fine debutante script: Chicken Kiev, Suprême de Veau aux Morilles, Boeuf en croute aux Truffes, Coulibiac de Saumon, Poulet à l'estragon. Wedged up in a corner, she sees "Boeuf à la méxicaine." That one, she says, pulling at the cold white box.

"I do microwave," says Carmen. "What time you eat?"

"Now, please," says Florence.

Carmen brings out the boeuf à la méxicaine, which turns out to be chili, in a glass bowl on a voile doily on a Sèvres plate on a silver plate on a silver tray to Florence in the smallest of the three living rooms, which is a red one. Florence has turned on the TV to see the news.

"A three-alarm fire in the Bronx this afternoon . . ."

Carmen straightens up suddenly and goes to the phone.

"It's for you," says Carmen. "Lady."

"But how did you know it was ringing?" asks Florence.

"Light goes on. Mrs. Russell deaf, phone ring with light."

It's Sylvie, who wants to know if Florence is free. Before Florence can lose herself in speculation as to the ultimate meaning of the word, Sylvie adds, "for dinner."

"Maybe," says Florence.

"Don't give me that. You're coming out with me and Thierry."

Florence accepts.

"Sylvie, who is this Mrs. Russell?" she asks.

"I'll tell you at dinner. Wear something nice. And by the way, you can keep my jacket."

Florence gives up on the boeuf à la méxicaine; she takes the tray into the kitchen. Carmen is standing there, tying mail into bundles with rubber bands.

"I leave soon," says Carmen.

Florence dreads being alone in the house.

"Fine," she says. It is a free roof over her head. She must remember that, be grateful and calm.

"I show you key," says Carmen, and leads her to the front door. There are four keys and two front doors, a detail Florence failed to notice when she arrived. Carmen laboriously explains the sequence in which the locks must be opened and closed, which leaf of the double door must be pulled open, and how to triple-lock the Medeco before the Fichet. Florence notices the little white box of an alarm by the door. "And that, do I put that on?" she asks.

"No, they broke. We no use," says Carmen. She gives Florence a bunch of keys with a silver dachshund hanging from a chain.

"How long does it take to get in?" she asks.

"Five minutes, not more," says Carmen.

Once Carmen has gone, Florence goes upstairs to take a bath. As she goes up, she feels the energy draining from her with each step. She runs a full bath in the pink bathtub and only when she has undressed and put her foot in does she realize that the water is icily tepid.

On her way out to meet Sylvie at the hotel, she tiptoes down the stairs. She doesn't want to disturb the maniacal ordered weather of Mrs. Russell's house. She has the first key in the first keyhole to get out of the house, when she sees the light blinking on the phone on the far side of the living room. With a glance at the key in the door she runs across the living room, and pushes all the white buttons as she picks up the receiver.

"Yes?" She's out of breath.

"May I speak to Mrs. Ellis?" It's a man's voice, prodigiously loud.

"She's not here." She has never thought of herself as Mrs. Ellis. She finds a knob on the phone and manages to turn the volume down.

"Well, could you give her a message?"

Something is working slowly in Florence's travel-sogged brain. "I'm sorry, did you say Russell or Ellis?" she asks.

"Mrs. Ellis." He's being polite, he's very kind, he's . . .

"Paul?"

"Florence?"

"How did you get this number?"

She is in the dark, she forgot to ask Carmen where the light-switches are, but oh God, he has found her. Here in this strange house where she doesn't belong.

"I called you at home, and a grumpy man told me to call Sylvie Ambelic at some hotel, so I did that, and she told me . . . what are you doing?"

But she can't tell him she's left home. If she does he'll take fright and flee, he won't save her if he knows how badly she needs him.

"What am I doing?" she repeats, to find out what he means.

"Like right now."

"Right now I'm sitting in the dark in a house on Sixty-third Street."

"Well, turn on the light."

"If only I could. I can't find the switches."

"You know," he says, "there's a particular innocence about you that I find very appealing. Have you tried, on the lamps?"

"On the . . ."

"There's usually a switch on a lamp. Or a little chain, made of silver balls with a sort of silver tassel on the end."

She finds the chain on a large pot next to her, topped with a gold paper shade. She pulls. Light.

"Oh, yes," she says.

"Better now?"

"Yes, thank you."

"Well, now that I've helped you turn on a lamp, would you like to have dinner?"

"I've got a . . . I'm supposed to meet Sylvie."

"Sylvie. The woman in the hotel. Do you want to have a drink afterward?"

"Yes," she says. "I'll need it."

"Where will you be?"

She has no idea. She tells him she'll meet him at midnight at Sylvie's hotel, in the lobby.

"I see we already have a tradition," he says. "By all means, let's keep it up."

The party that Sylvie takes her to is in the Metropolitan Museum. The car that takes them there is a limousine upholstered, once again and to Florence's delight, in blue velvet. Thierry is the man from the restaurant, months ago. Finally Florence is living the life she thought she deserved. She is wearing her best and only party dress, the ambassador dress. She hopes the ambassador will be there, she wants a chance encounter. "Oh, hello. How are you?" Your hands were on me, in me . . .

But she sees no ambassador. Heads of tanned men and powdered women, of the same species as the ones she met at dinner a week ago, before Paris, but not the same people. Crowds of shoulders; silhouettes of men in dark suits conversing by the statues that lead to the room where tables have been set up. "Come, come," says Sylvie, as if impatient to pull Florence through the crowd, as if she had a destination in mind. Squadrons of young men in black tuxedos holding round black lacquer trays on which are arranged twelve or ten snow peas.

"Snow peas?" asks Florence, taking one.

"It's delicious, they do it at every party," says Sylvie.

Florence bites into the green pod to find cream cheese has replaced the peas.

"Herbed," says the waiter. She takes another as Sylvie drags her through a thicket of brocade dresses.

"Where are we going?" she asks.

"I'm looking for Bruno, he's here somewhere," says Sylvie.

"Whose party is this?" asks Florence.

"It's a charity thing and I'm on the committee," says Sylvie. They have reached the end of the approach and are in the room where tables are set up.

"But it's seated, there isn't any room for me," says Florence.

"Yes, there is," says Sylvie, who is still pulling her along. "Here's my table. Look." And she points to a place card. On it is written: Miss X.

"That's me?" asks Florence.

"Yes, yes, we needed an extra girl. Now that you know where the table is, I can leave you. Go talk to people. We eat when the gong strikes."

Miss X. She had been merely anonymous; now she is Miss X. Not a bad pseudonym for a temptress. She looks at the palm fronds curving over the tables and the bread rolls sticking out of the pale brown napkins, the candles floating in water in the glass cups of tall chalices hung with orchids. "What's the cause?" she asks Sylvie, but Sylvie has lit a cigarette and is nervously fingering her hair while peering back toward the entrance.

"I just don't know where he is, he said he'd meet me here," she says.

"Is Thierry at our table?" asks Florence.

"No, yes, I can't remember where I put him," says Sylvie.

"Well, who are these people?" asks Florence, pointing to the place cards either side of her own Miss X: Mr. Franklin and Mr. Esposito.

"You'll see," says Sylvie. "You always want to know everything in advance." She puts out her cigarette and heads for the door, and Florence follows her, smiling at every person Sylvie smiles at, so as to be charming.

General, functional, social. It's her turn to be those things.

Sylvie introduces her: "Florence just got back from Paris," and Florence feels the contours of her glamorous life, and says the weather was good, but not as good as in New York, it really is a remarkable spring.

It's time for champagne: "What about a drink?" she mutters to Sylvie, whose anxious casting about for Bruno has led them from the coatcheck nook to the row of pillars in the big entrance hall.

The waiters in black are everywhere, young men with beautiful features, clean cheeks, bright eyes, short hair. Hundreds of them. A gray-haired man with glasses and a freckled bow tie hugs Sylvie. "Look at the boys tonight, aren't they gorgeous?" he says. "The Italians are all saying they want to take them home."

"Well, that's what they're here for," says Sylvie.

Florence takes a closer look; the waiters are all the same height, and slim, well-presented, eager, polished, homosexual . . .

"Thank God, I see one with champagne. *Ici!*" shouts Sylvie.

Champagne. A waiter glides over with a trayful, and Sylvie takes one, and Florence reaches out and clasps the cold thin bulb of the champagne glass and as she lifts it off the tray something stings her attention, solicits. It's the face of the waiter holding the tray. She takes a sip and while his head is turned, he's serving someone else, she details stringy blond hair, well cut to show off the shape of the head, and gently sagging cheeks that reveal cheekbones, an attractive bony look to the face that is the best a thirty-five, thirty-six-year-old could aspire to. A handsome faggot her own age, with a pointed nose that makes her think of a sail on a small sailboat, one of the toy boats for the basin in the Tuileries. Only the mouth is out of place, a mouth shrunken by years of disdain, of sulking, of little sneers. She knows that face. His eyes meet hers and stare back, sly, mocking . . .

"André?"

"*Oui?*" As if he expected everyone to know his name.

"André Routière?"

"Florence." The small mean mouth opens into a smile. He seems almost glad to see her.

A gong is struck, a loud brass wave reverberates across the crowd. Sylvie grabs Florence's arm. "That's dinner, and I still can't see Bruno."

"Don't worry," says Florence, with her eyes still on André, who stands in one spot with the tray as Sylvie pulls her back toward the dining room, "everyone turns up, eventually."

12

No SLEEP AND MORE champagne. The glances she receives from the men on each side of her prove they are enchanted with her company; she looks at the little card that says Miss X and it doesn't seem that it will be too bad, being a single woman in New York, filling empty seats at charity dinners, jet-lagged, wanted, courted . . .

She throws her head back because she knows that her neck makes a perfect curve when she displays it that way. The ambassador told her so. She runs a distracted hand through her short hair, to make the men want to do the same. Stretching like a cat on a sofa, waiting to be caressed. If Paul can bother to catch up with her, all men will want her. His interest works on her like a blessing. She knows she shouldn't use it to try to seduce other men, but then who will punish her? Who makes the rules, anyway? There are no more rules, they broke. She once more glances across a dinner table at Sylvie and sees perjury and foolishness rewarded. Sylvie is ecstatic, gazing into the eye of a sad Italian who turns out to be Bruno. Me too, thinks Florence, I'm allowed that too: all of it, everything.

Franklin on her left, Esposito on her right. Franklin owns sky-scrapers. Esposito says he just moved his money to New York, and does she know Venezuela? "Where do you live in New York?" she asks. "Oh, I don't live here," says Esposito. "But I thought you said . . ." she answers. "No, I moved my money. New York is a good place for money. I live in London."

Franklin on her left asks if she has children and adds, rubbing his smooth hands together while looking at a young girl at the next table, that she must be thinking about her biological time clock. No, she tells him, she hasn't thought about it. She adds: "And anyway, I'm only twenty." Franklin thinks he's heard wrong, she looks young, but no way is she twenty; still, he paid a thousand dollars for his seat at this dinner table and he isn't going to waste it—even if most of it is deductible—getting into a fight with a woman who doesn't know how old she is. Miss X.

"I just got back from Paris," she tells Esposito, to brandish some glamour. "I have a good friend in Paris," he says. "It's easy to fall in love there. It's a good place for older women." She doesn't know if he means she's older, or that his friend is older, and sees no way to ask. She's trying to keep pace with the champagne, not let the empty glass gain on her. If it's always full she won't suffer. "I was in love there too," she says, handing over her most protected secret as easily as passing the salt. "But here," says Esposito, launched, "no one falls in love. They don't have time. I've tried, but it's no use. All the women are looking for something better.

"Oh, I'm sure you're good enough," she says, "really."

Esposito gives a little cough, looks away, and then says, nervous: "I have a wife, of course, but I like to fall in love."

Now what have I done? she wonders.

Franklin is smiling at her, a little lopsided. "What do you call that?" he asks.

"A dress?" she asks.

"It's got some other name."

"Oh, a coat dress."

"That's right. Very nice."

She pulls herself straight and lets one shoulder fall forward, the ambassador effect.

Franklin, staring into her cleavage, shakes his head. "What a pity," he says.

"A pity?"

"I have a meeting early in the morning. I have to get a full night's sleep."

But I thought you wanted to stare at my breasts, she thinks. She doesn't say anything: why did he talk about his early morning meeting, when all she did was lean forward a little?

"If you give me your number, maybe I'll call you sometime and ask you out to the country," says Franklin. "I'll send a car."

Her turn to shake her head. "No, really, thank you, I . . ."

Esposito turns to her. "Is there a lot of disease in New York?" he asks.

"What kind of disease?" Old people on the street, their scalps peeling from radiation treatments; their arms crossed with white Band-Aids where blood was taken, heaving along the street on anodized chrome walkers, low, portable metal fences, or babies with whooping cough, ghetto rickets, hepatitis, the flu?

"I'm told there is a lot of disease," he says.

"I hear it's not too nice in your shantytowns either," she snaps.

"That thing, that thing, what is it called? Men had it first, now women and drugged people, prostitutes? No one recovers from it?"

"Oh, that," she says, and then stops to think. They will all die of it. Those who have fun, let go . . . "Yes. There's a lot of it. I hear."

Esposito stares at her as if she were a poisoned apple, and he were Snow White. "I have to be careful, I have a wife."

She nods. "No, no, you're right." And for some curious reason wants to apologize.

And turns to Franklin, who is removing a piece of basil from his plate.

"It causes cancer," he says.

"What does?" she asks.

"Basil. I read it in a medical journal. It's true."

The perfect oval leaf falls to the gold lamé tablecloth. Florence says, "You've got to be joking. Basil is wonderful. One of the best things about New York is that you can get basil here all year."

"I wouldn't eat it, if I were you," says Franklin, and he gallantly reaches over with his fork to scoop a green leaf off her plate and save her from cancer.

Esposito feels he has to explain. "Temptation isn't the same anymore," he says, his hand covering hers. She removes hers as politely as she can. "Things are too dangerous these days. You do understand."

But I wasn't offering myself to you, she wants to say. I was. How does she know? That's what it's supposed to be about, seduction, expensive dresses, Miss X at a charity dinner, confidence. . . . She will have to get out of there by midnight to meet Paul, his name sidles away from her each time, his voice was good on the phone tonight, but now she's seen André and to think of Paul while André is around would be like breathing near a toadstool, she must be careful to forget everything she really wants while that bad air is somewhere near her.

But André is not waiting on her table. She turns in her chair to see, and wonders how many of the handsome waiters are dying, but André is not in this part of the room, maybe it wasn't André after all. At eleven forty-five by the bronze watch—five forty-five in the morning Paris time—she shrinks herself to pass between the two seats, she takes the narrow uneven alleys between the tables at a graceful and near miraculous clip, she gets to the door and then down the corridor past the statues—"not museum quality," she thinks as she passes—to the great hall, a beach of gloom.

She stops in front of a pillar between two doors. She doesn't know which to choose, the left or the right, and hesitating there at the grating, her satin heel gets caught in the square hole of the underfoot grid, and now as in some fable her hesitation prevents her from moving at all. She has to step out of her shoe and kneel and pull it out of one little trap.

She chooses the left for no good reason, and goes straight through.

The open sweep of stone outside is wide and slow to the high-heeled foot. She turns to look back at the museum as she heads for the steps, and over the door she didn't take, the one that was on the right from the inside and is now on the left, over it hangs a huge black banner with red letters, and the red letters say, THE GATES OF HELL.

Underneath is written Rodin, but she doesn't pay attention to that. That was the door she didn't take. She didn't see the banner when she went in, she didn't know about it while she was inside, and now that she has read the words, she's out. Of course, she thinks, let André rot in hell. And Sylvie. It seems as good an answer as any. She gives a little giggle. She is drunk.

She has her eye on the dry stream of Fifth Avenue, scanning for taxis. She has to get to Sylvie's hotel; at this hour of the night on

Fifth Avenue it's not easy, there are no cabs. The heels are too high to contemplate walking there. And her dress too expensive not to be afraid of the dark.

She hears a soft noise from her left, and turns to make sure it is neither a beggar nor a thief, and it's a man in a dark suit, a tall blond man going gray, and his legs snap straight as he stops on the steps above her, a look of delight across his face.

Paul.

"What are you doing here?" she calls out, the first to speak, unfeminine, suspicious, afraid.

"I was looking for someone, but she's left," he says.

"Where are you going?" she asks.

"I have to go meet this woman," he says.

"Who is she?" she calls out.

"I don't know yet."

They resume walking down the stairs, but he comes no nearer to her. She faces him. "I thought you were going to meet me at Sylvie's hotel," she says.

"I am, but why should I tell you? I don't know you."

The relief of a man who knows there is no such thing as truth.

"I don't understand," she insists on saying.

"Nor do I," he says, and takes her hand.

There's the shock of truce in the contact of their skin. She remembers this as the point from which you stop lying, you stop pretending. All surrender comes when the hands touch, no it doesn't, it comes later. When the kiss comes. Or when the bodies touch? And what surrender? To give in as an animal, a skinned eel, to give in to the ambassador, open, wet and flailing on a strange couch, is that the culmination of desire, or is it disgrace?

They are walking. Then they are somewhere with a little table between them, and tall glasses on that table, and she looks at his hands, now isolated on the table, and finds them strangely mystical hands for a businessman, smooth, conical. "What kind of science?" she asks in a squeak, with no control of how her breath is allotted.

The hands reach out for her and with the contact of skin there is no need for an answer.

His forefinger runs along her cheek. She sees how his mouth curls a little, the upper lip raised over white teeth, and realizes that it's a smile. His blond-gray hair rides out a little from his head, and curls back in, the ends touching his nape. The blue eyes are really more than blue, their irises circled in darker gray. He is watching her.

He doesn't look like anyone she knows.

He closes his hands around her wrists, fine wrists for so tall a woman; he can feel the pulse beat in the estuary veins, river green, under the transparent skin. He almost knows the circuits of her blood.

She touches his temple, where the bone juts out. Where the wing would start, if he were Morpheus.

The puzzled look is still on her face.

"What is it?" he asks. Hesitation is charming to a point, no further.

"It's all going very fast," she says.

"Nothing has happened yet," he says.

"It's still too fast," she says. "And maybe it isn't a good idea."

"Stop trying to think," he says. "It won't help you."

But she wants to put everything on the little table between them before it starts, before anything starts, her father and Felix, and Julia and Felix, and Felix, and her wish on the candle, and Ben, and the ambassador, and push them all across at him, like so many sharp transparent vertical impediments, used glasses, a shining wall of empty vessels.

She tries: "I woke up in Paris this morning, I'm not even home, it's later than the middle of the night for me, I don't know where I'm living, I'm so tired I could have been drinking cough medicine, and now this," she says.

"Cough medicine?"

"I'll explain. Never mind. It's just another thing I'll have to explain." There are tears in her eyes from the effort.

"But what makes you think you have to explain anything? I'm not asking for a résumé."

"I'm keeping you from your sleep, and I might give you a disease, and I'm almost too old to have babies, and Paris is for older women, and no one has the time to fall in love in New York, anyway," she says in one breath. And keeps her eyes on him.

"And we may get hit by a cab coming out of here," he adds, "and the bomb may fall tomorrow, or there will be an earthquake, and lightning could strike too. What are you afraid of? Why are you so afraid?"

Helpless hands, hers, reach out to fan the air.

"You're not afraid?" she asks.

He shakes his head.

She narrows her eyes. He could be a carrier. He could be . . .

"Are you a homosexual?" she asks.

"What!" he says, peering at her. The romantic gloom of the bar now a sticky darkness. "You mean, do I have AIDS?"

"No, I mean, do you know my father?" The question is so irrational that he ignores it, and goes on:

"You'd like to know if I've had a blood test? Is that it?" He is offended; what does she think he is? And behind that, a vague sense that true responsibility, these days, might go as far as a blood test. The things one doesn't think about . . .

"I mean: do you know my father? It's important," her hand on his arm, and an urgent tone that convinces him the question is important. He'll try.

"I don't think so," he says. "Should I?"

She leans forward, palms on her knees: "You have to understand. It's very complicated, but you have to understand." She is crying in frustration, uses a bar napkin from the little table between them to wipe her eyes and then blow her nose. She keeps her eyes on him, as if he could absolve, explain.

"Do you want me to understand everything from the start, or am I allowed to find out things gradually? I agree with full disclosure, but there should be an order to the way things happen."

He's hanging on to this woman who looks like a boy, this woman with the fresh walk of an eighteen-year-old, unsteady in high heels, defensive and utterly sincere.

"I want it to fit," she is saying, very carefully, her words slurred despite her effort. "I want it to make sense. Whatever it is, whatever happens between us. My life has been very complicated, and either you're part of what's already happened, or you're something new.

I have to know which, you see. It can't be both. I wish you looked like someone I knew. I don't want to go just on blind trust. Pretend that I think everything is going to be all right."

She pauses to take a breath. He hands her a glass and she takes a sip, startled at the taste of quinine, and goes on.

"Everything is booby-trapped. Everything. Everything I touch is already poisoned, addled, and slanted, you know? Slanted so that it just naturally rolls away."

"I'm not going to roll away," he says.

If she pretends it means nothing, it will be like Venice. "I've done it without thinking, and it's wrong. It's the wrong feeling. I don't mean morals, I mean balance. Can you understand?"

Paul is immobile in his seat. This is the second time he's seen her take him for her confessor. He could say I'd love to help, but . . .

But he loves her. The absurdity of the feeling. The woman is half mad, suspicious, illuminated, mystical. Mad, but not banal.

She wants to hand herself over to him, and she wants to give him nothing.

"And why aren't you exhausted? It's late," she says.

"I'm in a different time zone, too, just like you. But I came in from California today. It's early for me."

"And late for me. Too late."

"Don't whine," he says. She smarts from the sharp little snap of those words, and likes it. If it were just that between them, she could keep him, it, the feeling, in check.

"I'm very, very bad," she says. To hear that whip again.

"Bad at what?" he asks. "Games, tennis, housekeeping?"

"No, bad," she says. "I've killed someone. I want you to know that. I killed someone."

She was probably made to kneel on the stone floors by nuns, he thinks. A Catholic child, cheating and beaten. He knows how to deal with that.

"It's not a sin," he says. The energy gone out of his voice, because he's said it so often before. Back on familiar tracks.

"Killing someone isn't a sin?" she answers.

"No, making love," he barely articulates. He doesn't want it to be easy. Everything has always been so easy, and this is getting easy now, and less interesting. Not interesting at all.

"I'm not talking about that. I killed someone."

"Abortion isn't a sin. You mustn't worry about that." That's what it usually is, with Catholics.

"He was my father's lover and he left me for my best friend. I wished him dead; I killed him with a candle and he fell off a cliff. I am bad," she says. And her face is wet, she turns wide strange eyes on him: "I'd love to be able to love you, but I'm bad, you can't want me. I'll cause you harm and you've been so nice. I can't help it."

He sees her rub her hands across her face; her features are in perpetual flux, and what she thinks and what she says are irreducible to psychology. What she's saying makes no sense at all. But he can tell she believes it, and that is what fascinates him. It sounds like a fairy tale.

He sits forward and she pulls back. Maybe this time, she thinks, it will be her turn to be harmed.

He's never been in a fairy tale before.

"If," she says, she's trying to say, "if you could have been sent to punish me . . ." But the words drift away into the dark.

"Tell me later," he says. "It's okay."

She would like to jump into his eyes and stay there forever. It would be so safe.

His hands run up her arm, inside the stiff black sleeve. She shivers to feel him touching the bare flesh beneath her clothes.

She looks so strangely like a boy, and he never thought he was like that. The short hair and the clean bare skin, all the way down inside the cold hard dress.

Their mouths move, silent, toward each other.

Once the breath is shared a pact begins. Arms laid down. To turn all the vacillating questions into the firm texture of lips, the bulky battleship to satin.

But it is not enough for Florence: she puts her hand up to hold the top of his arms, as if testing a wall to see how thick, how strong, how enduring. The answer cannot be only soft and blind; it must be safe and capable too. It must promise not to die. She cannot close her hands over his shoulders, they are too broad. His body is brave. She senses an intimation of sports, of patrician football on a green lawn by the sea. He will be brave, he is of that race.

The mouth again; each is soft, no way to tell which is softer, or which is which. A confluence of breath and privacy coming to join. A mouth like home. Satin. There is no sound, no smell, no taste. When water is at blood temperature it is no longer wet. Her body sails into the swell of their rhythm. She pulls him to her. She wants.

To jump in and swim in her forever, in him. She could live in his skin and he in hers. As fast as that.

And then a wave rears back, and her face pulls away from his. This was in the plot, this was what I wanted, but can the rest be over? He feels her elbows and shoulders suddenly sharp bone, refusal. "What's wrong?" he says.

"I wished him dead, and he died," she says.

"Maybe you wished me alive," he says. He'll play Prince Charming. That's what she wants. And the moment he thinks he's grabbed the role, the ready-made solution, she slips away.

"No," she says. "You have to know. I didn't wish for you. I never thought of wishing for you."

"Oh?" he says. A little taken aback. He tries to gather arguments in his favor. "I'm rich," he says, helplessly, feeling absurd. "I'm divorced, I'm free, I'm generally considered a good person, I have two children, I travel a lot, there's no madness in my family, I don't shoot heroin or sleep with men, I don't think there's anything for you to be afraid of. Why didn't you wish for me?"

She's frowning.

He doesn't know where he is, he's never had to talk like this before, it sounds like a marriage proposal.

"Well . . ." she says, embarrassed. She doesn't need to hear all that. He has made himself sound so solid there is no room for fear or much hope.

"What do you want?" she says, cold and a little mean.

He is amazed to find his chest tight. His head is hot and he's afraid he will lose everything if he says the wrong thing. He can outguess anyone, Paul, it's the secret of his success. In all fields. But here this laser judgment coming at him, and he can't reach out and touch her because she'll take it wrong, she'll take herself away.

"It's late," he says, trying to find what he knows, what he knows, what he thinks he might know, be able to understand, and he feels her so critical that his matching coolness rises to it.

"Well, what do you want?" he asks, to conclude and be done with this strange interrogation.

"I think I want to go home," she says.

He walks her back to the empty house, waits between the two little trees on the steps while she tries to fit a key first into one lock, then another. The sound of keys stabbing on the door irritates him, so he takes the bunch from her hand and inserts the first key into the right lock. Florence hears the metal clasp give a sort of bark as it releases the metal bar, and the penetration, metal into metal, shocks and fascinates her.

Bravely, she steps into the vestibule between the doors, and turns to face him. "I'll be fine now," she says, "I just need to sleep."

"I didn't think there was anything wrong with you," he says, gamely. "Good night."

And he steps back into the street.

"Will you . . ." she begins. But he's already said, "I'll call."

"You have the number?"

"If this is where I called you earlier, I do," he says.

And her "of course" comes in on his "earlier." Such a jumble of words. I'm sorry, she thinks, but doesn't say it.

Of course she can't remember where the switches for the lights are; only the big lamp in the living room by the phone is on. She peers up the stairs; the grandfather clock is now giving a loud tick; in daylight it was silent.

She tiptoes up the stairs, afraid to touch the banisters in case there are other hands on them. Shrill and grim with fear, heart stopped in her chest, afraid to breathe. Turns at a landing, feet silent on a thick beige carpet, past the locked door with a glance at the empty dog basket. One more flight. There is a slice of pink light coming from an open door, she left a light on. She wants to run in, to throw the door closed behind her, gives in, takes the last three treads in one step, and is inside the pink room, panting like a dog.

How many floors above her, another two? And two below, and a basement, probably, too. Are the windows locked in the back, is the glass strengthened? Her ears alert to every possible effect of shattering glass, a crash, a clink of falling chinks, the scrape of diamond across a pane. Her whole body wired like an alarm to catch the differing breezes of intruders. Intruders penetrating the house. The intruders are gifted, in her mind, with the power to climb the sheer brick face of a brownstone, and break a window by flicking an index against a gloved thumb; to dangle from the roof on the light white cables for subscription TV.

It's so hot. She gets across the room to open a window and stops herself, feeling for safety catches, wishing there were more, surveying the access to the narrow sill and horrified to see a balcony outside the bathroom. Anyone could get up there, anyone roaming undetected in the secret space behind the big houses, anyone who can shinny up walls in a shining black leotard.

She flicks on the air conditioner set into the window, she'll have artificial air instead. But it starts with a roar that subsides to a hum so insistent that it interferes with her own radar.

I could be home, she thinks, safe in bed with Ben. I could be with Paul. But she won't go home, and though she makes an involuntary lurch toward the phone, she doesn't have Paul's number.

Because—she has to take deep breaths to calm her breathing, and she sits on the edge of the bed to bend her body out of its rigid cast—this is where I am now. She gets up to turn off the air conditioner and returns to sit at the edge of the bed, her ordained spot. And when her breathing is regular, slow, she rises and takes off her makeup in front of the sink, and watches her eyes in the mirror.

And then she slips naked into the peach sheets, which have the slick texture of less than real cotton. She lies there, listening, and then reaches up to put out the light.

Either I'm safe, or I'm not, she thinks. Whatever happens, happens.

13

"SYLVIE CALL THREE TIMES," says Carmen by the door in her white uniform.

Morning. Bright sunlight. It's late.

Florence pulls herself out of the well of peach sheets and heaves her back against the pillows and the hard bolster.

"I tell her you asleep, but now is noon."

"Could I have some breakfast?" asks Florence.

"I bring now," says Carmen, with a smile.

What a new day this will be. Florence feels brave because she was brave last night, and the night passed away without attacking her. She sees the phone blink by her side, and picks it up.

"So?" asks Sylvie, in a low, nervous tone.

"Good morning," says Florence.

"You sound happy. How was the rest of your evening?"

"It was good," says Florence. "I think it was good."

"Well if it was, why are you there? Or is he next to you?"

"Don't be so basic," says Florence. "How are you?"

Sylvie's voice whispers on the phone: "Wait a minute while I check if he's sleeping." Florence hears the tension and fear of being found out, the tectonic plates of Sylvie's arrangements crashing, crushing together in all the wrong ways.

"In a state. In all my states. Claudia is arriving today with her father when I thought they were arriving tomorrow. Bruno's still asleep but I have to get him to leave. You see how bad it is. They'll be here in a little while. Why don't you come over and have something with me here? We can talk and then you can meet Claudia."

"I'd love it," says Florence.

She isn't afraid of anything anymore. It isn't the old occasional feeling of being held up by some outside grace; it has to do with having a backbone of her own. The knight's long vigil, but she was let off easy; she was able to sleep.

"I'll be over soon," she says.

She bathes and washes her hair and tries to make it stand up a little, in tune with fashion. She is whistling, and she feels good. Sylvie's problems, a sandstorm of fluff.

Before she leaves the house she calls Ben. Not from inclination, but a sense that deference must be paid, certain acts performed, words said. Something she earned or something she owes.

"You're with Sylvie," he says, "running around."

"No, I'm not," says Florence.

"I knew it was going to happen," he says.

"That's for me to say. You're the one who . . ." She chokes over the words. They are so much not true. She longs to be able to say she loves him, but she doesn't love him.

He knows what happened is just an excuse. He knows. But he gave her the excuse.

"I'm sorry, Florence," he says.

"Don't be sorry," she says, "be glad."

"I want to fix up the apartment," he says.

"You don't have to," she says. "I'm not coming home."

"For me," says Ben. "For me."

They could hang up. They stay on the line.

"Did you get much work done while I was in Paris?" she asks.

"Yes," he lies. "Did you have fun?"

"Yes," she lies.

"Well, what happens now?" he asks. Stunned at her cruelty.

"I'm not coming home," she says.

"I didn't ask you to."

"Good," she says, and she hangs up. Without goodbye.

She shouldn't have called. She was doing what she thought she should do. But the mere accomplishment of duty has sullied her instead of shining her armor. She looks less happy in the mirror. She can't believe she is hurting Ben, she doesn't want to. It might have been kinder to disappear entirely.

She walks up to Sylvie's hotel, to get some air. She is two hours late. The city looks new and oddly appealing.

As she turns off Park she finds herself walking behind Marc, and she walks faster to catch up with him.

"Ah, Florence," he says. "How pleasant to see you. I just got back."

"I did too, yesterday. It was wonderful, you did something wonderful for me."

He clasps her shoulders and looks at her tenderly. "It was my pleasure. What use is money unless it can help people?"

She walks alongside him. "Sylvie tells me you've left home, you're living at mad Mrs. Russell's. I hope you weren't too scared last night."

"Scared?"

"In the house alone. Mrs. Russell is terrified of sleeping there alone, she never comes to New York without a houseguest. I used to stay there. The front door, the alarms . . . it's impressive."

"It is," says Florence.

"If you get frightened, you can always sleep at my office. I have a bed there. Just let me know."

"I will," says Florence.

"And there's no need to tell Sylvie. Just between you and me, all right?"

"Fine," says Florence.

"You're a brave girl, leaving your husband. Not everyone dares do that."

Florence nods. Never leave a man unless you have another. These people all share the same views on human husbandry.

They are at the door of the hotel. He takes her hands in his, approaches his stomach to hers.

"You may need help, you will. Ask me, don't go through Sylvie, ask me directly."

"Help?" says Florence.

"Money," says Marc. "If you need anything like that, money, just ask me." He's holding a little packet of hundred-dollar bills, and pushes it at her.

She looks down at the money. There is that tinge of shame, of sluttish disgrace.

"Thank you," she says. "But I don't need this. I'll be fine." She hands it back to him and starts to go in the hotel door.

"Aren't you coming?" she asks. To be polite.

"No, I have to attend to some things first," says Marc. "I'll see you later." The money thick in his hands.

"Goodbye," says Florence. "Thank you for Paris."

The concierge nods at her, the elevator boy smiles at her; he's the same as yesterday. Outside Sylvie's door she hears laughter, young laughter. She presses the bell. She is late.

"And that's . . ." she hears Sylvie say, in a dangle of coin bracelets. Sylvie's graceful step toward the door, and Sylvie's bouncing hair and a smile such as Florence has never seen. It's the first time she's seen Sylvie happy.

"I can't say you're not late, she's here already," says Sylvie, pulling Florence by the crook of her elbow and releasing her into the living room, where a young girl with dark hair is kneeling by an open plaid suitcase.

The girl looks up. A round face with a pointed chin, and eyebrows that go up at the edges, and a headband over her hair. Long limbs, and black tights and dancing shoes.

"Claudia, this is Florence, my oldest friend," says Sylvie, her voice warm with pride.

Claudia stands up. Florence's heart is beating uncontrollably. The girl comes over—she's as tall as Sylvie, wears a boy's white shirt and under it, it seems, another shirt—and her eyes are large almond ovals, perfect shapes.

"*Bonjour, madame*," she says, and strikes out her hand. Don't curtsy, thinks Florence, please don't curtsy.

"I can't believe it," she says, "it's like meeting you all over again." She feels time curve in on itself, cut back, join at the break.

A small hand in hers, a small soft hand. Maybe it's only when you're older that the skin of children begins to feel like petals. When your own grows loose, dry.

Claudia stands there, removes her hand from Florence's, turns to her mother. Florence is arrested by the round cheek curving into jaw, by the narrow shoulders. Is it possible that at that age you are already longing for other worlds, indifferent to the clean new chance in this one?

"You look wonderful," says Sylvie to Florence, to catch her attention.

"I just saw Marc downstairs," says Florence, pulling herself back to now.

"Oh, is he back?" asks Sylvie.

"She's so much like you," says Florence. She can't take her eyes off the girl.

"Oh, no, she doesn't look like me," says Sylvie, laughing, her earrings sparkling, "she looks like her father."

There is a noise from the bedroom, the phone is replaced, and Florence realizes someone in there was having a murmured conversation.

Sylvie turns to the open door and says, "Come out, Florence is here."

A tall shape fills the door, against the light; he's all shadow. She sees dark hair and a thin neck in an open shirt, a white shirt, and the light behind him catches the bold curves of the cheekbone on the edge of his skull. A tall thin man, with tanned skin and deep straight lines across his forehead, and the traces of a rictus grin etched where dimples would be; a dark bangle hanging on one wrist, and a nervous equine twitch to the head as he looks first at Sylvie with a certain impatient scorn, and then at Claudia with an accomplice's smile.

Claudia ambles over to him and asks, *"Papa, tu restes?"*

And Sylvie speaks, pushing her hair forward to hide her eyes.

"Felix, this is Florence, remember I've told you about my friend Florence?"

Florence stares at him, from twelve feet across the room, her breath held in, and while she tries to focus—are his eyes underlined in black, and why is his shirt open so low?—he blurs, the image blurs as when you try to focus in a dream and can't see anymore.

"You'd better get moving, Marc will be back soon and we know what happens when the two of you are in the same room," says Sylvie.

But Felix just stands there without moving, resting his elbow on the side of the door frame. Tendons taut in his neck, and his eyes alarmed, ringed with dark.

Florence is so afraid that she cannot move.

Felix gives a kind of jerk and moves out of the door frame toward her. He is wearing a gray suit, wrinkled cotton, but she sees it as green. His hair is short and a little sparse, combed forward, but she sees it long below his ears.

She can barely look at the man approaching her. His progress is irregular, he is limping. His mouth is thin with effort.

"Hello, Florence," he says, and gives her his hand.

She lets him take it. A shape in front of her, gray-green and now a collection of bones she once knew in the palm of her hand.

Of course he's thin, he's dead.

Her skin waits for the chill of the grave, but his hand is hot and dry.

Sylvie's eyes are wide open on them both, and Claudia has returned to her suitcase, but has not knelt down, is there watching her father and her mother's best friend.

Florence looks as if she is about to scream.

Sylvie cannot catch the tone she needs to say, "You've met?" A cough comes out instead of words.

"But you died," says Florence. "My father told me you'd died."

She isn't going to tell him she killed him. He might not know.

"I never died, I only went away," he says.

"You know Felix?" Sylvie manages to stammer.

Florence doesn't even glance at her. But she looks at the child by the suitcase, and at its father. She could have been mine, she thinks.

"I'd like you to leave us alone," says Florence in a firm voice; Sylvie is dismissed.

"Come on, Claudia, let's go unpack in your bedroom, come on, take your case," says Sylvie. She picks up the key to Claudia's room.

She knows she has to get out of here. Claudia hesitates, so Sylvie scoops the two open sides of the bag together and heaves it toward the front door. "Let me in when I come back," she shouts, and to Claudia: "Come on, Claudia, come on!"

"*J'arrive, Maman*," she says obediently, and follows Sylvie out the door, which closes behind them.

Florence's blood is dry, molecules run wild, scraping inside her veins.

She tries to put out her arm but is afraid to touch him again. This is the plot: They brought him back to stop her heart, just when she thought she'd earned one.

If he breathes on her, she'll die. She backs away, a mere fraction, just enough to feel safe.

"Elise," he says, in a tender voice. "Elise."

"I'm Florence," she says.

He gives a short laugh. "I know that. I knew that."

"Where did you go, Felix?"

If you had come back a week ago . . . But now I'm making my peace with the present. Why did I never ask Sylvie? I couldn't mention your name. Afraid of naming you and naming my crime. It was because I loved you that I wanted you dead.

"Where did you go, Felix?"

He is almost too late. Standing near me and breathing.

"Florence," he says. The accent is subtly changed, but you don't remember the voices of the dead. I can't remember Julia's voice. My voice is gone. His accent is oiled rocks knocking together under a strange colonial twang.

His suit is green his hair is long his face is smooth and young. The dead don't age. A scratch turned to scar along his cheek is a deliberate mistake.

"I had to get away," he says.

I'm trying to look into his eyes, and they have no expression, they are not like his eyes were in the dreams I used to have before he died. And they are rimmed with dark pencil.

"Are you wearing makeup on your eyes?"

"Just a little. I was in Marrakesh. Just kohl."

"You live there?"

"Other places, too."

But where, and how? I reach for the rubbery black bangle around his wrist.

He looks down, at his bracelet or my hand, I'm not sure.

"Kenya. A souvenir of Kenya."

He hasn't changed. Death should improve people. If someone comes back from the dead, they bring messages. That's why they come back.

"How's Julia?"

"My God," he says, "you know everything."

See, he could be dead.

He gives a sigh that turns into a little cough, and turns his face to the window, the best light in the room. His eyebrows come together and his eyes start to shine and he moves forward to the window at a strange uneven gait.

The daylight at the window is hard, like stone, white stone. And now I can see his face is wrinkled from the sun, his teeth are going bad, and the skin at the neck is loose and red. He's aged. He must be alive. He's not the Felix I knew.

"I knew this would happen," he says. "Sylvie told me you were here." He's looking away. He doesn't want to look at me.

"Sylvie knew you weren't dead all along," I say.

"Yes."

"And she's seen you, all these years . . ."

"It didn't matter to her, and there was Claudia."

"But why didn't she ever tell me you were alive?"

He is looking at the window. Silence.

And he turns to me, with a smile that's almost sly. "What did she say when you asked her?"

"I never asked her. I couldn't . . ."

"Why not?"

Oh Lord, Felix. Because I thought I killed you. No, I can't say it. You are proof that my wish did not kill, and still I cannot name it.

"Oh, because . . ." I say. And I thought I was brave.

"Florence," he says, "if only you had told me your real name the day you met me, everything would have been all right."

14

I WENT HOME TO get the ring; I went home to Ben but he was not there. The ring was in its little yellow box in the top drawer of the chest in the bedroom. The bed was made and there was a flower in a pot by its side. We'd never had a flower there before. I had slept in that room for years, but it was so much less mine than the Rue du Bac, where I had lived for just fifteen months. The bare floors made the place more a schoolroom than a bedroom, and I don't know what I learned there. It's more what I forgot.

I held the instant. Just to put my keys on the counter in the kitchen and turn on the TV and make a cup of tea and lie on the bed watching the evening news; not to go out again. To pretend that the last few days and last few weeks had never happened, and when Ben came back from wherever he was, we'd talk about dinner. Not about Katy's dark hair on the pillow next to him, or how the only thing I wanted was to leave. I stood on the little podium that makes the entry, stood there and tried to grasp it: what one is supposed to do and where one is supposed to go, and whether there are things one cannot escape and whether there are great white torsos up there among the stars deciding what will happen to us, and whether any invisible being bothers to figure out, by reasoning or throwing dice, which of a thousand pathetic footpaths we are to take. And what was right and what was wrong. There was no answer of course, and no voice, and nothing, even, in the book I took at random from the shelf, which opened to a recipe for eggplant caviar. I just knew I wanted to leave.

I went without writing a note, I had nothing to say. The doorman handed me an overnight package from Paris; my father must have sent it the day I left. I put it into my bag. For once I didn't want to know. After all this time what was so urgent it had to follow me home on the next plane? Maybe it was money. I didn't need whatever Jacob had sent.

I bought a bunch of peonies on the way down to Mrs. Russell's, and when I came into the house—there now was memory in the locks, and the keys were easy—I saw the living room as welcoming. That stranger's big room was a place I wanted to know and to keep, because I had tamed it in my sleep. It had kept me safe. And the big black phone had brought good news once and could do it again.

I gave the peonies to Carmen and asked her to put them in a vase.

I went up to the pink bedroom and took the new, half-linen sheets out of the suitcase, and pulled the candlewick spread off the bed, and the beige blanket. I pulled off the peach sheets and folded them carefully and hid them in the closet, and then I spread my own new sheets on the bed. I pulled the corners tight and put away the blanket and the spread; it was too hot for covers. The bed looked cool, white and simple, like an operating table. Winding sheets, a shroud for Felix, to bury his death in.

"I help you?" asked Carmen. She was standing at the door.

I felt dizzy and saw by my watch that it was past four. "I put my own sheets on the bed," I said, as if it were something I always did.

I had forgotten to eat.

I asked Carmen to heat up one of the concoctions from the freezer.

"Which one you want?" she asked.

"I don't know," I said. "You decide. Whatever tastes best. And I'd like some toast with butter, and half a bottle of wine."

"You hungry," she said.

I ate alone, privately, quickly, on a tray in the living room, like an actress between acts.

And after I brought the tray in to Carmen I went back to the living room and sat on the sofa looking at the peonies in their blue vase, and after a few minutes I knew I was waiting for Felix, waiting again for Felix. And the bed was waiting for him upstairs.

It wasn't the doorbell that rang, but the phone; I saw the white light blinking Morse.

"Florence." I'd never heard him say that on the phone.

"Felix." Just to say the name again was an insane privilege, a miracle. He was downtown, he told me. In a friend's loft.

"I'm ready to come up to you," he said. "Where is your house exactly?"

I looked around the living room and up the stairs. He would come in and see the flowers I used to have in Paris. I had done what I could to stop time. But it wasn't right.

"Let's meet outside," I said.

A silence. I went on:

"A hotel, there's a little hotel on Central Park South where we can meet. It has two entrances, you can go in on Fifty-eighth Street." I gave him the name of the hotel and told him I'd meet him there in an hour.

I didn't want to see him here.

After he hung up and I'd heard his voice again, his slow voice on the phone, and given him an appointment like an ordinary mortal, I knew he was alive. Sylvie's suite might have been a trick, full of smoke and mirrors. Mrs. Russell's house was solid. I didn't want to see him here. But I had to see him before I could go on.

I went upstairs and put pink on my cheeks and black around my eyes. And then I took it off again because it made me look too much like him.

I heard the doorbell; I was afraid for an instant that he had come here, but then I heard Carmen saying, "Ellis? Ellis?"; I went to the landing, and leaned over. There was a boy carrying a large white paper package.

"That's me, Carmen," I shouted down. Carmen looked up, nodded, and signed a slip of yellow paper. She carried the package in and started up the stairs.

"No, no, I'm coming down," I shouted.

I pulled the paper open. It was a bunch of yellow roses, with a card. I'm not sure if I like yellow. I imagined for a second that they were from Felix. The card said, "Can we please have dinner at a decent time tonight? These late hours are killing me." And it was signed Paul.

Maybe, I thought.

It was a short walk to the hotel. I had the ring in my bag, I was taking the ring to Felix. Aware of the arch of my feet in my high heels, of the heat.

I walked down the long marble entrance, the floor the color of sand, but so hard and shining that I slipped once and almost fell.

Felix was there, waiting, sitting in one of two armchairs that perched around a little table, in the center of the lobby. The walls reached up thirty, forty feet.

He was drinking a beer. His legs thrust out in front of him, a little askew. A waitress came over and I ordered tonic water, for the quinine. Then I looked at his legs, not at him but his legs.

"When did that happen?" I asked.

He looked down and moved his good leg over the bad one, embarrassed at his infirmity.

"It's full of metal," he said.

"Did it happen in Italy?" I asked, terrified of his answer.

"No," he said, sitting up a little, pulling his hips back in the chair. "In Kenya."

"Are you sure?" I asked. "When? How?"

"I was in a Land-Rover. I was trading rare woods, six years ago. The Land-Rover rolled over. I was in hospital four months."

Four months in an African hospital. Nothing to do with me. Two years after we moved to New York. Nothing to do with me.

"I missed you." It was Felix who said it.

"You did?"

"I wanted to call. I spoke to Sylvie. I didn't dare call you."

"Because of Jacob?"

"Because of Jacob, yes. Sylvie told me in Portofino who you were."

"But why did my father tell me you were dead?"

"That's what I wanted everyone to think. Florence, it was the only way. The situation was too hard."

"If you had called me it would have changed my life."

"It would?" he asked with a smile.

"Yes. Saved it."

"Well, but you got married? Sylvie said you were with an American."

"I don't want to talk about that," I said. "My father told me just a few days ago about Julia, Julia and . . ." That sentence had no way to end, either. So much to say and none of the words were right.

We sat there in silence. I drank my tonic water.

It was Felix who began. "Julia's Sundays were good," he said, "when the people came to lunch."

He brings it back. I don't know anymore whom I'm jealous of, her for having him, him for having her.

"You were there?"

"Well, yes." His eyes wide open, as if he's afraid of saying too much.

"It was a nice life in that house." I sound tinny, casual, false. I'm trying to draw him on. I have to hear more. All of her. I still need her so much, I still have to know. You'd think time would make a difference. It doesn't anymore.

"I didn't live with her," he says, "not really. I had my own room in Kensington. I never gave it up until after she was dead."

"Why not?" I ask. Inviting him into Julia's house. Make yourself at home. It was, almost, mine.

Felix takes a deep breath, curls his shoulders in against the back of his chair.

"Many reasons," he says. "My mother lived in one room in Vienna, one room. With a kitchen at the front door and a table next to the bed where she played cards with her friend, who sold vegetables in the market."

"Yes?" I don't want to understand. My winged being, and his mother with a man who sold vegetables.

"I didn't want to take advantage. You shouldn't take advantage of women. Julia was rich."

A breeze goes past me; the Aquilon, not the south wind. Money?

"She was a rich woman."

And colder still. You come back from the dead to tell me this.

"Until I met Julia, I was only with men. For a boy from Vienna, you know, to live in Rome and Capri and know that life was a miracle. I knew Jacob's friends before I knew Julia."

He pronounces it Yacob.

"Yacob." He closes his eyes and smiles. "Yacob and Julia. After she died . . ."

"You were in the car with her. Weren't you?"

"Yes." He looks down now. Down at his cowboy boots.

Please, Felix. You have to tell me. But Julia's death floats away from us now, leaves us stranded in the marble lobby.

"What were you doing in London? You never told me."

"My father was English. I was born in England during the Blitz, I told you that. My parents divorced after the war, but I went to school in England. I told you."

"You remember telling me?"

"Florence, do you think because you took another name that you didn't exist?"

I don't know. "I just waited for you."

"Yes," he says.

"Maybe I'm still waiting," I say. And once I've said it, it's as if I still didn't exist.

If we talk about her I'll come back to life. "Tell me about her."

"But where do I start?" he asks, his lazy Austrian voice helpless under the syllables.

"Julia."

"She was fifteen years older than me. She was beautiful. You know that. And alone."

"Except for Trevor Blake."

"Him." Our eyes meet over a common enemy, and that is a form of union.

"She said he was safe."

"She never told me that."

"Not you. It's not what you tell a child."

"Safe. What did she mean?" But as I ask, I know. Safe, like Ben.

"From the fires of hell. From passion."

"You were her passion." It comes out a whisper.

He gives a little shrug and reaches for his empty glass of beer.

Turns, and calls the waitress for a vodka. Rattles the ashtray, picks up my bottle of tonic water and bangs it against the marble table. There are no words for passion.

"I was going to make films. She had a friend at the BBC."

"I was going to study history of art at the Courtauld. She had a friend there too."

It's as if we were her lost children.

"Documentaries," he specifies, "on art."

Vying for favors from the dead.

"I was going to live with her after school," I said.

He pulls away from the table, stretches out his arms like an animal waking, and the black bracelet dances on his wrist. His leg twitches and he pulls it out, the heel hammers the marble floor just once. He runs a hand now through his hair; the profile is still good.

The way he holds his head back, his neck made long and almost smooth again, reminds me of someone. He glances at me from his position, his arms behind his head now, a languid feline. I know it so well.

He reminds me of me. Stretched out on offer, open to invite desire. The way I have offered myself, the thing I am just learning to be. What I am only just now learning was always his.

I want to reach out and touch him because I know from the inside how much he wants to be touched. His skin needs contact for his body to breathe. But he's too old for this, he's stale. A whore, using old tricks.

We too are twins, like Jacob and Julia.

I can't remember what we were saying, or who was talking. "I thought you were dead," I say, to find my way back.

"I had to go away."

"You were in Portofino."

"I needed a change. It was difficult with Jacob, he wanted to get me an apartment, and André kept warning me to forget Jacob, and you were always waiting . . ."

"André?"

"I lived with André."

I must have known that all along or I would not have feared André so much. And that's why he hated me, and the gypsy candle . . .

I start again: "So you picked up Sylvie in the street . . ."

"It's normal, that, you know. It's what we all do. You see someone in the street, and they look good, and you ask them for a light, or where they're going . . . that's how things happen. With boys."

"With me, too."

"Yes, you weren't like Sylvie. Sylvie immediately wanted to know everything. Where I lived and who I was and what I did, and my phone number, everything. You were more like a boy. You didn't invade. You were simpler."

"And so you went away with Sylvie. I should have invaded."

"Then I probably would have married you," he says, with a chuckle. A resigned, rude chuckle. And he goes on: "I wanted to marry Julia. I wanted her to have my baby."

He sits forward; his vodka arrives but he ignores it, and goes on.

"I didn't live with her because I didn't want to be her pet. I didn't have money like she did."

"What did you do? What do you do now?"

"I trade, I sell things. Now it's rare woods, from Africa. That's why Marrakesh. It used to be miniatures, things from the East. One time I sold some temple sculptures from Cambodia and made money. I bought Julia an amethyst necklace."

"I remember it." The one that lasted four months, that was not a good investment.

"She cried, you know. Then she said, 'Felix, you can't afford it.' "

"She did have a practical side," I said.

"I wanted to marry her," he says, and this time it sounds thin. "She didn't want a baby."

"A first child after forty, it's not easy, and it was harder then," I say.

The side of his mouth turned down, he reaches for his vodka. The ice is crystal. It looks so cold. He takes a sip and looks at me and his eyes too are ice.

"Didn't you ever want a child?" he says.

"Yours." It comes out before I can stop it.

He looks down, grasps his glass in both hands, holds it steady to the table.

"After that, I never thought I would be a father."

"So Sylvie gave you a big surprise."

"I don't like women. They cause trouble."

"Trouble!"

"Months after Portofino, I call Sylvie because I can't call you, I don't want to stir up that Ellis nest. And she tells me she's going to have my baby."

"Didn't she think you were dead? Wasn't she shocked?"

"She was angry at Marc for making it up. It was his invention. I just walked down the cliff."

Oh, Sylvie, who believes everything she's told. But things don't fit. I stare at him; the kohl is running slightly now, gummy beneath the eye.

"He made it up," Felix continues. "Marc's little games. You know Marc. I knew he was watching me with Sylvie in that house in Portofino. Watching us at night."

As he would watch me asleep in his office. Or somewhere else.

"So why didn't you move in with Julia?" I ask, and I'm as cold as he is.

"Her niece was coming to stay. That was you. She said she couldn't concentrate on both of us at once."

I'm glad.

"She kept making delays to keep you away."

"Yes, 'there are too many things going on,' and 'pass your exams,' and 'don't riot.' All that was because of you?"

He smiles, proud. The cuckoo in my nest. I have an urge for fire and light a cigarette from his pack on the table; he motions for me to give him one, to hand it across his knees to him. "So what happened?" I ask, match in hand.

"I loved America, you know." Hunched over his cigarette, he feels the cold wind too. "I used to come here and play pool . . ."

"With the Indians, I know, you told me. In the Southwest."

"Arizona, Flagstaff, Phoenix, New Mexi—"

"And?" I don't want this hippie travelogue.

"I went away. She said no. I went away to Arizona so she could think, so she could miss me. And when I came back the keys to her car were in a bowl in the front hall, and she wasn't there. She was at Trevor Blake's in the country." A falsetto rise for the name of

Trevor Blake. "I found the phone number in the big book in the kitchen, and I called her. I told her I was coming up to get her. To take her back."

"Wait, when was this?"

"Winter," he says. "January."

Oh God.

"She said, 'Don't come.' But I went, and called her from the village, and she was ready to leave. She made me wait until five in the morning"—he has a smile on his face—"a superior woman, a beautiful, rich woman, and she was sneaking from a stately home in the middle of the night to be with me."

Triumphant. "A world-class beauty," he says.

The cold crunch of tires on frosty gravel, the twin gateposts of Stanley, Trevor's house. With the eagles bearing shields on top of stone globes. But this is not my Julia.

"She wanted to drive. She pushed me out of the driver's seat. She said, 'It's my car.' "

Gone slack now, shoulders fallen without even the effort of a shrug. Over his cold vodka, which is almost dry. The ice in it wintry, a nighttime glow from the glass.

"And?" I need to hear the worst.

He shakes his head, looks up at me under his eyelids. As if he were scared. "We talked."

"Then?"

"The car went off the road."

Is that all.

"She was dead. My side of the car wasn't touched. I got out and went around and tried to open her door, but I couldn't. Her eyes were shut. I waited for a while, a long time."

He looks at me; there are tears. I have the feeling of someone holding my hand, palm pressed against mine, and I feel a hot breath in my ear, and the weight of an impatient body on mine: the palm-to-palm pressure of the invisible hand, and the heat. My ears are burning. He is talking about Julia's death, and there is a hot breath of life on me.

"That's all I can say."

"You left?"

"I knew there would be problems when the police came. I couldn't do anything for her, so I left. I survived and she was dead. I was alive, it was my fault. I tried to call Geraldine in London, but she said, very English, 'It's best that I don't see you.' "

Imitating her accent. Without success.

"Geraldine," I say. "She named the baby Julia."

"I wanted to be with someone who knew her, who loved her. I used to speak with Jacob on the phone. He was nice, he was funny. I knew his friends, I didn't know him."

"You had a lot in common," I said.

"Don't be sarcastic," says Felix.

I will have to apologize for wishing him dead.

"I didn't have his number, but I knew the shop was called Jacob Ellis et Compagnie, that it was on the Rue Jacob. So I went to Paris."

Or maybe I won't.

"He looked so much like her. He said he'd been waiting for me. It was . . . strange. We went out for a walk, and he cried. He cried in the street."

My father cried?

"He loved her so much. He could do that with me. Between men, sometimes, it's easier than with women."

Between men. I have to let go. I have to tell him, and let go. He is like that, he always was.

"Women cause problems. Men are simpler. It's friendship. And, you know . . ."

"Yes?"

"He missed her even more than I did."

"So did I."

"You never talked about her. He did. He talked about you too, the problem child. You were a bad girl, leaving home."

"But when we met? You didn't know who I was? You never saw a picture?"

That nice picture of me, by Dad's desk at home.

"I never went to Jacob's apartment. Because of Michel. Jacob took a room near the République . . ."

"I don't want to know any more," I said.

"You keep asking. Of course you want to know, you want to know everything."

"Felix, for fifteen years I thought you were dead. Sixteen years."

"But you get over things. I did. I managed to forget Julia."

"But I was in love with you. You were magic to me, you were the most wonderful thing that had ever happened to me." He looks pleased. "Felix, I loved you so much that I tried to . . ."

Don't tell him, says the voice. The voice is back again, firm, sure.

But I'm trying to tell him, I have to tell him something about love.

The ring might explain it. I take out the little yellow box.

He leans forward to peer at the ring, half closes his eyes, and then smiles. "Oh, I remember this. You showed it to me once in Paris."

"Look at what is on it," I say. "Look at the woman and the swan."

"Oh, yes," he says, but he isn't looking at the stone, the chipped blue agate. He is looking at a couple across the hall. A young couple, blond, foreign, tall. A man and a woman.

"Sometimes," he says, "you want to be both of them, to know what love is like from both sides."

I see his eyes glitter, and I've heard those words before.

"You already know, Felix," I say.

I turn the engraved image toward me.

"Uhmmn?" says Felix, turning back toward me, returning to the ring.

"Look!" I say, and hand him the ring.

He takes it, smiles, appraises its weight, brings it nearer to his eyes. It's not for sale, I want to say.

I point at the stone, and the movement of my hand jolts his arm.

"Oh," says Felix.

The ring falls from his fingers onto the marble floor. The sound of bronze on stone like gunshot.

My knees are on the marble. My hand is on the ring, my fingers grappling for its edges. I pick it up.

"Look," I say.

I won't give up.

"What?" he says.

I turn the ring to me.

The inset stone is gone.

I see my hand around the ring, and the bronze like a blind socket around the missing image.

Scattered black crystals, shards of agate like coal dust glitter on the floor beyond his feet. And by my hand his foot in its cowboy boot, the boot ridged to an ungainly point tipped in silver.

"I'm sorry," he says.

I get up off my knees and sit down in the chair again.

I hold the ring in my hand but I can't look at where the stone is missing.

"I loved you, Florence," says Felix, "when you were young."

"When you were young, you mean," I say.

The cool white sheets waiting for us at home. The winding sheets, the linen shroud.

"I can come back with you now," he says, "we've talked enough."

But I should confess.

"I thought you were dead."

"Stop talking about that. It was something Marc made up, to scare Sylvie. It suited me fine."

"But there was a body."

"Why don't you ask Sylvie? She's your friend."

"I was too scared to bring it up, Felix. Because I thought . . ."

He gives a snort and sits up, defensive now.

"What do you think? Think, think? What?"

"But who was the boy who fell off the cliff?"

"It wasn't . . ." he says, and I know he's going to say, "me."

He says, "My fault."

And now the ice and the tiny slivers of black stone converge in my veins. And he goes on:

"I didn't push him. He fell."

"Who?" No. "What? Who was he?"

"Just a boy, a boy on a cliff. A boy I met there. Walking along the cliff, a handsome young boy."

"You mean someone you picked up? Like me, like Sylvie?"

"A boy"—his voice is raised—"a boy, it's simpler with boys."

"But why a boy? You were there with Sylvie . . ."

"God, women never understand! Sylvie told me about you, her

best friend Florence, Jacob's daughter. The apartment on the Rue du Bac. I understood who you were. I went for a walk to calm down, and there was a boy. It was quick, like that. But afterwards he wanted money, he"—and here, he laughs—"he even had a knife. So I had to defend myself."

"You pushed a boy off a cliff?"

"No, he fell. No one understands, he fell." He puts his hand against his temple, shakes his head, and now he glares at me.

I put the blind ring back in its yellow case, and the case in my bag.

"So now you know. Accidents happen around me," he says.

"I have to go now."

"Don't you want me to come to your house?"

"It's not my house," I tell him.

He has his hand on my arm. "Florence."

"I must go."

"There's one more thing you should know," he says, "just one. About me and Julia."

I'm standing and trying to get free, his hand tight on my arm. I don't want to know any more and I uncurl his fingers from my arm. At his jaw I see a muscle twitch, stand out.

"It wouldn't have been her first child. I tell you that. Remember it."

He looks like an old woman sitting there, his hair in disarray, his mouth tight and his makeup running.

"I'm going now," I say. "Someone's waiting for me."

15

FLORENCE OPENS HER EYES on dancing molecules; she sees the radium glow of a travel clock, parked at an angle on a table near her. The heave and sigh of curtains in a light wind lets in uneven parcels of street light, sodium sparkle rising and falling with the wind. The middle of the night is deeper than geology; nature returns to its chemical components.

The air pales while she sleeps again, and then she hears a garbage truck, but the metallic whir now purrs. Machinery had been tamed or she's in a better part of town, with newer, cleaner trucks.

She wants to know. She can make out a pile of books, a bottle of vitamin C, the contour of a lamp. The open closet doors cast shadows in the shadow. Dark frames stand out against the wall, but the pictures inside them remain indistinct.

She puts her feet on the floor, gets out of bed, and wanders to the door and out into a corridor, and into a study on the other side. Piles of mail on the desk, addressed to Paul; photographs of him in a white polo shirt, with dogs and children on a lawn by the sea, in a wind-cheater on a boat; she pulls open a drawer and sees treasure, color photographs slipping in untidy piles, a bill that says, "Rhine-lander Florist." Everything is open, laid out. Even, if she wanted to know, the price of her bouquet. So much information just under her fingers: letters from a bank, from a law firm, cards from Chile and Brazil and Greece. Lawyer's briefs with paper clips on the long paper, a collection of message slips. All she would have to do is sit down and read, and she'd know everything. But the wealth of evidence

333

releases her from curiosity; since it's all laid out, she can let it be.

Her father's express envelope protrudes from her bag in the hall. She takes it and breaks the seal, but stops herself before she reads. It can wait.

Outside and very near she sees the green trees of the park. She is naked; it strikes her as indecent to pry without clothes. She leaves the letter on the desk, and finds a bathroom, untenanted save by guest towels, where she splashes her face. Then she returns to the dark bedroom.

A pale arm reaches up to her from the bed, a warm hand pulls her down into it. His hand covers the cold space at her shoulder blades. Calves clasp. Dry lips catch on skin; they could rub together and catch fire again, but they subside into alert erotic drowse. Eyes shut, her hands on him, she is carried from uncritical desire back to wary self-preservation: diastole and systole. Breathing in, she wants his body; breathing out, she fears his life. Come into me, heat, weight, pressure, tension, flexion, pulsion, pain, release; the lozenge of hair on his chest scrapes her shoulder: the green lawn by the sea, now verified by photographs, and if it goes well she'll have a station wagon and get to know the kids, and if it really goes well they'll like her. And she'll sign his last name on the bottom of her checks, and dye her hair a little lighter in a few years. Come into me I want your cock, break over me like a wave, we'll ride each other, marrow to marrow we'll crash together, and end scattered like pebbles over a thousand miles of shore; vertebrae curve back to fit along the top of an arm, and she'll have a baby at thirty-seven, thirty-eight, or forty, and get to know Paul too well: she'll know his every story, know which gray face in the school photograph is his, third from the right bottom row, and the whims and fortunes of his ancestors, and she'll break a crystal cup from his first marriage on a bad day by the sea. But we'll have real lives.

Then the light turns warm, and he is awake too.

She touches the line that runs down from the navel, the line along which the egg first divided, the indelible seam of the mold. The maker's mark. Each of us split in two so that we might begin to exist.

114 Chester Street
London SW1

May 8, 1958

Dear Jacob;
She's up there drawing on the table; I hope not on *the table, but on the paper.*

Sweet thing; she says she hopes she's not in the way, and do you know how that makes me feel?

Maybe we should have done it the other way around; I could have kept her and you would have been the uncle in Paris. But you're the one who has a real family life, though real and family and life are words that seem a little strange applied to you and Michel, and no, this is not a criticism. I do forget to eat except on weekends, and I was the one who was going to marry a lord. A good marriage. We all wanted it, didn't we? Olivia especially, and Lady Radford would have been such a lady. No flat shoes for her. And since Olivia thinks that Florence is a Radford bastard anyway, and since everything we do is to avoid scandal, it's probably best this way. I hate it. I want to tell her, all the time, but she wouldn't understand. Maybe everything stopped when she was born because that's what was supposed to happen, her birth, and nothing else. You say I have my work, and I do. You'll see, I'll do well. Just to show everyone.

I would have said it wasn't possible, like dogs and cats, but Doctor Emery says she's fine. Exceptionally, she's a freak because she's fine.

We will tell her one day, won't we? When she's old enough to take it?

Oh, Jacob, I'll hate seeing you grow old—I just had a flash of us telling her and we were both so old, so old—and I don't want to grow old either. No one else can understand about us. I know we broke a rule but it doesn't have to break us. Did it? Michel is what you wanted, isn't he? (Say hello to him.) Have her work well in school, and don't let her get grim and tough like those French children, those tiny middle-aged people. Right now I don't want to send her back at all, but she said (Yes, I did suggest it: Why don't you have her stay here with me?) "Is that because Papa wants to be alone in Paris?" So what could I do? So keep her for now, but I swear, when she's eighteen she's going to come and live with me. And if you don't want me to tell her I never will. I swear.

Your Julia

P.S. Are my shoes ready at Mancini yet? I ordered green crocodile, don't say it's extravagant because it's the most amazing green, and they're pumps so they're practical.

About the Author

Joan Juliet Buck was born in California and raised in Paris and London. She has lived in the United States since 1979 and now divides her time between Paris and New York. She is a Contributing Editor to Vogue, and her work appears regularly in *Vanity Fair*. Her first novel, *The Only Place To Be*, was published in 1982.